spectacle

· BOOK THREE ·

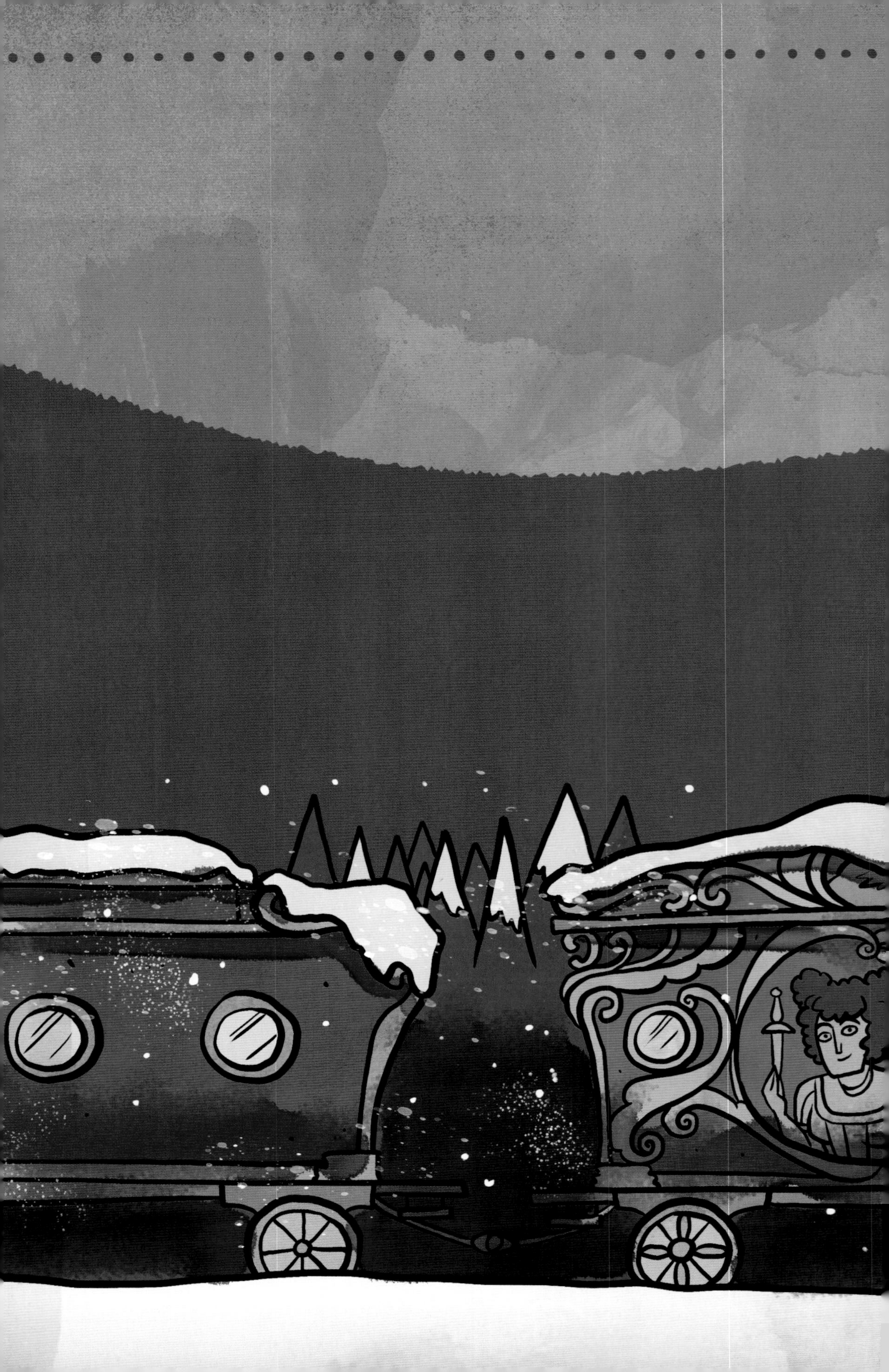

spectacle

· BOOK THREE ·

- MEGAN ROSE GEDRIS -

Designed by Hilary Thompson
Edited by Ari Yarwood with Zack Soto

PUBLISHED BY ONI-LION FORGE PUBLISHING GROUP, LLC
James Lucas Jones, president & publisher
Sarah Gaydos, editor in chief
Charlie Chu, e.v.p. of creative & business development
Brad Rooks, director of operations
Amber O'Neill, special projects manager
Harris Fish, events manager
Margot Wood, director of marketing & sales
Jeremy Atkins, director of brand communications
Devin Funches, sales & marketing manager
Tara Lehmann, marketing & publicity associate
Troy Look, director of design & production
Kate Z. Stone, senior graphic designer
Sonja Synak, graphic designer
Hilary Thompson, graphic designer
Angie Knowles, digital prepress lead
Shawna Gore, senior editor
Robin Herrera, senior editor
Amanda Meadows, senior editor
Jasmine Amiri, editor
Grace Bornhoft, editor
Zack Soto, editor
Steve Ellis, director of games
Ben Eisner, game developer
Michelle Nguyen, executive assistant
Jung Lee, logistics coordinator
Joe Nozemack, publisher emeritus

1319 SE Martin Luther King, Jr. Blvd.
Suite 240
Portland, OR 97214

onipress.com | lionforge.com
facebook.com/onipress | facebook.com/lionforge
twitter.com/onipress | twitter.com/lionforge
instagram.com/onipress | instagram.com/lionforge

rosalarian.com
twitter.com/rosalarian

First Edition: May 2020

ISBN 978-1-62010-770-6
eISBN 978-1-62010-732-4

1 2 3 4 5 6 7 8 9 10

Library of Congress Control Number: 2019952538

Printed in China.

SPECTACLE, BOOK THREE. RELEASED MAY 2020. PUBLISHED BY ONI-LION FORGE PUBLISHING GROUP, LLC, 1319 SE MARTIN LUTHER KING JR. BLVD., SUITE 240, PORTLAND. OR 97214. SPECTACLE IS ™ & © 2020 MEGAN ROSE GEDRIS. ALL RIGHTS RESERVED. ONI PRESS LOGO AND ICON ™ & © 2020 ONI-LION FORGE PUBLISHING GROUP, LLC. ALL RIGHTS RESERVED. ONI PRESS LOGO AND ICON ARTWORK CREATED BY KEITH A. WOOD. THE EVENTS, INSTITUTIONS, AND CHARACTERS PRESENTED IN THIS BOOK ARE FICTIONAL. ANY RESEMBLANCE TO ACTUAL PERSONS, LIVING OR DEAD, IS PURELY COINCIDENTAL. NO PORTION OF THIS PUBLICATION MAY BE REPRODUCED, BY ANY MEANS, WITHOUT THE EXPRESS WRITTEN PERMISSION OF THE COPYRIGHT HOLDERS.

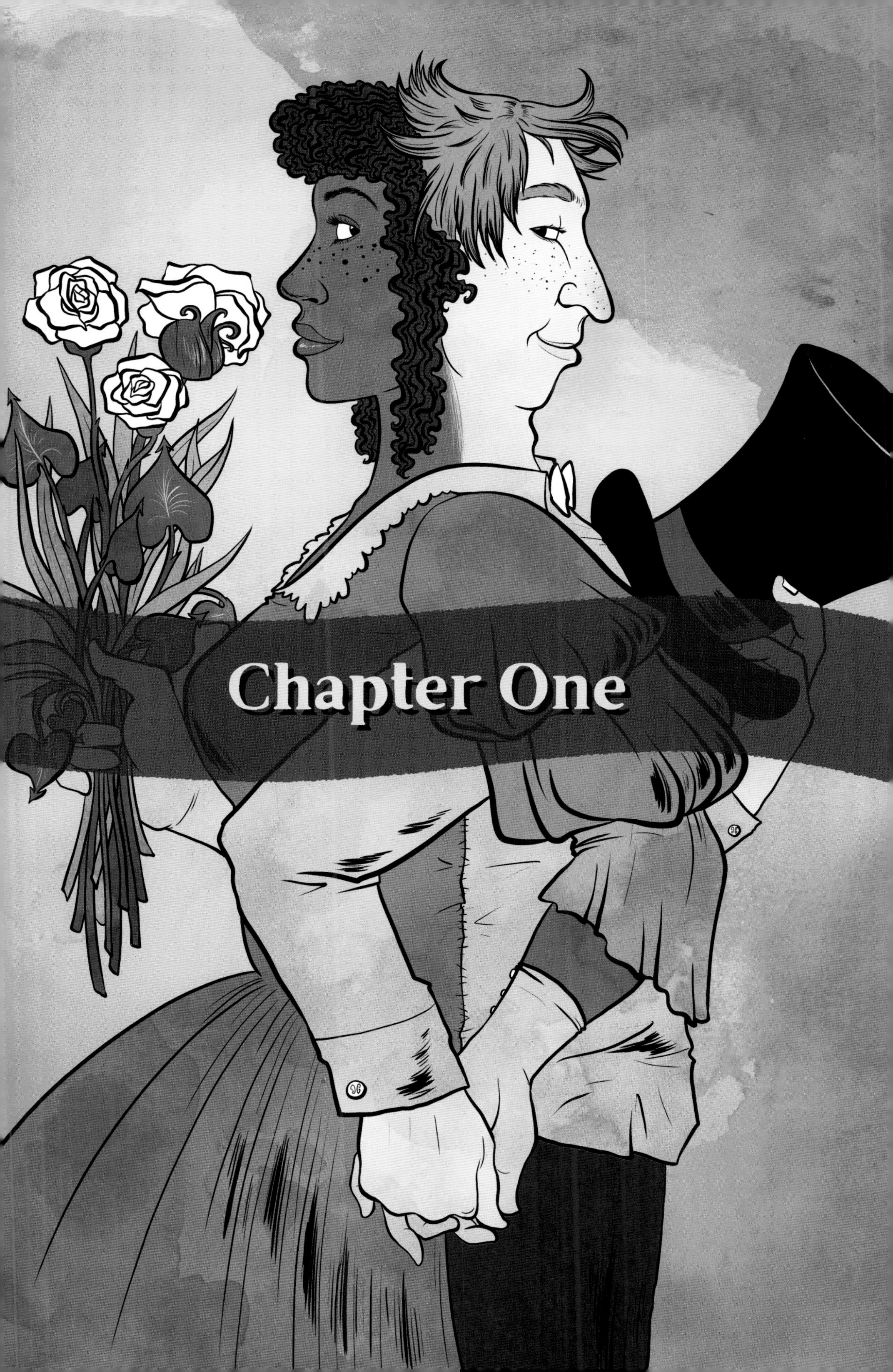
Chapter One

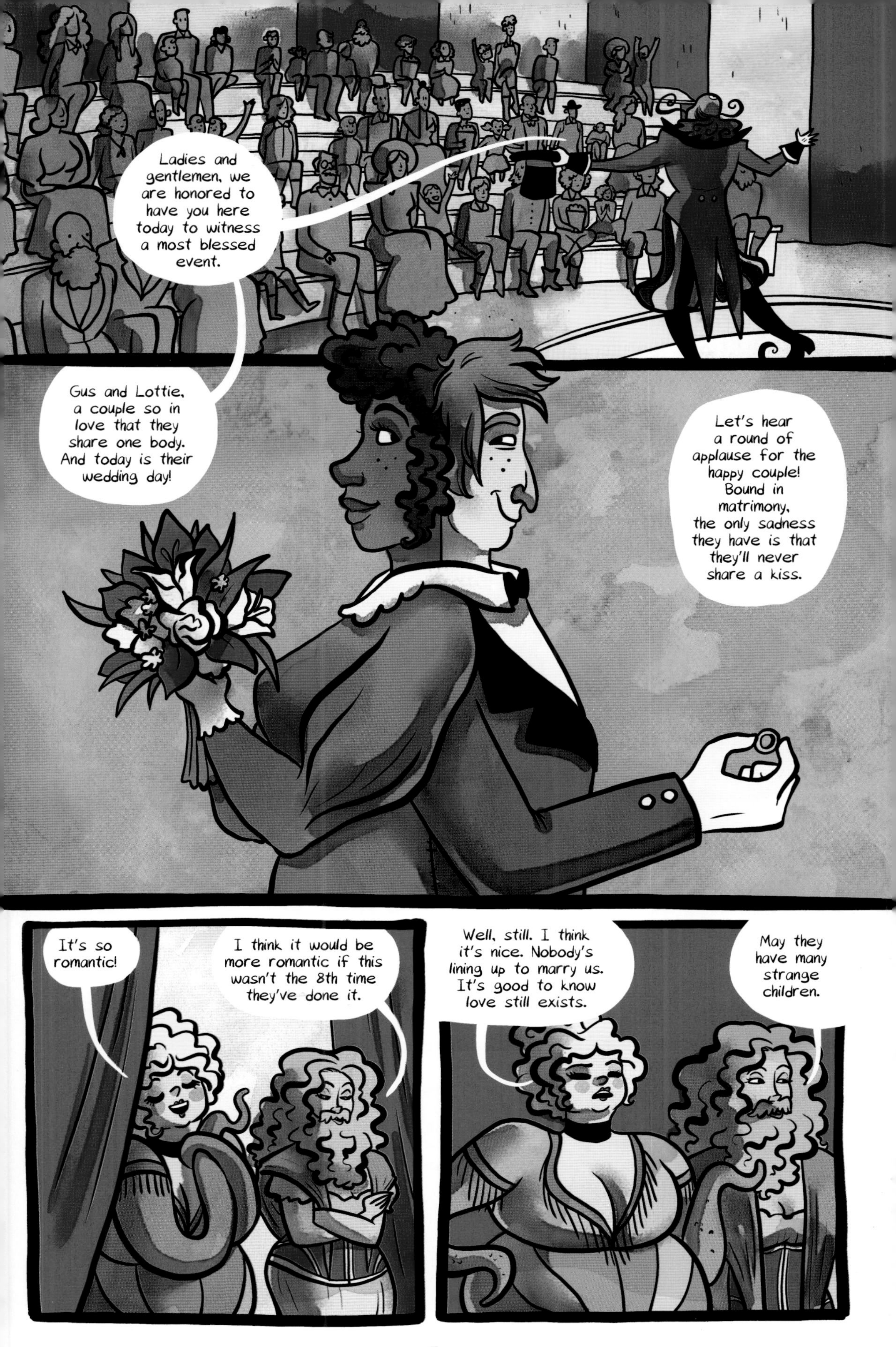
Ladies and gentlemen, we are honored to have you here today to witness a most blessed event.
Gus and Lottie, a couple so in love that they share one body. And today is their wedding day!
Let's hear a round of applause for the happy couple! Bound in matrimony, the only sadness they have is that they'll never share a kiss.
It's so romantic!
I think it would be more romantic if this wasn't the 8th time they've done it.
Well, still. I think it's nice. Nobody's lining up to marry us. It's good to know love still exists.
May they have many strange children.

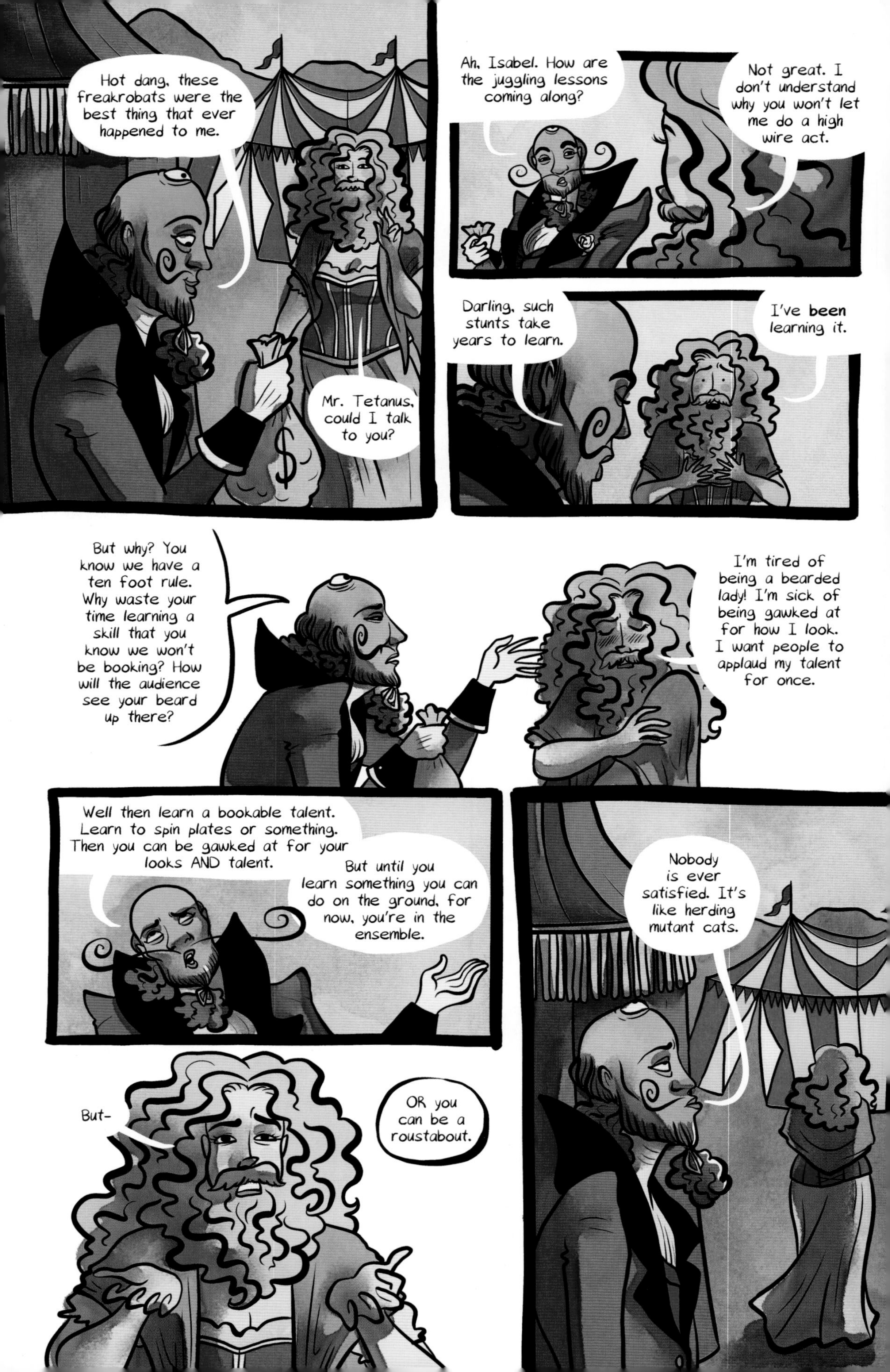
Hot dang, these freakrobats were the best thing that ever happened to me.
Mr. Tetanus, could I talk to you?
Ah, Isabel. How are the juggling lessons coming along?
Not great. I don't understand why you won't let me do a high wire act.
Darling, such stunts take years to learn.
I've **been** learning it.
But why? You know we have a ten foot rule. Why waste your time learning a skill that you know we won't be booking? How will the audience see your beard up there?
I'm tired of being a bearded lady! I'm sick of being gawked at for how I look. I want people to applaud my talent for once.
Well then learn a bookable talent. Learn to spin plates or something. Then you can be gawked at for your looks AND talent.
But until you learn something you can do on the ground, for now, you're in the ensemble.
But-
OR you can be a roustabout.
Nobody is ever satisfied. It's like herding mutant cats.

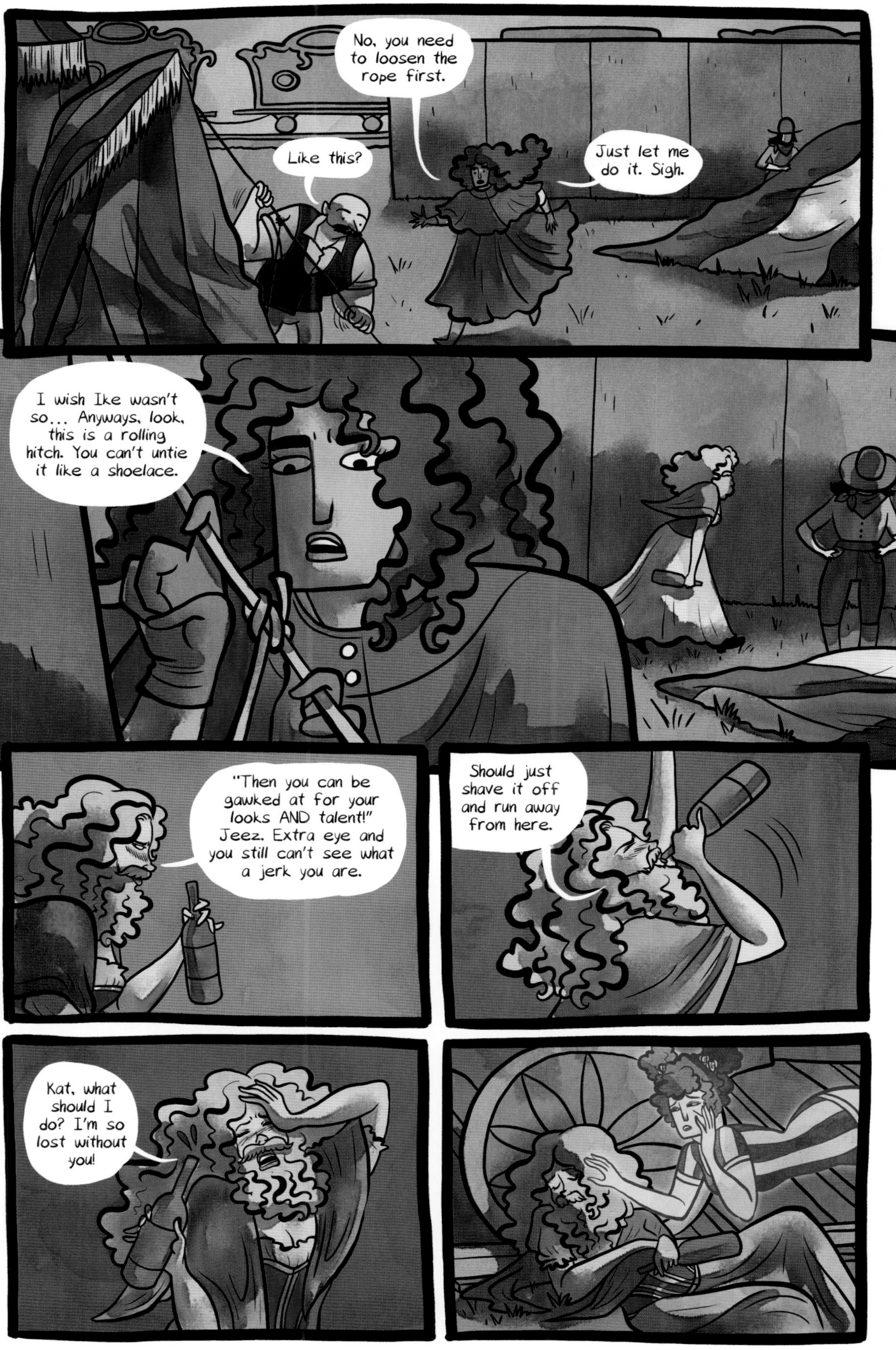
No, you need to loosen the rope first.
Like this?
Just let me do it. Sigh.
I wish Ike wasn't so... Anyways, look, this is a rolling hitch. You can't untie it like a shoelace.
"Then you can be gawked at for your looks AND talent!" Jeez. Extra eye and you still can't see what a jerk you are.
Should just shave it off and run away from here.
Kat, what should I do? I'm so lost without you!

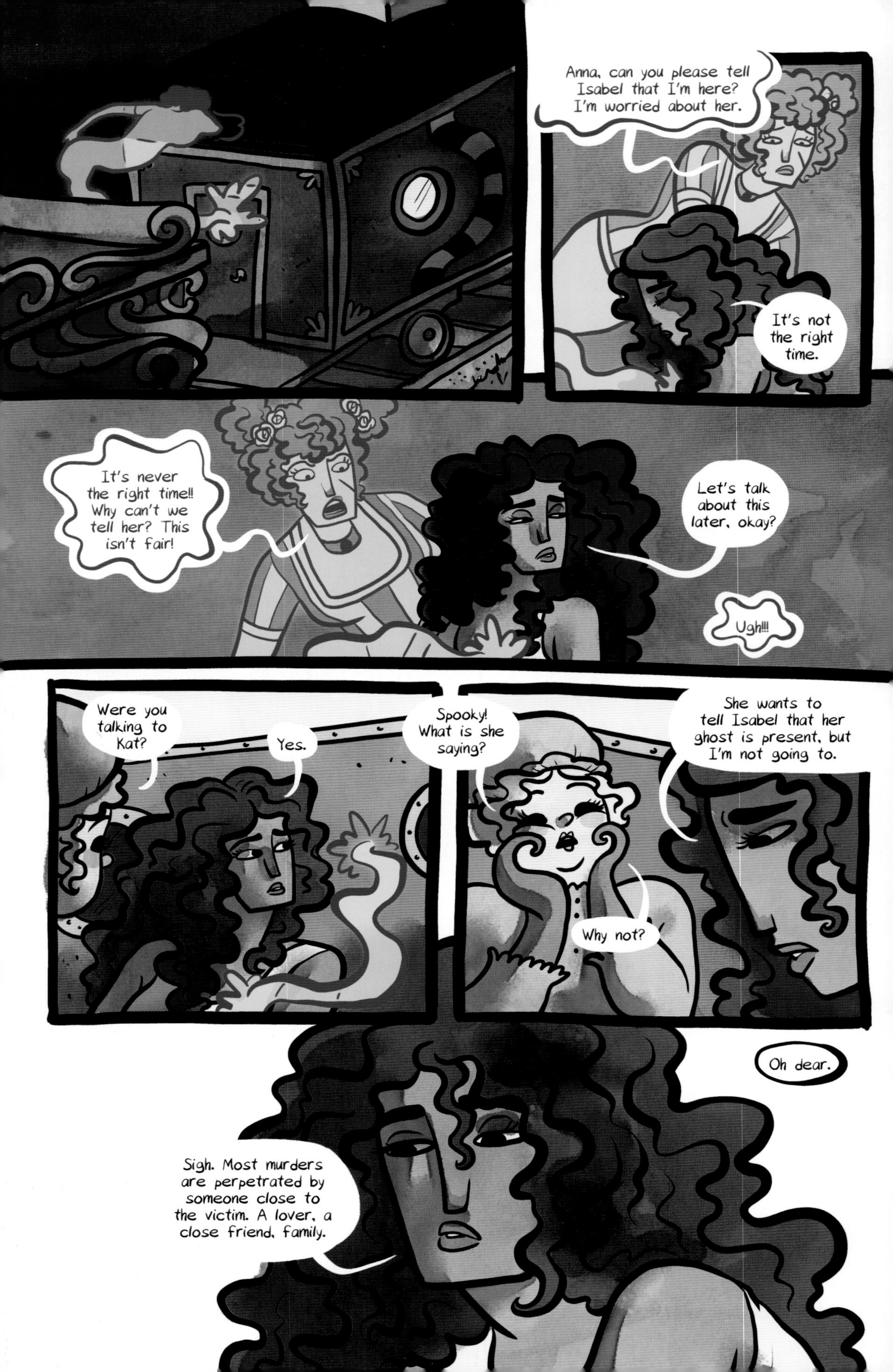

Anna, can you please tell Isabel that I'm here? I'm worried about her.
It's not the right time.
It's never the right time!! Why can't we tell her? This isn't fair!
Let's talk about this later, okay?
Ugh!!!
Were you talking to Kat?
Yes.
Spooky! What is she saying?
She wants to tell Isabel that her ghost is present, but I'm not going to.
Why not?
Oh dear.
Sigh. Most murders are perpetrated by someone close to the victim. A lover, a close friend, family.

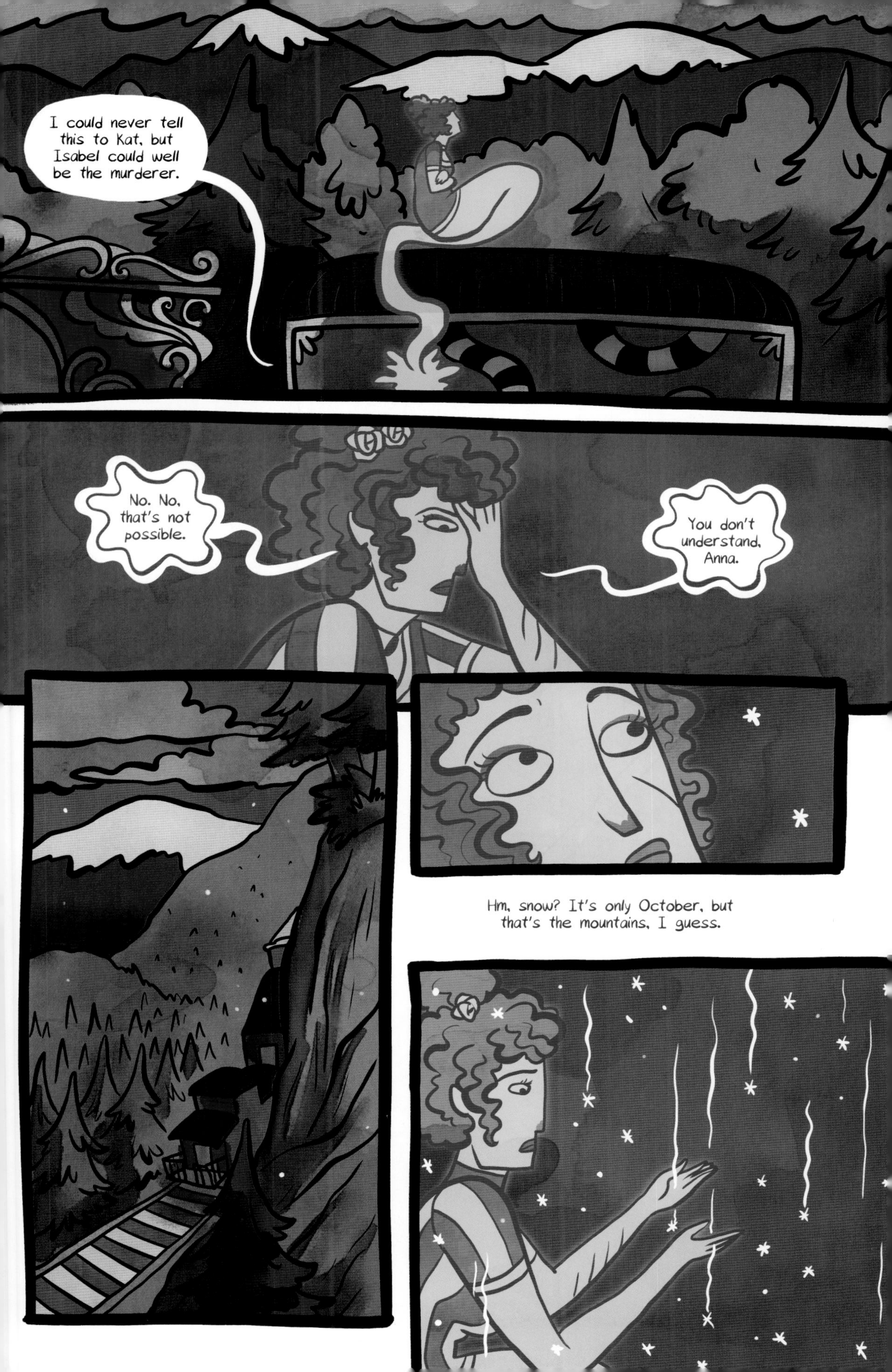
I could never tell this to Kat, but Isabel could well be the murderer.
No. No, that's not possible.
You don't understand, Anna.
Hm, snow? It's only October, but that's the mountains, I guess.

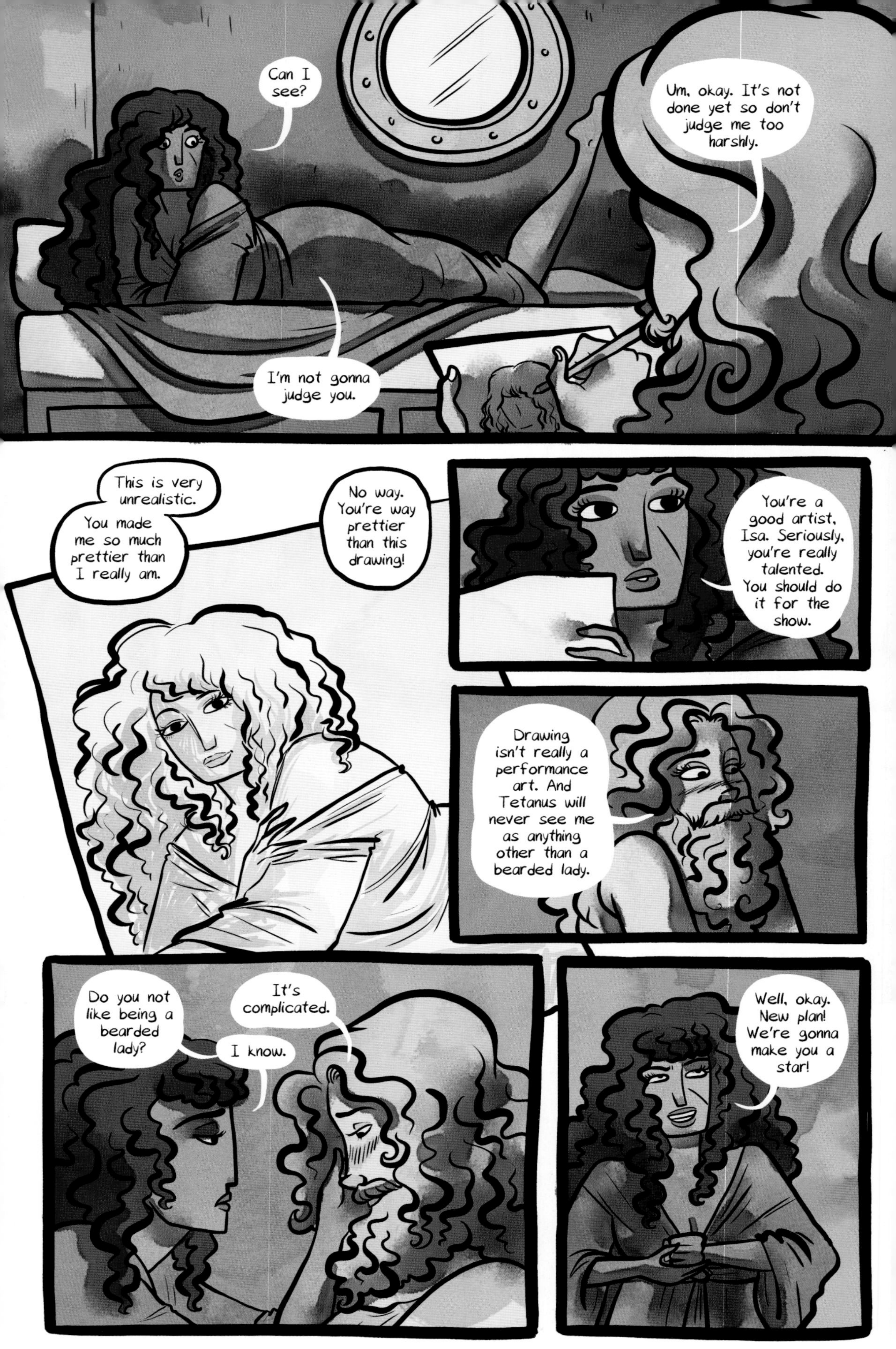

Can I see?
Um, okay. It's not done yet so don't judge me too harshly.
I'm not gonna judge you.
This is very unrealistic.
You made me so much prettier than I really am.
No way. You're way prettier than this drawing!
You're a good artist, Isa. Seriously, you're really talented. You should do it for the show.
Drawing isn't really a performance art. And Tetanus will never see me as anything other than a bearded lady.
Do you not like being a bearded lady?
It's complicated.
I know.
Well, okay. New plan! We're gonna make you a star!

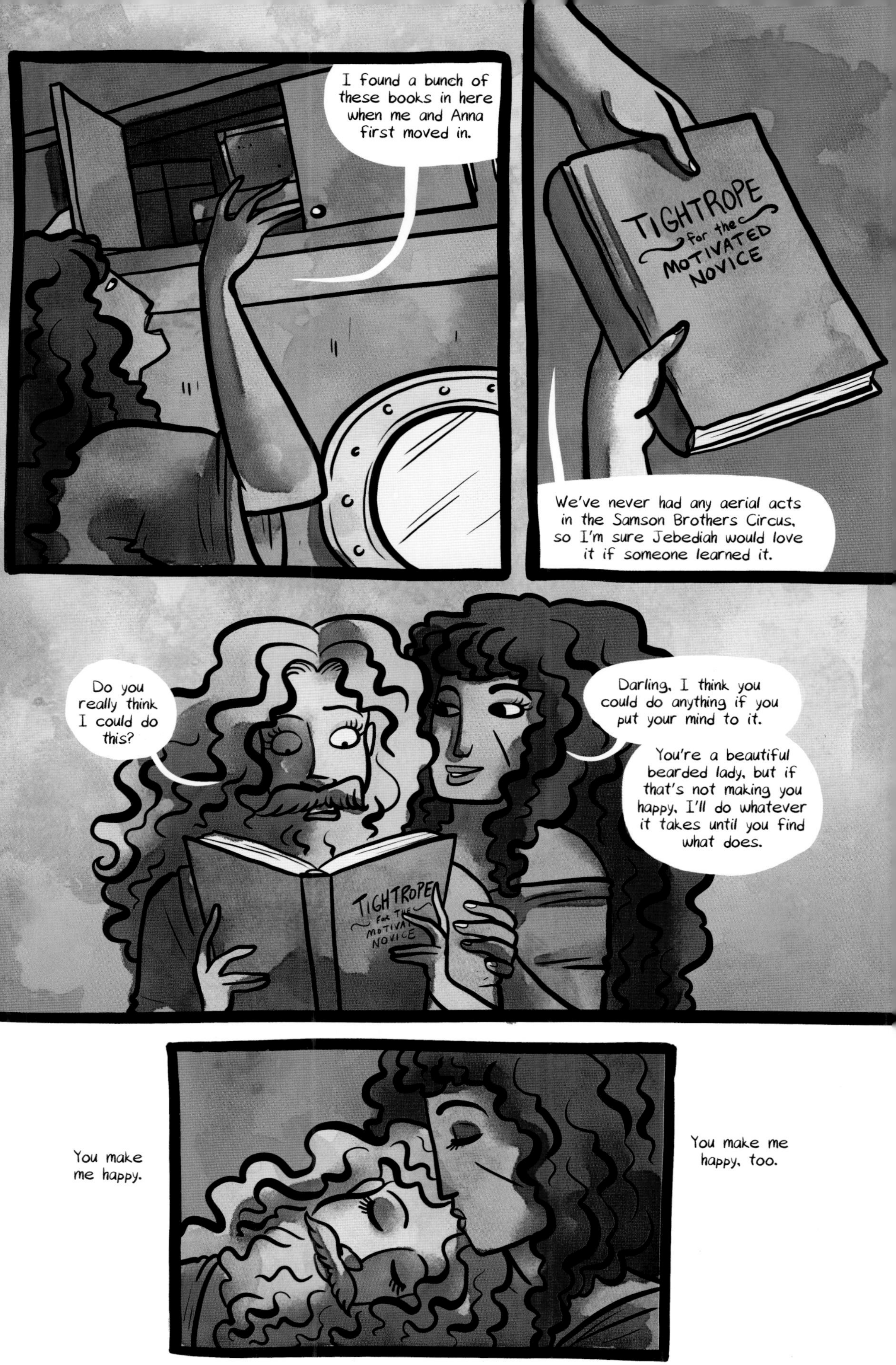

I found a bunch of these books in here when me and Anna first moved in.
TIGHTROPE for the MOTIVATED NOVICE
We've never had any aerial acts in the Samson Brothers Circus, so I'm sure Jebediah would love it if someone learned it.
Do you really think I could do this?
Darling, I think you could do anything if you put your mind to it.
You're a beautiful bearded lady, but if that's not making you happy, I'll do whatever it takes until you find what does.
TIGHTROPE
You make me happy.
You make me happy, too.

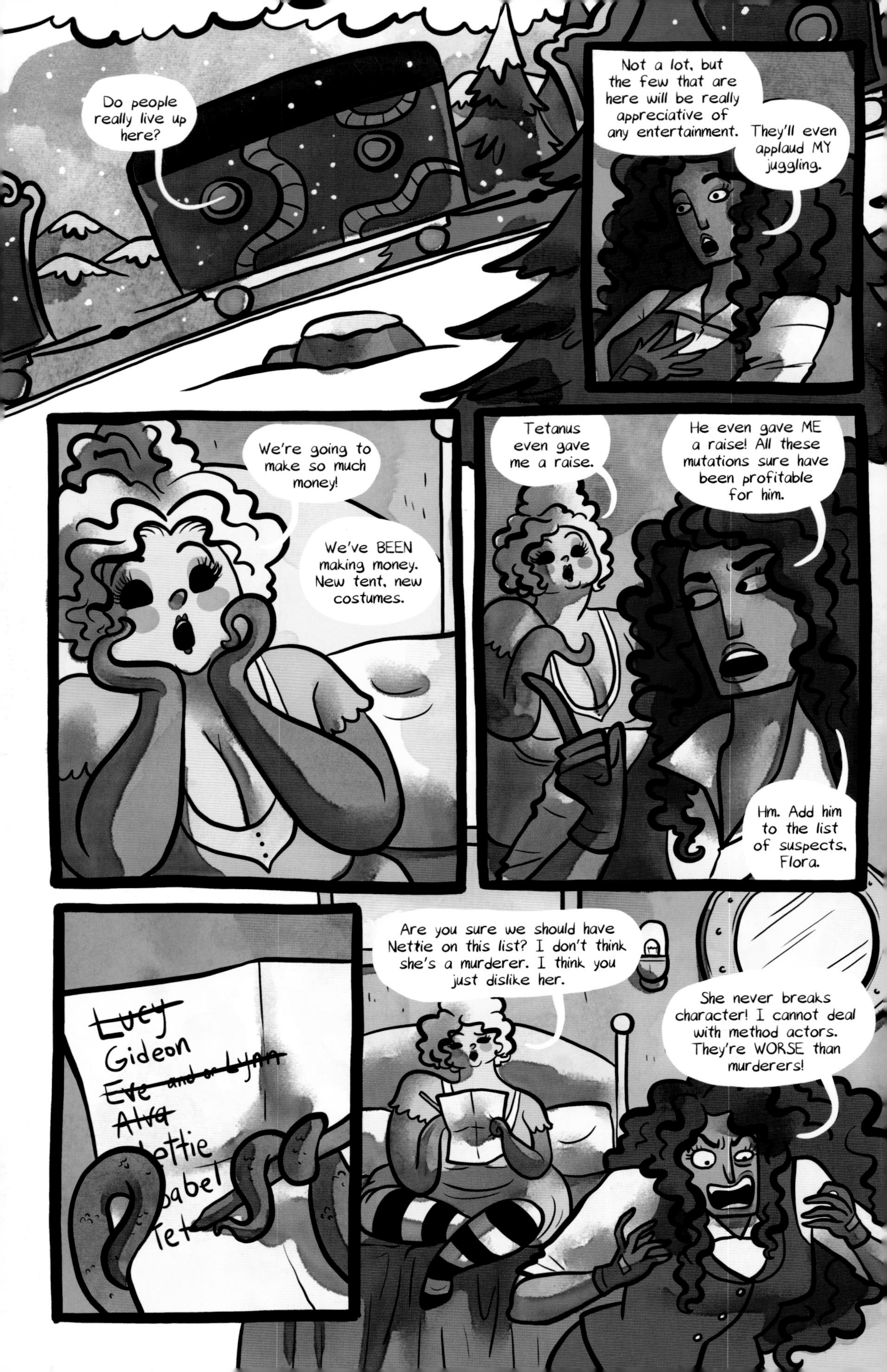
Do people really live up here?
Not a lot, but the few that are here will be really appreciative of any entertainment.
They'll even applaud MY juggling.
We're going to make so much money!
We've BEEN making money. New tent, new costumes.
Tetanus even gave me a raise.
He even gave ME a raise! All these mutations sure have been profitable for him.
Hm. Add him to the list of suspects, Flora.
Lucy
Gideon
Eve and or Lynn
Alva
Are you sure we should have Nettie on this list? I don't think she's a murderer. I think you just dislike her.
She never breaks character! I cannot deal with method actors. They're WORSE than murderers!

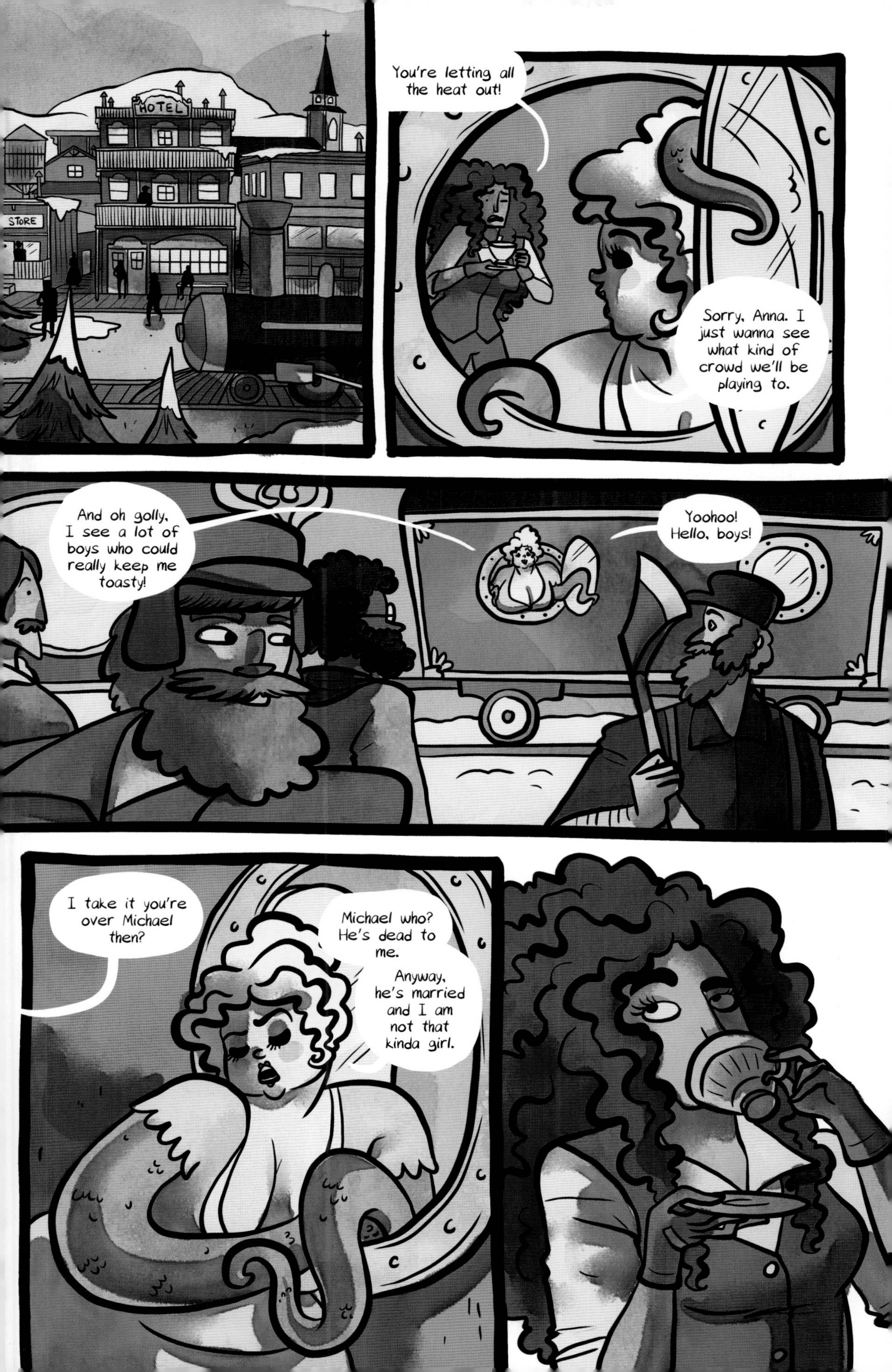
HOTEL
STORE
You're letting all the heat out!
Sorry, Anna. I just wanna see what kind of crowd we'll be playing to.
And oh golly, I see a lot of boys who could really keep me toasty!
Yoohoo! Hello, boys!
I take it you're over Michael then?
Michael who? He's dead to me.
Anyway, he's married and I am not that kinda girl.

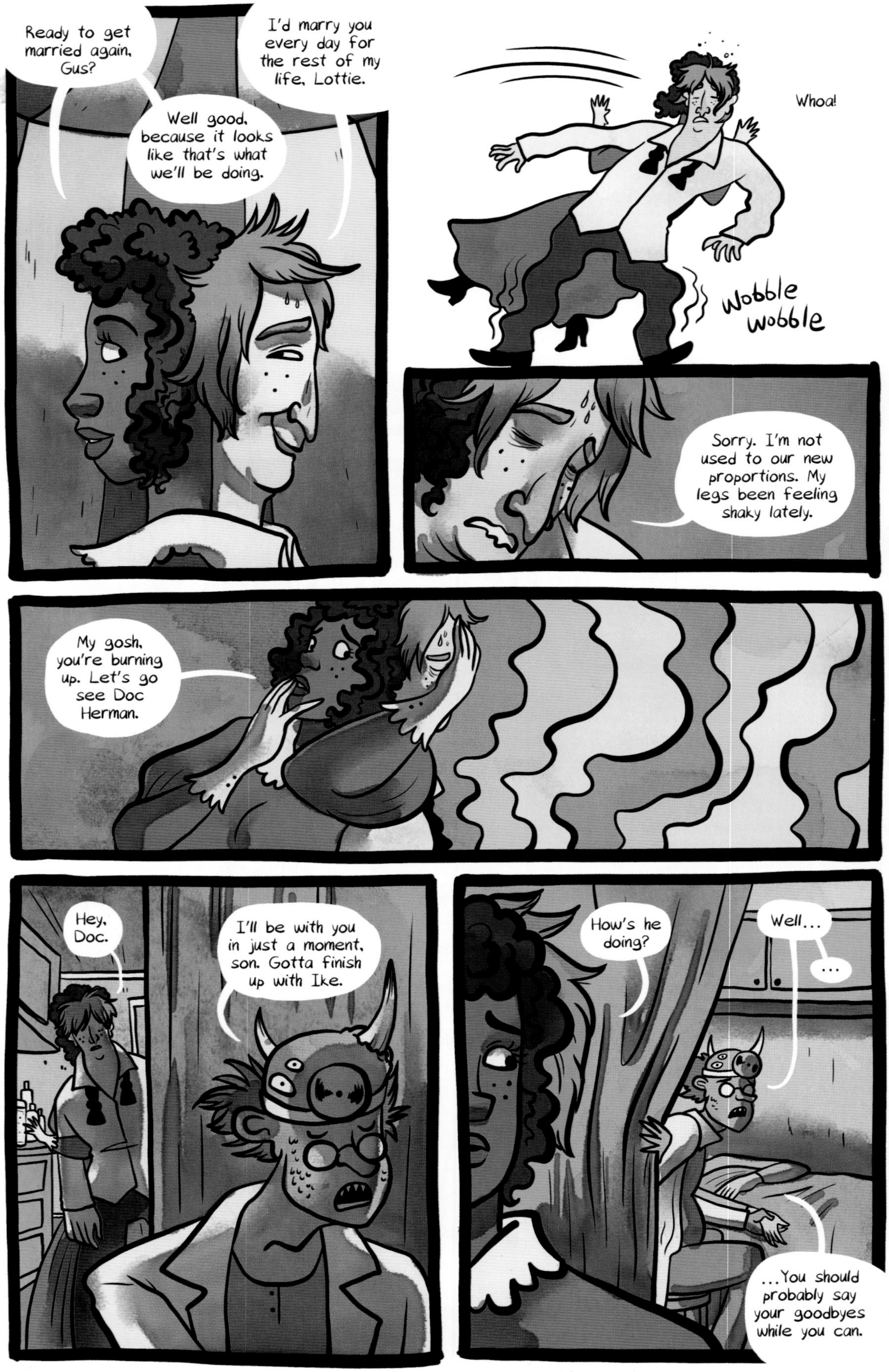
Ready to get married again, Gus?
I'd marry you every day for the rest of my life, Lottie.
Well good, because it looks like that's what we'll be doing.
Whoa!
Wobble wobble
Sorry. I'm not used to our new proportions. My legs been feeling shaky lately.
My gosh, you're burning up. Let's go see Doc Herman.
Hey, Doc.
I'll be with you in just a moment, son. Gotta finish up with Ike.
How's he doing?
Well...
...
...You should probably say your goodbyes while you can.

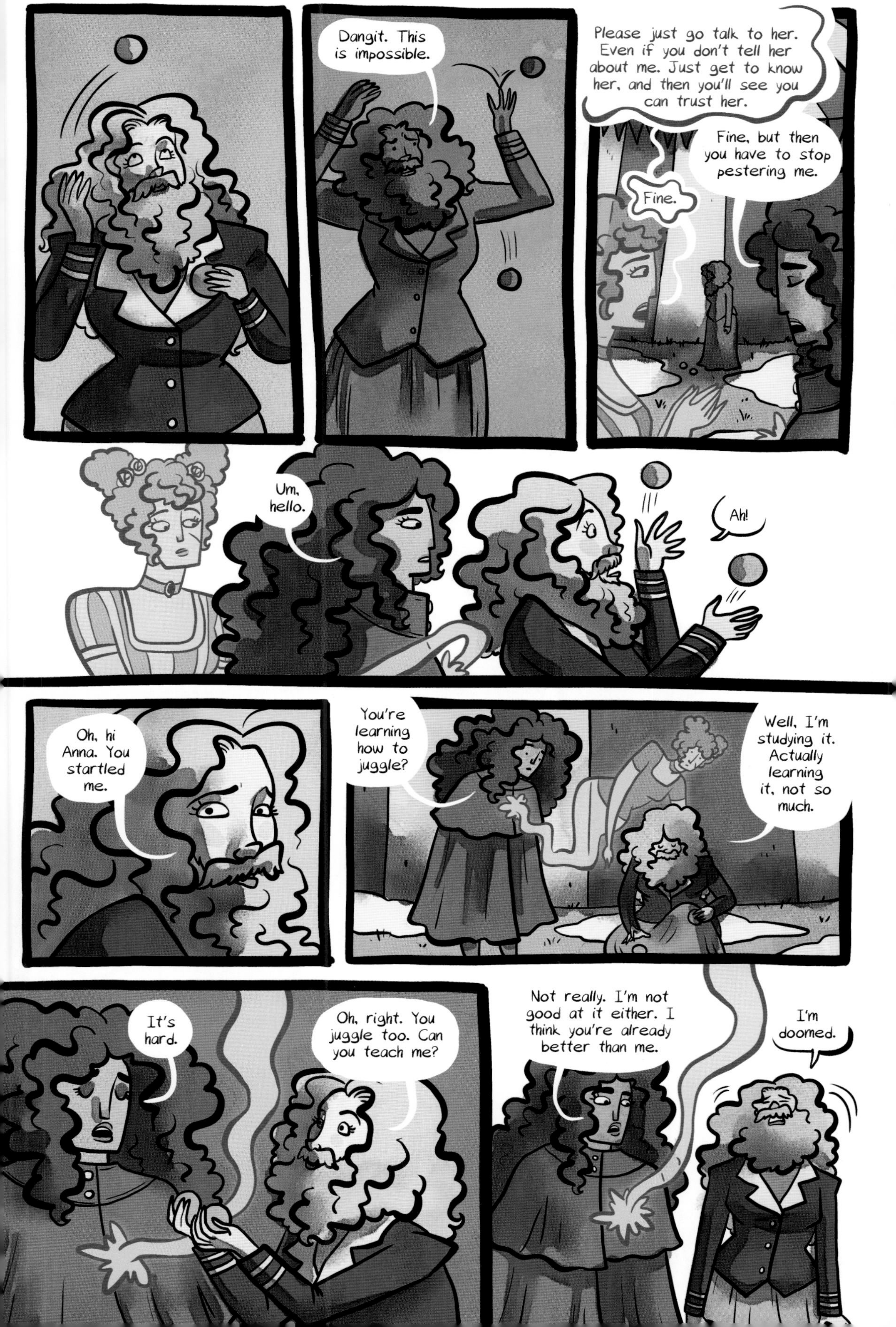
Dangit. This is impossible.
Please just go talk to her. Even if you don't tell her about me. Just get to know her, and then you'll see you can trust her.
Fine, but then you have to stop pestering me.
Fine.
Um, hello.
Ah!
Oh, hi Anna. You startled me.
You're learning how to juggle?
Well, I'm studying it. Actually learning it, not so much.
It's hard.
Oh, right. You juggle too. Can you teach me?
Not really. I'm not good at it either. I think you're already better than me.
I'm doomed.

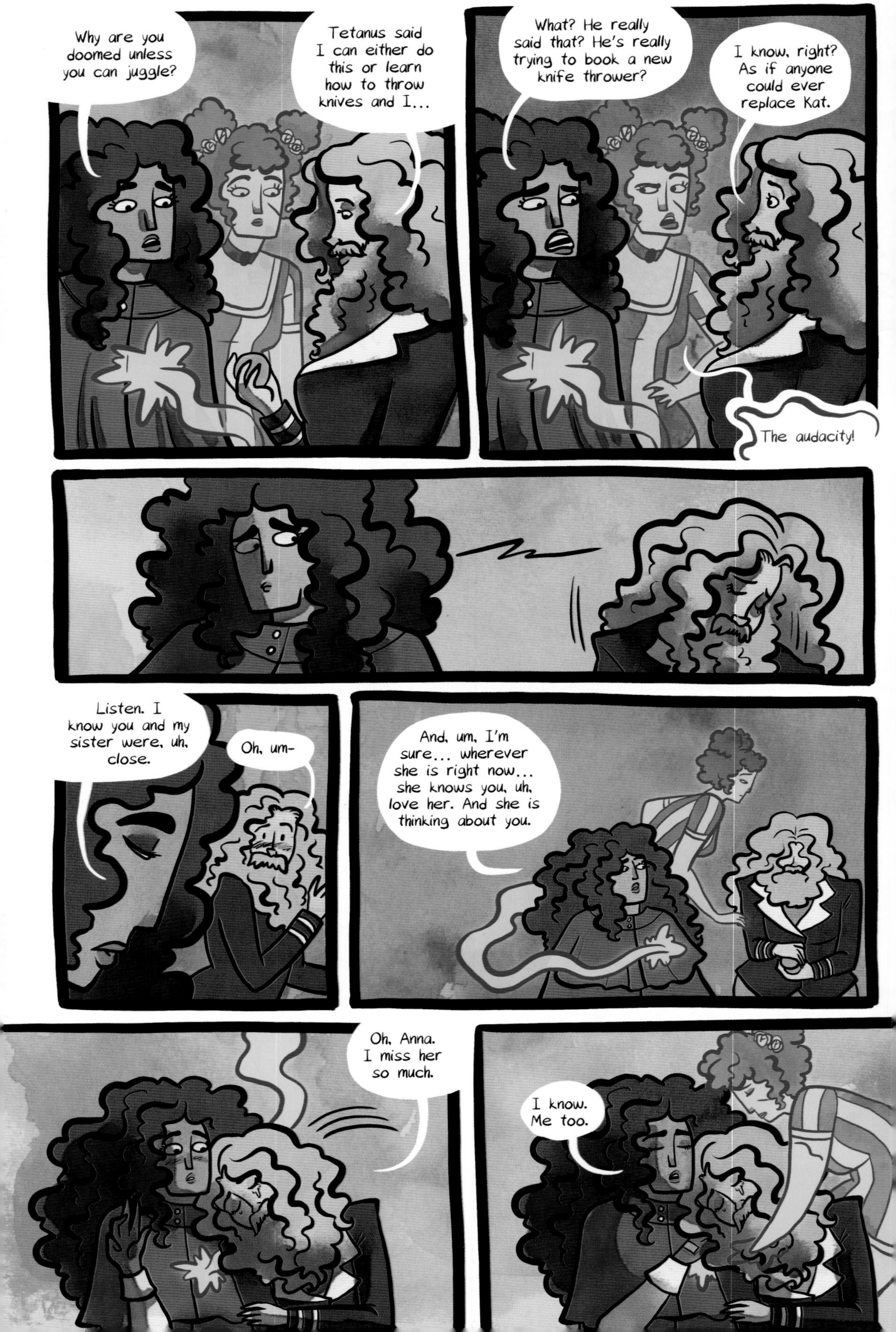
Why are you doomed unless you can juggle?
Tetanus said I can either do this or learn how to throw knives and I...
What? He really said that? He's really trying to book a new knife thrower?
I know, right? As if anyone could ever replace Kat.
The audacity!
Listen. I know you and my sister were, uh, close.
Oh, um-
And, um, I'm sure... wherever she is right now... she knows you, uh, love her. And she is thinking about you.
Oh, Anna. I miss her so much.
I know. Me too.

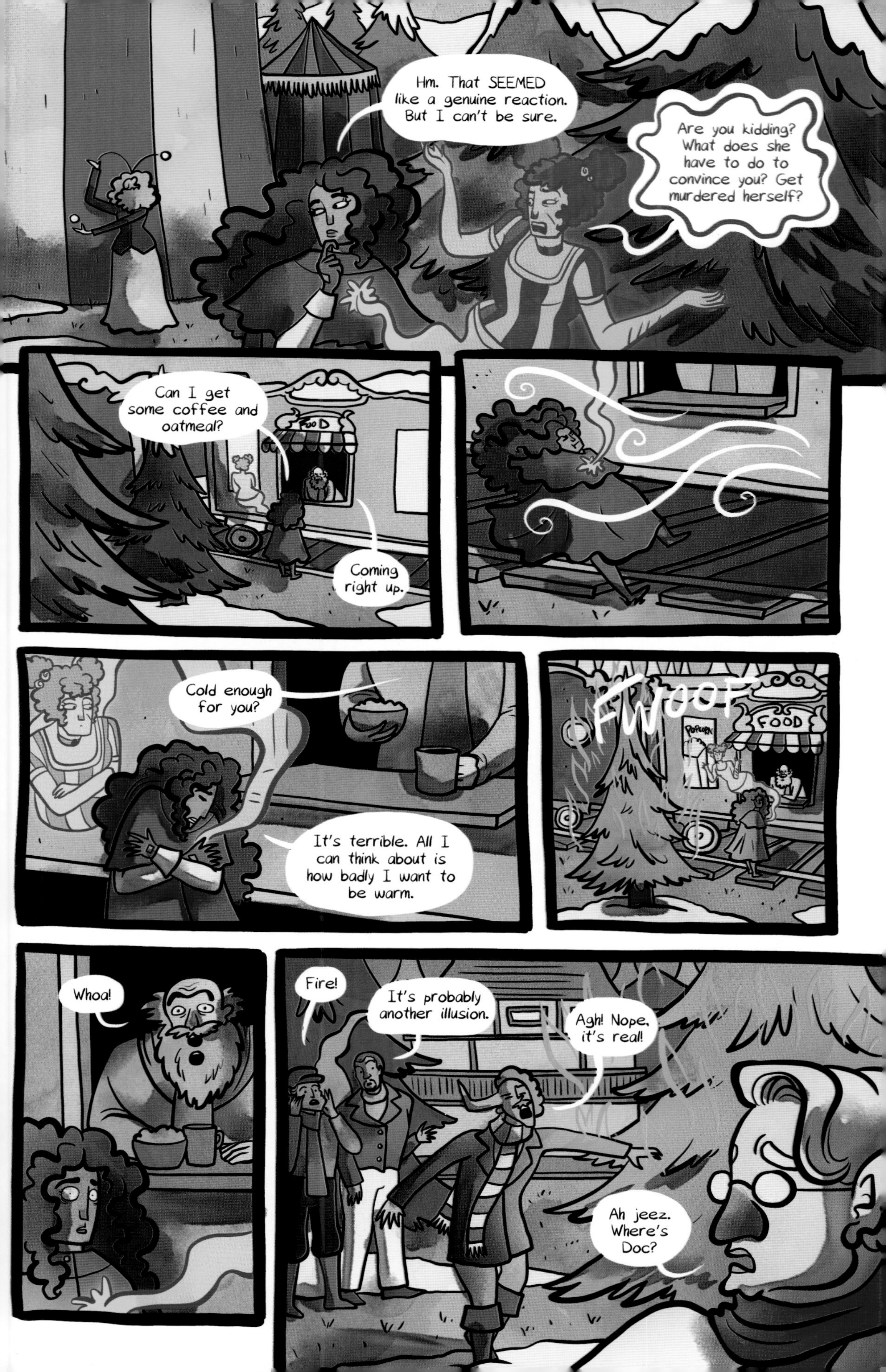
Hm. That SEEMED like a genuine reaction. But I can't be sure.
Are you kidding? What does she have to do to convince you? Get murdered herself?
Can I get some coffee and oatmeal?
FOOD
Coming right up.
Cold enough for you?
It's terrible. All I can think about is how badly I want to be warm.
FWOOF
POPCORN
FOOD
Whoa!
Fire!
It's probably another illusion.
Agh! Nope, it's real!
Ah jeez. Where's Doc?

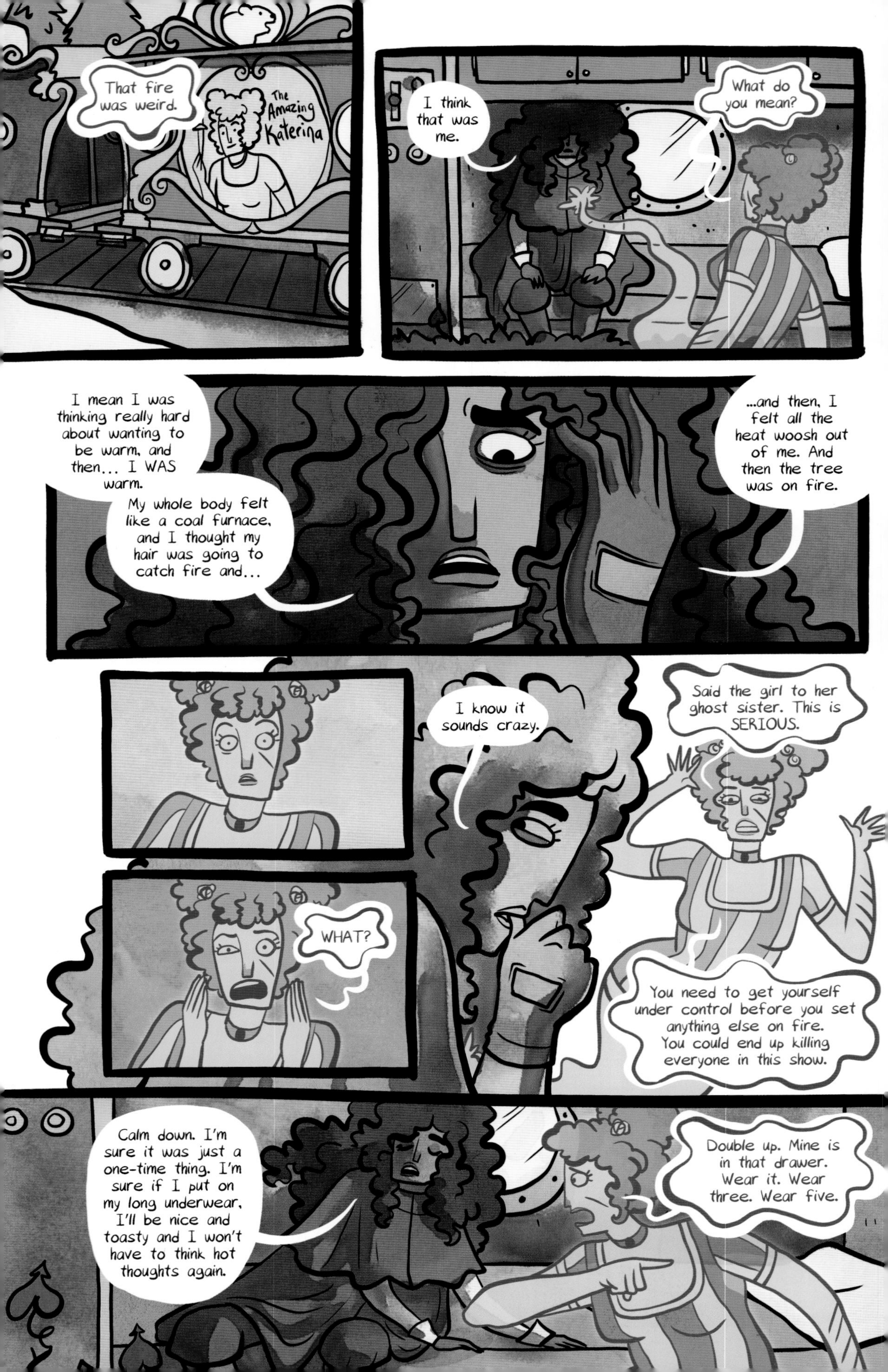
That fire was weird.
The Amazing Katerina
I think that was me.
What do you mean?
I mean I was thinking really hard about wanting to be warm, and then... I WAS warm.
My whole body felt like a coal furnace, and I thought my hair was going to catch fire and...
...and then, I felt all the heat woosh out of me. And then the tree was on fire.
WHAT?
I know it sounds crazy.
Said the girl to her ghost sister. This is SERIOUS.
You need to get yourself under control before you set anything else on fire. You could end up killing everyone in this show.
Calm down. I'm sure it was just a one-time thing. I'm sure if I put on my long underwear, I'll be nice and toasty and I won't have to think hot thoughts again.
Double up. Mine is in that drawer. Wear it. Wear three. Wear five.

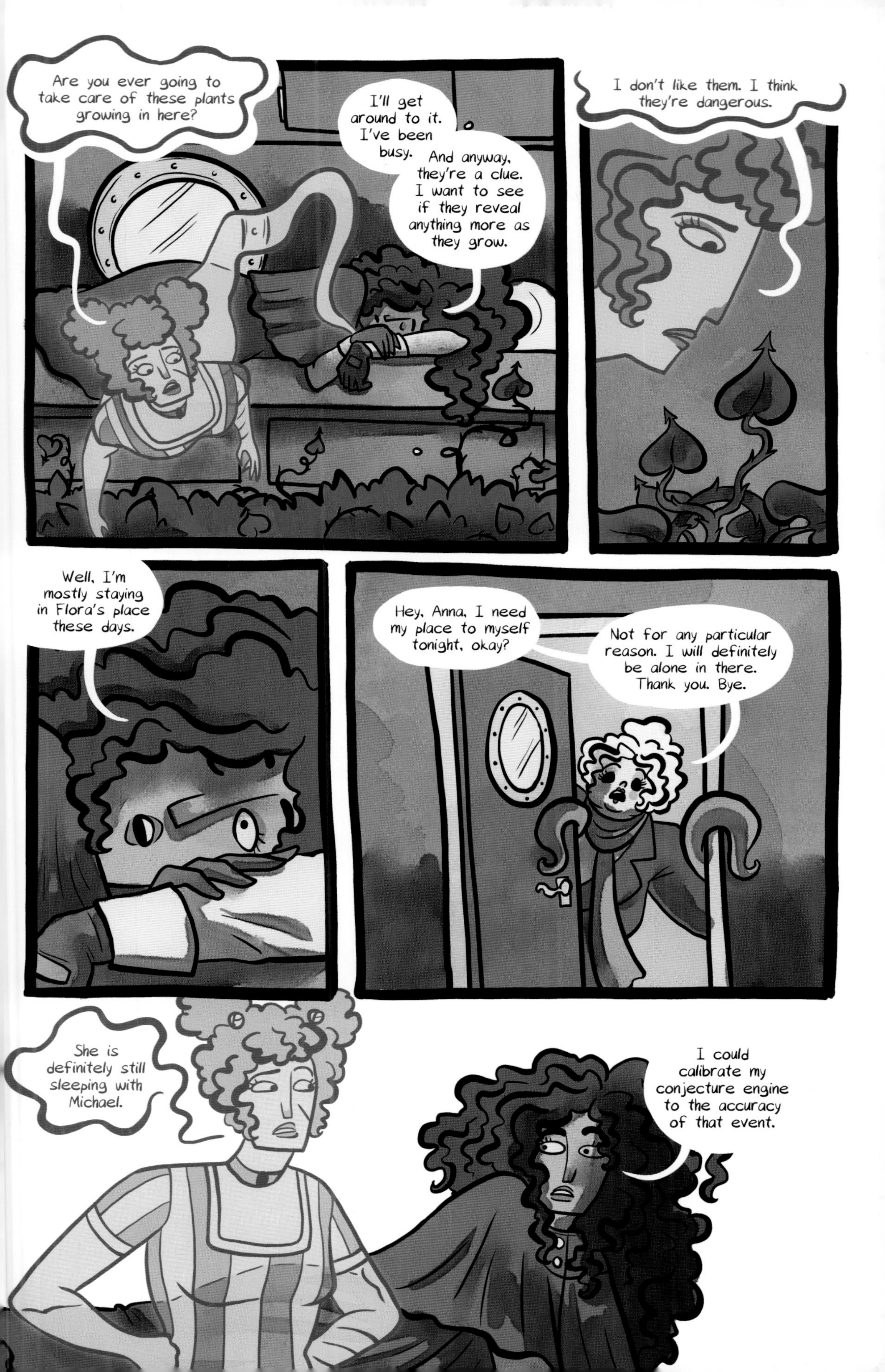
Are you ever going to take care of these plants growing in here?
I'll get around to it. I've been busy.
And anyway, they're a clue. I want to see if they reveal anything more as they grow.
I don't like them. I think they're dangerous.
Well, I'm mostly staying in Flora's place these days.
Hey, Anna, I need my place to myself tonight, okay?
Not for any particular reason. I will definitely be alone in there. Thank you. Bye.
She is definitely still sleeping with Michael.
I could calibrate my conjecture engine to the accuracy of that event.

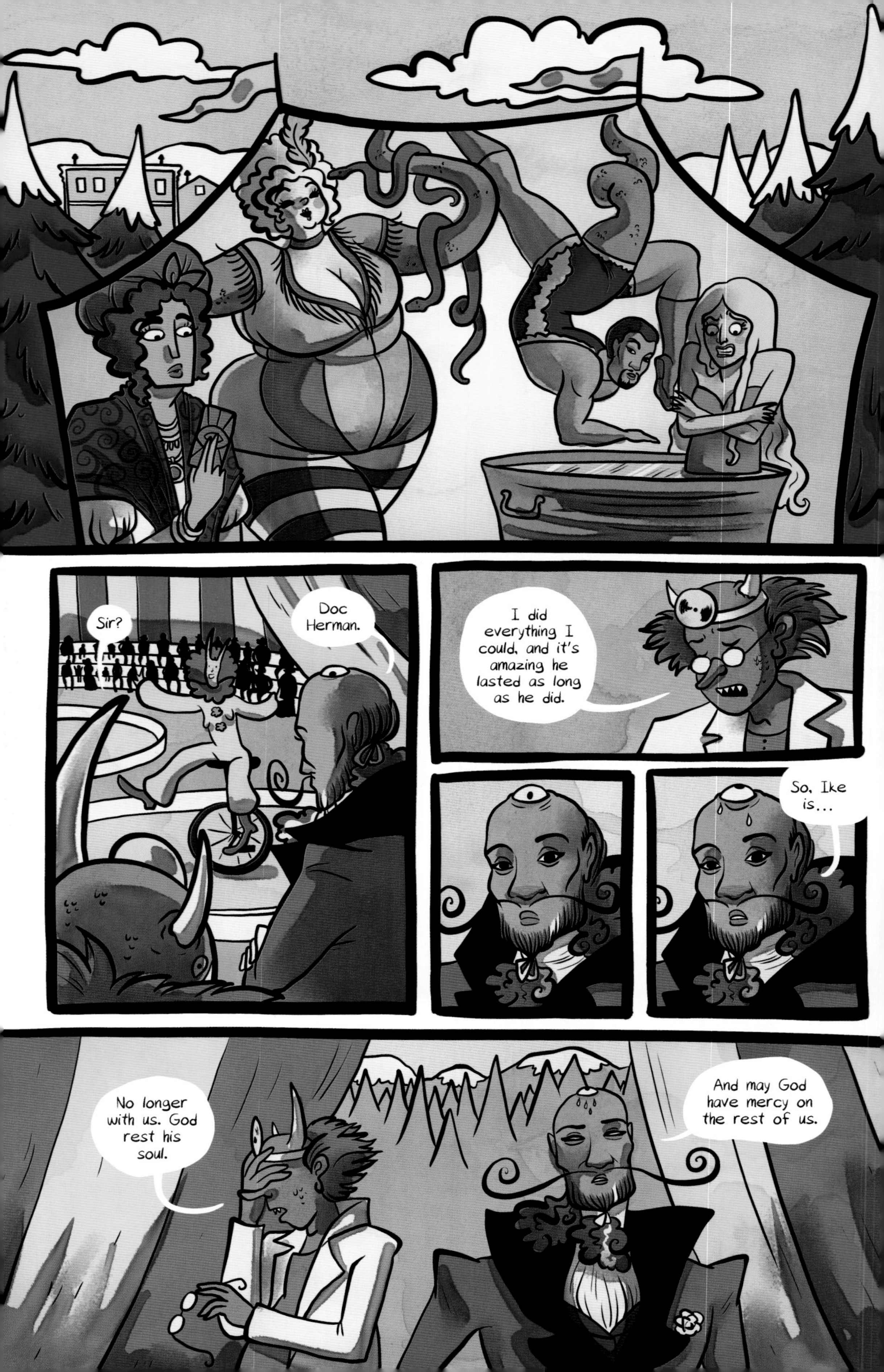
Sir?
Doc Herman.
I did everything I could, and it's amazing he lasted as long as he did.
So, Ike is...
No longer with us. God rest his soul.
And may God have mercy on the rest of us.

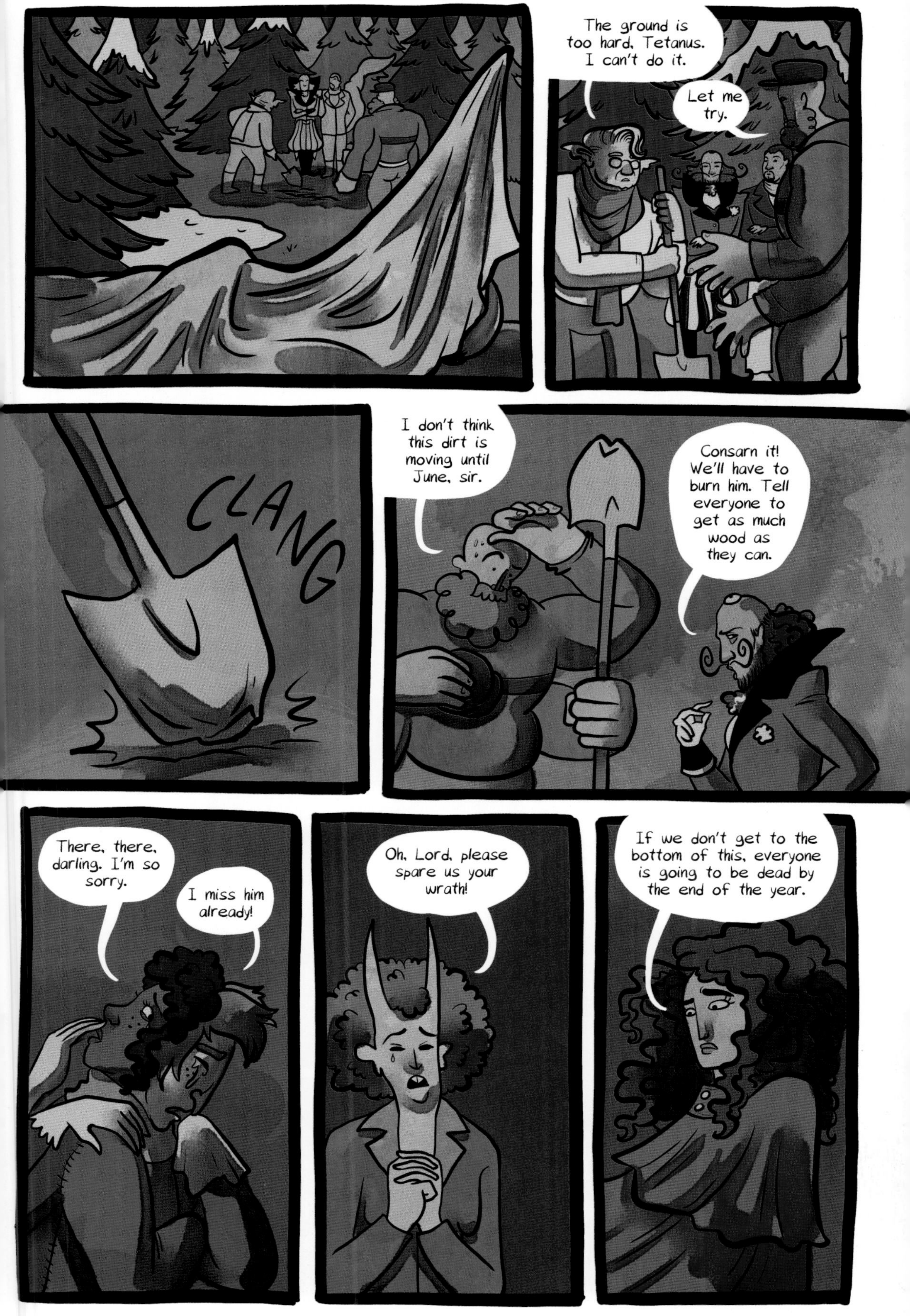
The ground is too hard, Tetanus. I can't do it.
Let me try.
CLANG
I don't think this dirt is moving until June, sir.
Consarn it! We'll have to burn him. Tell everyone to get as much wood as they can.
There, there, darling. I'm so sorry.
I miss him already!
Oh, Lord, please spare us your wrath!
If we don't get to the bottom of this, everyone is going to be dead by the end of the year.

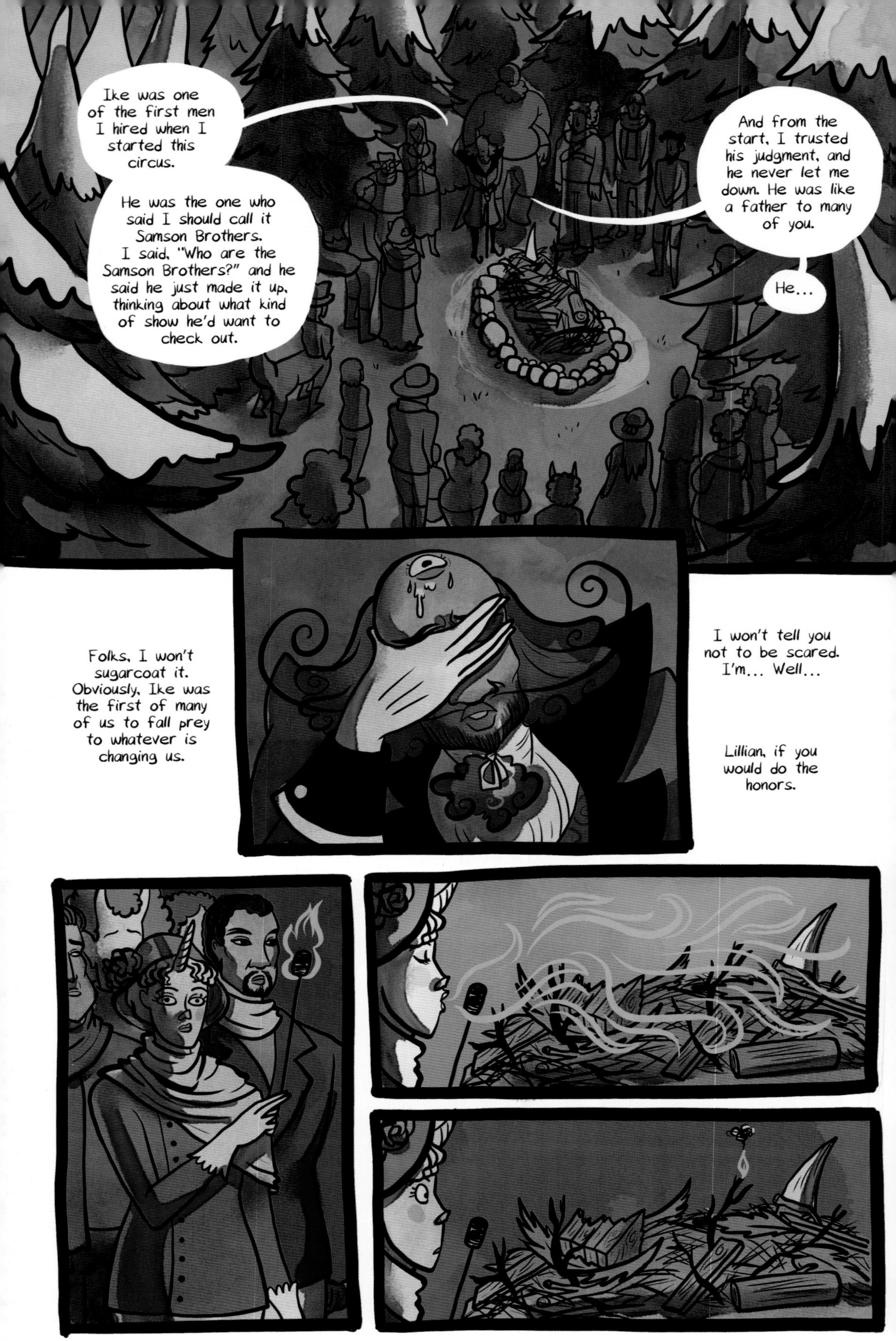
Ike was one of the first men I hired when I started this circus.
He was the one who said I should call it Samson Brothers. I said, "Who are the Samson Brothers?" and he said he just made it up, thinking about what kind of show he'd want to check out.
And from the start, I trusted his judgment, and he never let me down. He was like a father to many of you.
He...
Folks, I won't sugarcoat it. Obviously, Ike was the first of many of us to fall prey to whatever is changing us.
I won't tell you not to be scared. I'm... Well...
Lillian, if you would do the honors.

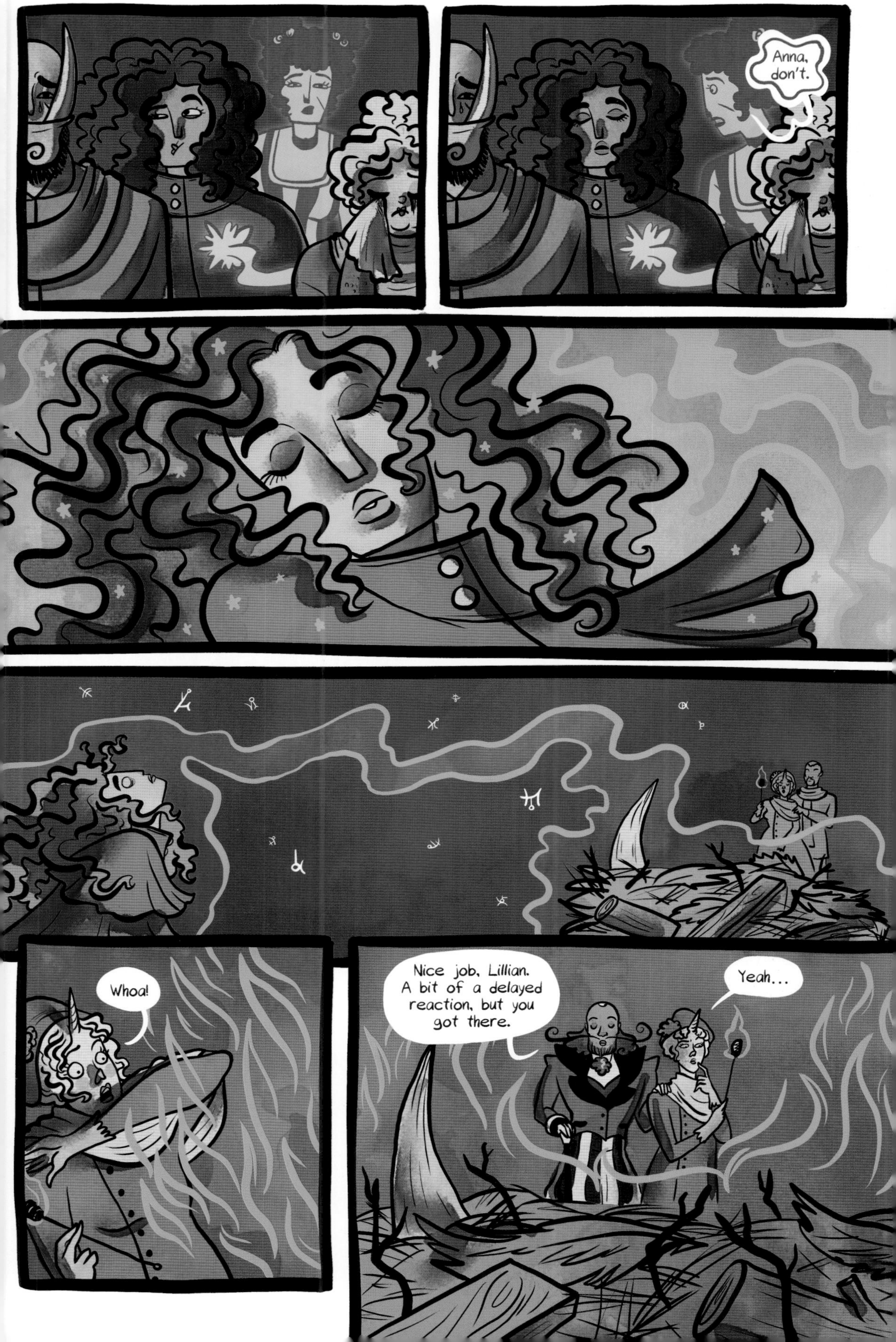
Anna, don't.
Whoa!
Nice job, Lillian. A bit of a delayed reaction, but you got there.
Yeah...

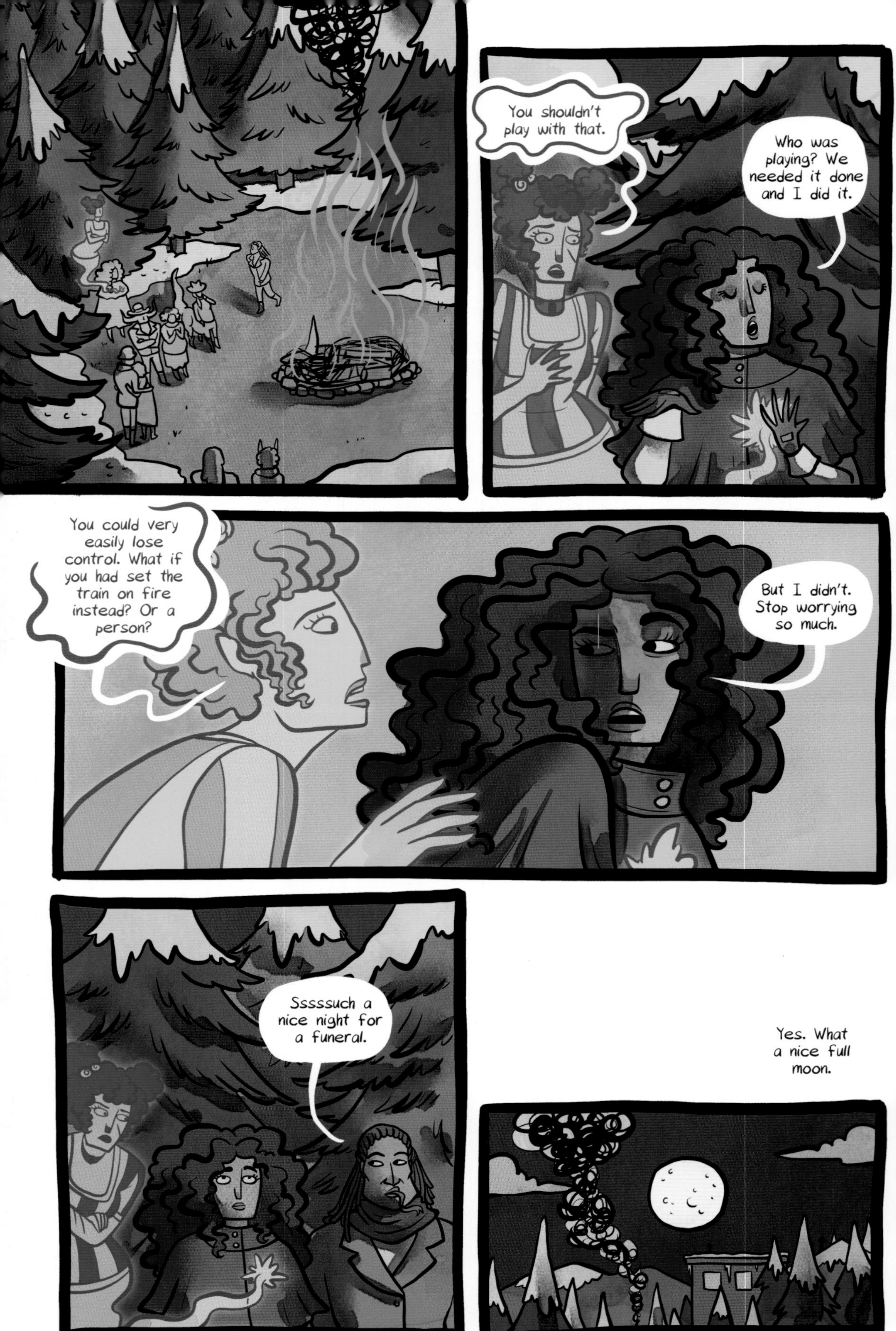
You shouldn't play with that.
Who was playing? We needed it done and I did it.
You could very easily lose control. What if you had set the train on fire instead? Or a person?
But I didn't. Stop worrying so much.
Sssssuch a nice night for a funeral.
Yes. What a nice full moon.

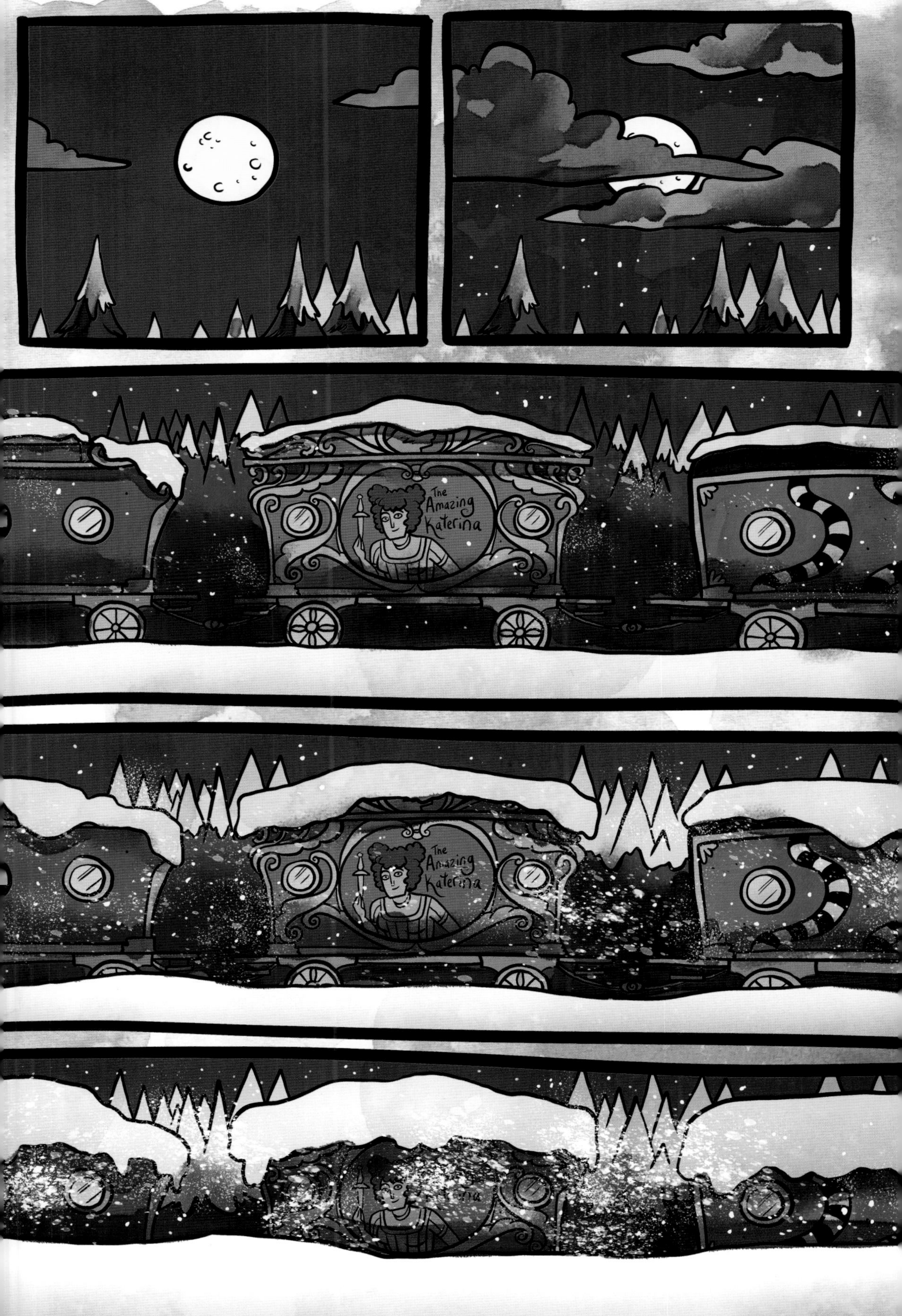
The Amazing Katerina
The Amazing Katerina

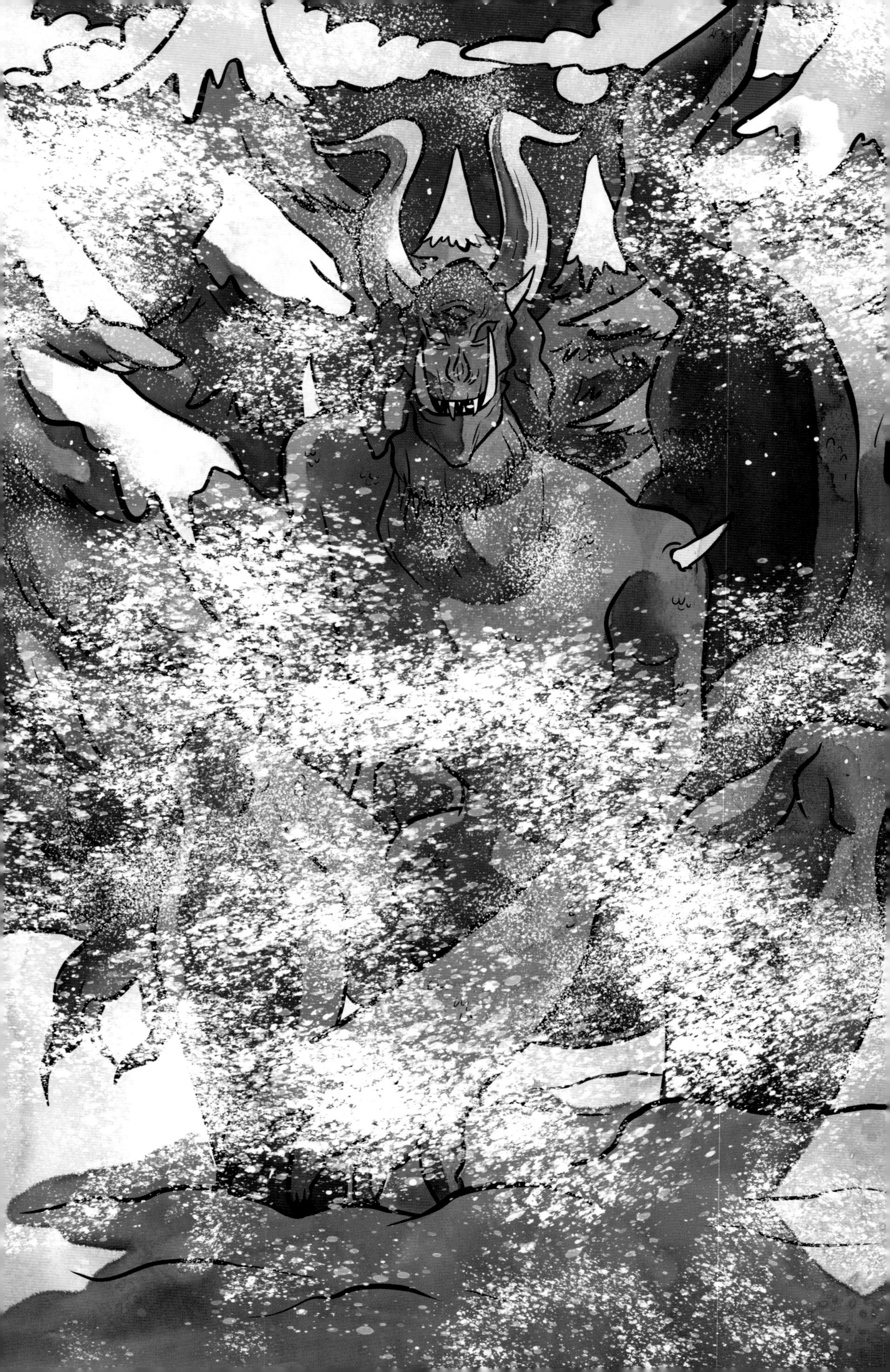

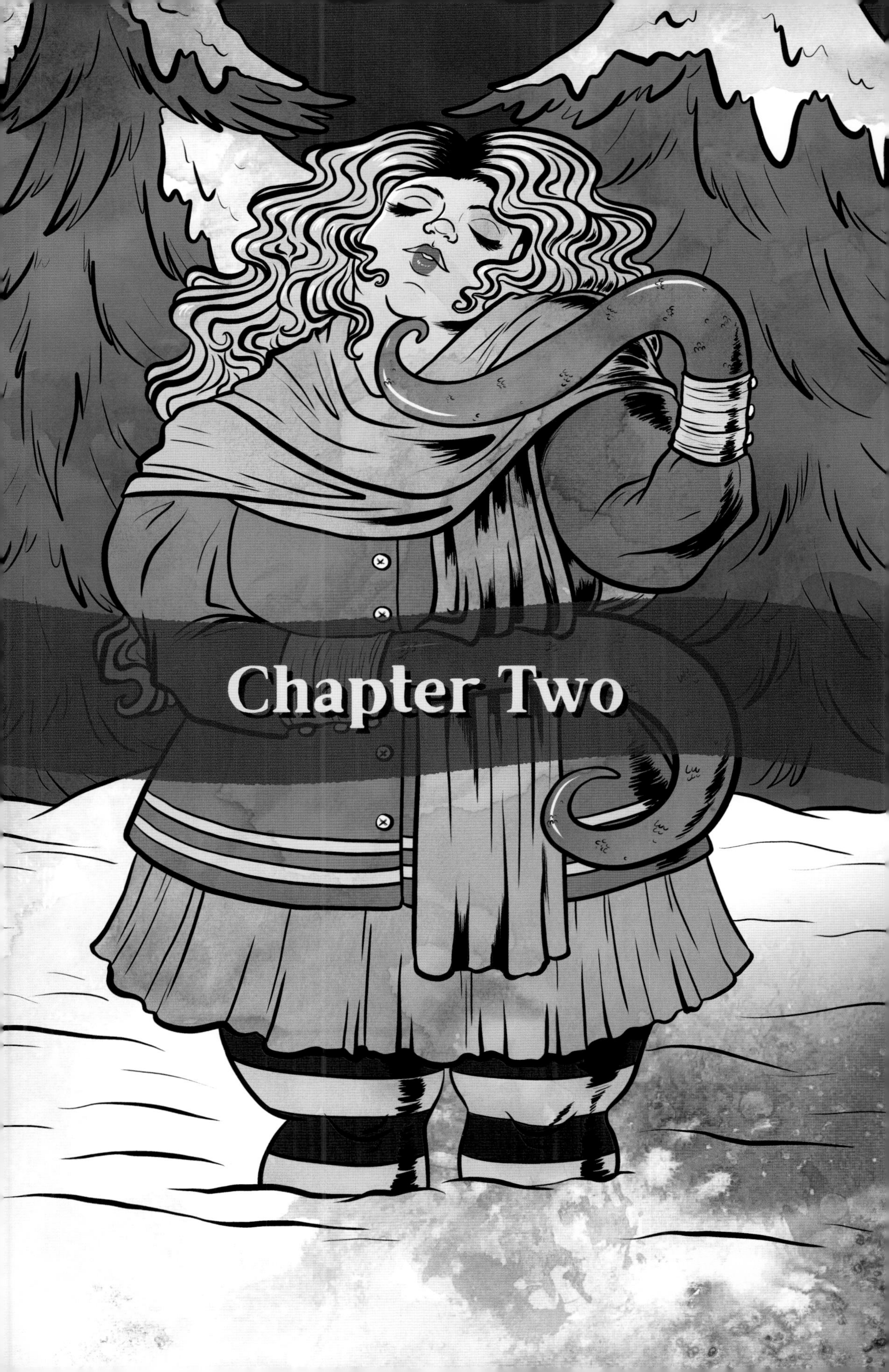

Chapter Two

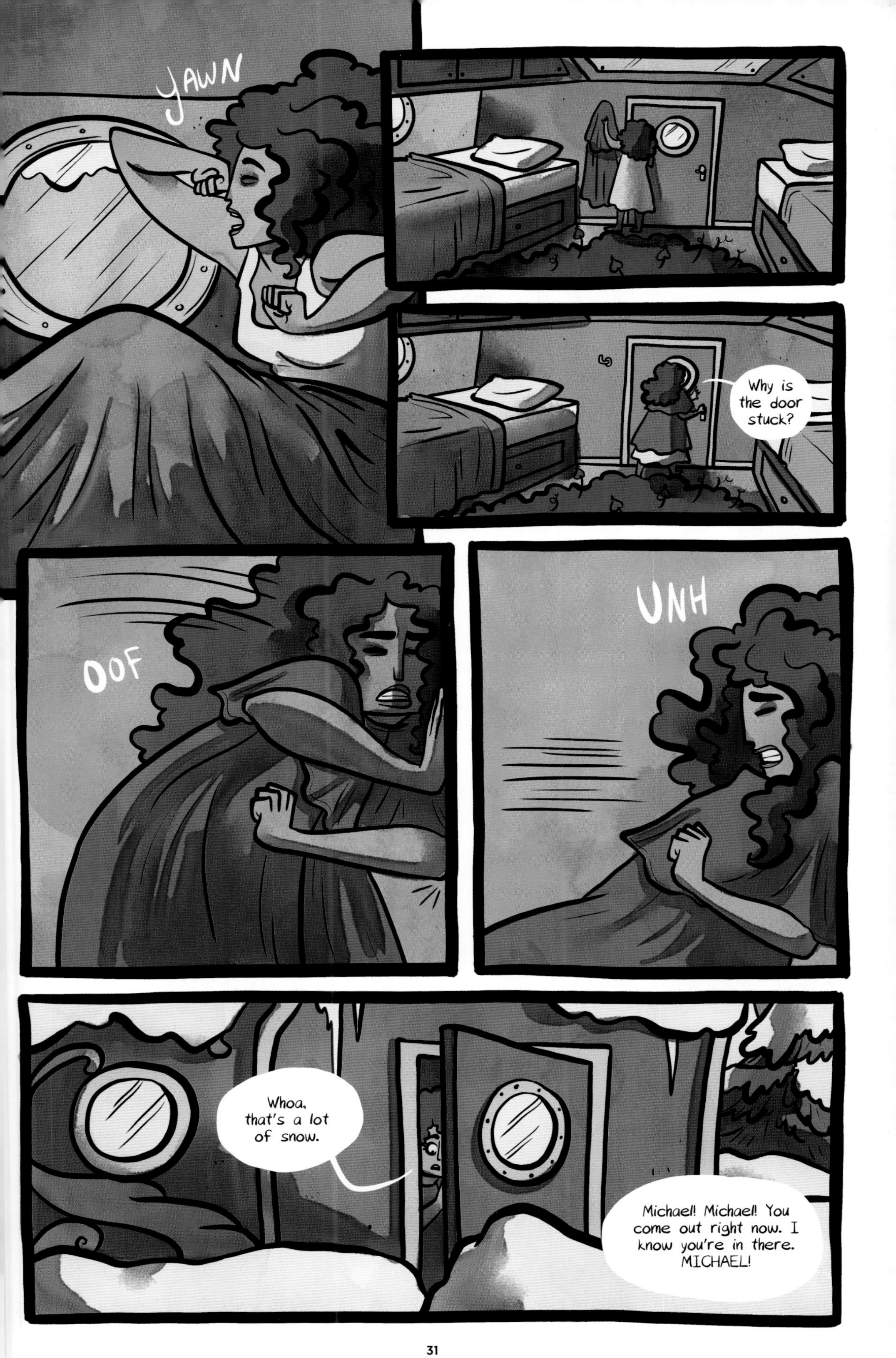
YAWN
Why is the door stuck?
OOF
UNH
Whoa, that's a lot of snow.
Michael! Michael! You come out right now. I know you're in there. MICHAEL!

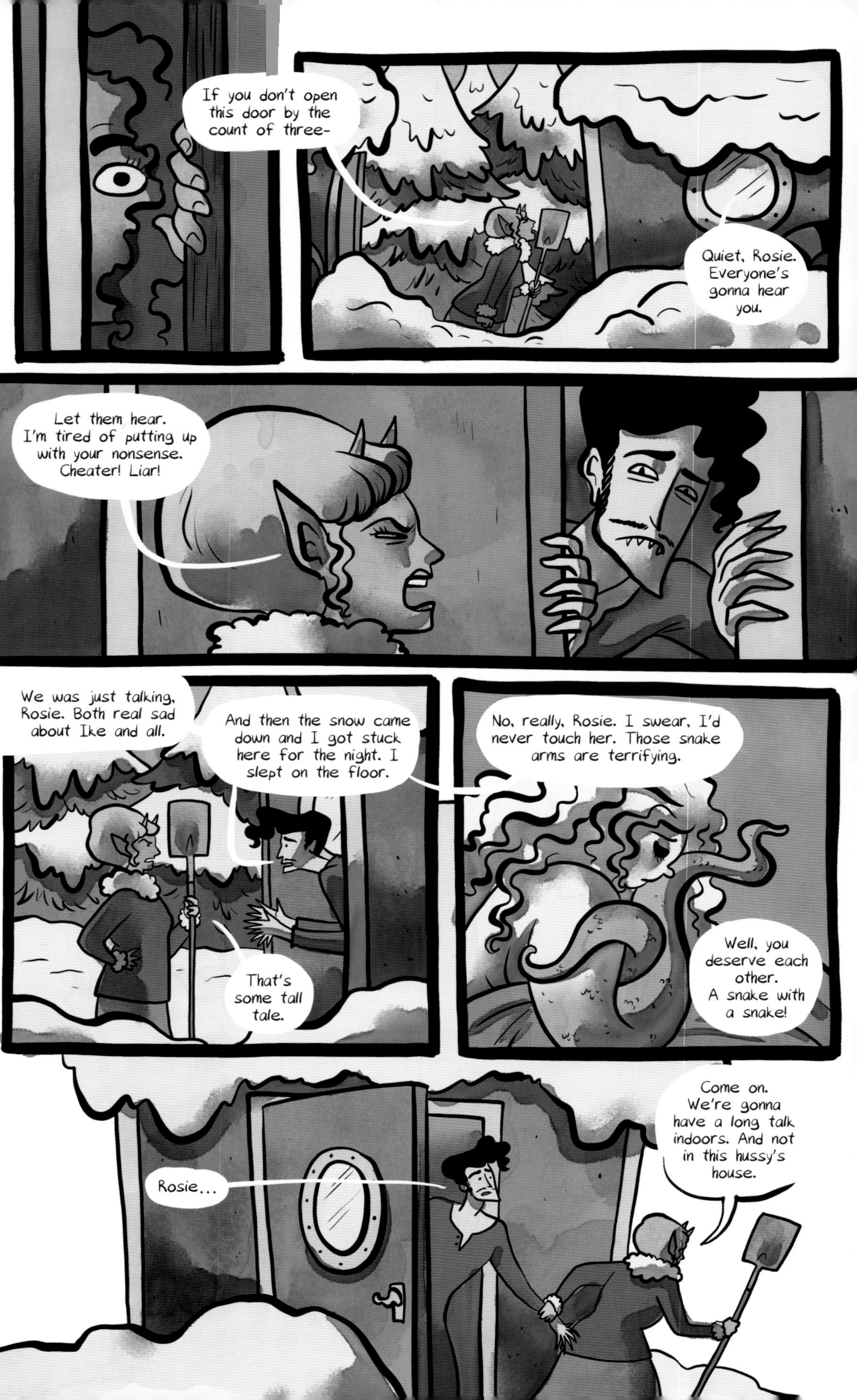
If you don't open this door by the count of three-
Quiet, Rosie. Everyone's gonna hear you.
Let them hear. I'm tired of putting up with your nonsense. Cheater! Liar!
We was just talking, Rosie. Both real sad about Ike and all.
And then the snow came down and I got stuck here for the night. I slept on the floor.
That's some tall tale.
No, really, Rosie. I swear, I'd never touch her. Those snake arms are terrifying.
Well, you deserve each other. A snake with a snake!
Come on. We're gonna have a long talk indoors. And not in this hussy's house.
Rosie...

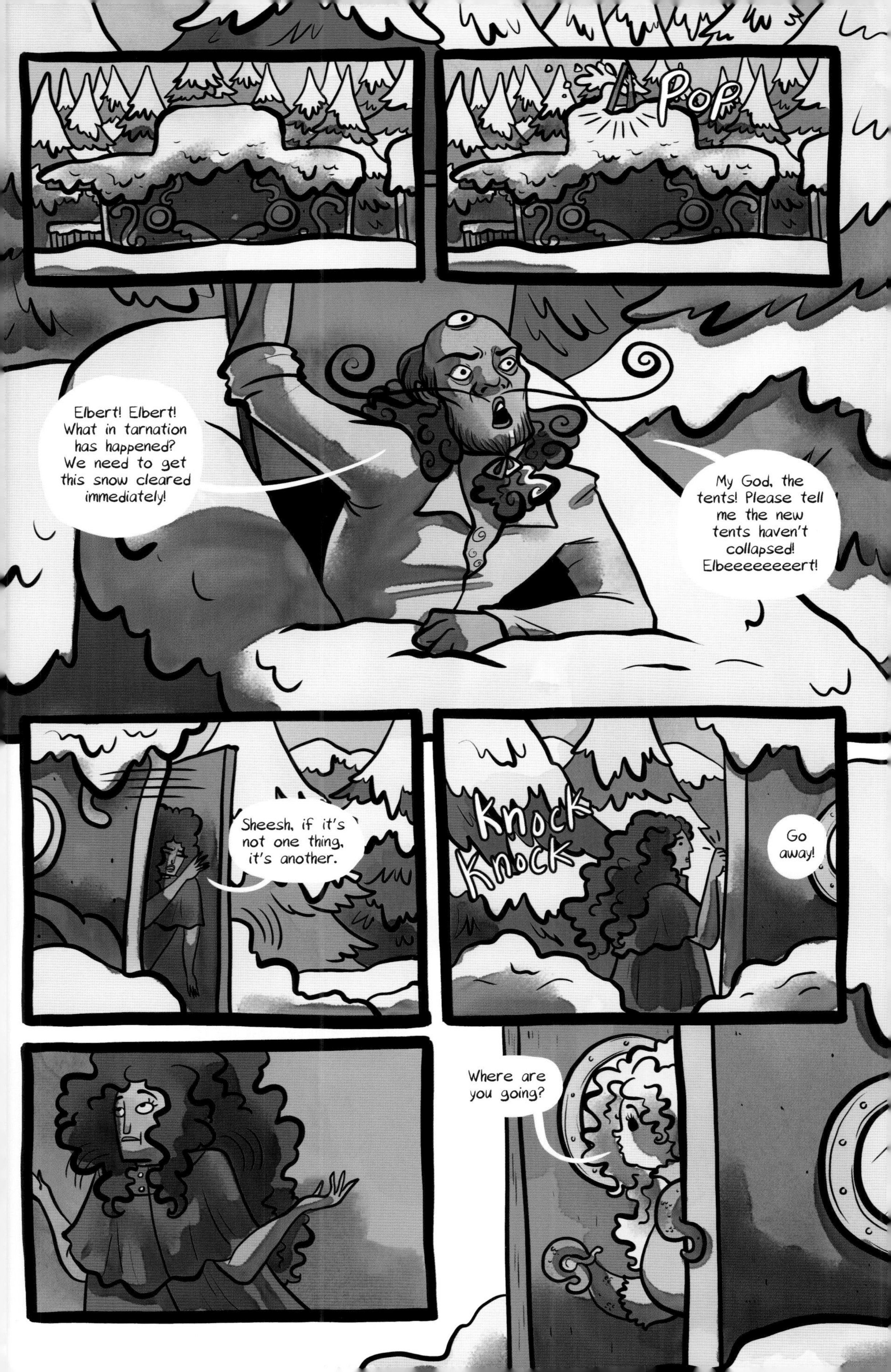
POP
Elbert! Elbert! What in tarnation has happened? We need to get this snow cleared immediately!
My God, the tents! Please tell me the new tents haven't collapsed! Elbeeeeeeeert!
Sheesh, if it's not one thing, it's another.
Knock Knock
Go away!
Where are you going?

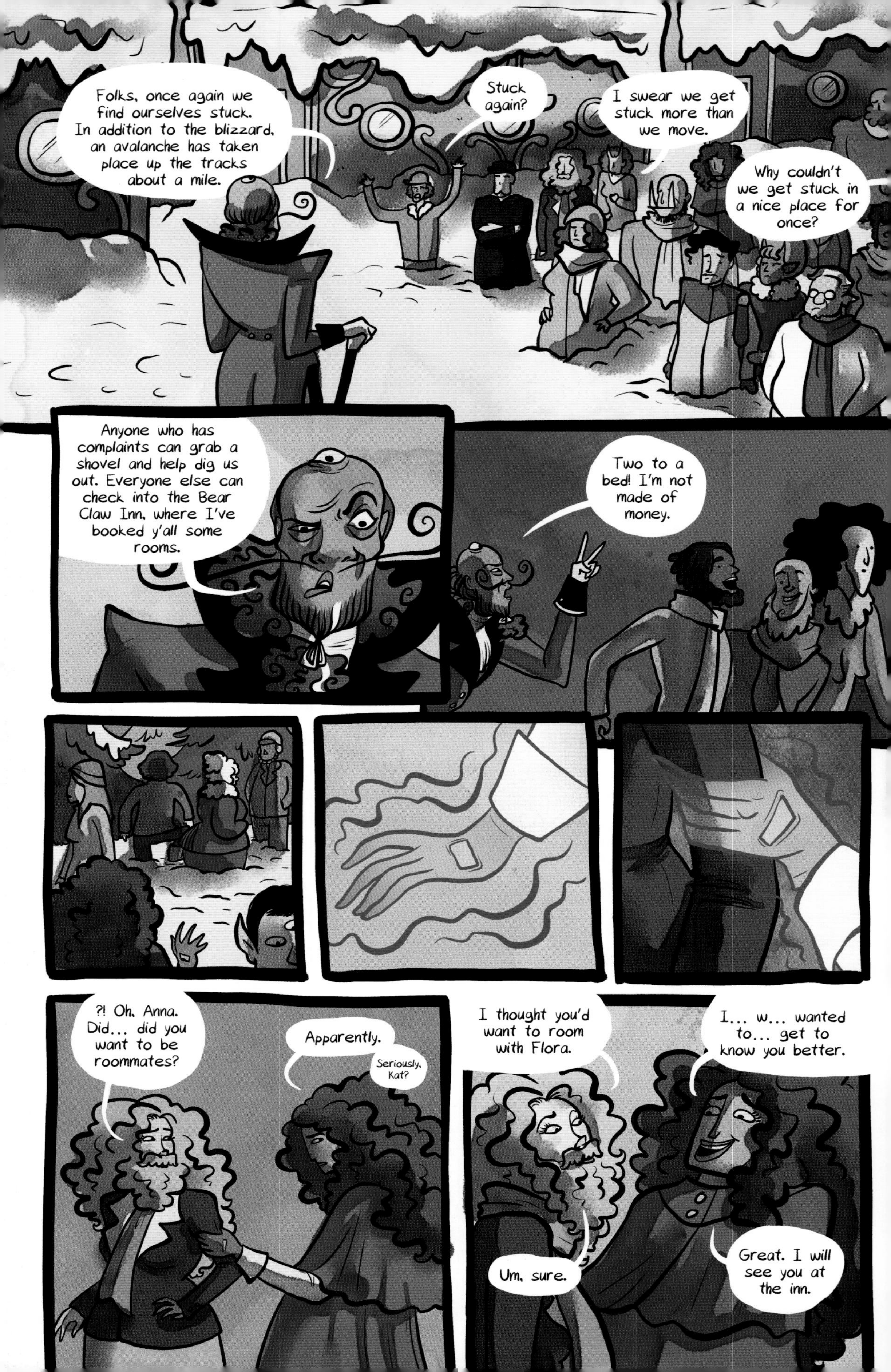

Folks, once again we find ourselves stuck. In addition to the blizzard, an avalanche has taken place up the tracks about a mile.
Stuck again?
I swear we get stuck more than we move.
Why couldn't we get stuck in a nice place for once?
Anyone who has complaints can grab a shovel and help dig us out. Everyone else can check into the Bear Claw Inn, where I've booked y'all some rooms.
Two to a bed! I'm not made of money.
?! Oh, Anna. Did... did you want to be roommates?
Apparently.
Seriously, Kat?
I thought you'd want to room with Flora.
I... w... wanted to... get to know you better.
Um, sure.
Great. I will see you at the inn.

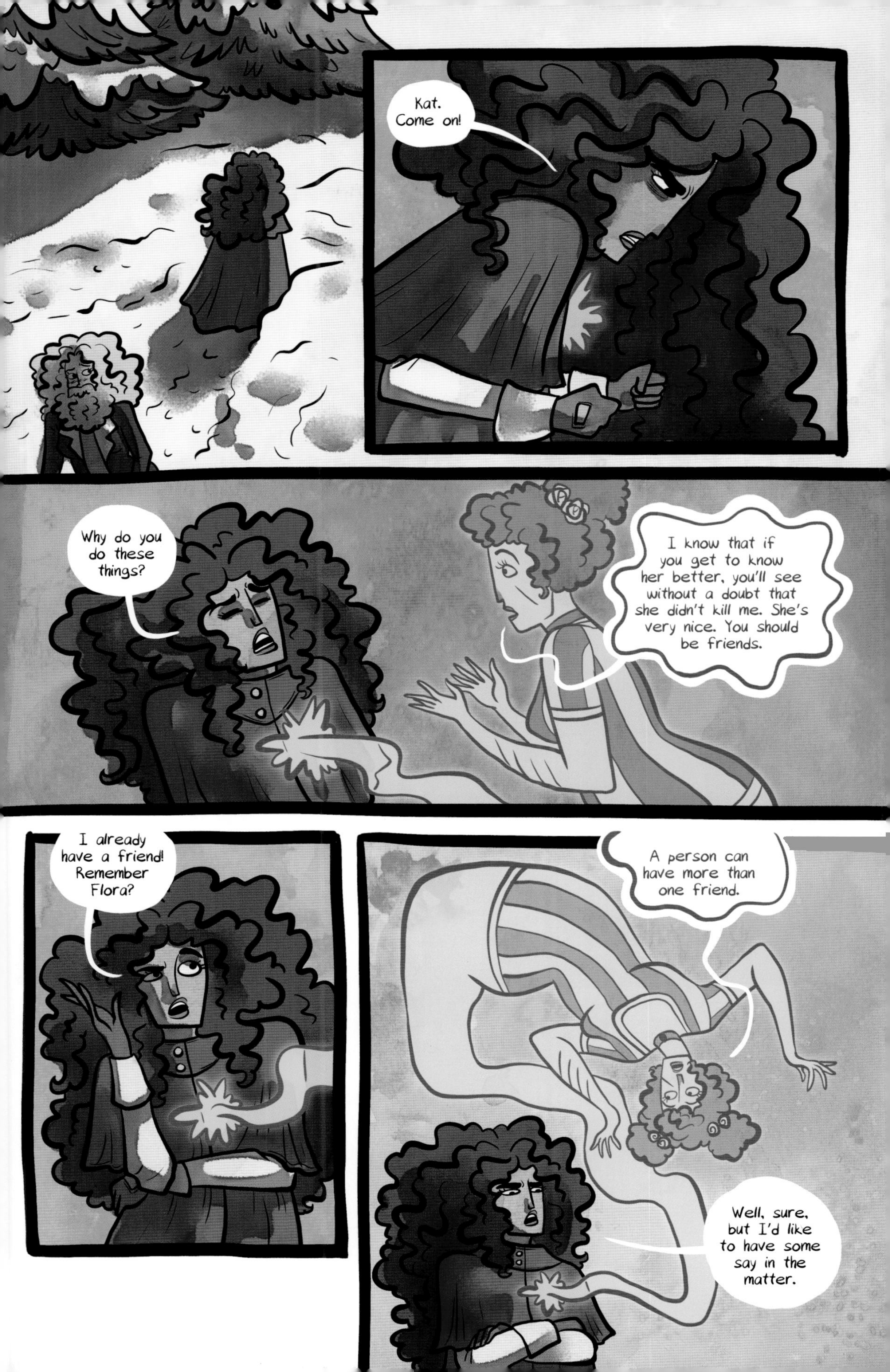
Kat. Come on!
Why do you do these things?
I know that if you get to know her better, you'll see without a doubt that she didn't kill me. She's very nice. You should be friends.
I already have a friend! Remember Flora?
A person can have more than one friend.
Well, sure, but I'd like to have some say in the matter.

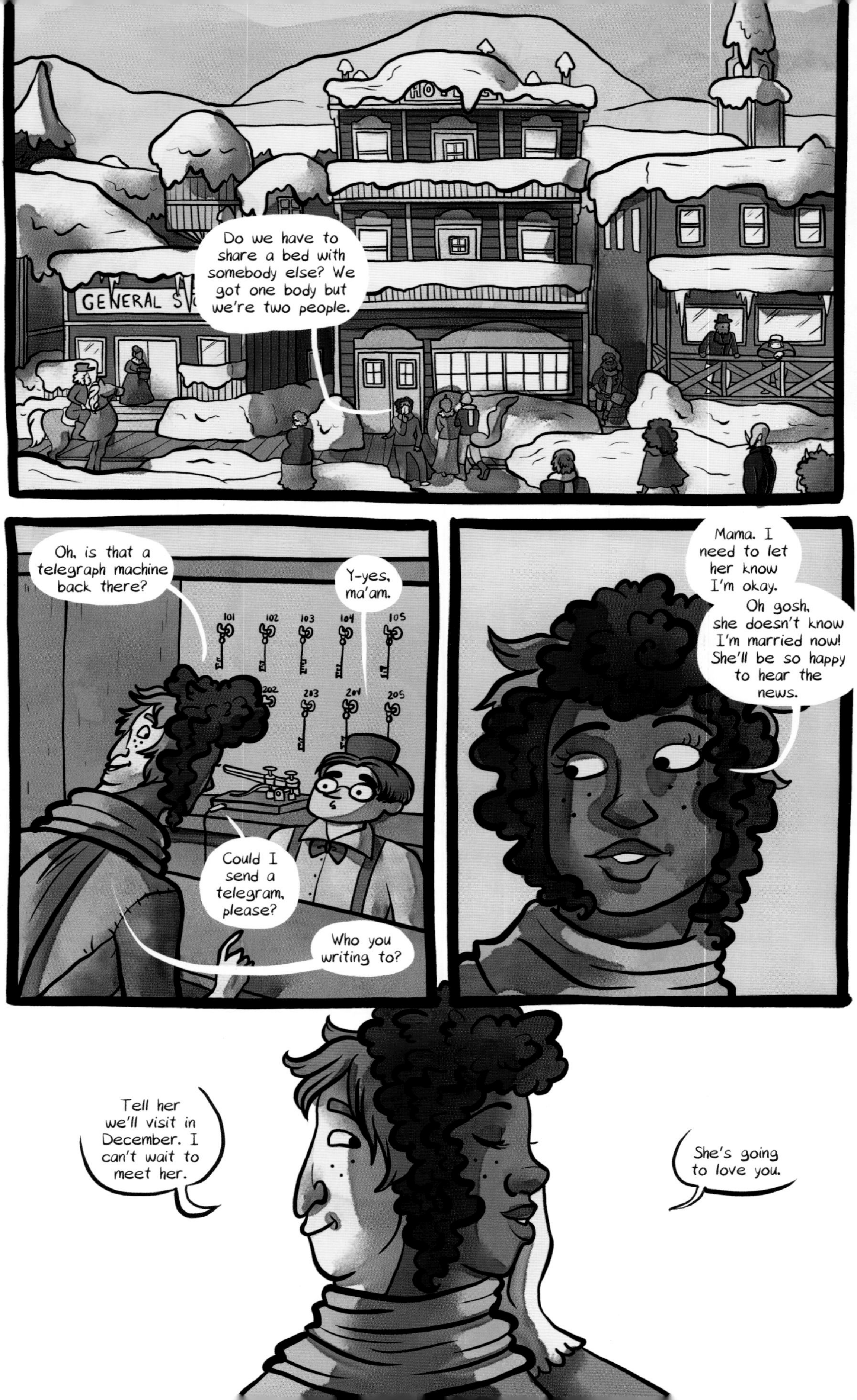
Do we have to share a bed with somebody else? We got one body but we're two people.
Oh, is that a telegraph machine back there?
Y-yes, ma'am.
Could I send a telegram, please?
Who you writing to?
Mama. I need to let her know I'm okay.
Oh gosh, she doesn't know I'm married now! She'll be so happy to hear the news.
Tell her we'll visit in December. I can't wait to meet her.
She's going to love you.

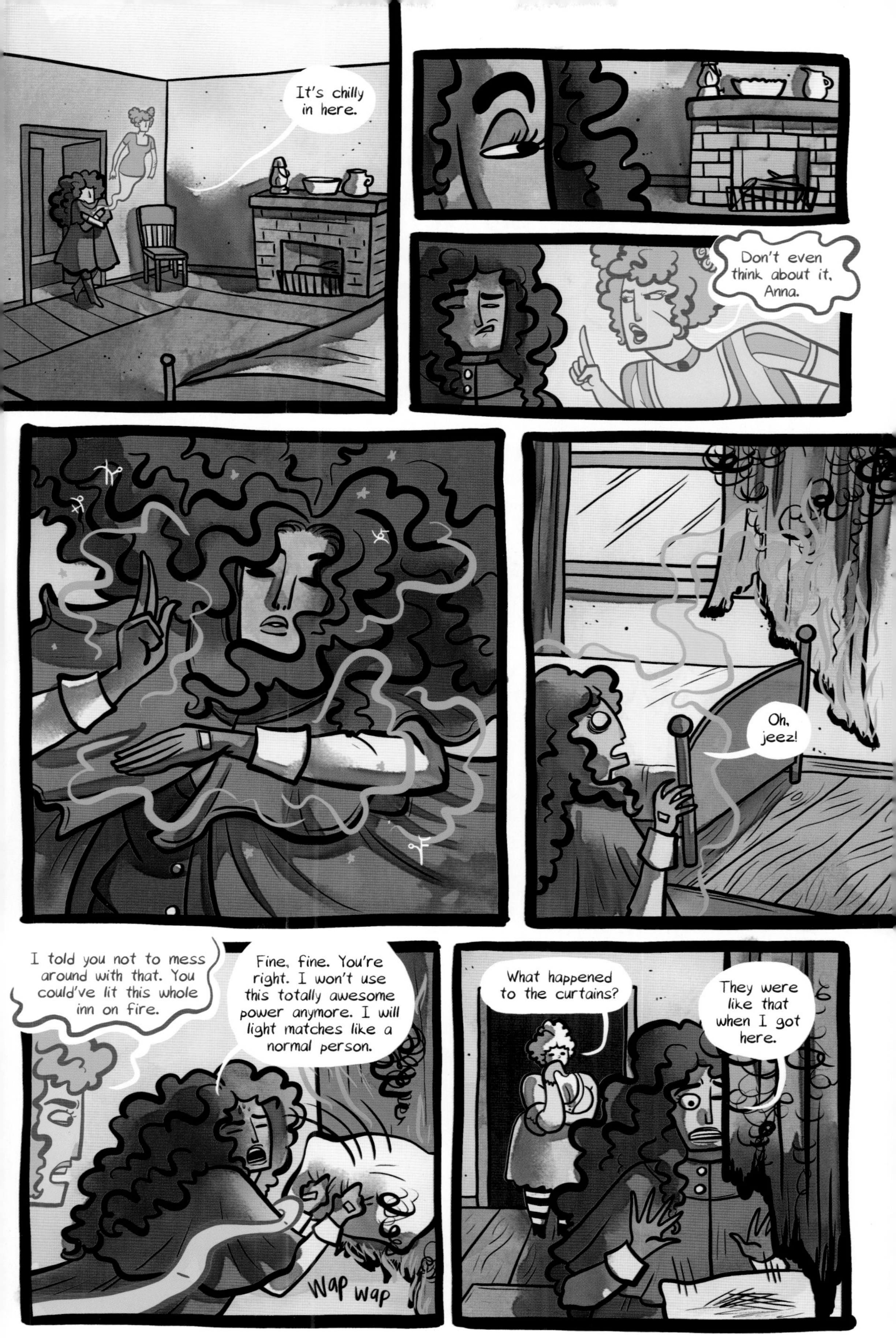
It's chilly in here.
Don't even think about it, Anna.
Oh, jeez!
I told you not to mess around with that. You could've lit this whole inn on fire.
Fine, fine. You're right. I won't use this totally awesome power anymore. I will light matches like a normal person.
Wap wap
What happened to the curtains?
They were like that when I got here.

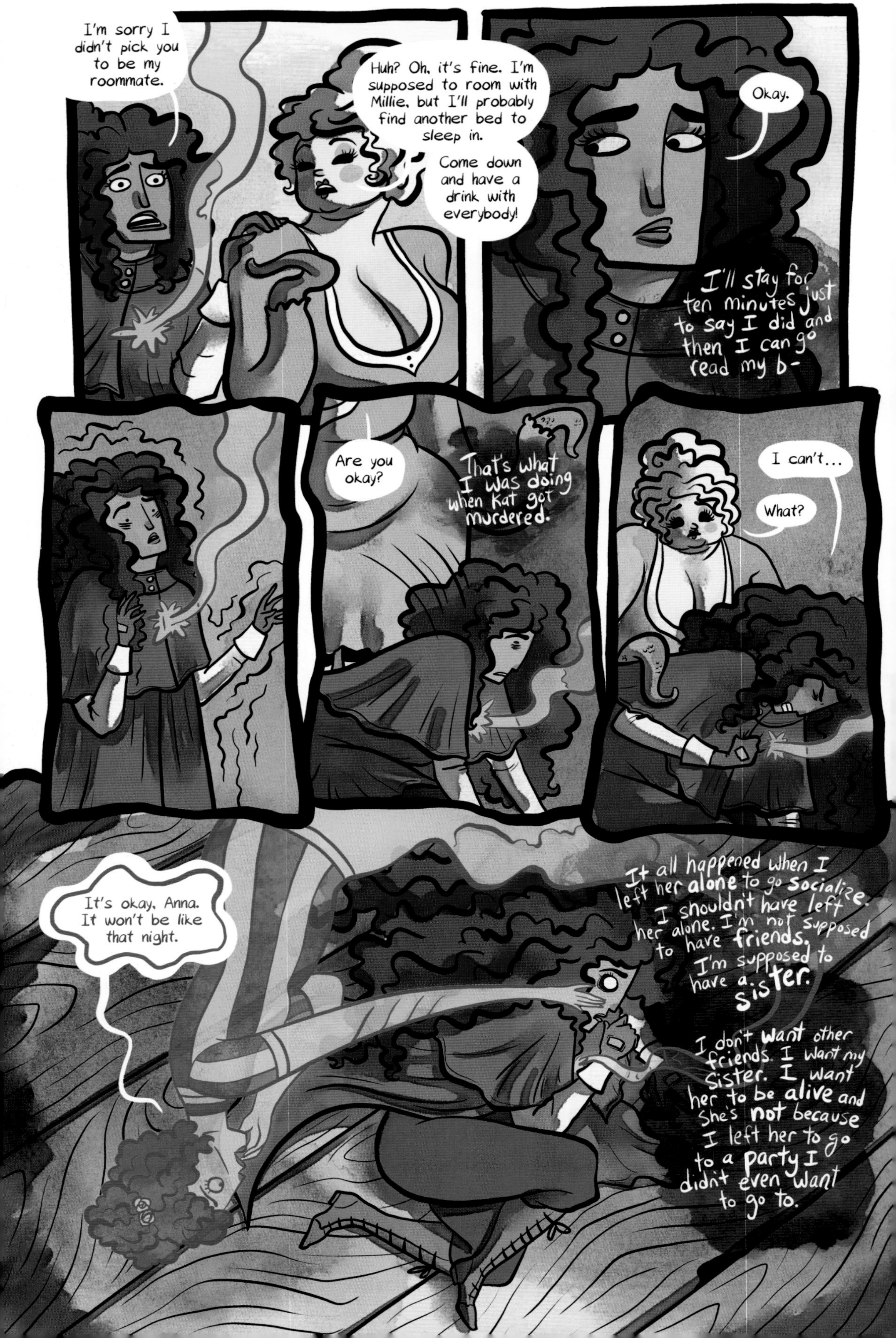
I'm sorry I didn't pick you to be my roommate.
Huh? Oh, it's fine. I'm supposed to room with Millie, but I'll probably find another bed to sleep in.
Come down and have a drink with everybody!
Okay.
I'll stay for ten minutes just to say I did and then I can go read my b-
Are you okay?
That's what I was doing when Kat got murdered.
I can't...
What?
It's okay, Anna. It won't be like that night.
It all happened when I left her alone to go socialize. I shouldn't have left her alone. I'm not supposed to have friends. I'm supposed to have a sister.
I don't want other friends. I want my sister. I want her to be alive and she's not because I left her to go to a party I didn't even want to go to.

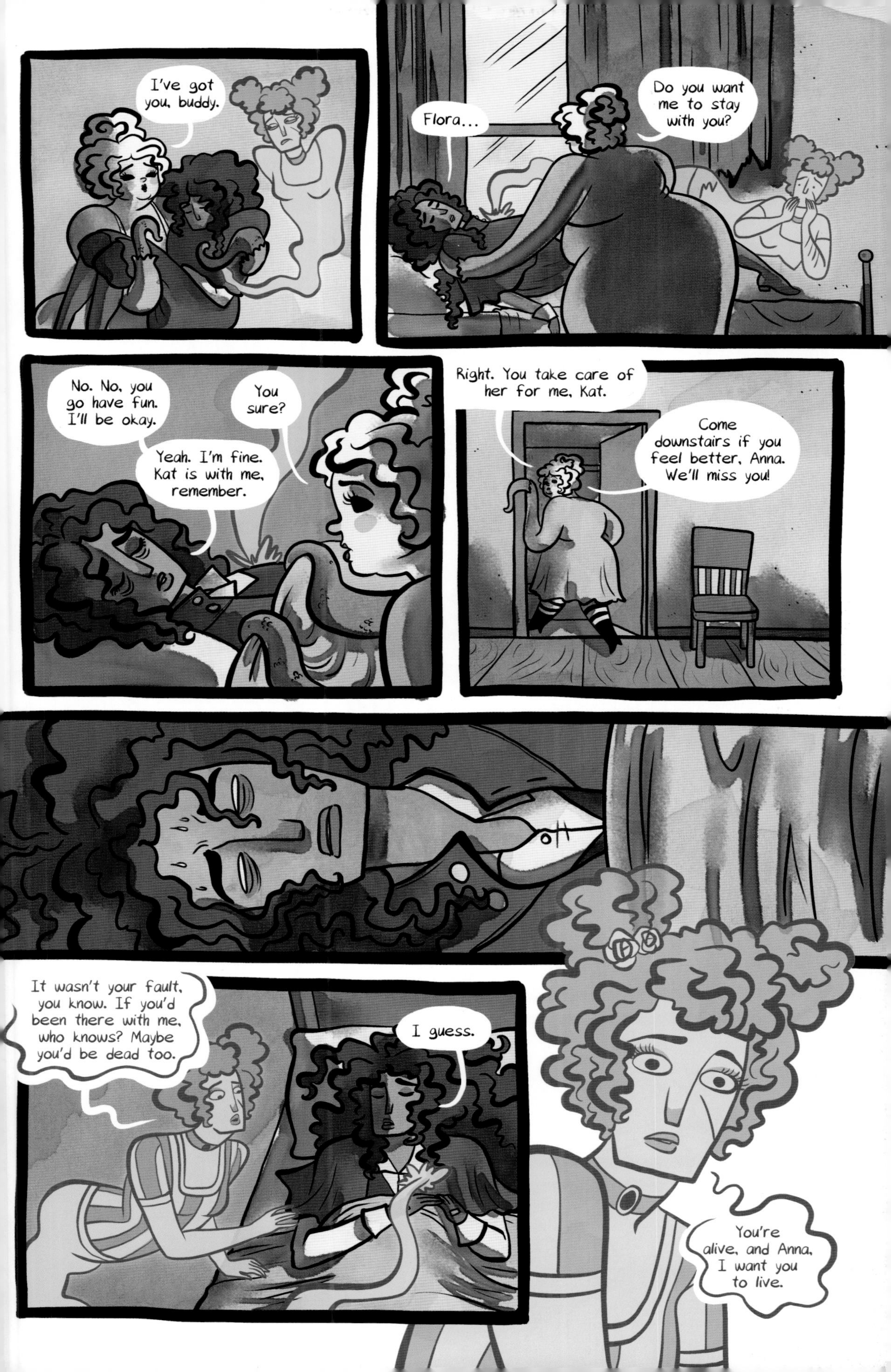
I've got you, buddy.
Flora...
Do you want me to stay with you?
No. No, you go have fun. I'll be okay.
You sure?
Yeah. I'm fine. Kat is with me, remember.
Right. You take care of her for me, Kat.
Come downstairs if you feel better, Anna. We'll miss you!
It wasn't your fault, you know. If you'd been there with me, who knows? Maybe you'd be dead too.
I guess.
You're alive, and Anna, I want you to live.

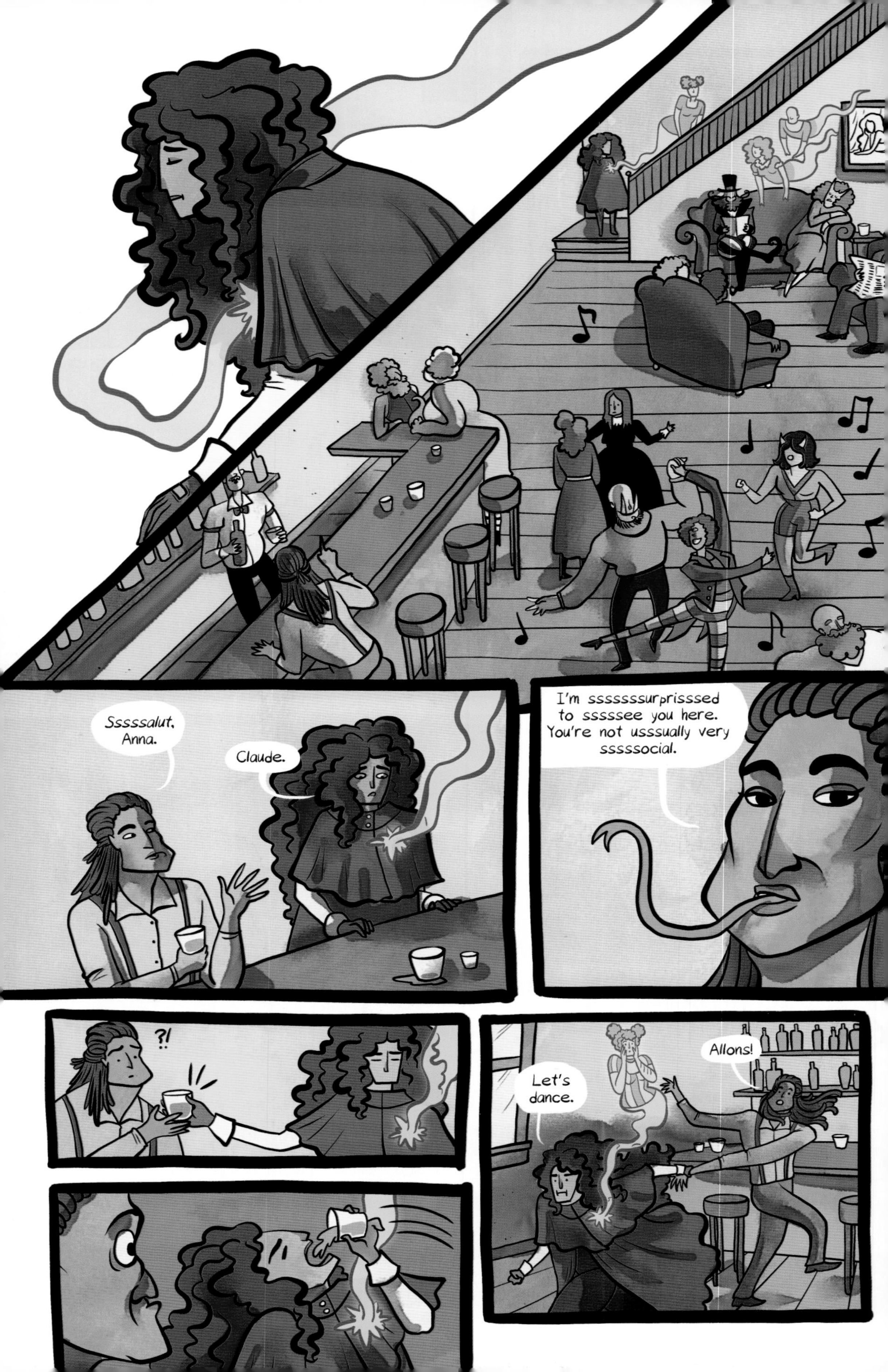
Sssssalut, Anna.
Claude.
I'm sssssssurprisssed to ssssssee you here. You're not usssually very ssssssocial.
?!
Let's dance.
Allons!

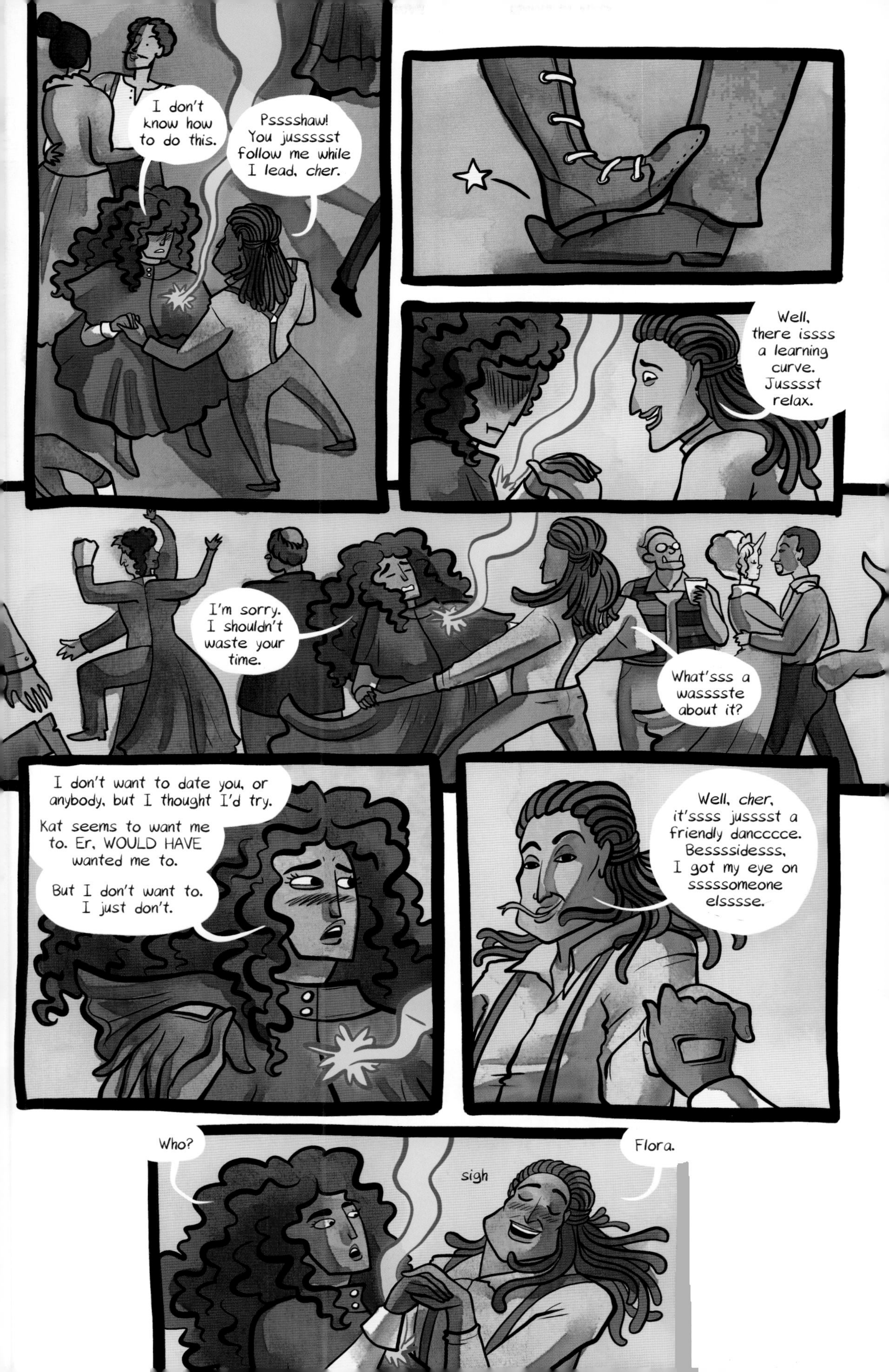

I don't know how to do this.
Psssshaw! You jussssst follow me while I lead, cher.
Well, there issss a learning curve. Jusssst relax.
I'm sorry. I shouldn't waste your time.
What'sss a wasssste about it?
I don't want to date you, or anybody, but I thought I'd try.
Kat seems to want me to. Er, WOULD HAVE wanted me to.
But I don't want to. I just don't.
Well, cher, it'ssss jussssst a friendly dancccce. Besssssidesss, I got my eye on sssssomeone elsssse.
Who?
sigh
Flora.

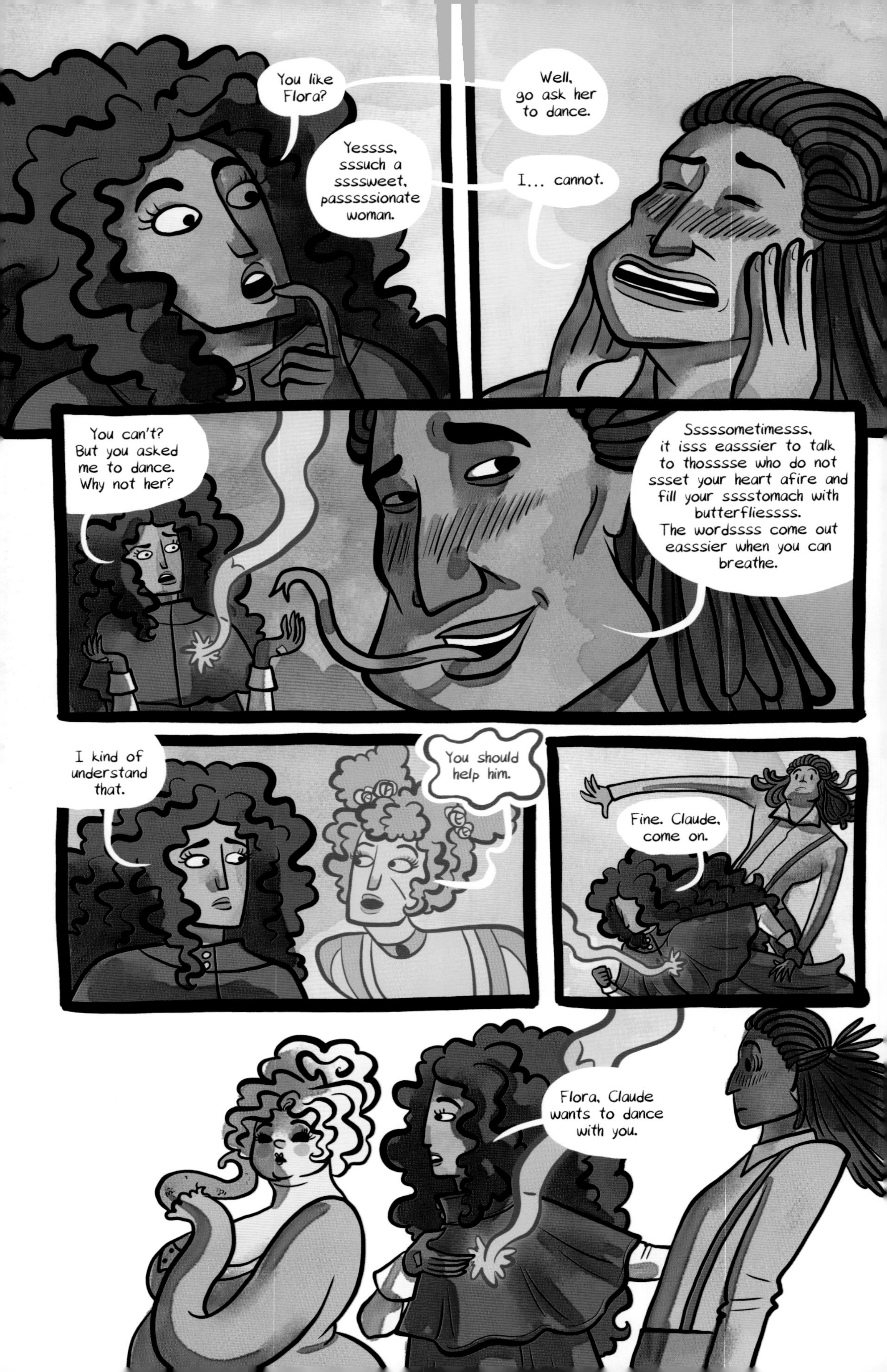
You like Flora?
Yessss, sssuch a sssweet, passsssionate woman.
Well, go ask her to dance.
I... cannot.
You can't? But you asked me to dance. Why not her?
Sssssometimesss, it isss easssier to talk to thosssse who do not ssset your heart afire and fill your sssstomach with butterfliesss. The wordssss come out easssier when you can breathe.
I kind of understand that.
You should help him.
Fine. Claude, come on.
Flora, Claude wants to dance with you.

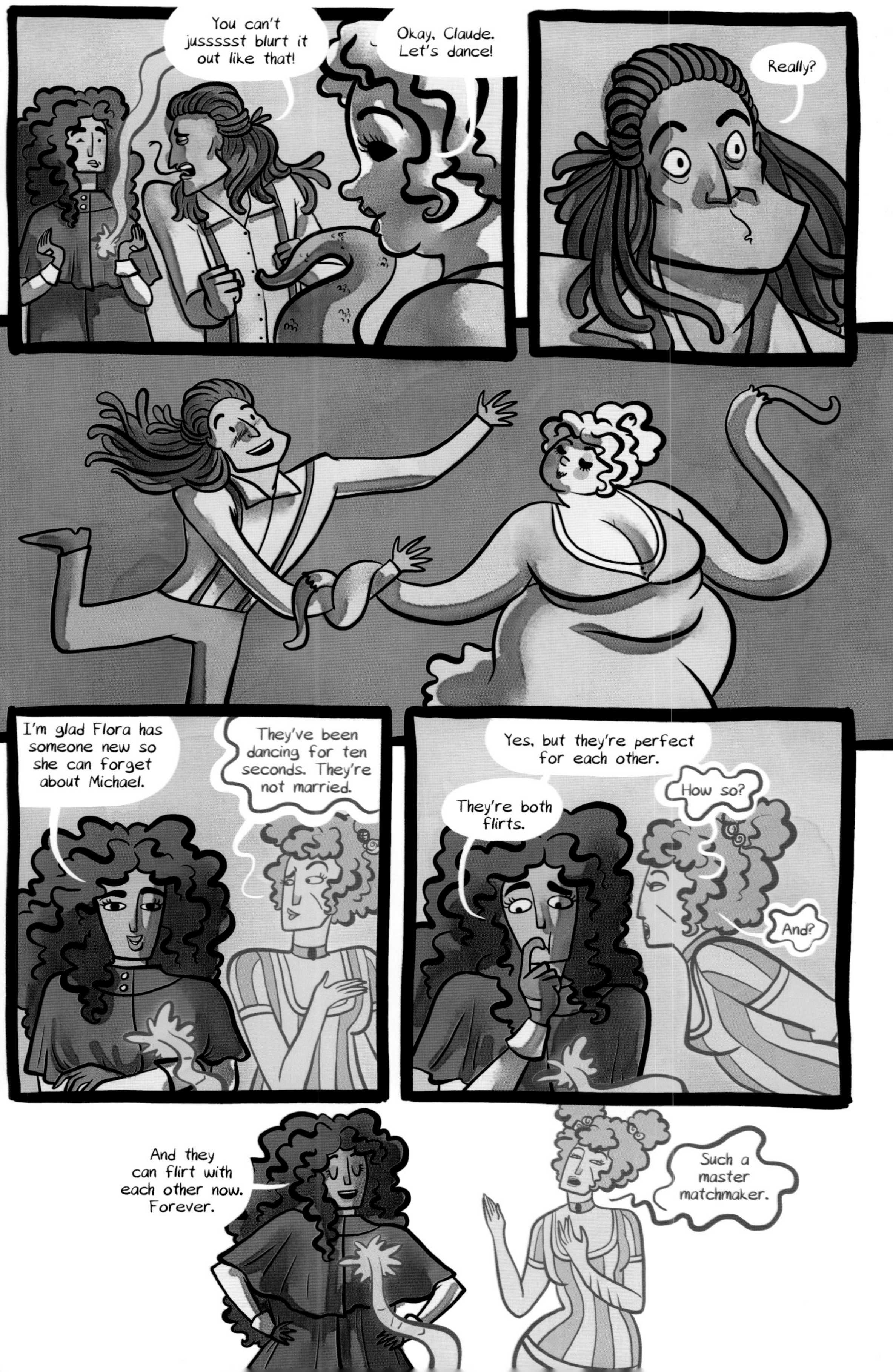

You can't jussssst blurt it out like that!
Okay, Claude. Let's dance!
Really?
I'm glad Flora has someone new so she can forget about Michael.
They've been dancing for ten seconds. They're not married.
Yes, but they're perfect for each other.
They're both flirts.
How so?
And?
And they can flirt with each other now. Forever.
Such a master matchmaker.

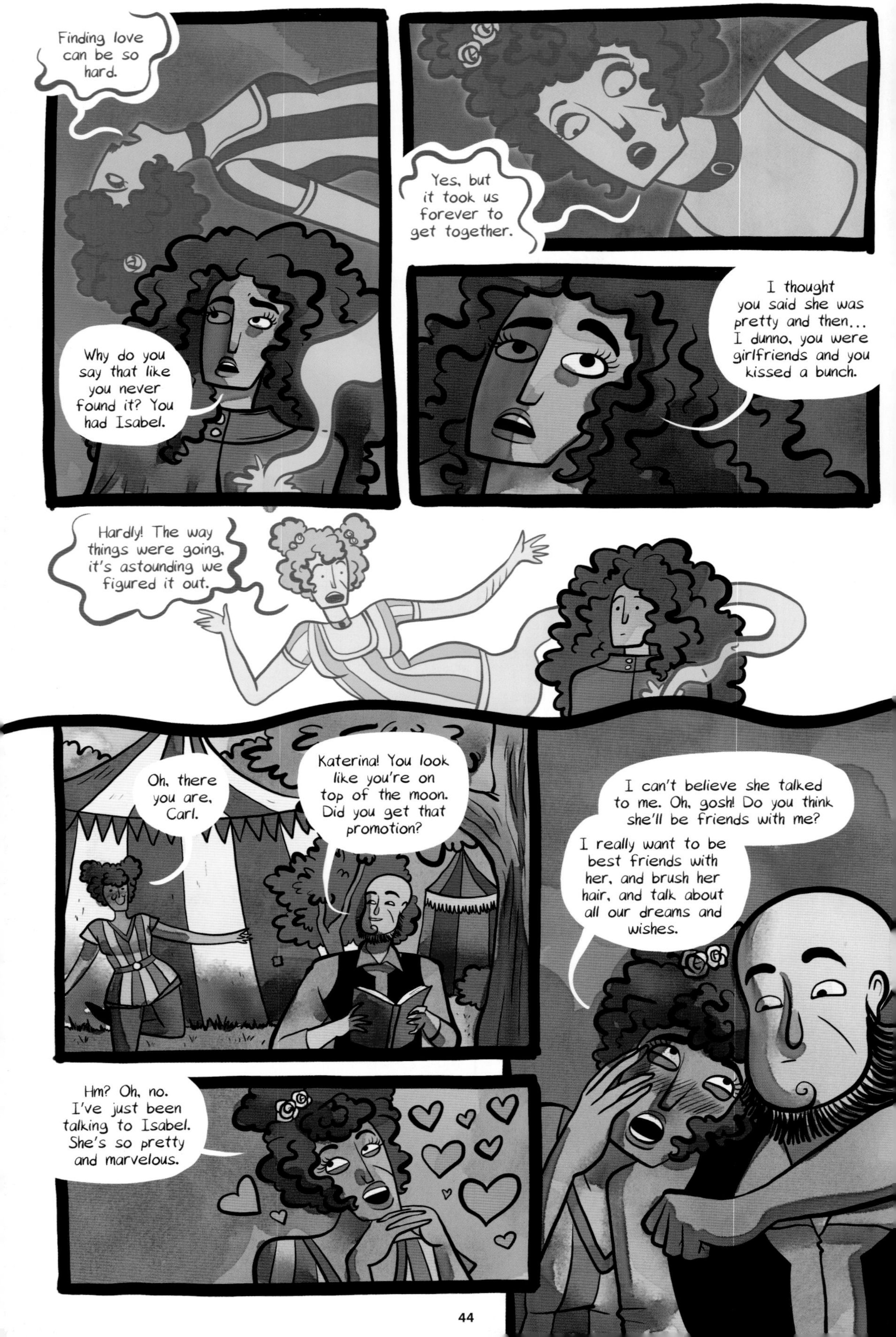
Finding love can be so hard.
Yes, but it took us forever to get together.
Why do you say that like you never found it? You had Isabel.
I thought you said she was pretty and then... I dunno, you were girlfriends and you kissed a bunch.
Hardly! The way things were going, it's astounding we figured it out.
Oh, there you are, Carl.
Katerina! You look like you're on top of the moon. Did you get that promotion?
I can't believe she talked to me. Oh, gosh! Do you think she'll be friends with me?
I really want to be best friends with her, and brush her hair, and talk about all our dreams and wishes.
Hm? Oh, no. I've just been talking to Isabel. She's so pretty and marvelous.

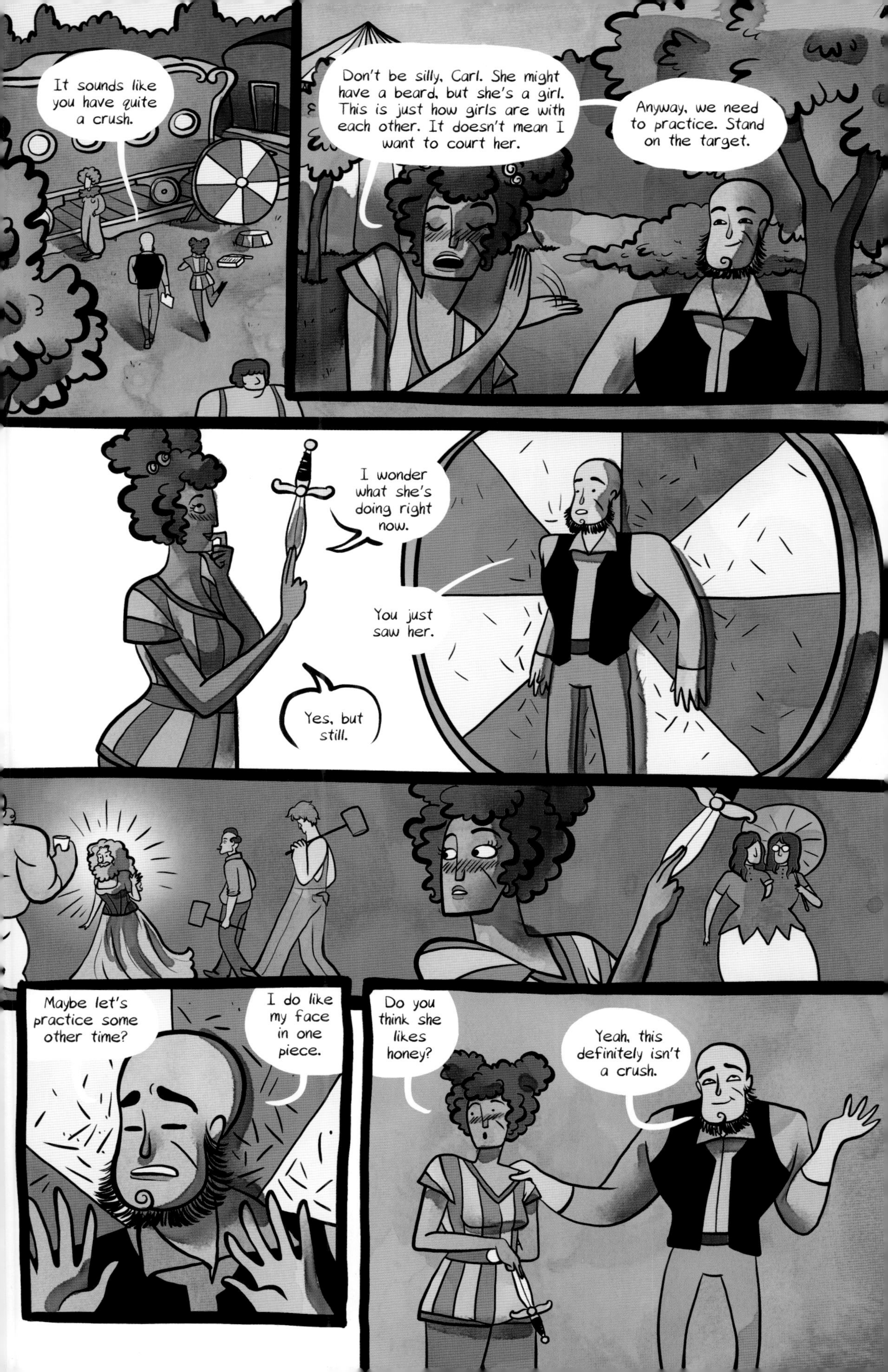
It sounds like you have quite a crush.
Don't be silly, Carl. She might have a beard, but she's a girl. This is just how girls are with each other. It doesn't mean I want to court her.
Anyway, we need to practice. Stand on the target.
I wonder what she's doing right now.
You just saw her.
Yes, but still.
Maybe let's practice some other time?
I do like my face in one piece.
Do you think she likes honey?
Yeah, this definitely isn't a crush.

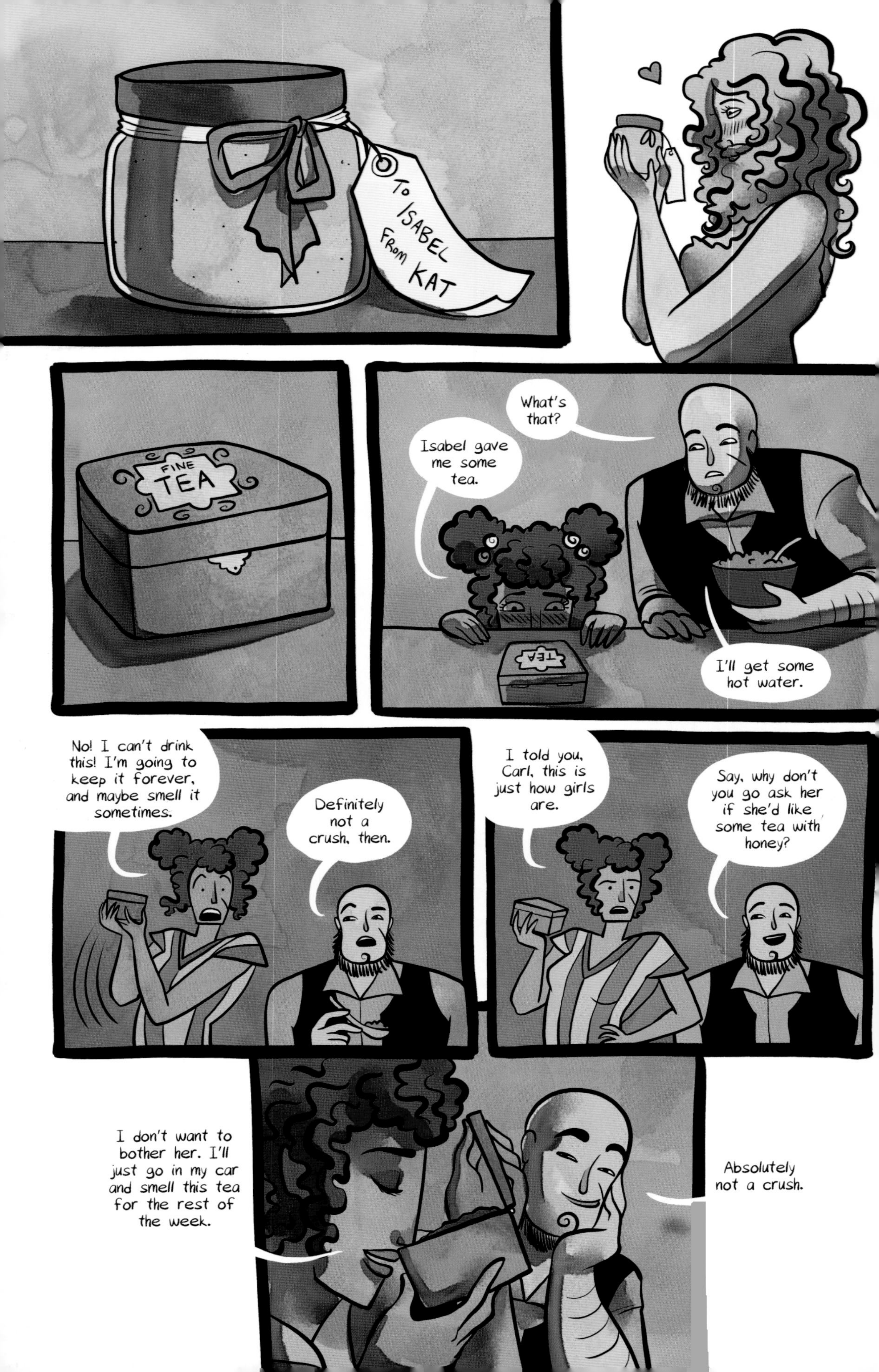
TO ISABEL FROM KAT
FINE TEA
What's that?
Isabel gave me some tea.
TEA
I'll get some hot water.
No! I can't drink this! I'm going to keep it forever, and maybe smell it sometimes.
Definitely not a crush, then.
I told you, Carl, this is just how girls are.
Say, why don't you go ask her if she'd like some tea with honey?
I don't want to bother her. I'll just go in my car and smell this tea for the rest of the week.
Absolutely not a crush.

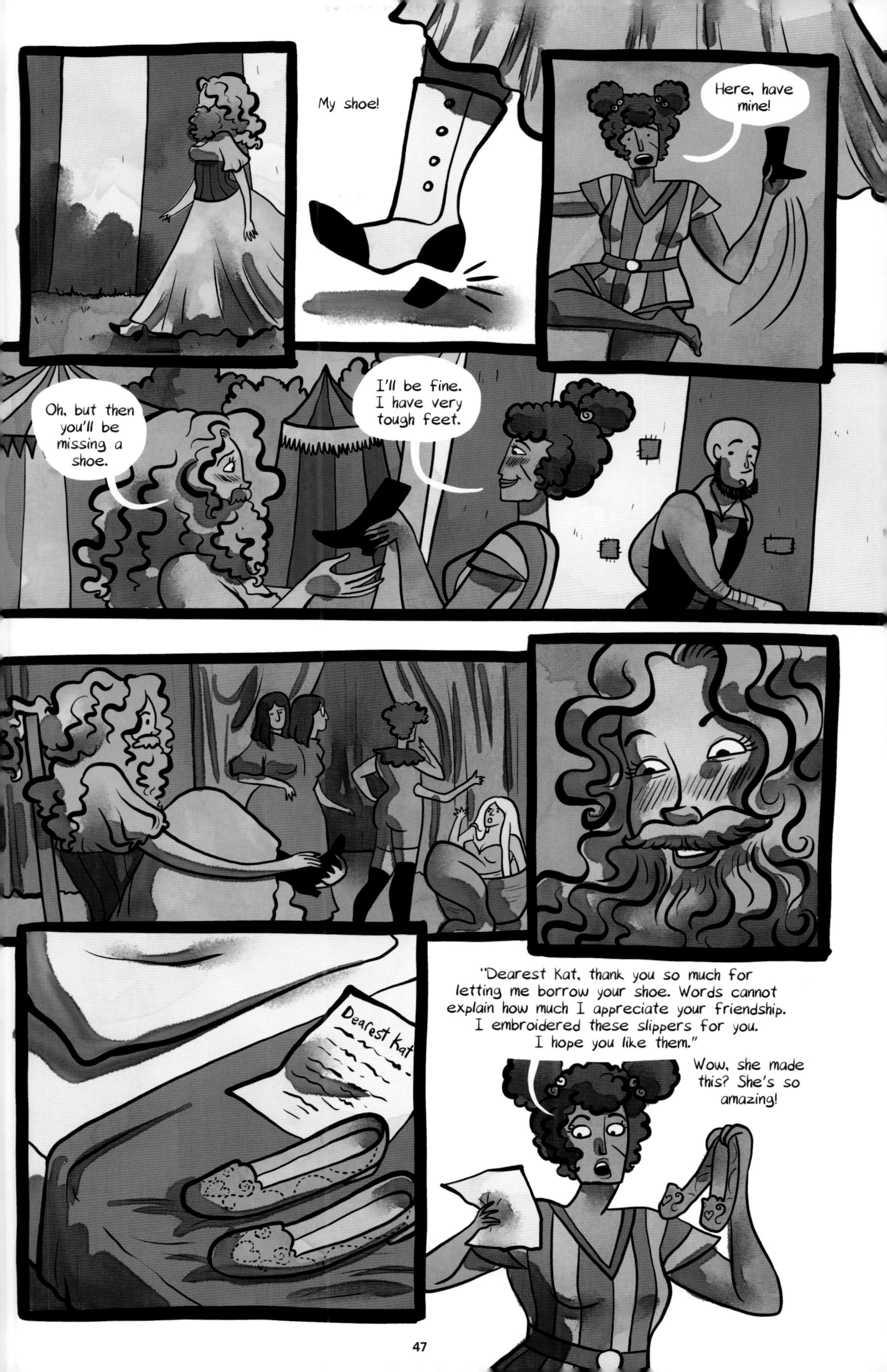
My shoe!
Here, have mine!
Oh, but then you'll be missing a shoe.
I'll be fine. I have very tough feet.
Dearest Kat
"Dearest Kat, thank you so much for letting me borrow your shoe. Words cannot explain how much I appreciate your friendship. I embroidered these slippers for you. I hope you like them."
Wow, she made this? She's so amazing!

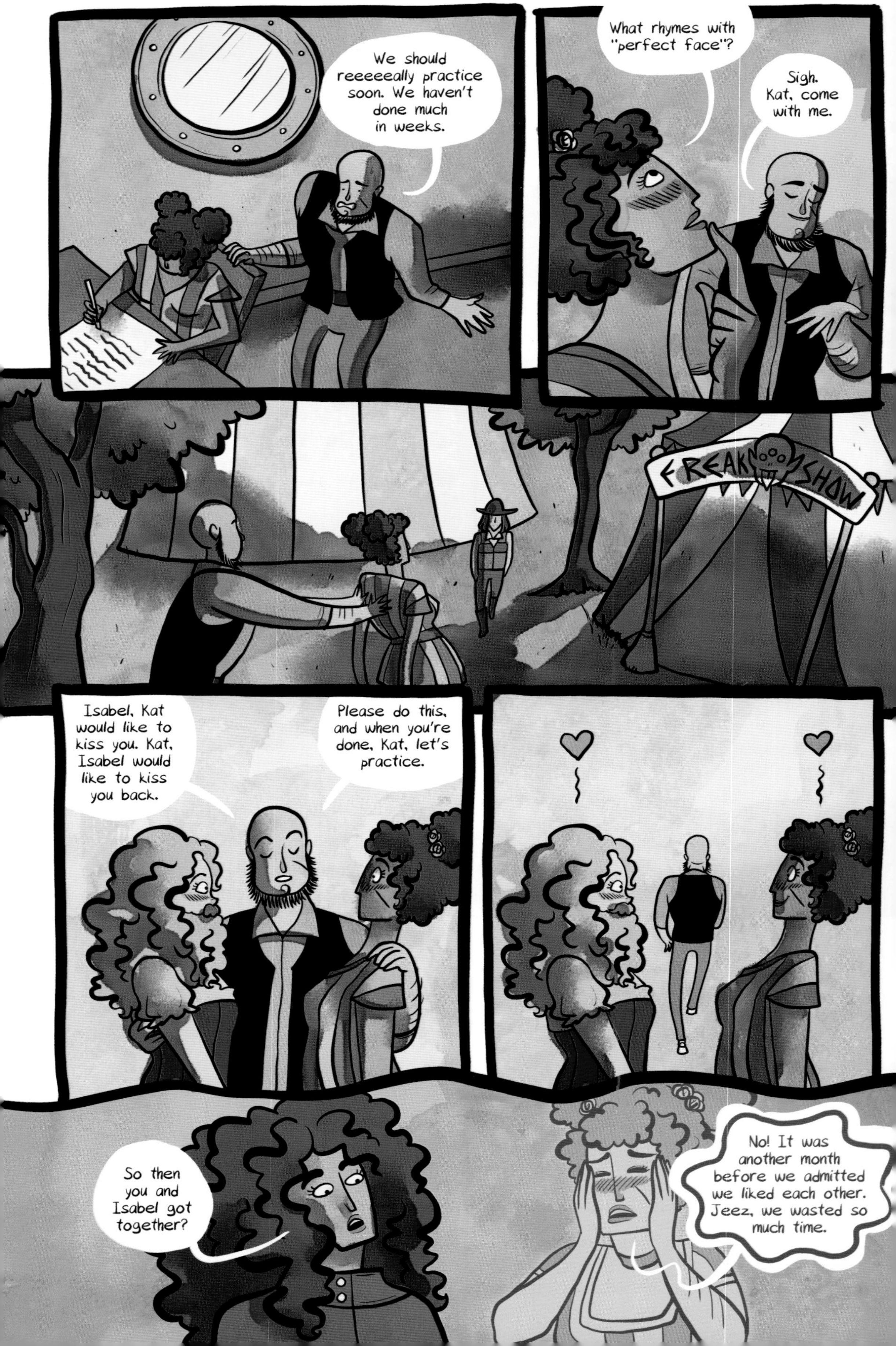
We should reeeeeally practice soon. We haven't done much in weeks.
What rhymes with "perfect face"?
Sigh. Kat, come with me.
FREAK SHOW
Isabel, Kat would like to kiss you. Kat, Isabel would like to kiss you back.
Please do this, and when you're done, Kat, let's practice.
So then you and Isabel got together?
No! It was another month before we admitted we liked each other. Jeez, we wasted so much time.

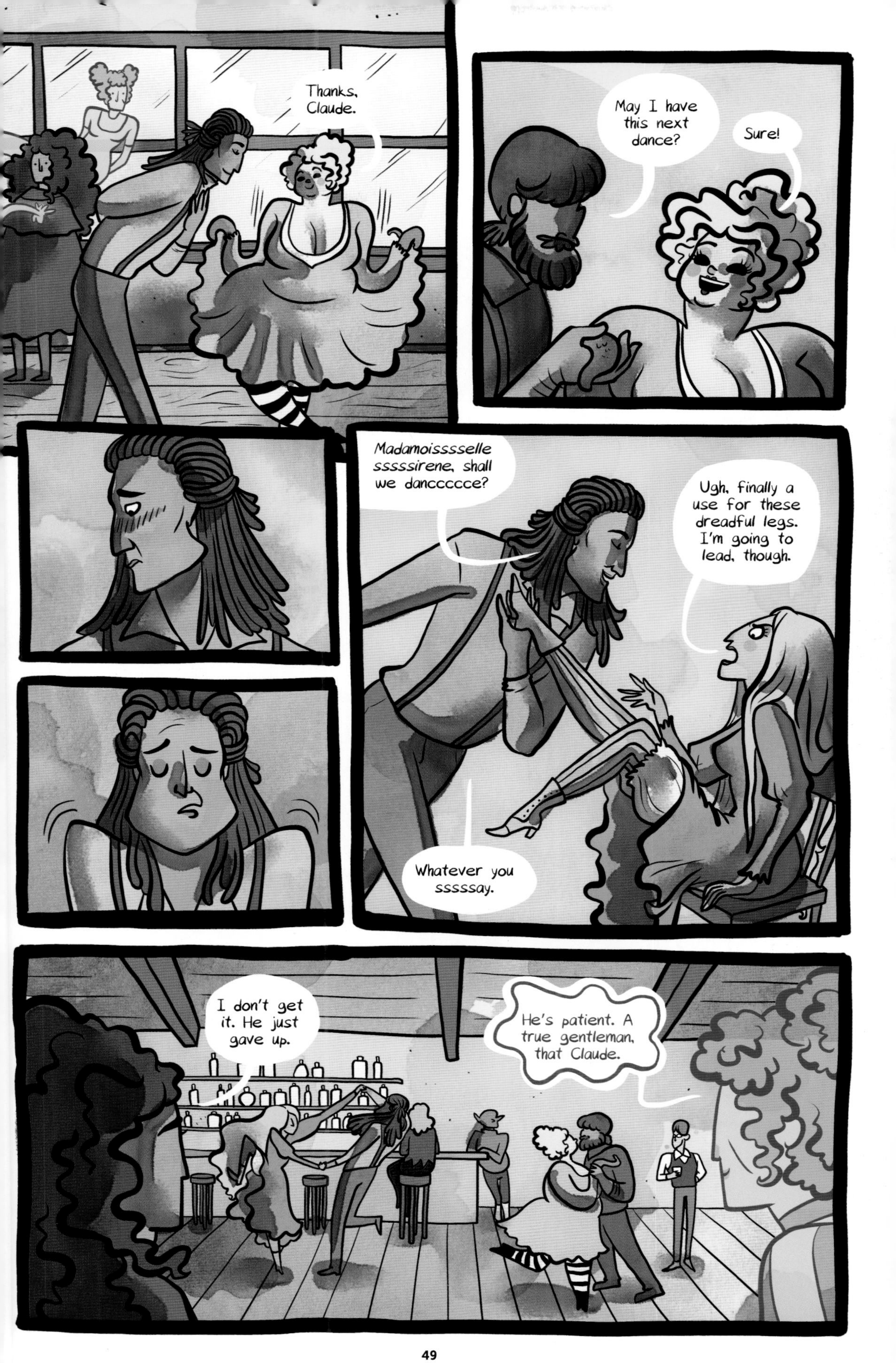
Thanks, Claude.
May I have this next dance?
Sure!
Madamoissssselle sssssirene, shall we dancccccce?
Ugh, finally a use for these dreadful legs. I'm going to lead, though.
Whatever you ssssssay.
I don't get it. He just gave up.
He's patient. A true gentleman, that Claude.

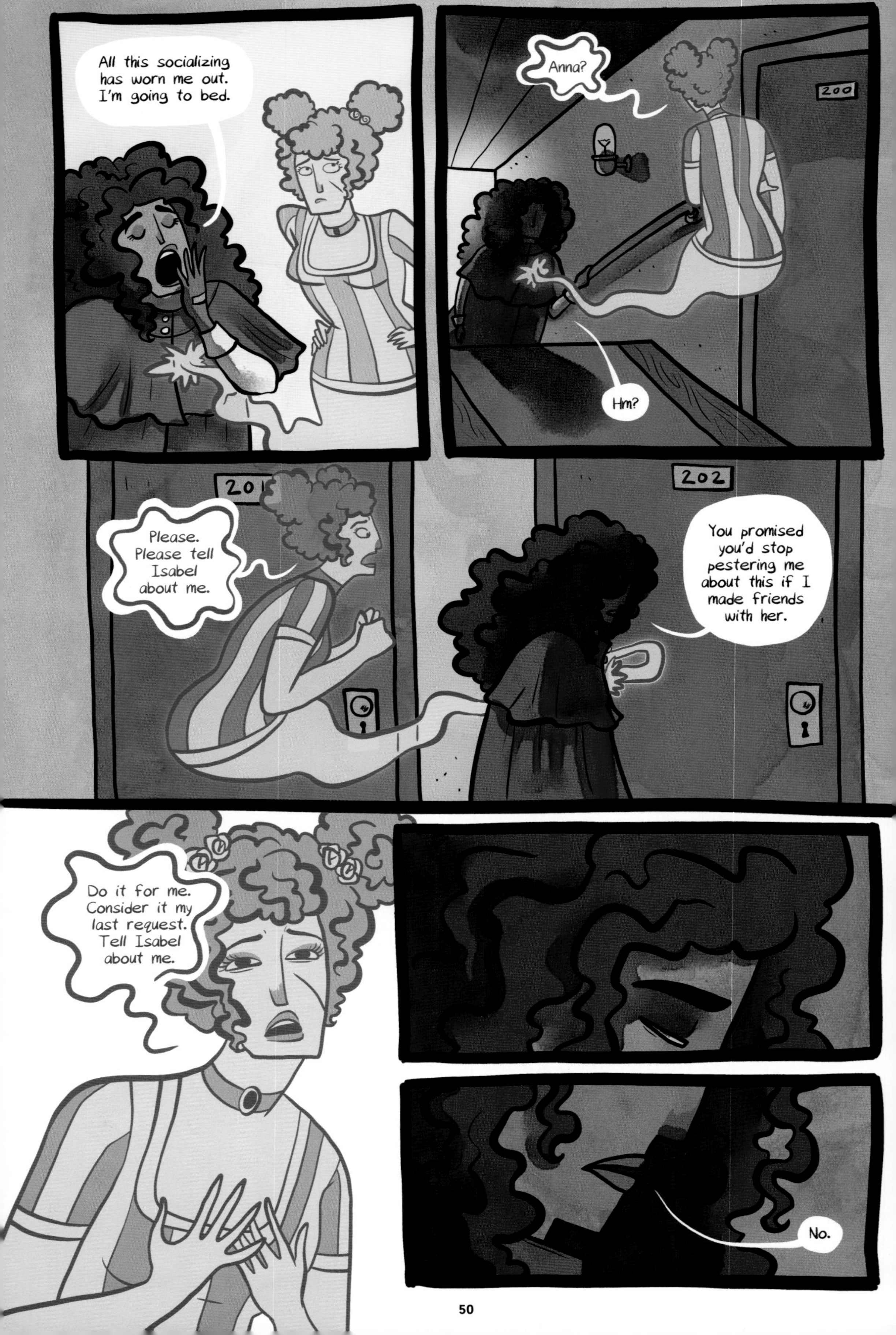
All this socializing has worn me out. I'm going to bed.
Anna?
200
Hm?
201
Please. Please tell Isabel about me.
202
You promised you'd stop pestering me about this if I made friends with her.
Do it for me. Consider it my last request. Tell Isabel about me.
No.

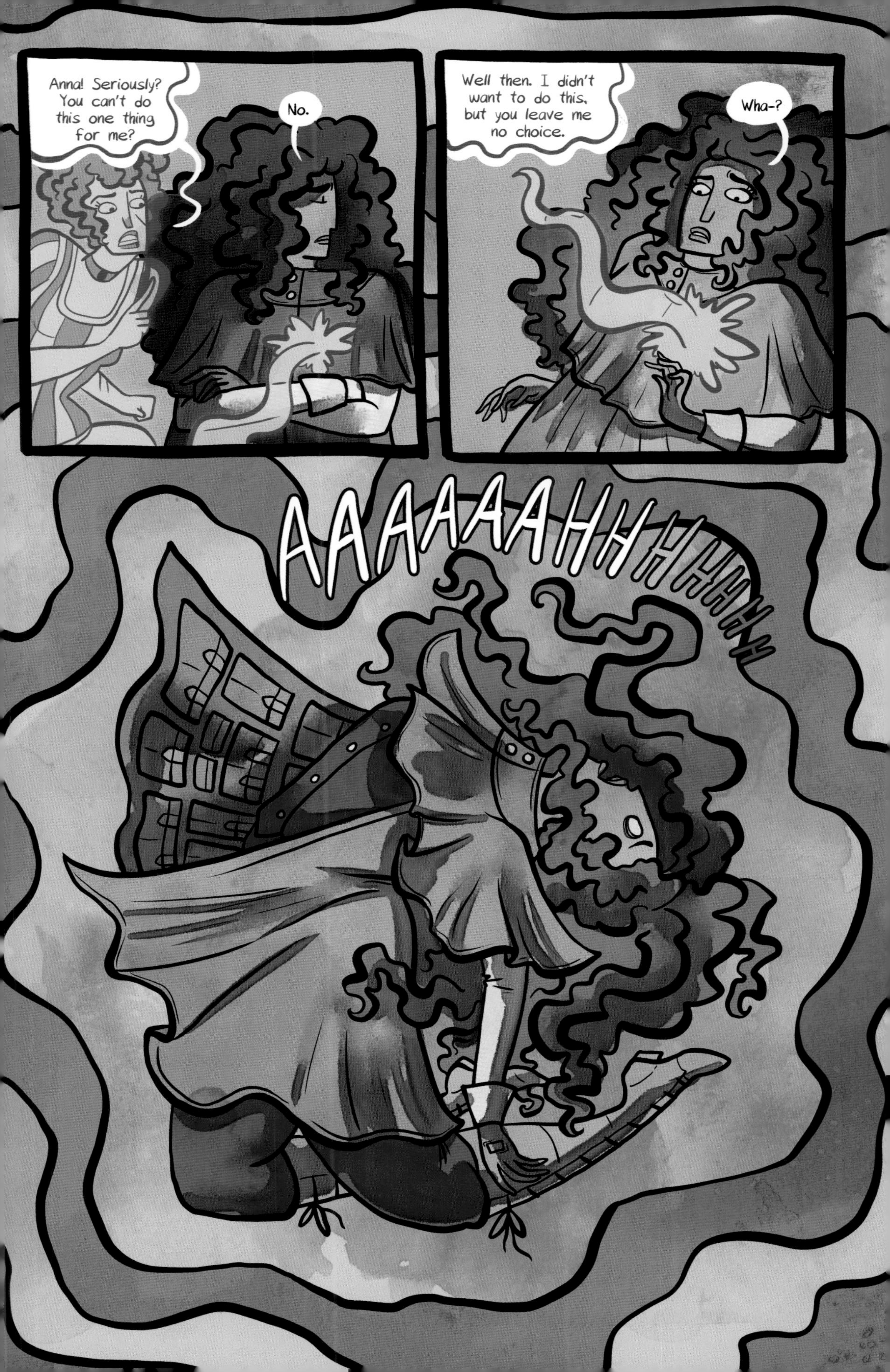

Anna! Seriously? You can't do this one thing for me?
No.
Well then. I didn't want to do this, but you leave me no choice.
Wha-?
AAAAAAHHHHHHHHH

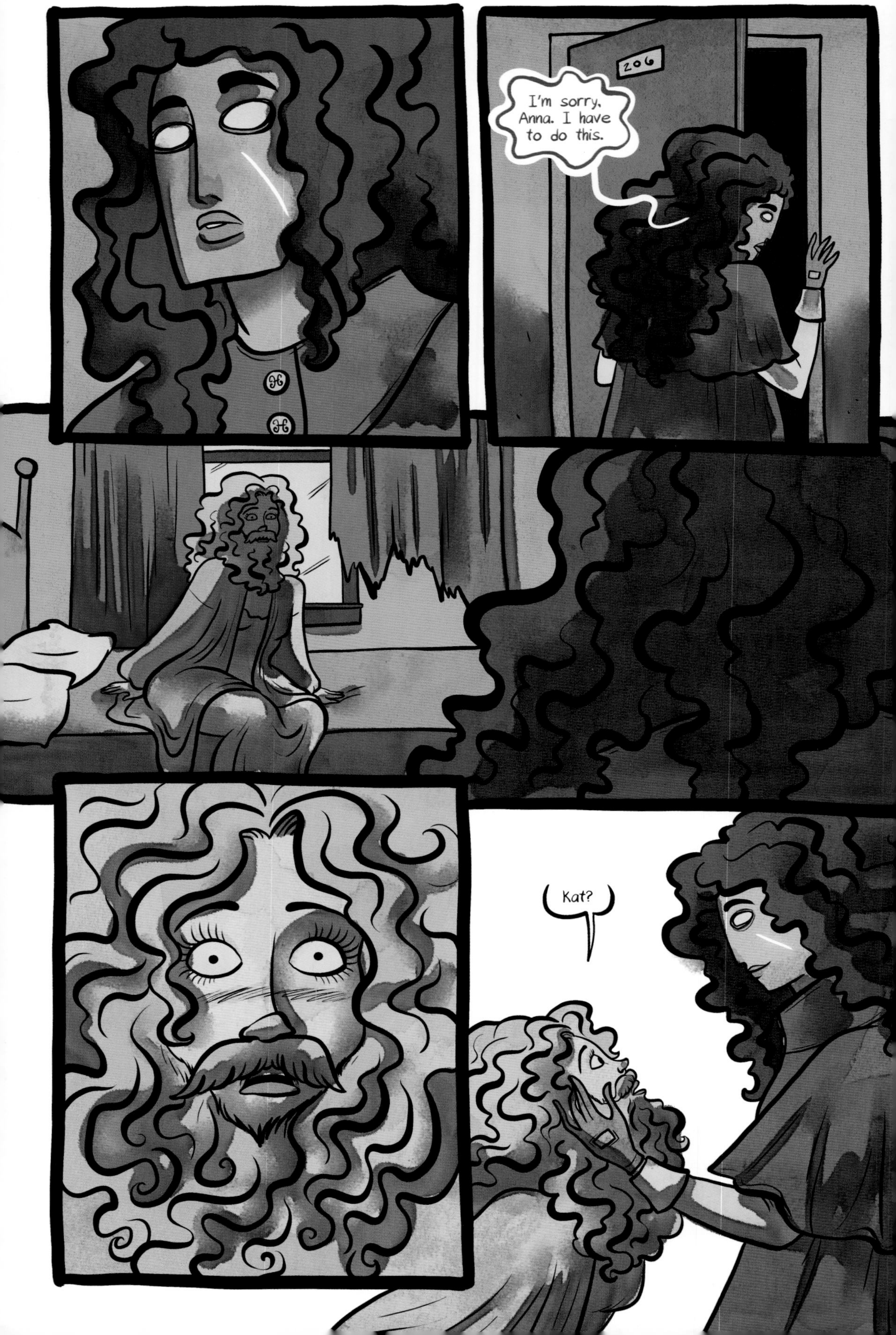
I'm sorry, Anna. I have to do this.
Kat?

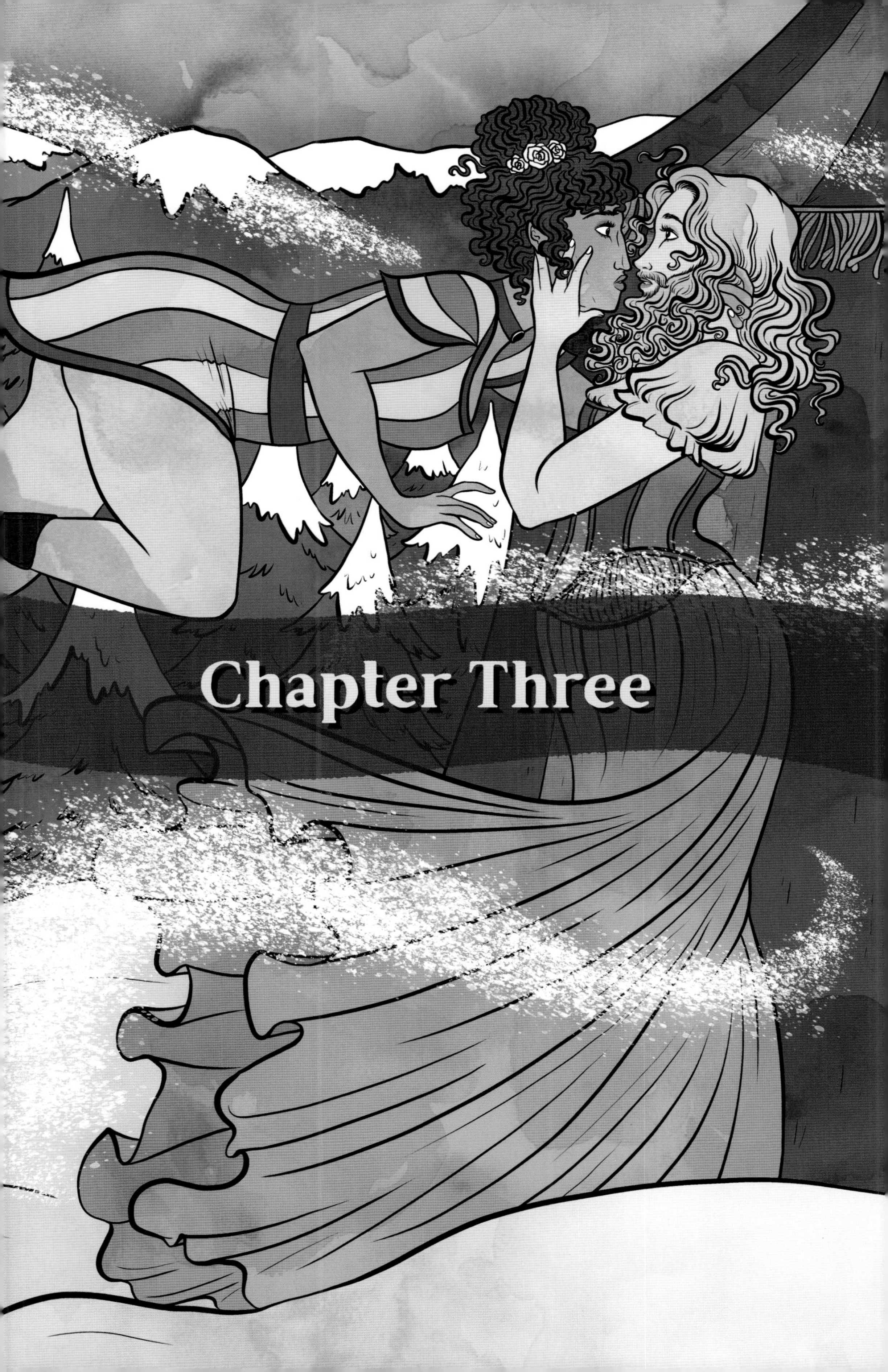

Chapter Three

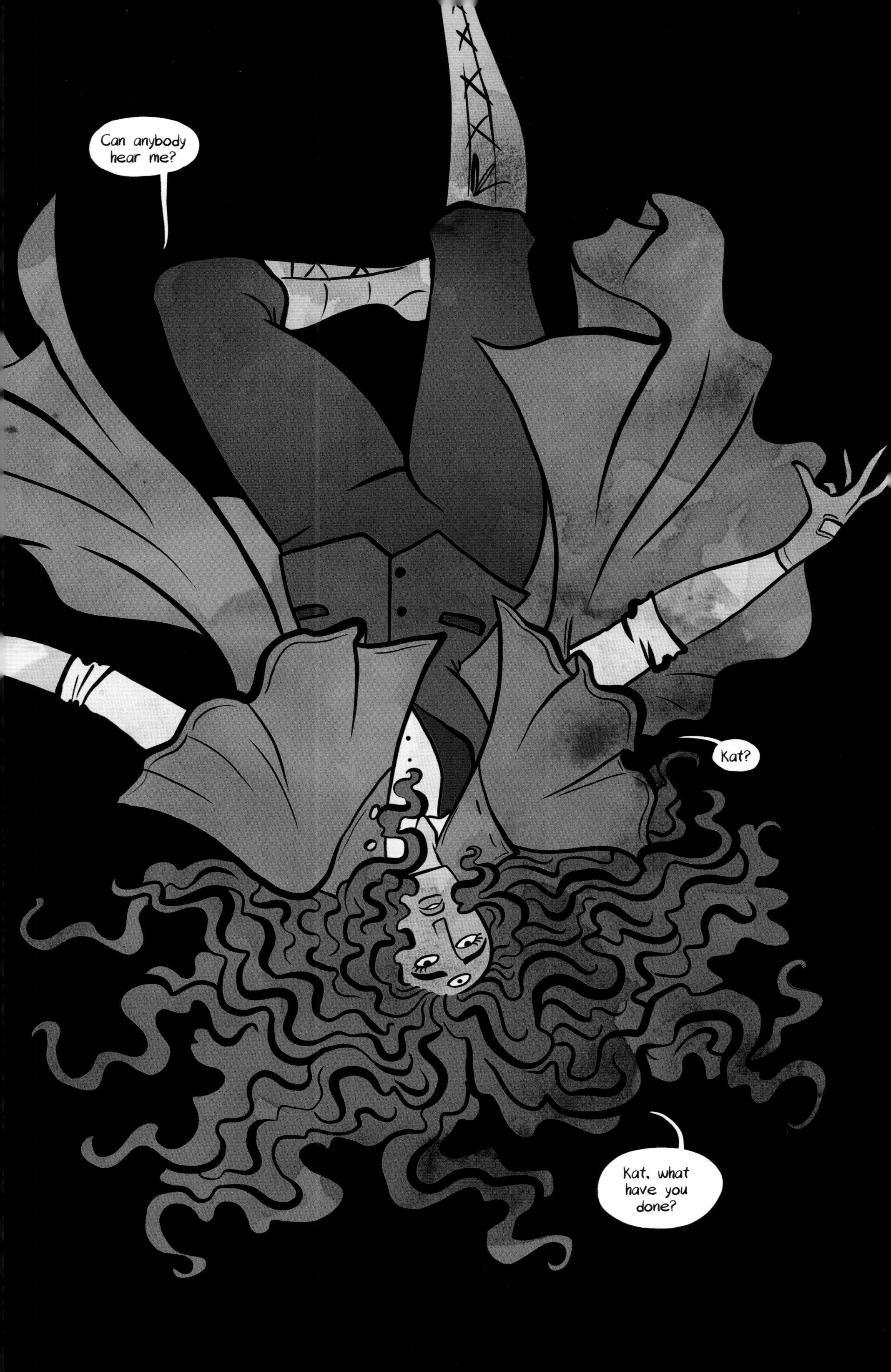
Can anybody hear me?
Kat?
Kat, what have you done?

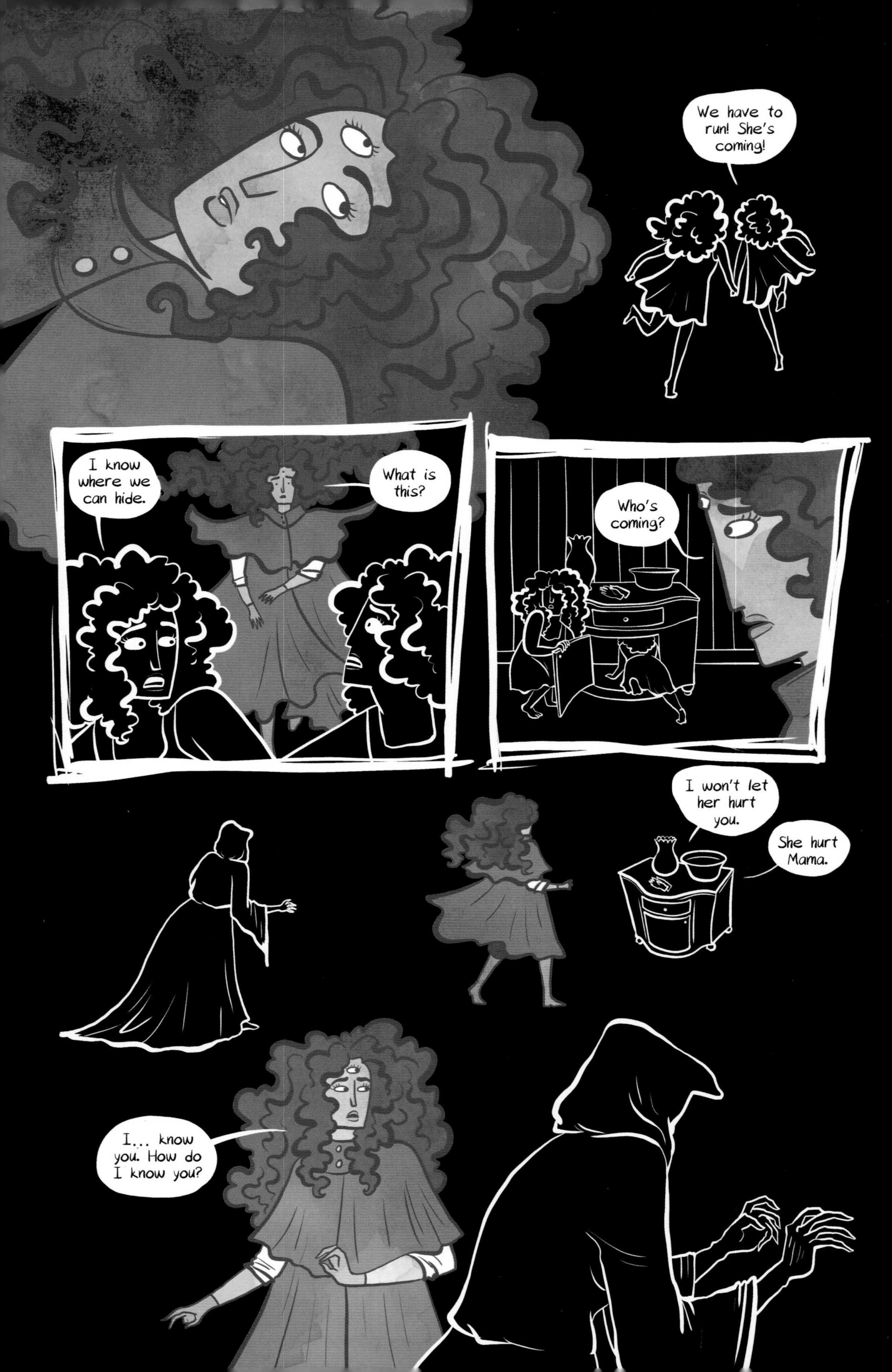
We have to run! She's coming!
I know where we can hide.
What is this?
Who's coming?
I won't let her hurt you.
She hurt Mama.
I... know you. How do I know you?

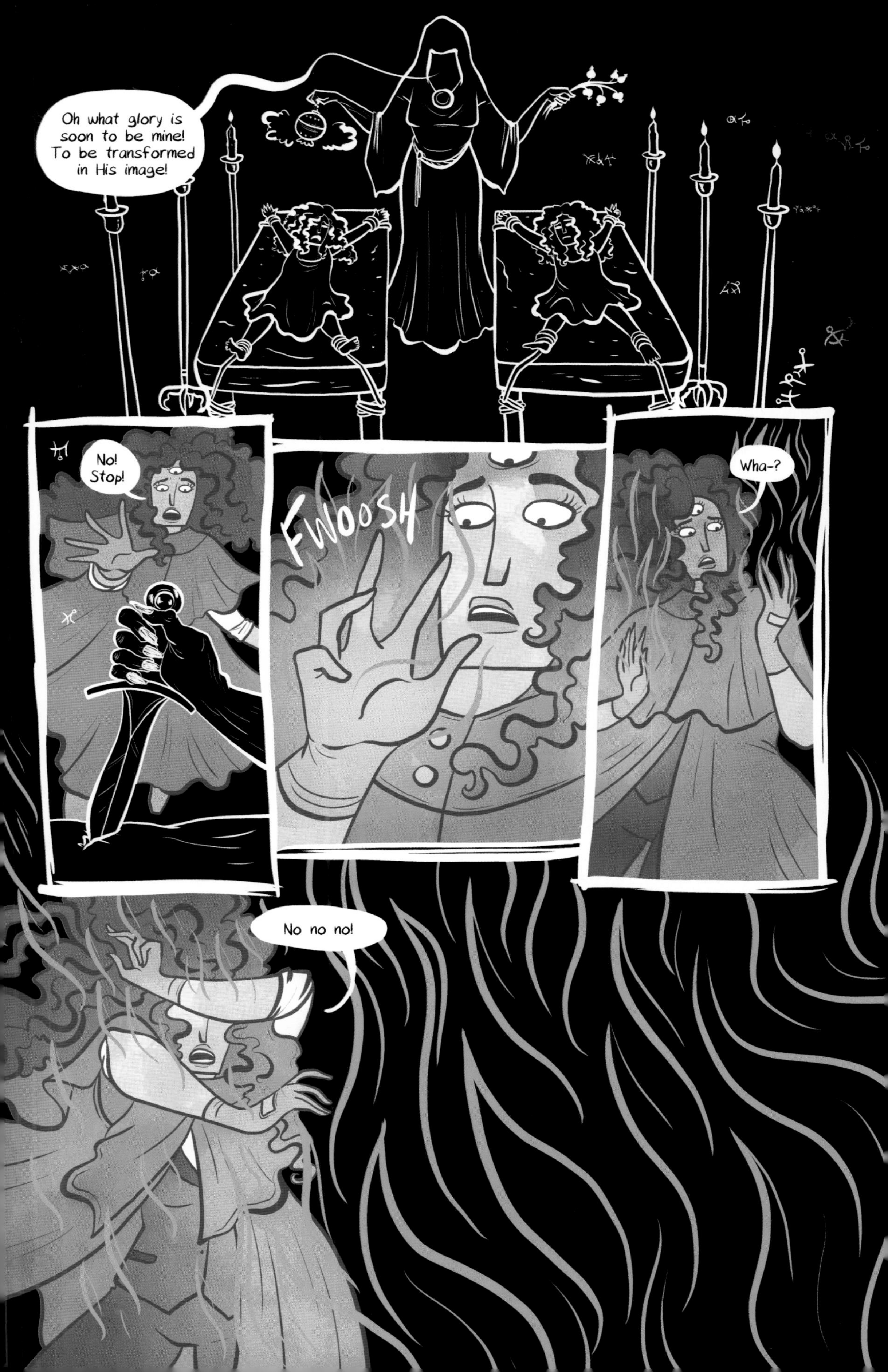
Oh what glory is soon to be mine! To be transformed in His image!
No! Stop!
FWOOSH
Wha-?
No no no!

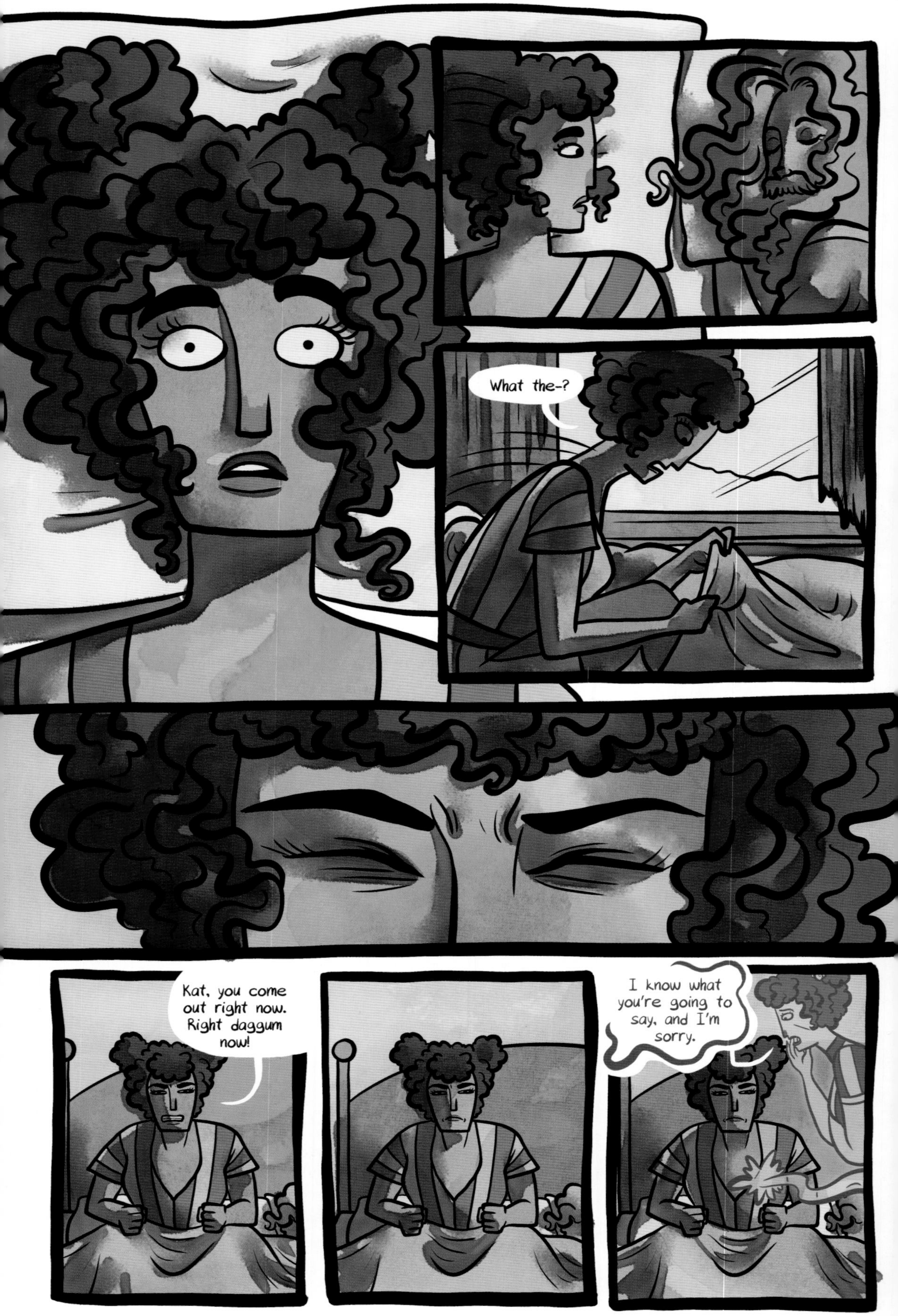
What the-?
Kat, you come out right now. Right daggum now!
I know what you're going to say, and I'm sorry.

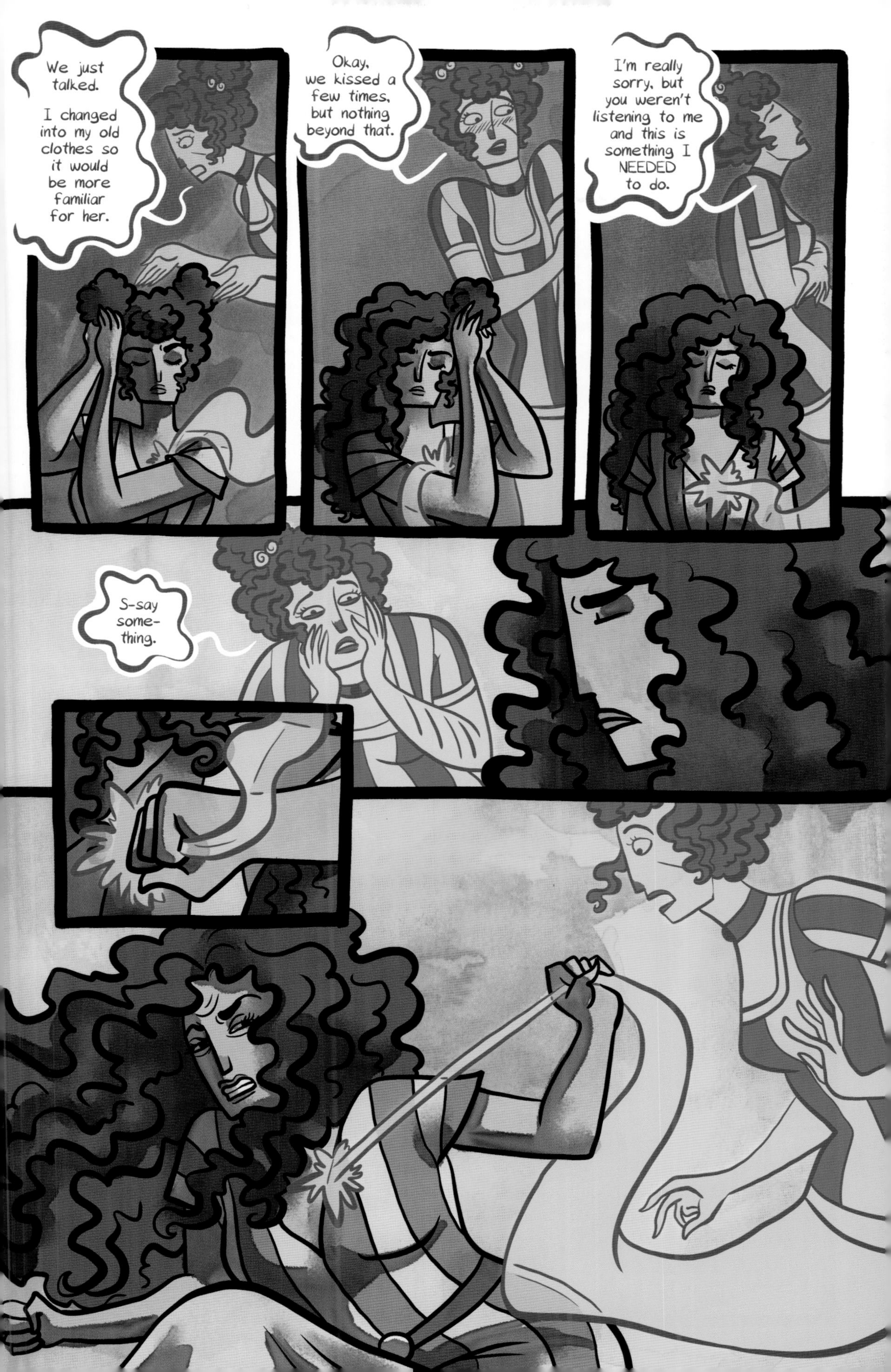
We just talked.
I changed into my old clothes so it would be more familiar for her.
Okay, we kissed a few times, but nothing beyond that.
I'm really sorry, but you weren't listening to me and this is something I NEEDED to do.
S-say some-thing.

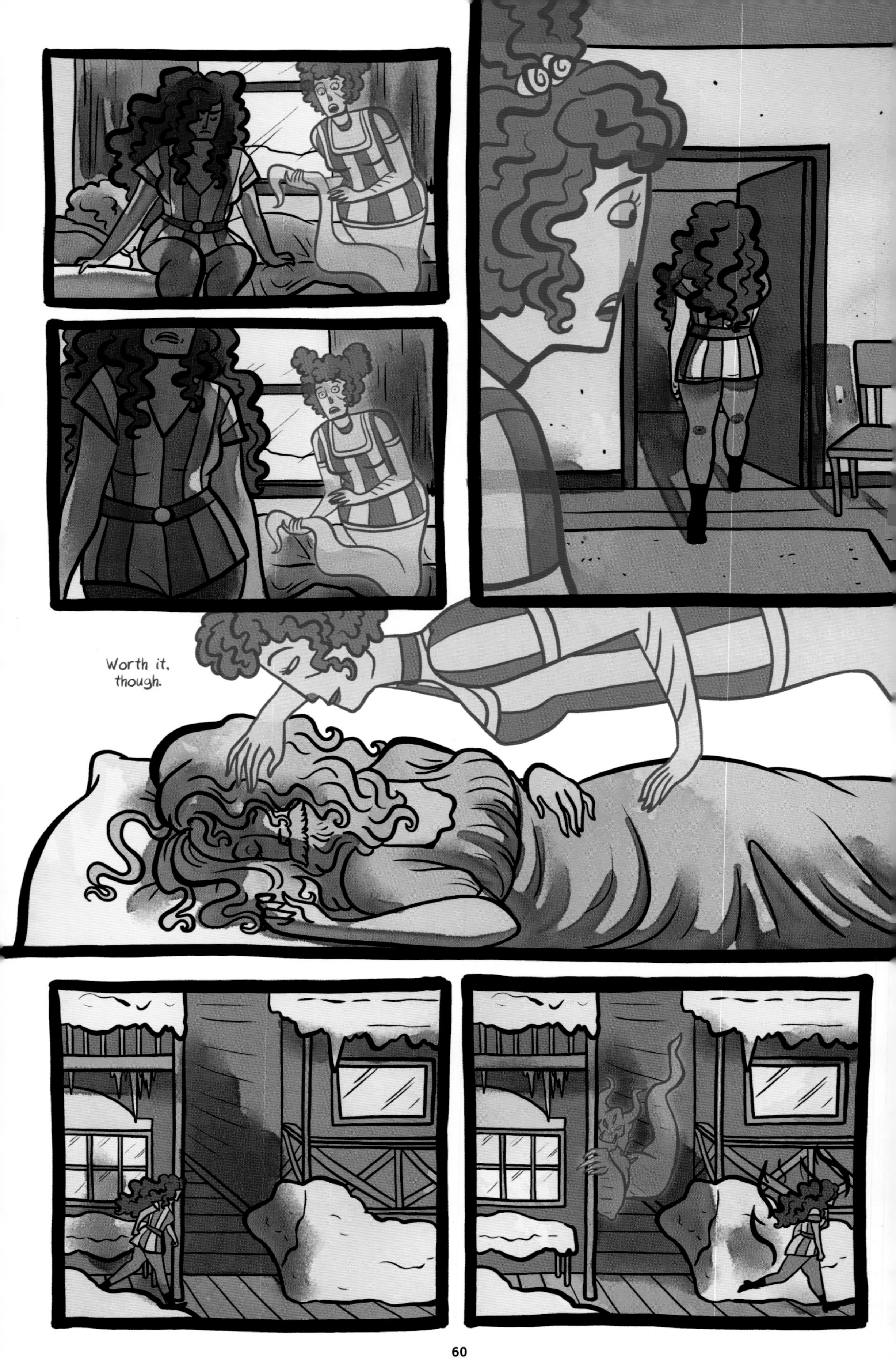
Worth it, though.

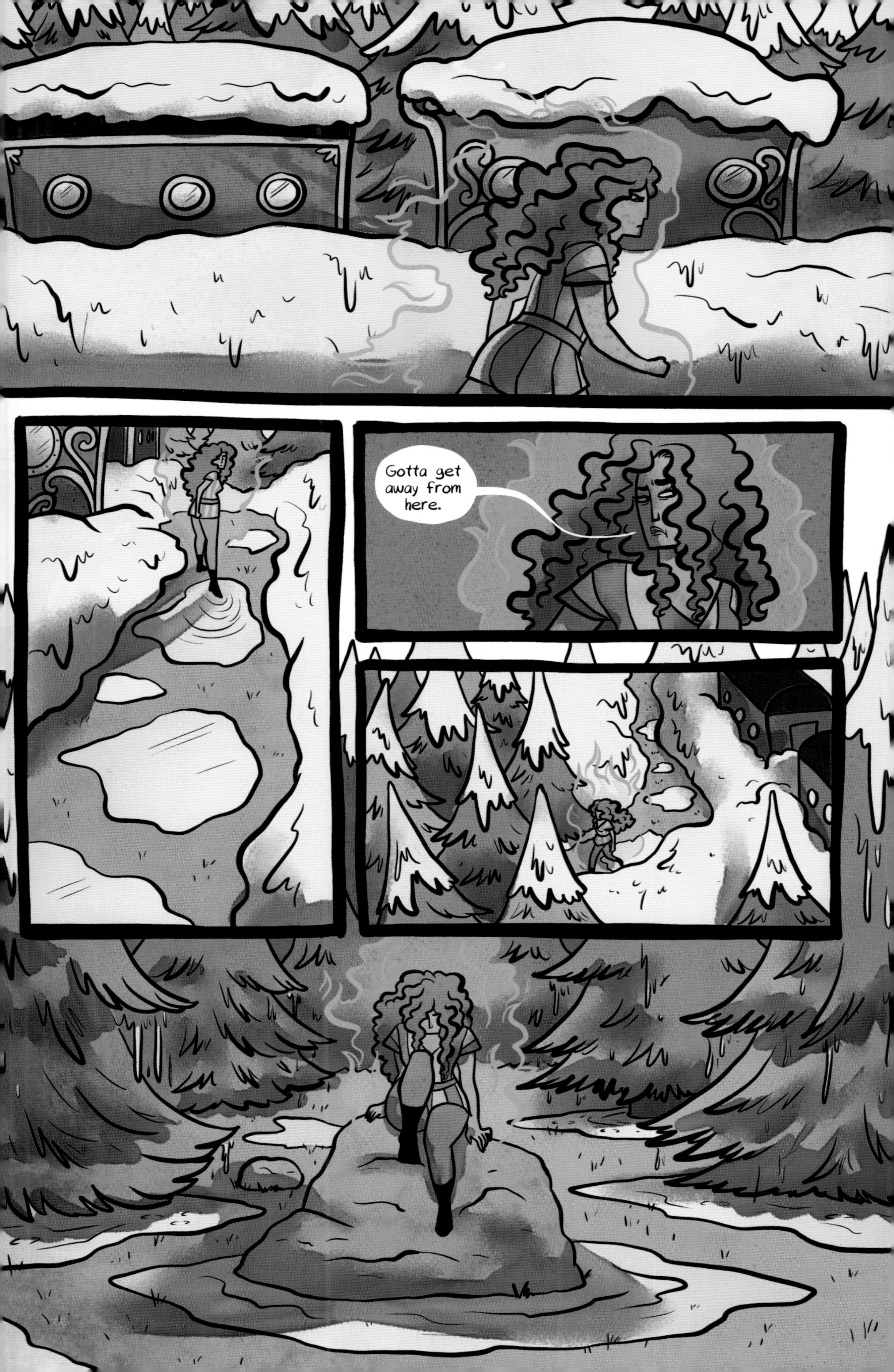
Gotta get away from here.

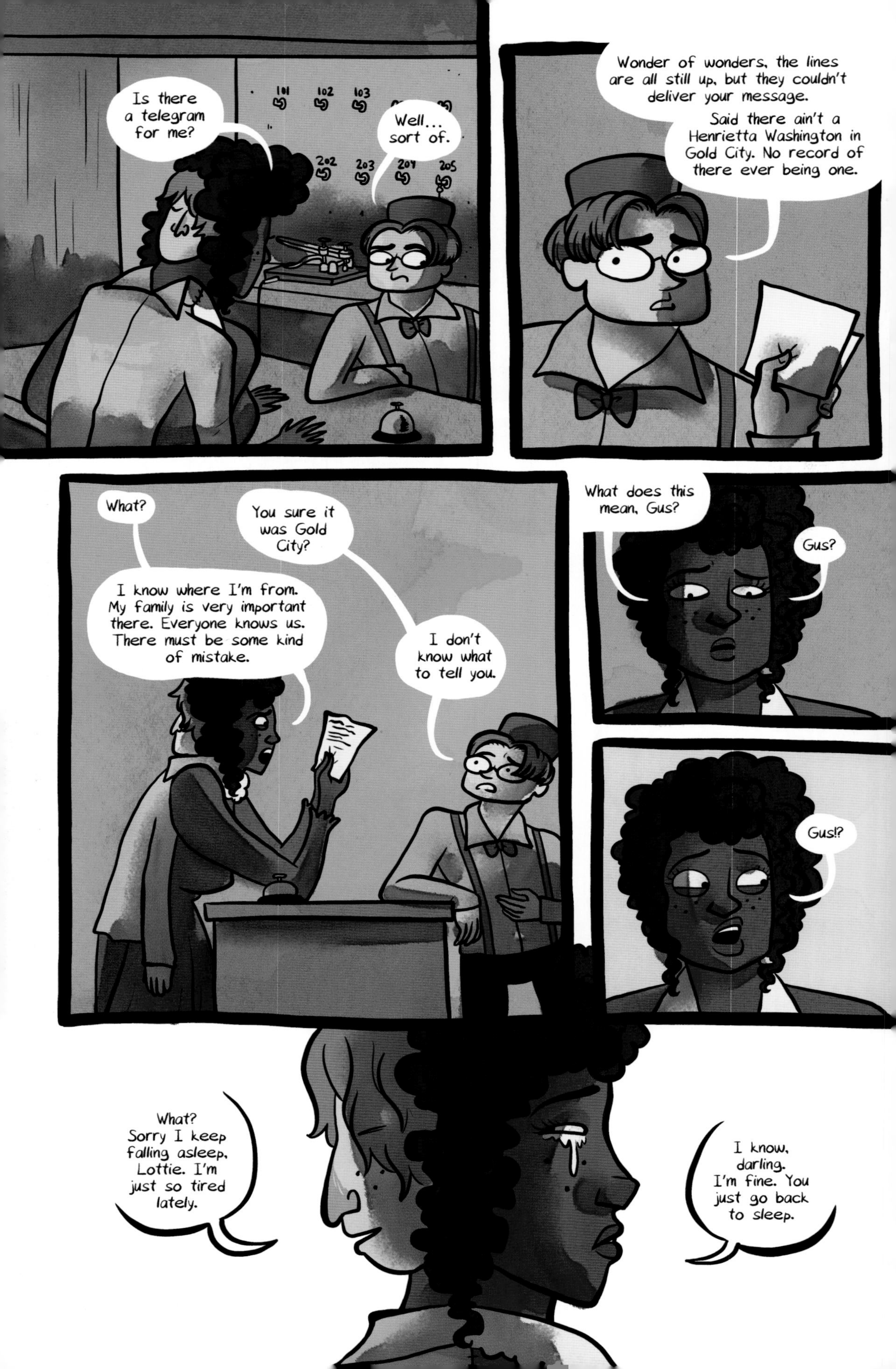
Is there a telegram for me?
101
102
103
202
203
204
205
Well... sort of.
Wonder of wonders, the lines are all still up, but they couldn't deliver your message.
Said there ain't a Henrietta Washington in Gold City. No record of there ever being one.
What?
You sure it was Gold City?
I know where I'm from. My family is very important there. Everyone knows us. There must be some kind of mistake.
I don't know what to tell you.
What does this mean, Gus?
Gus?
Gus!?
What? Sorry I keep falling asleep, Lottie. I'm just so tired lately.
I know, darling. I'm fine. You just go back to sleep.

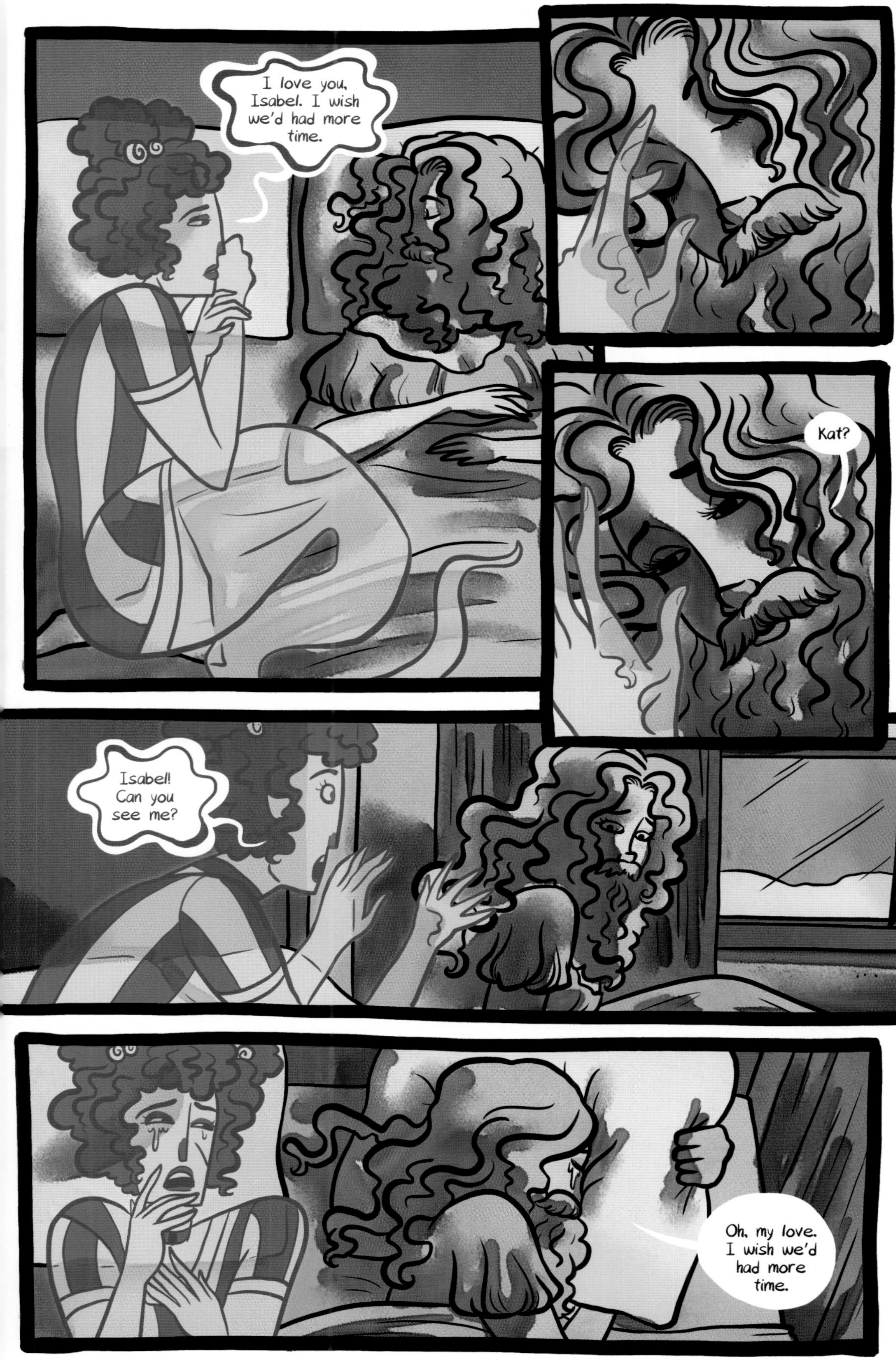
I love you, Isabel. I wish we'd had more time.
Kat?
Isabel! Can you see me?
Oh, my love. I wish we'd had more time.

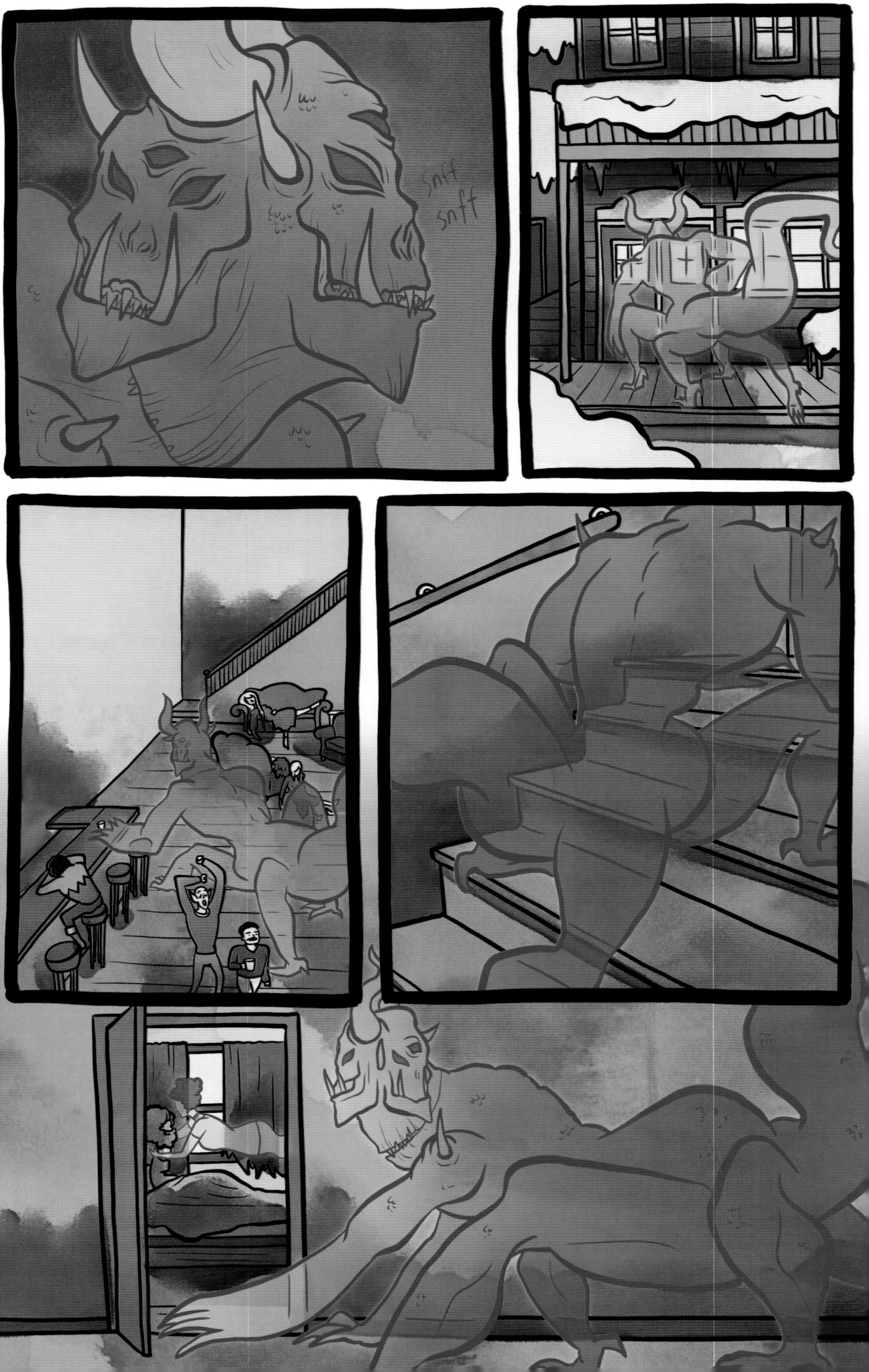
snff
snff

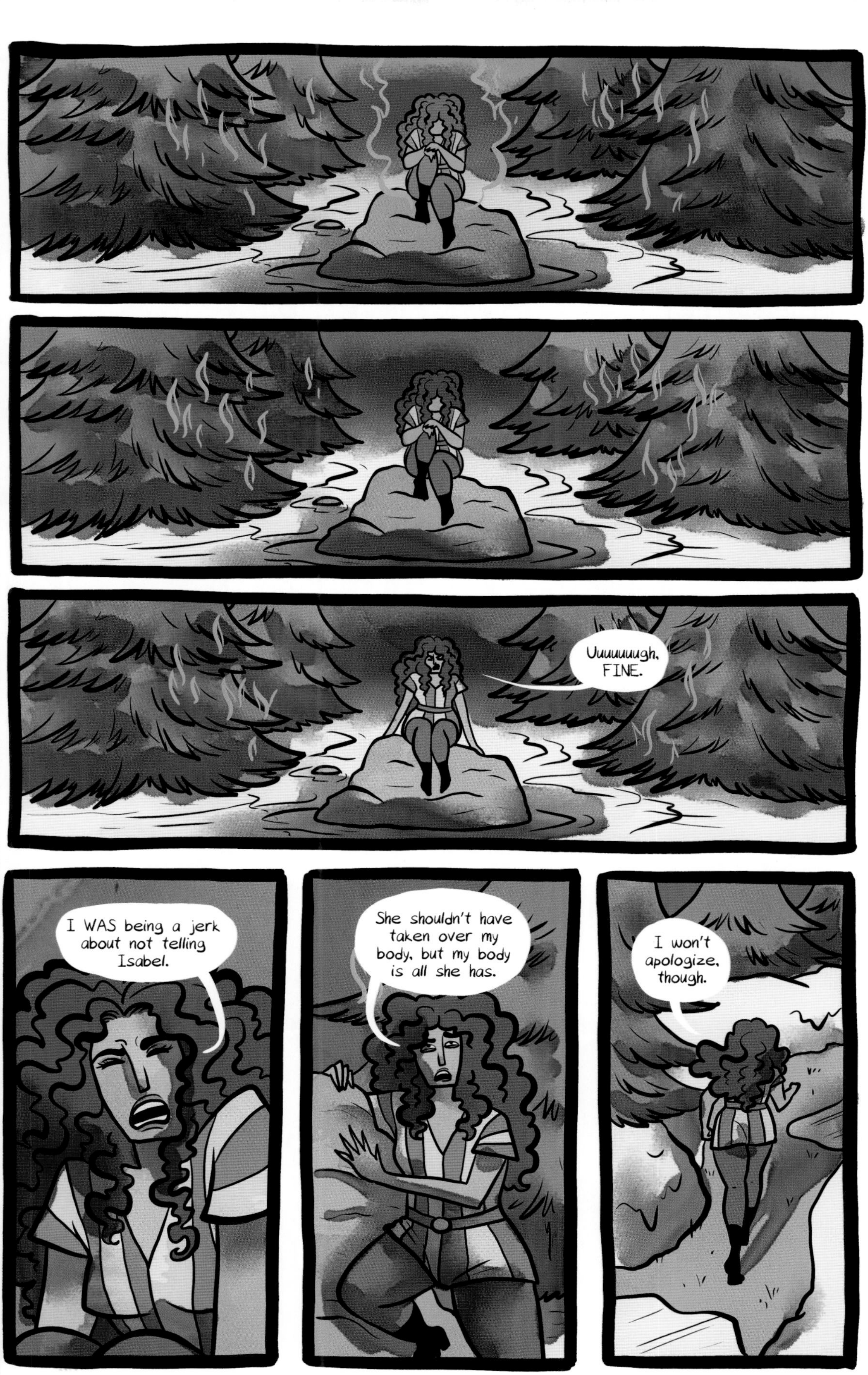
Uuuuuuugh, FINE.
I WAS being a jerk about not telling Isabel.
She shouldn't have taken over my body, but my body is all she has.
I won't apologize, though.

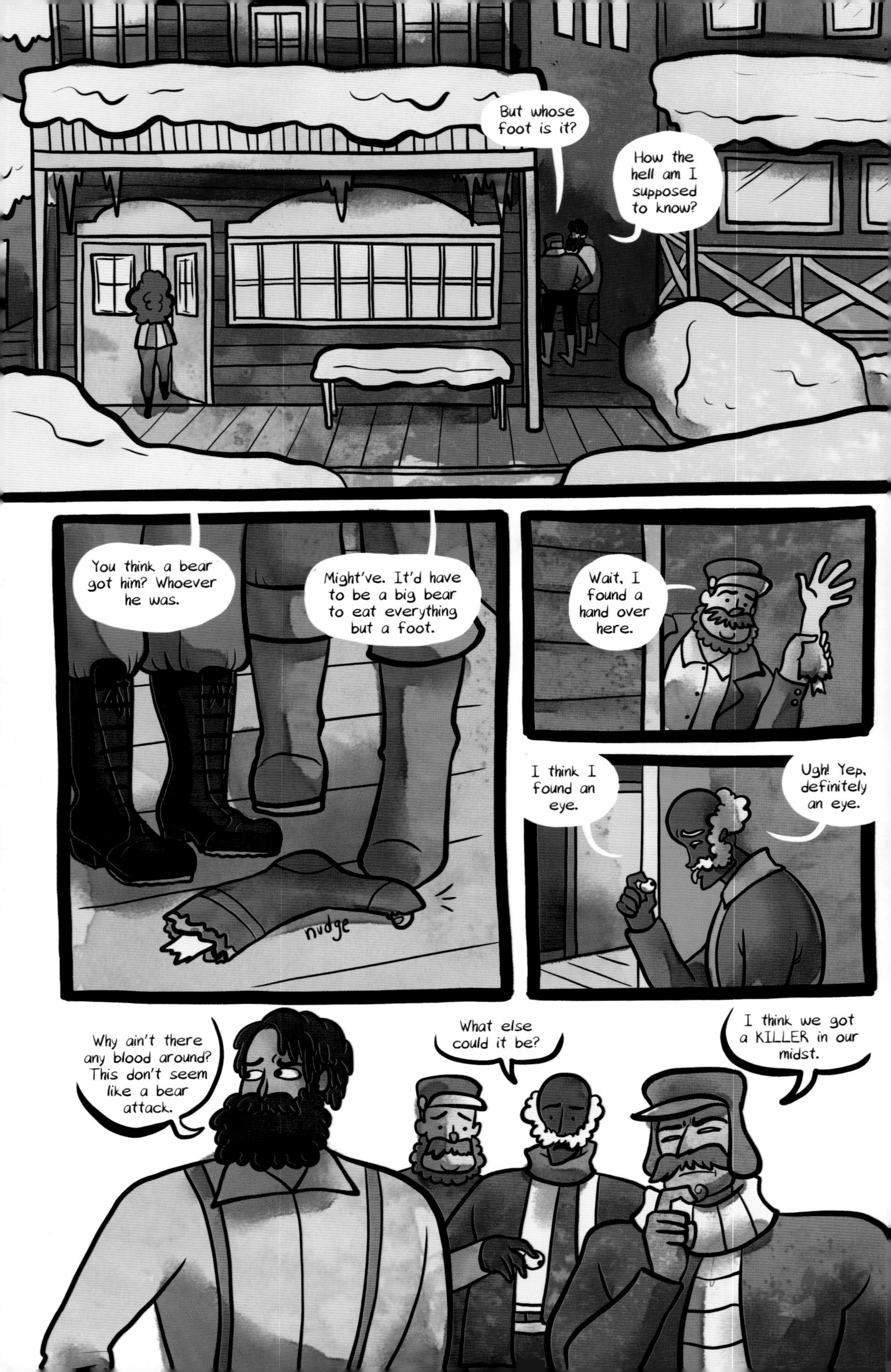

But whose foot is it?
How the hell am I supposed to know?
You think a bear got him? Whoever he was.
Might've. It'd have to be a big bear to eat everything but a foot.
nudge
Wait, I found a hand over here.
I think I found an eye.
Ugh! Yep, definitely an eye.
Why ain't there any blood around? This don't seem like a bear attack.
What else could it be?
I think we got a KILLER in our midst.

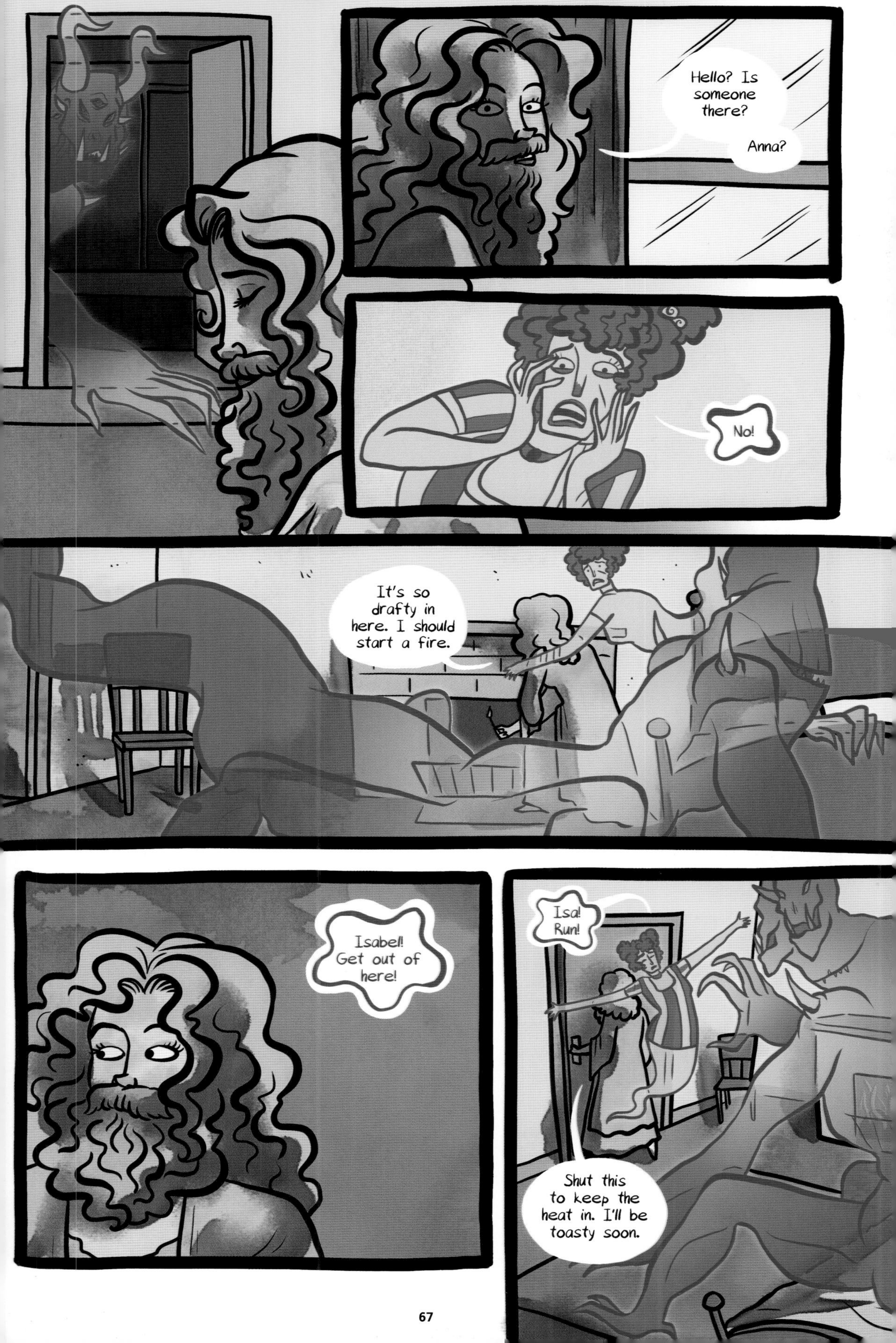
Hello? Is someone there?
Anna?
No!
It's so drafty in here. I should start a fire.
Isabel! Get out of here!
Isa! Run!
Shut this to keep the heat in. I'll be toasty soon.

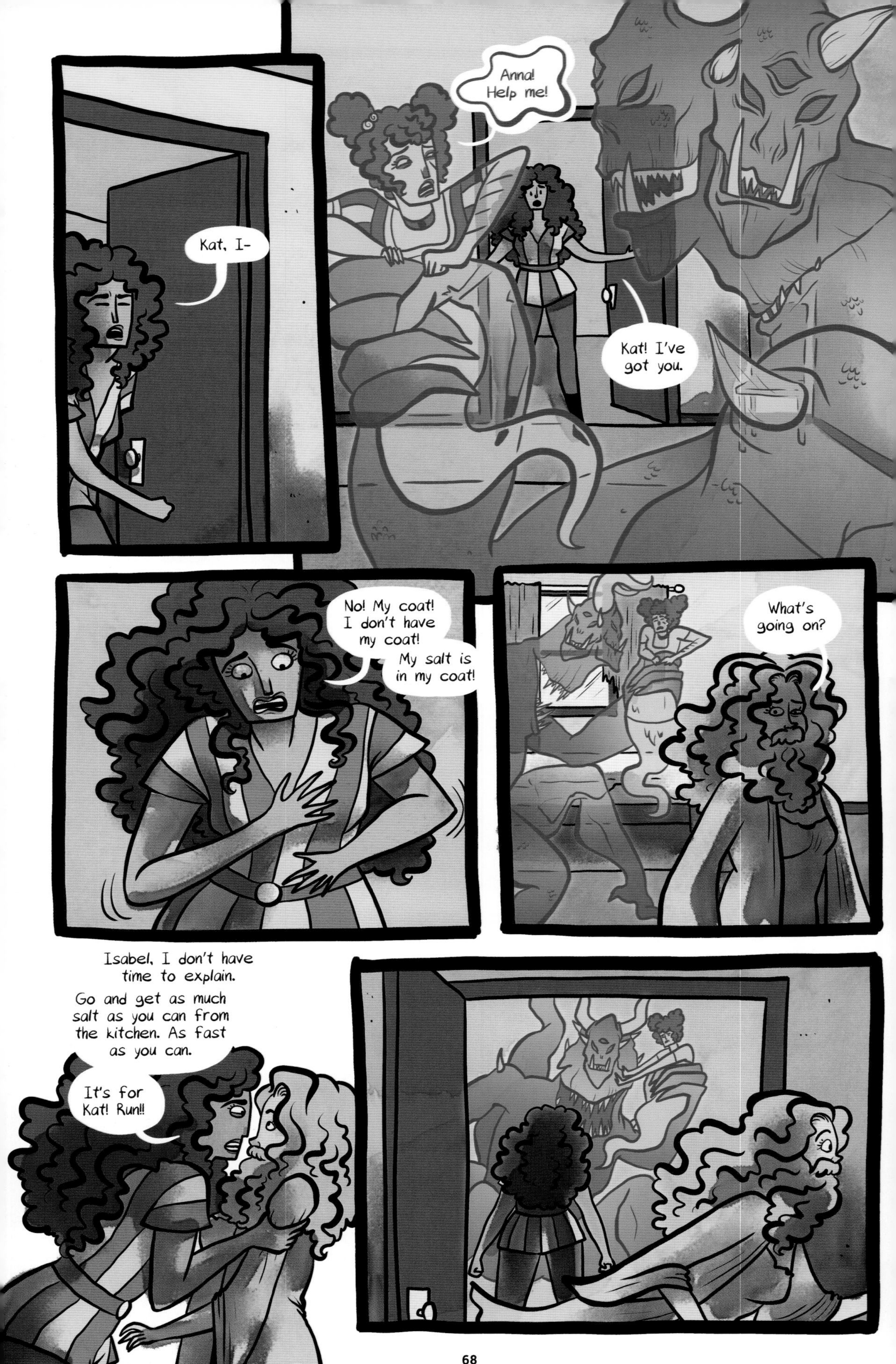
Kat, I-
Anna! Help me!
Kat! I've got you.
No! My coat! I don't have my coat!
My salt is in my coat!
What's going on?
Isabel, I don't have time to explain.
Go and get as much salt as you can from the kitchen. As fast as you can.
It's for Kat! Run!!

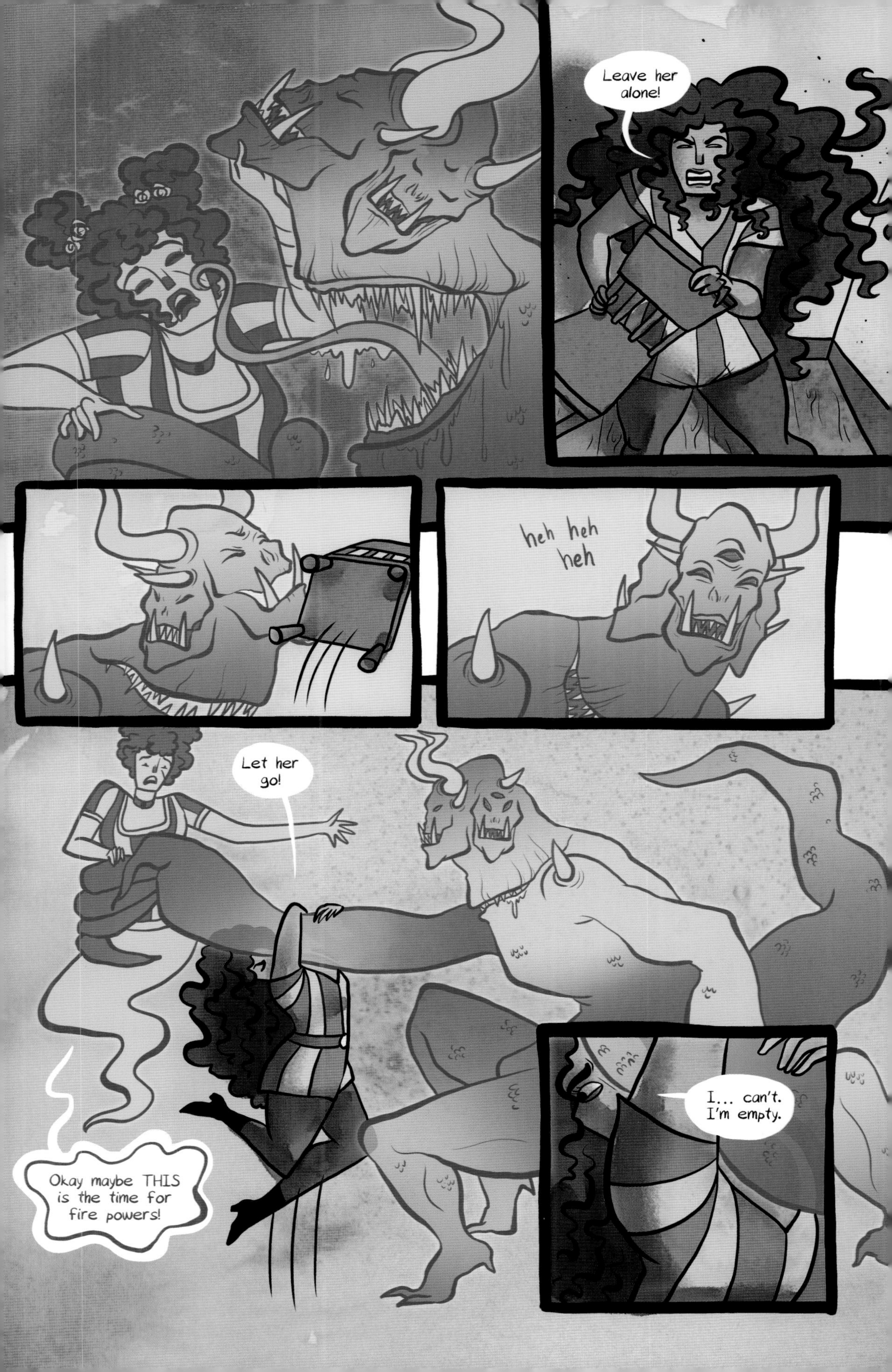
Leave her alone!
heh heh heh
Let her go!
Okay maybe THIS is the time for fire powers!
I... can't. I'm empty.

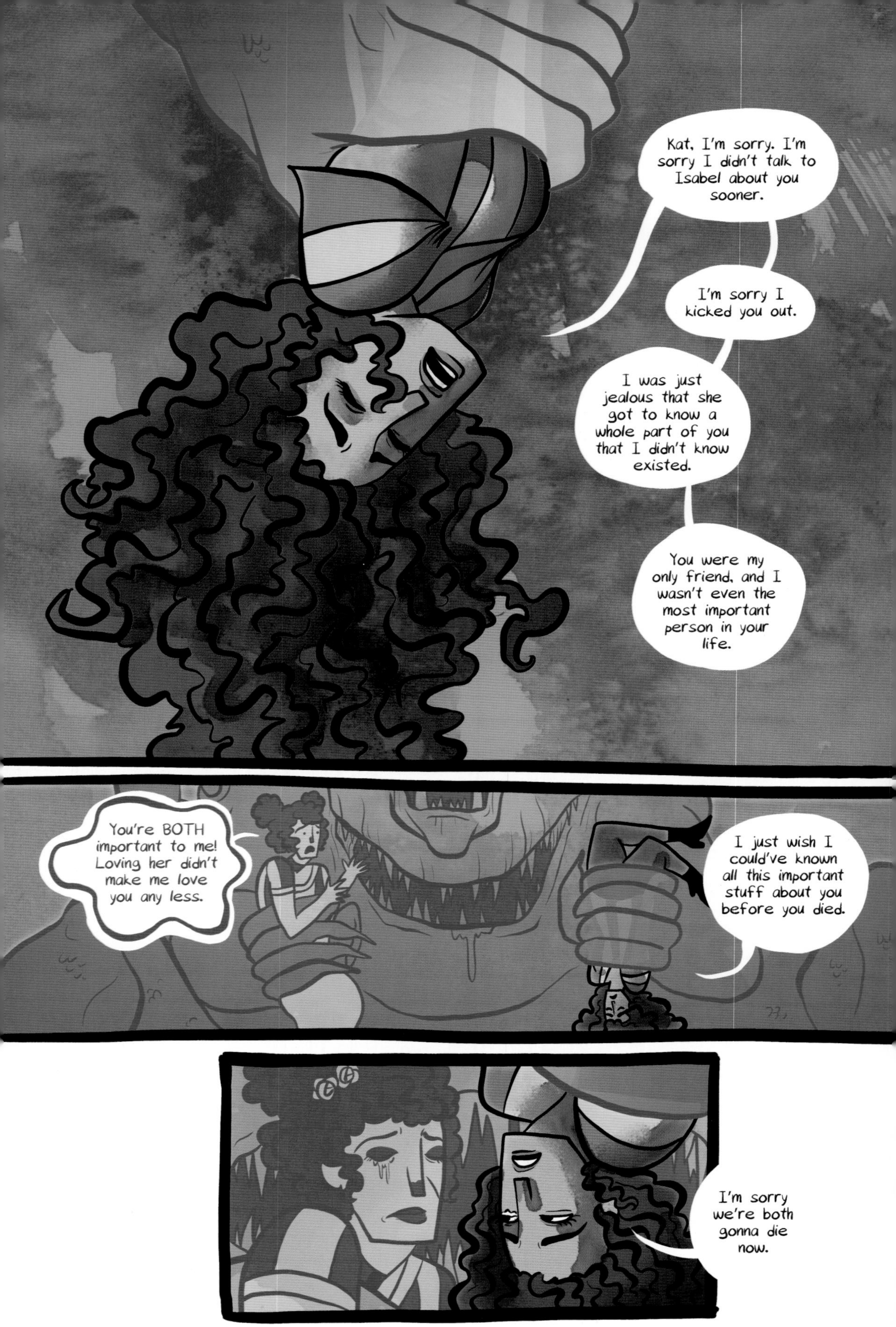
Kat, I'm sorry. I'm sorry I didn't talk to Isabel about you sooner.
I'm sorry I kicked you out.
I was just jealous that she got to know a whole part of you that I didn't know existed.
You were my only friend, and I wasn't even the most important person in your life.
You're BOTH important to me! Loving her didn't make me love you any less.
I just wish I could've known all this important stuff about you before you died.
I'm sorry we're both gonna die now.

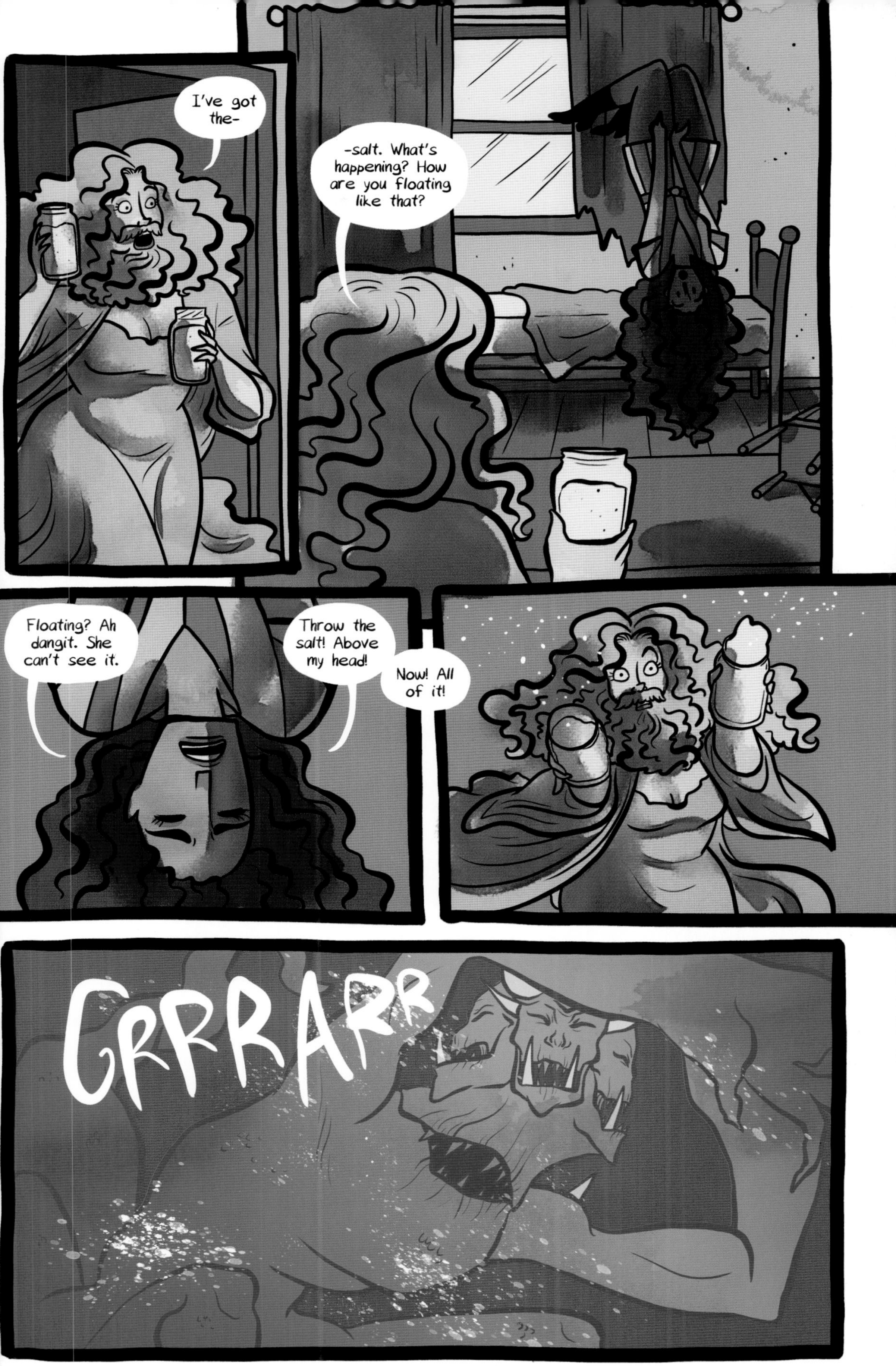
I've got the-
-salt. What's happening? How are you floating like that?
Floating? Ah dangit. She can't see it.
Throw the salt! Above my head!
Now! All of it!
GRRRARR

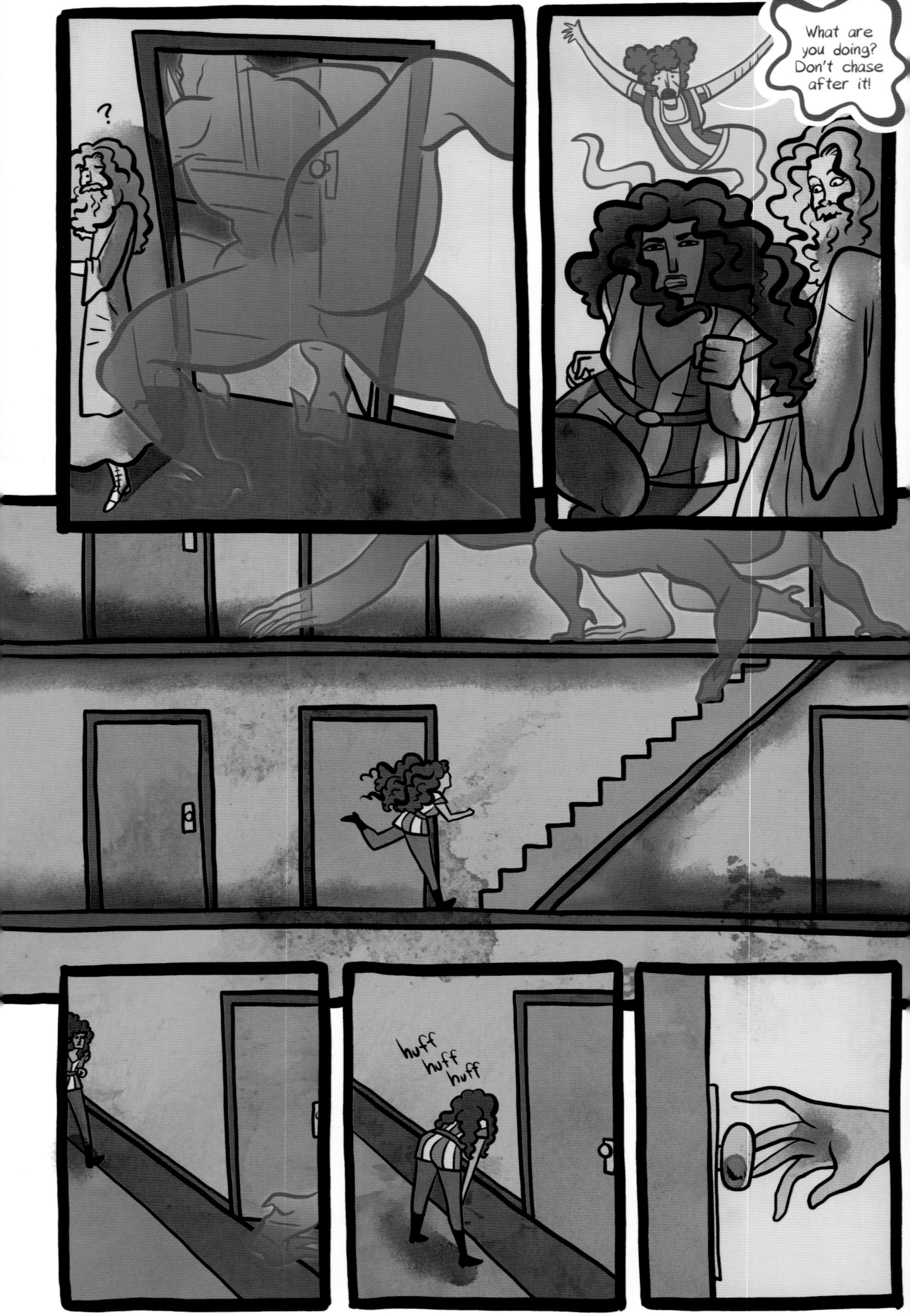
?
What are you doing? Don't chase after it!
huff huff huff

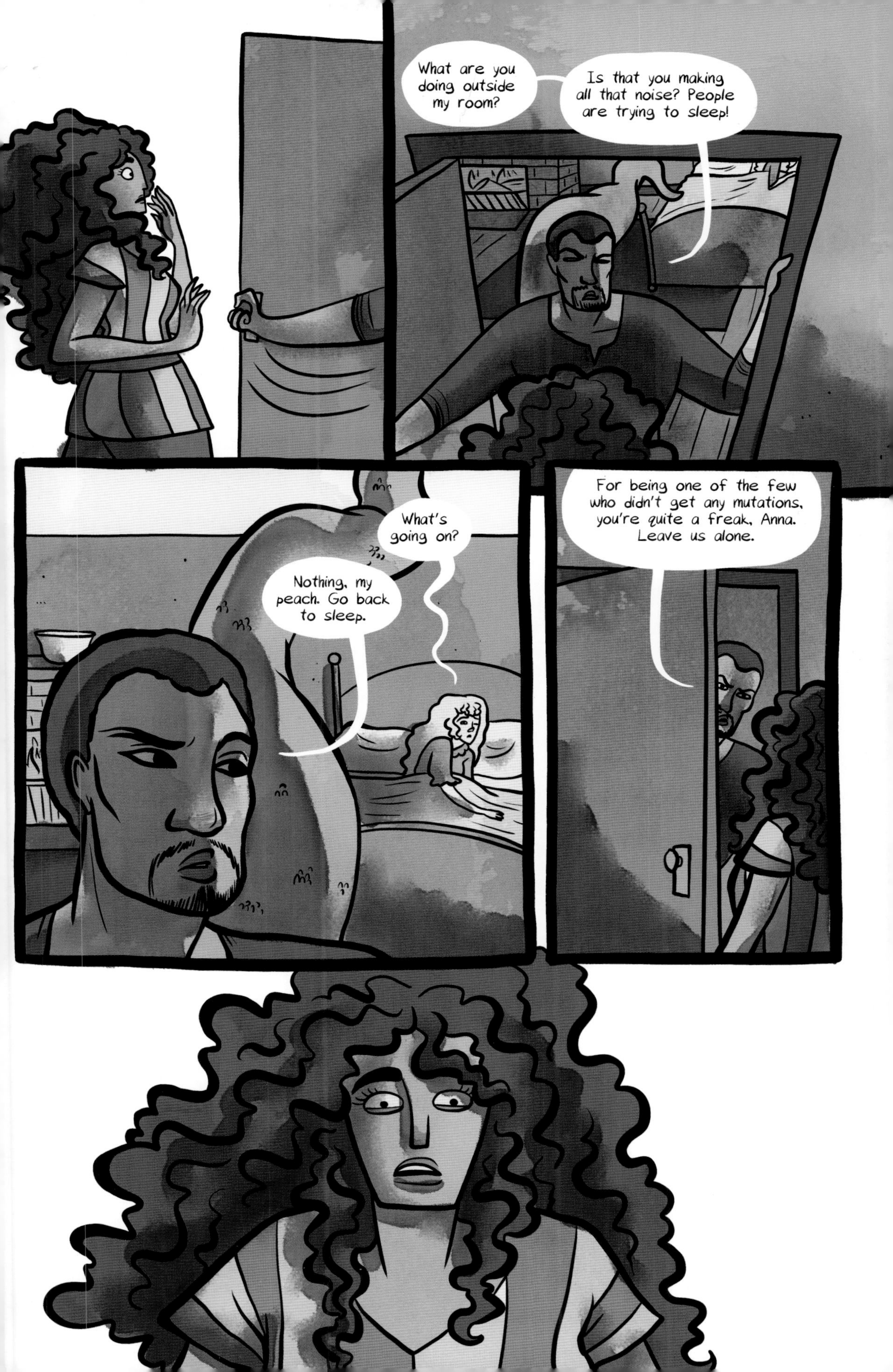
What are you doing outside my room?
Is that you making all that noise? People are trying to sleep!
What's going on?
Nothing, my peach. Go back to sleep.
For being one of the few who didn't get any mutations, you're quite a freak, Anna. Leave us alone.

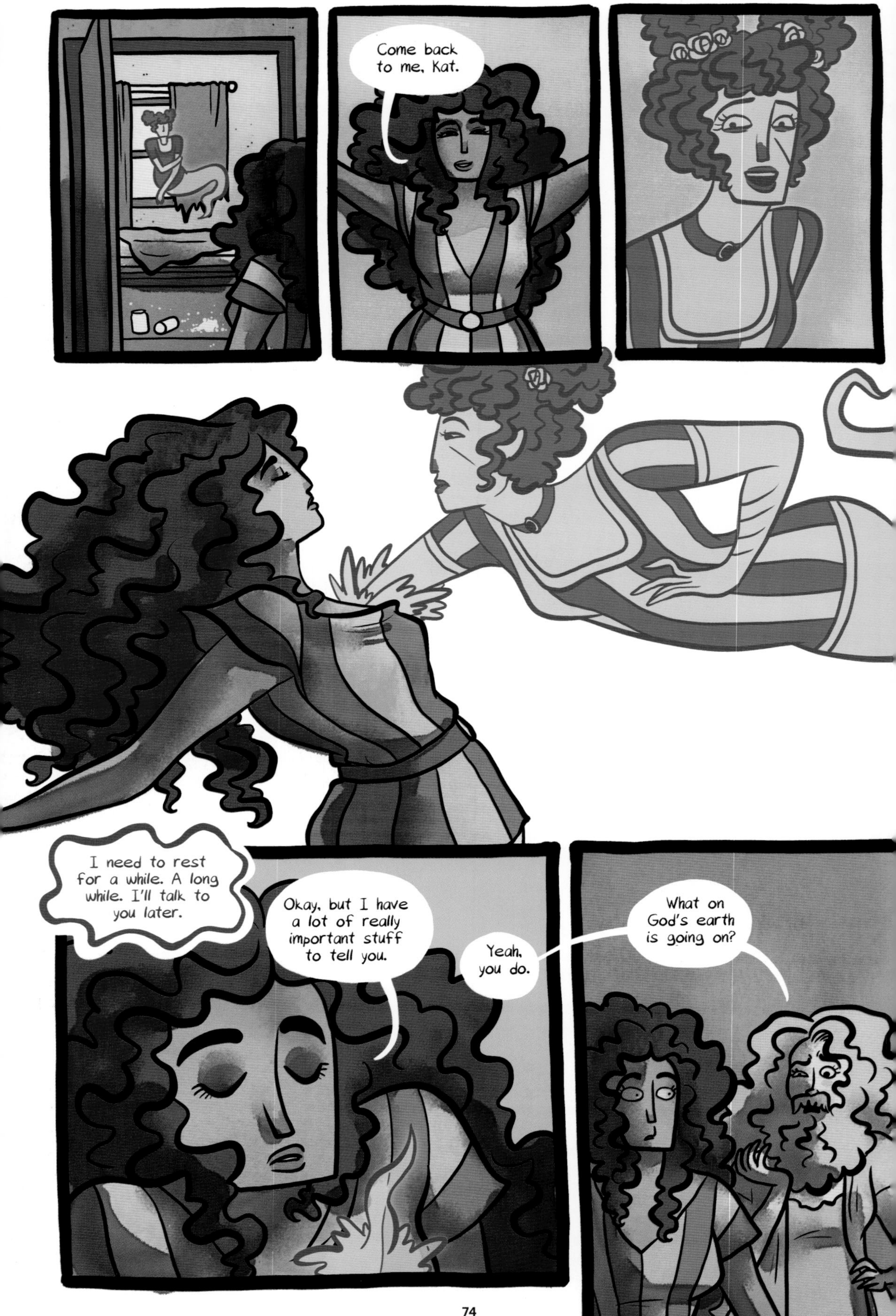
Come back to me, Kat.
I need to rest for a while. A long while. I'll talk to you later.
Okay, but I have a lot of really important stuff to tell you.
Yeah, you do.
What on God's earth is going on?

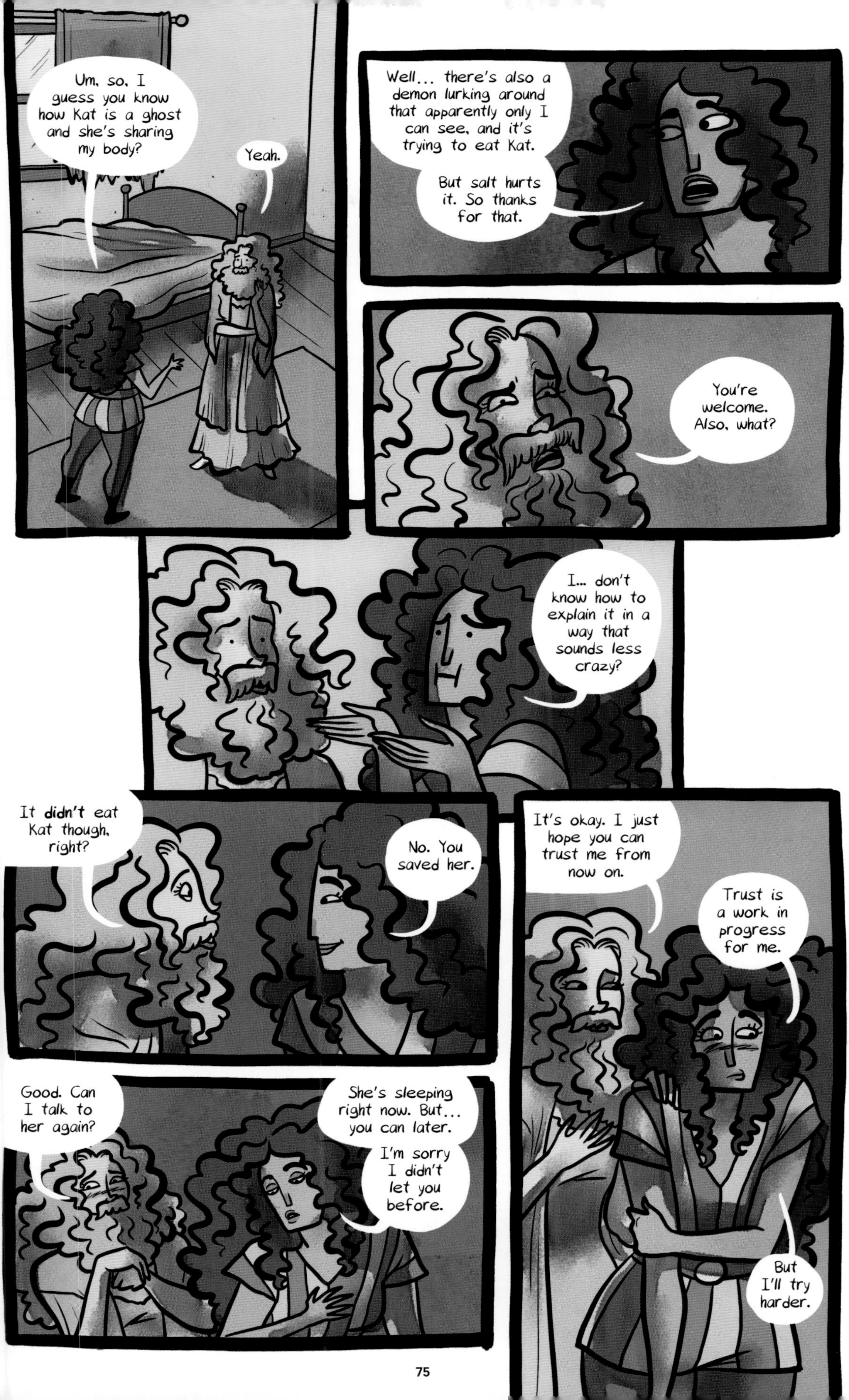
Um, so, I guess you know how Kat is a ghost and she's sharing my body?
Yeah.
Well... there's also a demon lurking around that apparently only I can see, and it's trying to eat Kat.
But salt hurts it. So thanks for that.
You're welcome. Also, what?
I... don't know how to explain it in a way that sounds less crazy?
It **didn't** eat Kat though, right?
No. You saved her.
Good. Can I talk to her again?
She's sleeping right now. But... you can later.
I'm sorry I didn't let you before.
It's okay. I just hope you can trust me from now on.
Trust is a work in progress for me.
But I'll try harder.

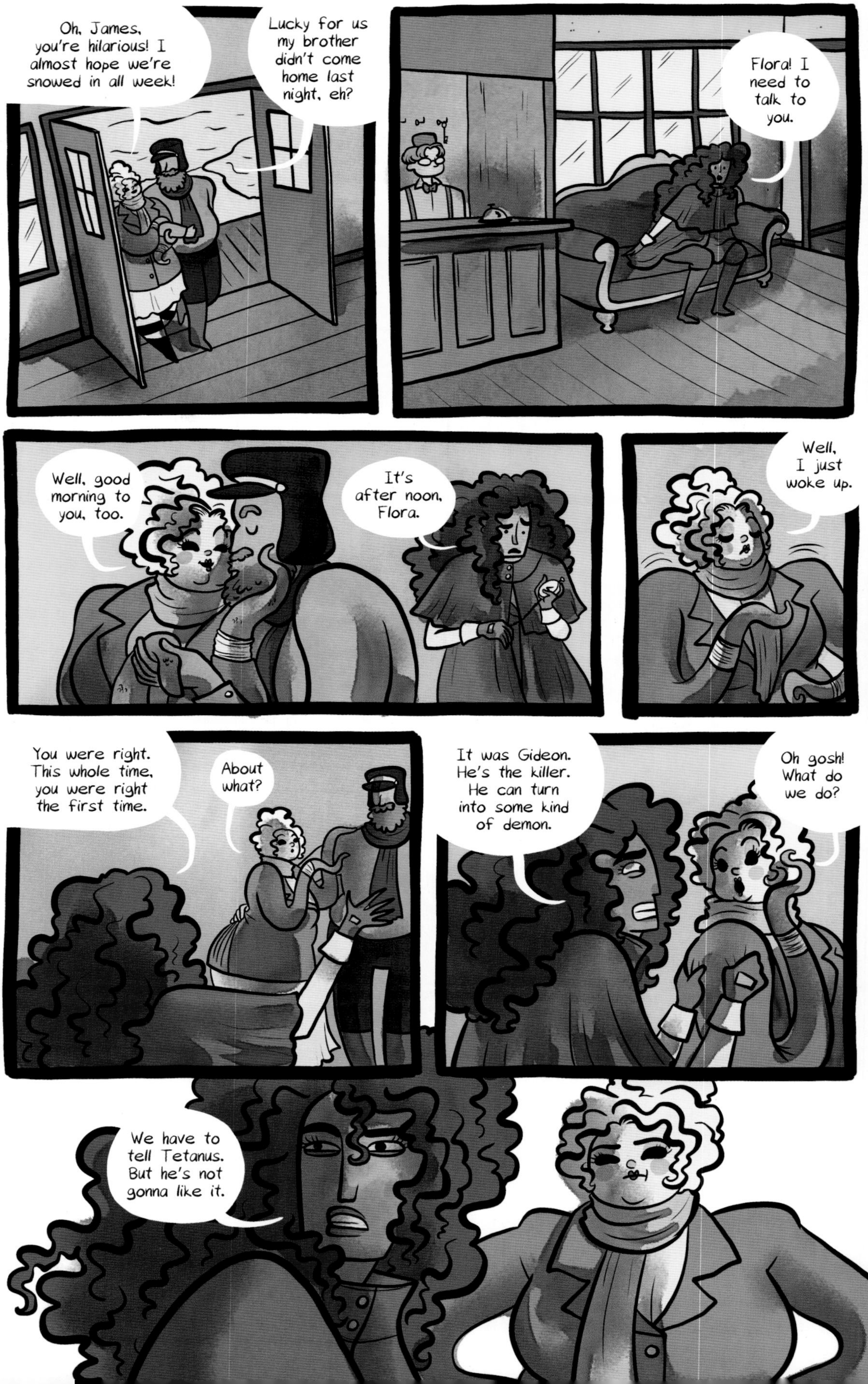
Oh, James, you're hilarious! I almost hope we're snowed in all week!
Lucky for us my brother didn't come home last night, eh?
Flora! I need to talk to you.
Well, good morning to you, too.
It's after noon, Flora.
Well, I just woke up.
You were right. This whole time, you were right the first time.
About what?
It was Gideon. He's the killer. He can turn into some kind of demon.
Oh gosh! What do we do?
We have to tell Tetanus. But he's not gonna like it.

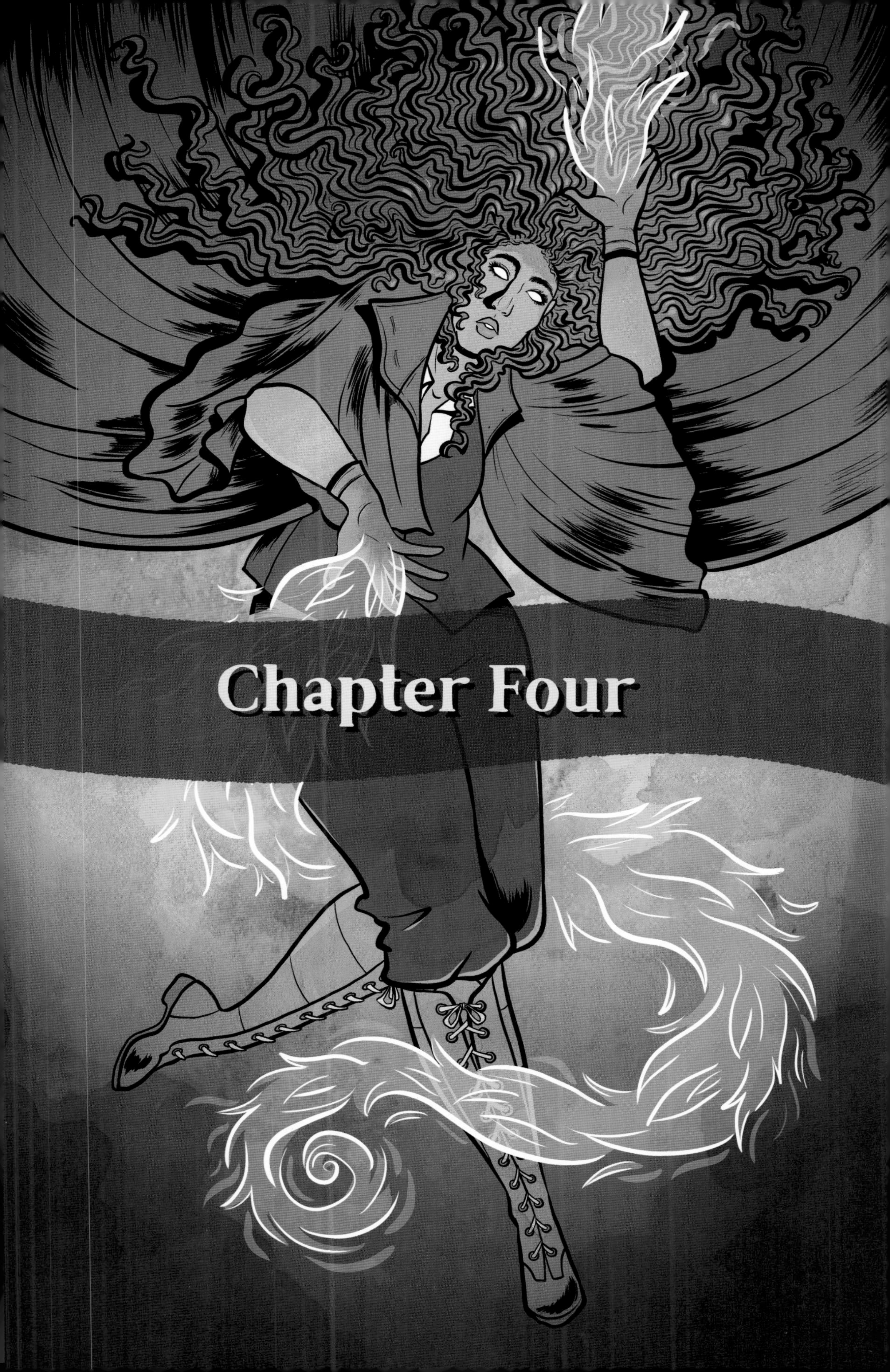

Chapter Four

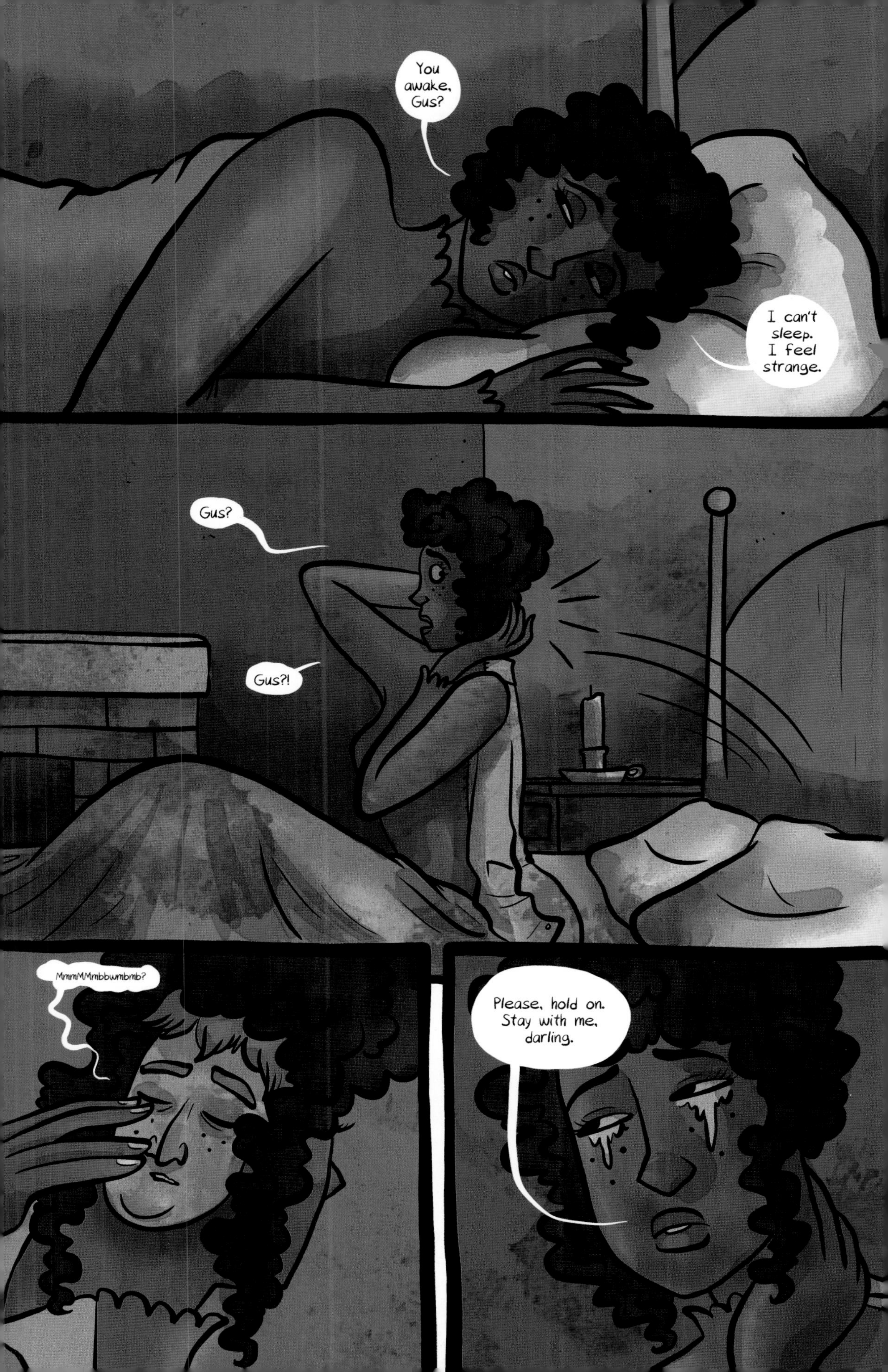
You awake, Gus?
I can't sleep. I feel strange.
Gus?
Gus?!
MmmMMmbbwmbmb?
Please, hold on. Stay with me, darling.

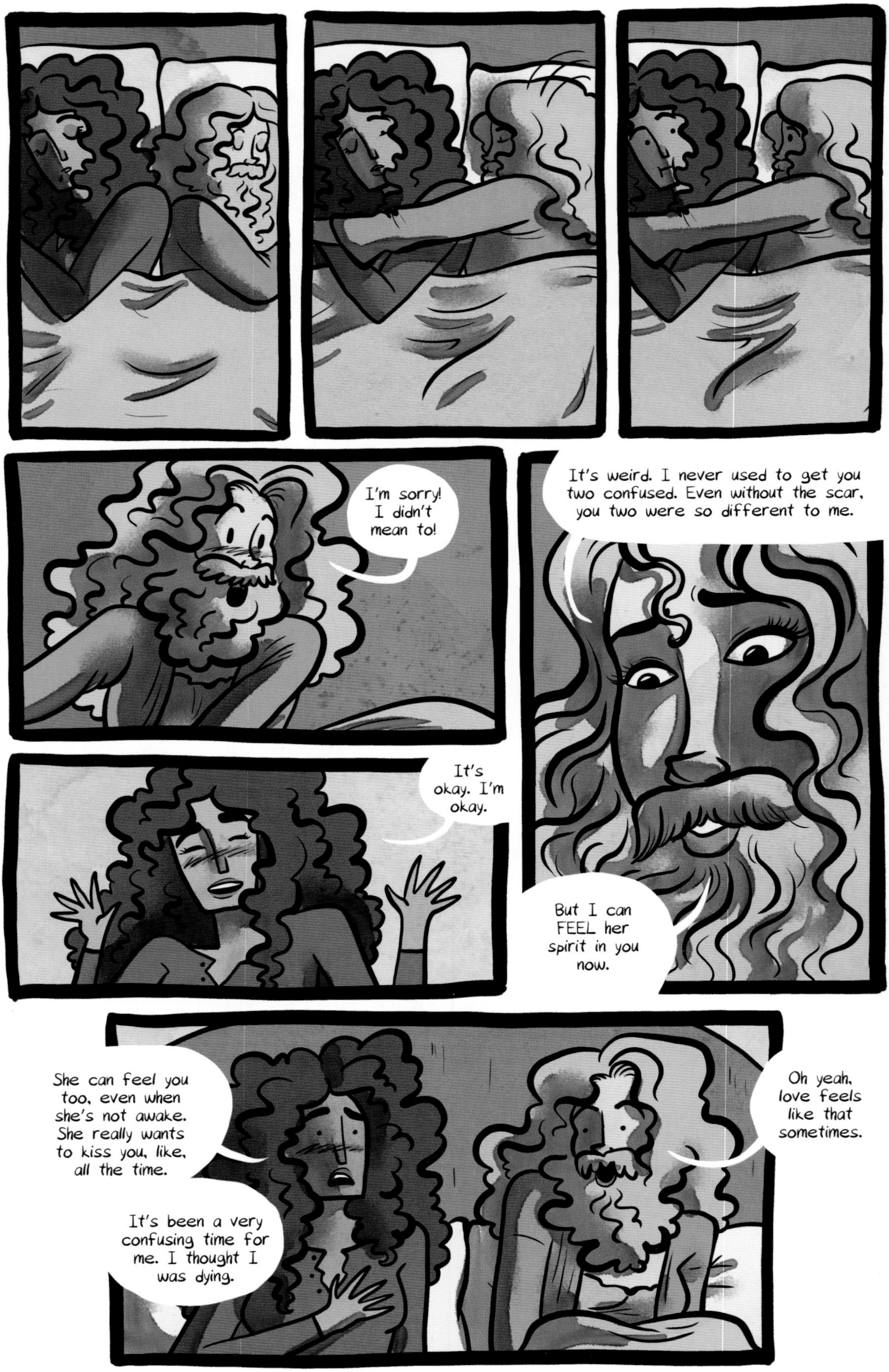
I'm sorry! I didn't mean to!
It's weird. I never used to get you two confused. Even without the scar, you two were so different to me.
It's okay. I'm okay.
But I can FEEL her spirit in you now.
She can feel you too, even when she's not awake. She really wants to kiss you, like, all the time.
It's been a very confusing time for me. I thought I was dying.
Oh yeah, love feels like that sometimes.

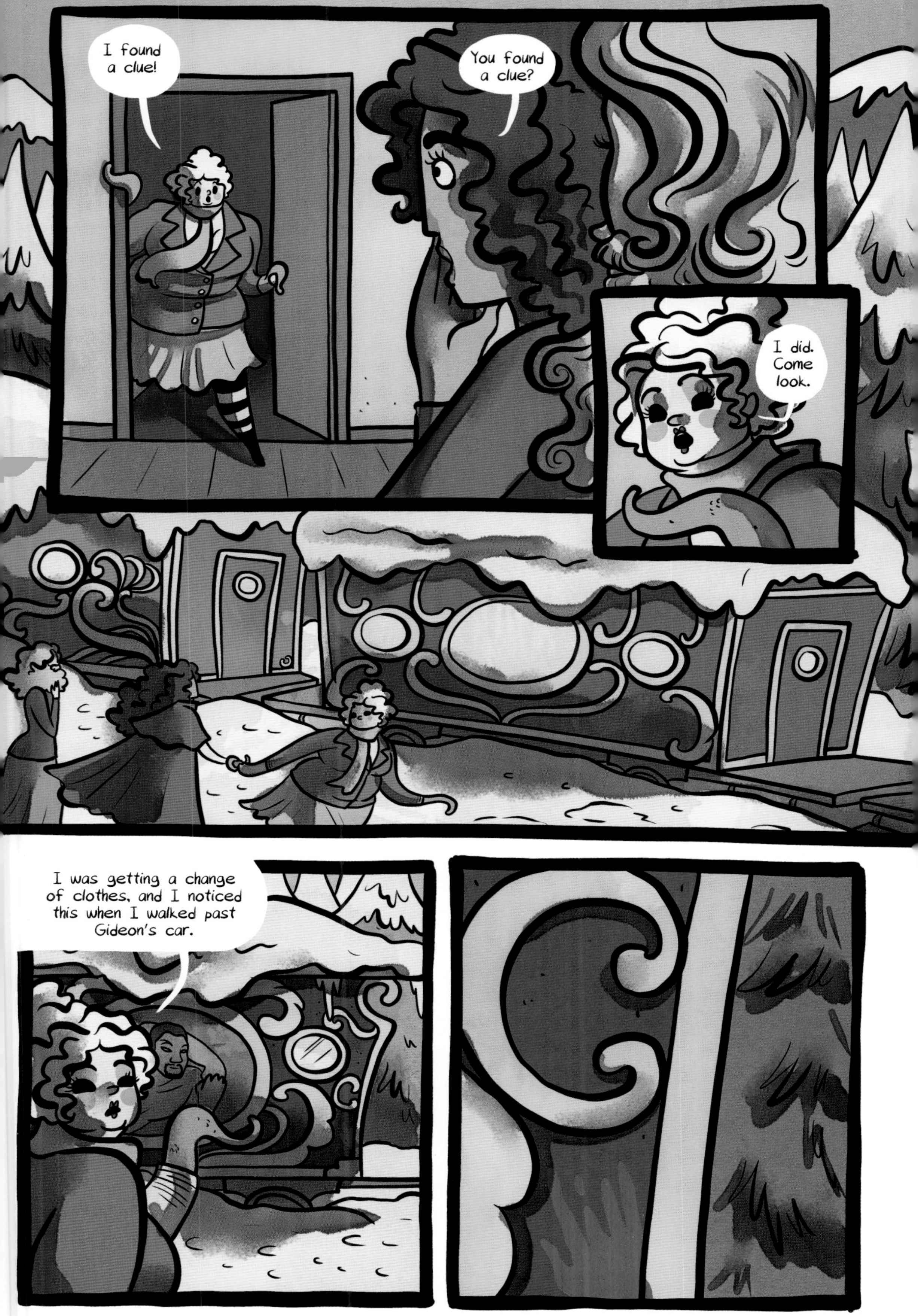
I found a clue!
You found a clue?
I did. Come look.
I was getting a change of clothes, and I noticed this when I walked past Gideon's car.

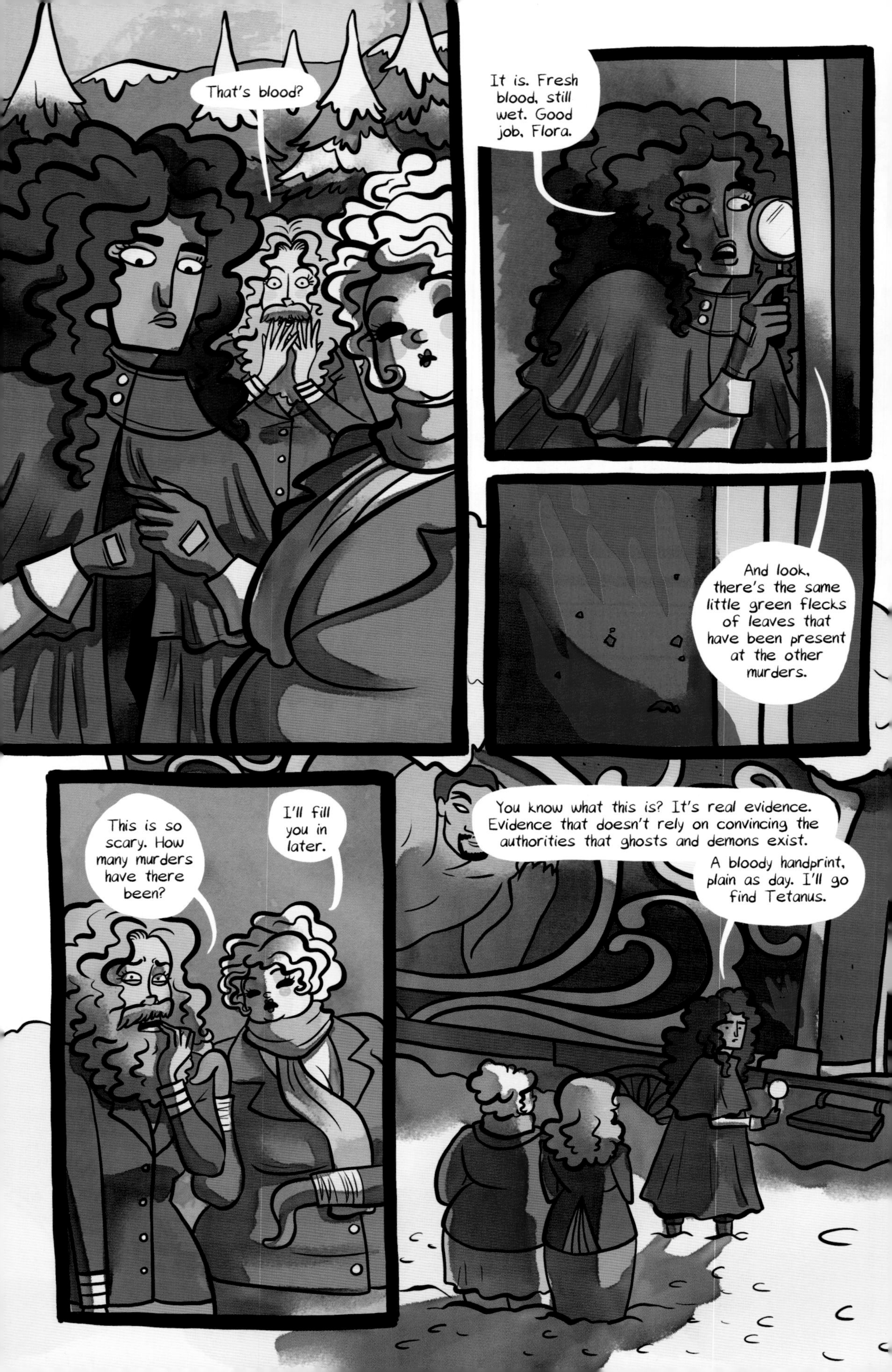

That's blood?
It is. Fresh blood, still wet. Good job, Flora.
And look, there's the same little green flecks of leaves that have been present at the other murders.
This is so scary. How many murders have there been?
I'll fill you in later.
You know what this is? It's real evidence. Evidence that doesn't rely on convincing the authorities that ghosts and demons exist.
A bloody handprint, plain as day. I'll go find Tetanus.

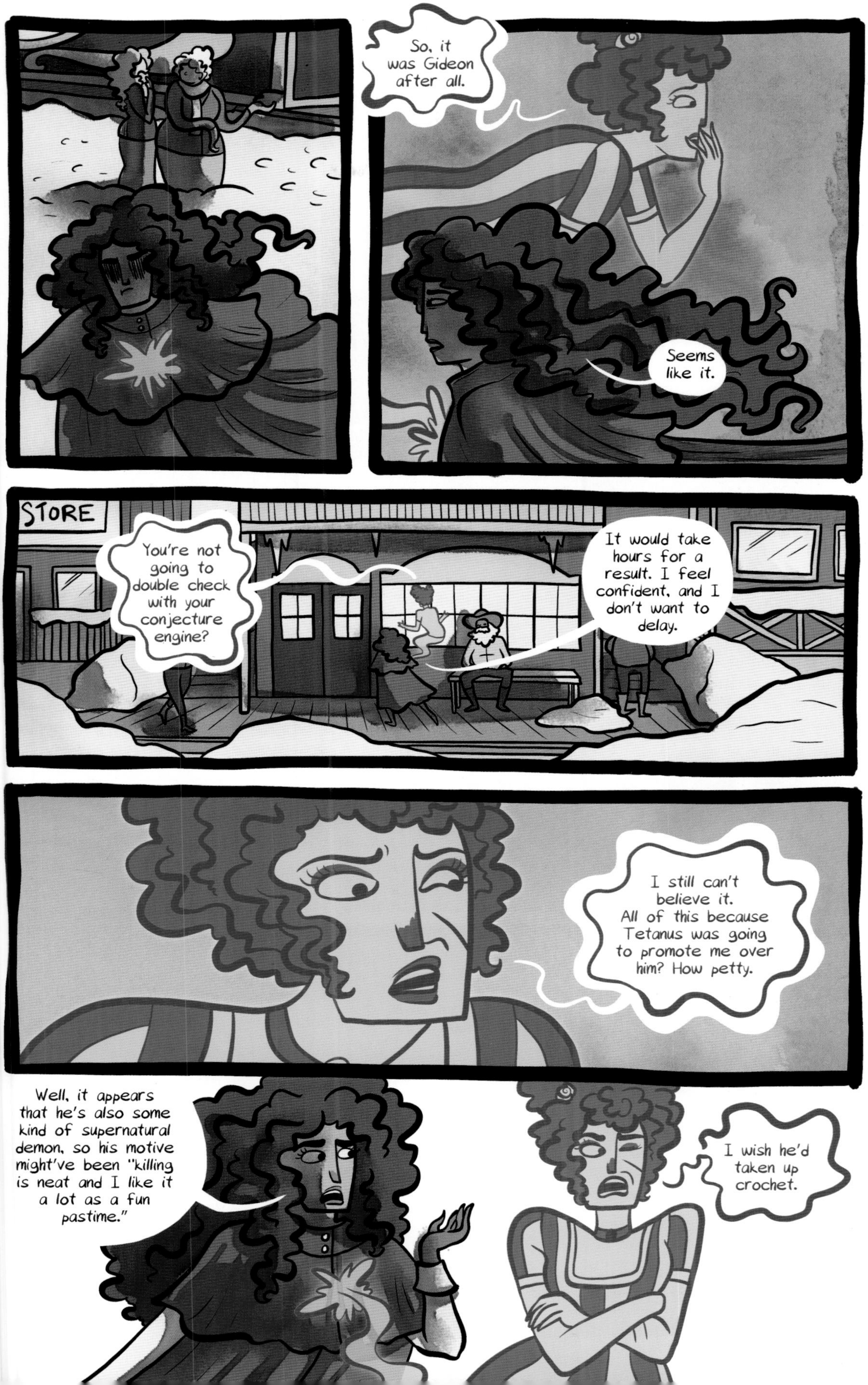
So, it was Gideon after all.
Seems like it.
STORE
You're not going to double check with your conjecture engine?
It would take hours for a result. I feel confident, and I don't want to delay.
I still can't believe it. All of this because Tetanus was going to promote me over him? How petty.
Well, it appears that he's also some kind of supernatural demon, so his motive might've been "killing is neat and I like it a lot as a fun pastime."
I wish he'd taken up crochet.

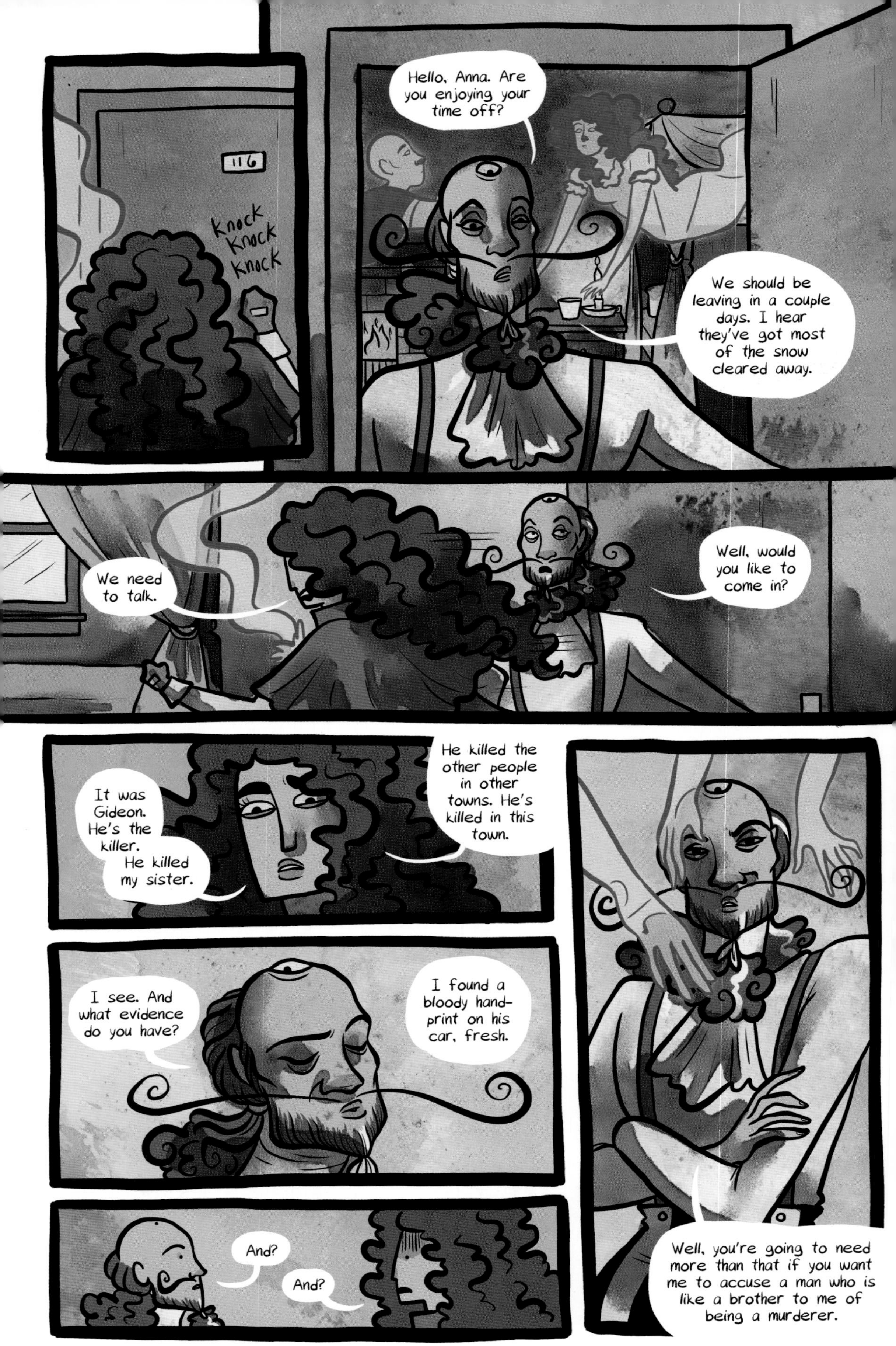

knock knock knock
Hello, Anna. Are you enjoying your time off?
We should be leaving in a couple days. I hear they've got most of the snow cleared away.
We need to talk.
Well, would you like to come in?
It was Gideon. He's the killer.
He killed my sister.
He killed the other people in other towns. He's killed in this town.
I see. And what evidence do you have?
I found a bloody hand-print on his car, fresh.
And?
And?
Well, you're going to need more than that if you want me to accuse a man who is like a brother to me of being a murderer.

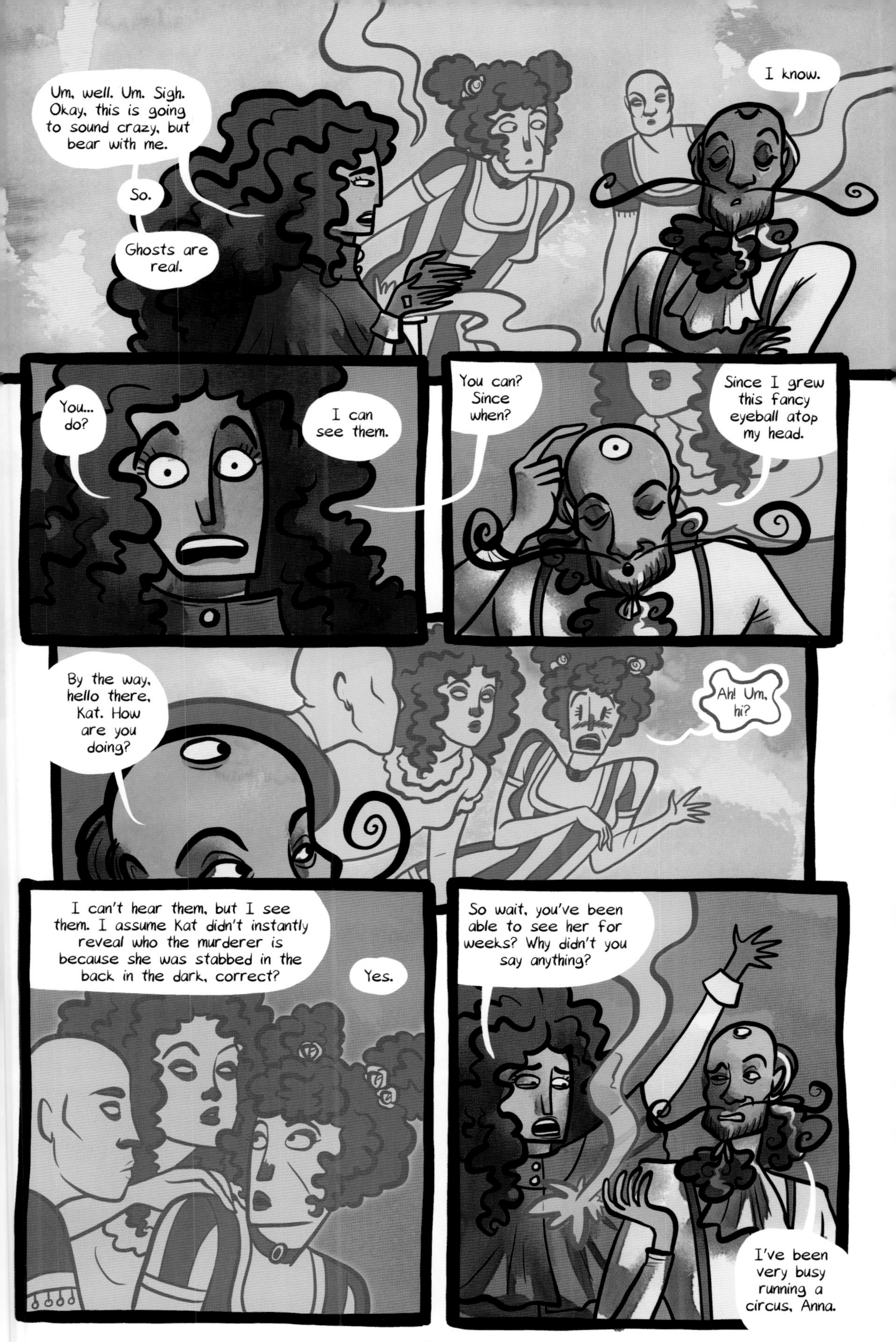

Um, well. Um. Sigh. Okay, this is going to sound crazy, but bear with me.
So.
Ghosts are real.
I know.
You... do?
I can see them.
You can? Since when?
Since I grew this fancy eyeball atop my head.
By the way, hello there, Kat. How are you doing?
Ah! Um, hi?
I can't hear them, but I see them. I assume Kat didn't instantly reveal who the murderer is because she was stabbed in the back in the dark, correct?
Yes.
So wait, you've been able to see her for weeks? Why didn't you say anything?
I've been very busy running a circus, Anna.

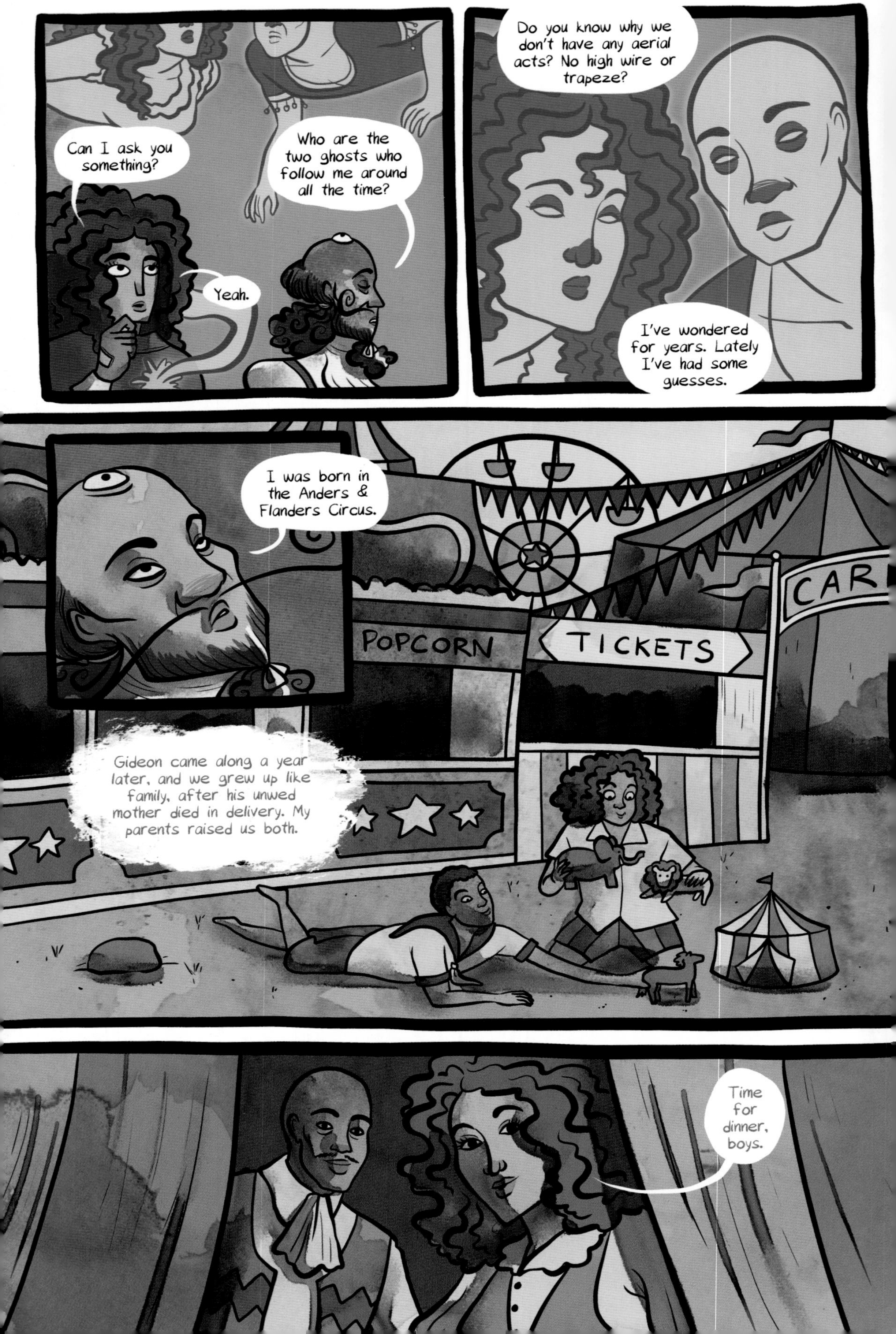
Can I ask you something?
Yeah.
Who are the two ghosts who follow me around all the time?
Do you know why we don't have any aerial acts? No high wire or trapeze?
I've wondered for years. Lately I've had some guesses.
I was born in the Anders & Flanders Circus.
POPCORN
TICKETS
CAR
Gideon came along a year later, and we grew up like family, after his unwed mother died in delivery. My parents raised us both.
Time for dinner, boys.

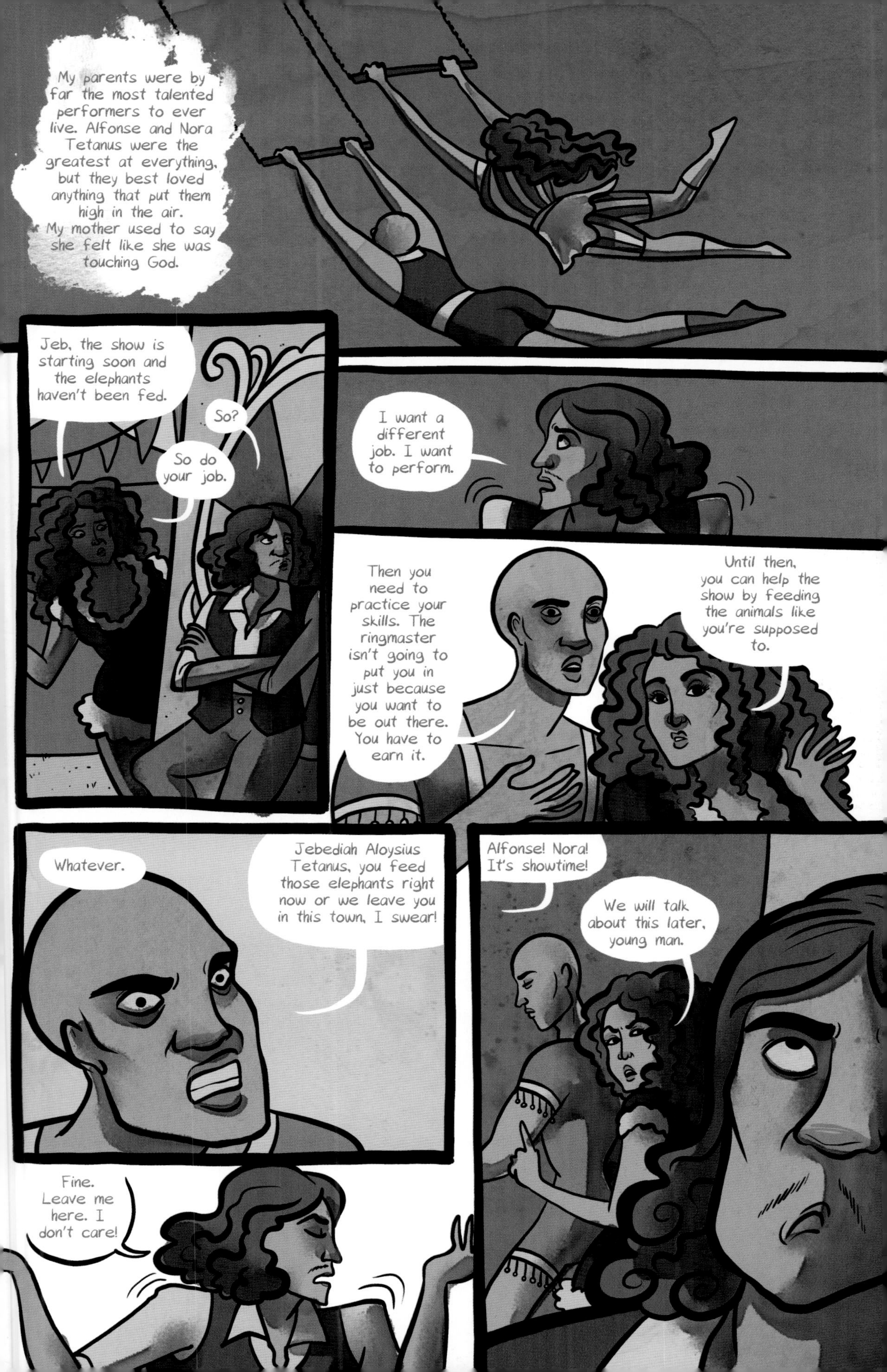
My parents were by far the most talented performers to ever live. Alfonse and Nora Tetanus were the greatest at everything, but they best loved anything that put them high in the air. My mother used to say she felt like she was touching God.
Jeb, the show is starting soon and the elephants haven't been fed.
So?
So do your job.
I want a different job. I want to perform.
Then you need to practice your skills. The ringmaster isn't going to put you in just because you want to be out there. You have to earn it.
Until then, you can help the show by feeding the animals like you're supposed to.
Whatever.
Jebediah Aloysius Tetanus, you feed those elephants right now or we leave you in this town, I swear!
Fine. Leave me here. I don't care!
Alfonse! Nora! It's showtime!
We will talk about this later, young man.

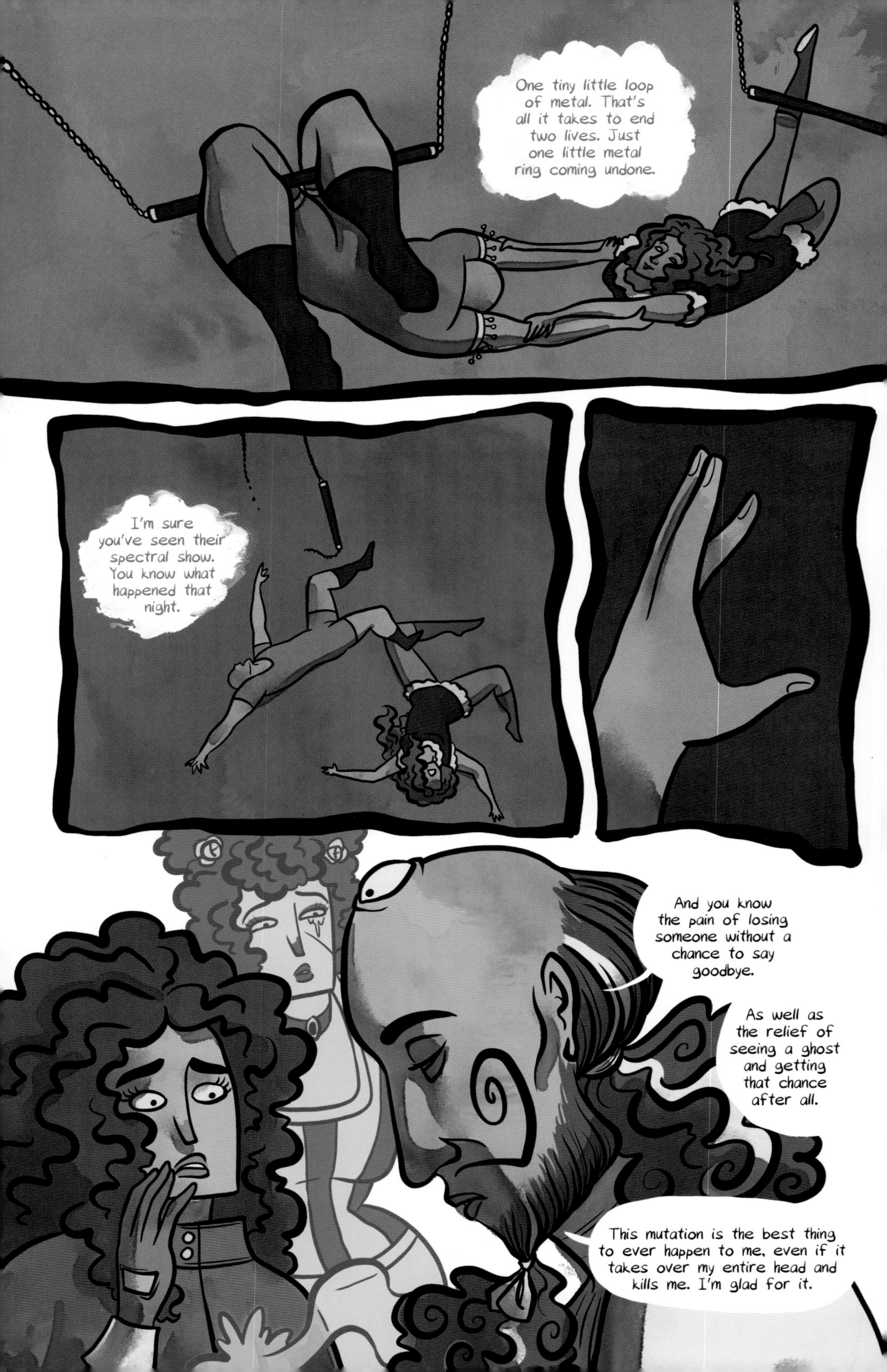
One tiny little loop of metal. That's all it takes to end two lives. Just one little metal ring coming undone.
I'm sure you've seen their spectral show. You know what happened that night.
And you know the pain of losing someone without a chance to say goodbye.
As well as the relief of seeing a ghost and getting that chance after all.
This mutation is the best thing to ever happen to me, even if it takes over my entire head and kills me. I'm glad for it.

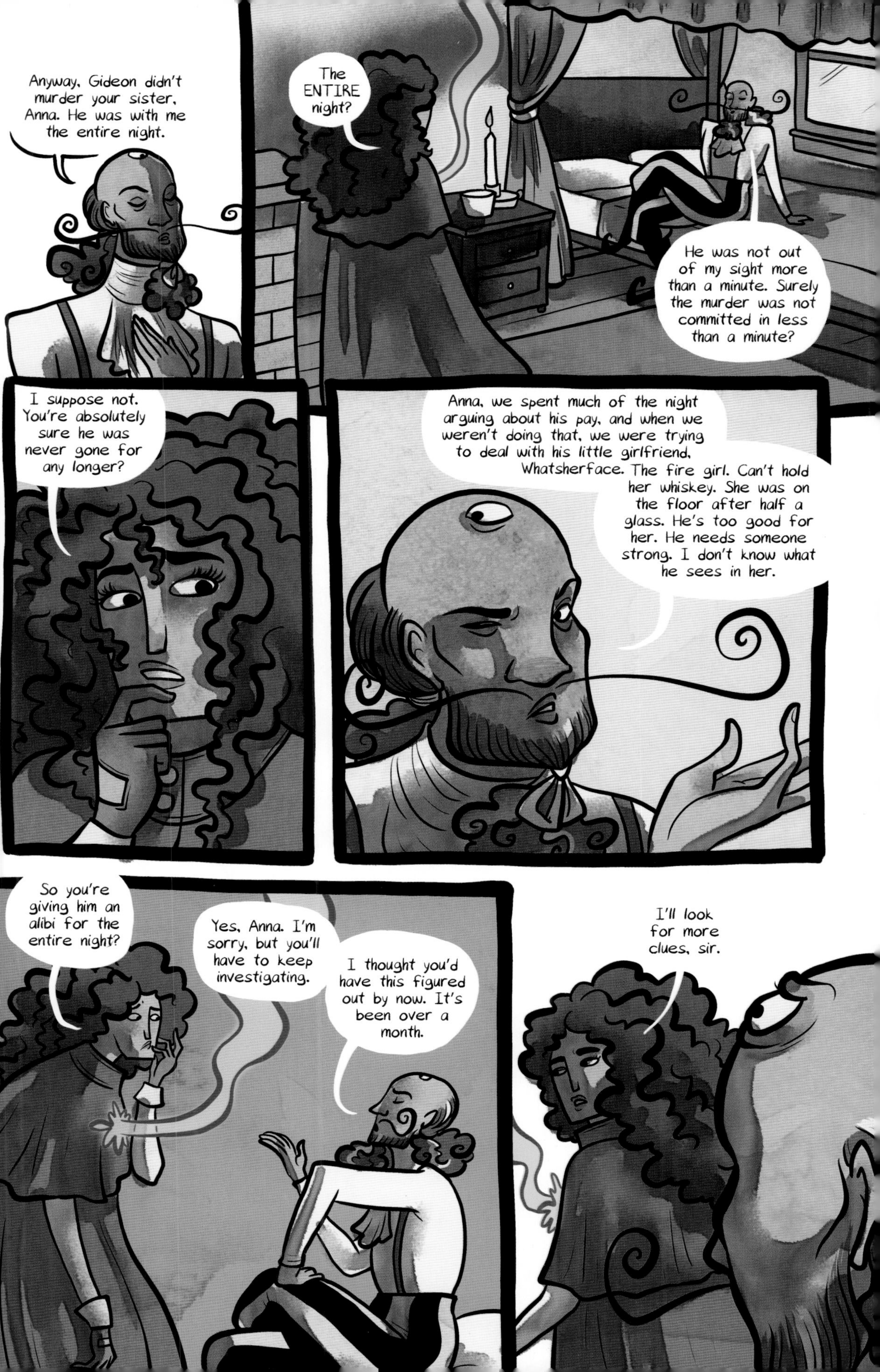

Anyway, Gideon didn't murder your sister, Anna. He was with me the entire night.
The ENTIRE night?
He was not out of my sight more than a minute. Surely the murder was not committed in less than a minute?
I suppose not. You're absolutely sure he was never gone for any longer?
Anna, we spent much of the night arguing about his pay, and when we weren't doing that, we were trying to deal with his little girlfriend, Whatsherface. The fire girl. Can't hold her whiskey. She was on the floor after half a glass. He's too good for her. He needs someone strong. I don't know what he sees in her.
So you're giving him an alibi for the entire night?
Yes, Anna. I'm sorry, but you'll have to keep investigating.
I thought you'd have this figured out by now. It's been over a month.
I'll look for more clues, sir.

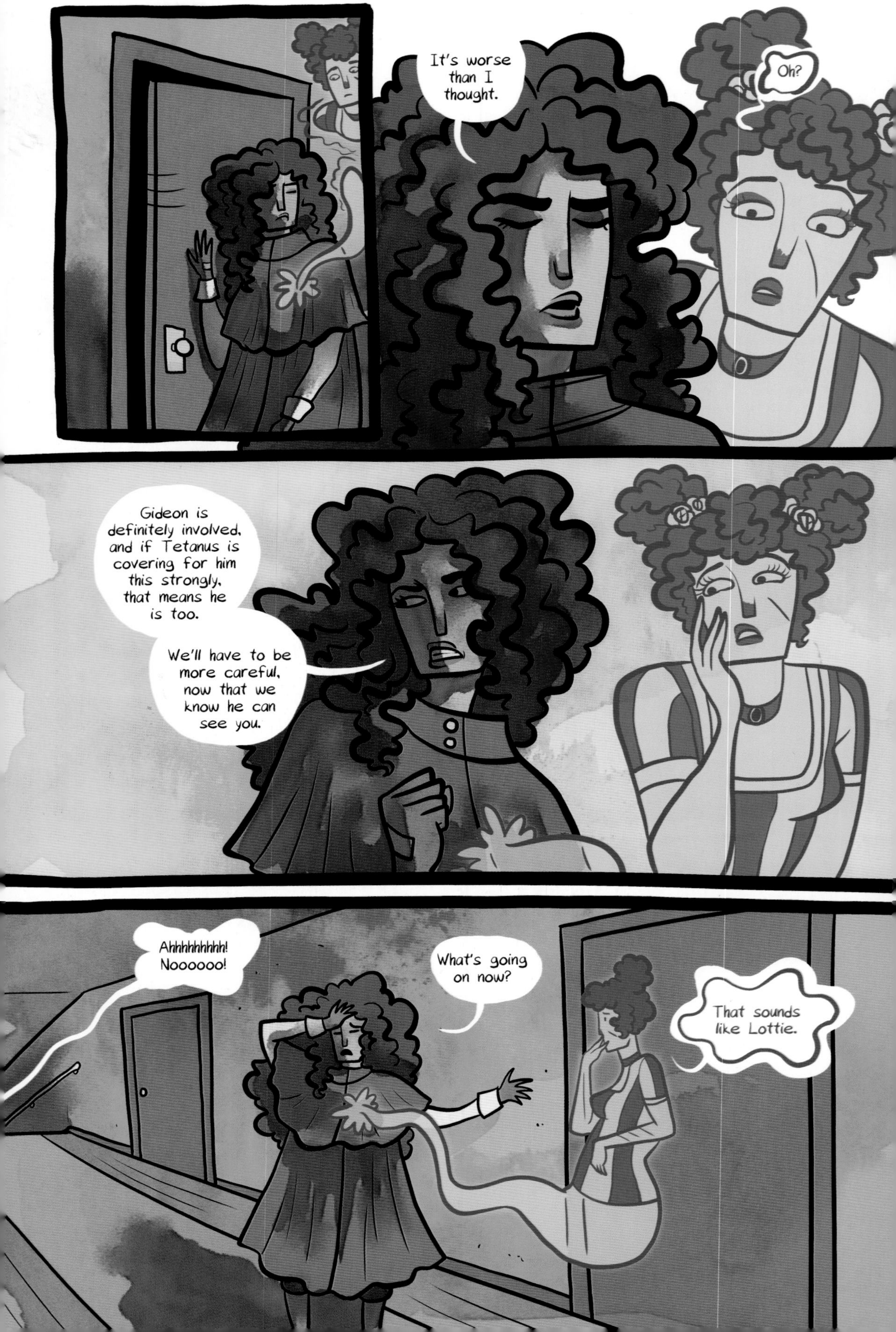
It's worse than I thought.
Oh?
Gideon is definitely involved, and if Tetanus is covering for him this strongly, that means he is too.
We'll have to be more careful, now that we know he can see you.
Ahhhhhhhhh! Noooooo!
What's going on now?
That sounds like Lottie.

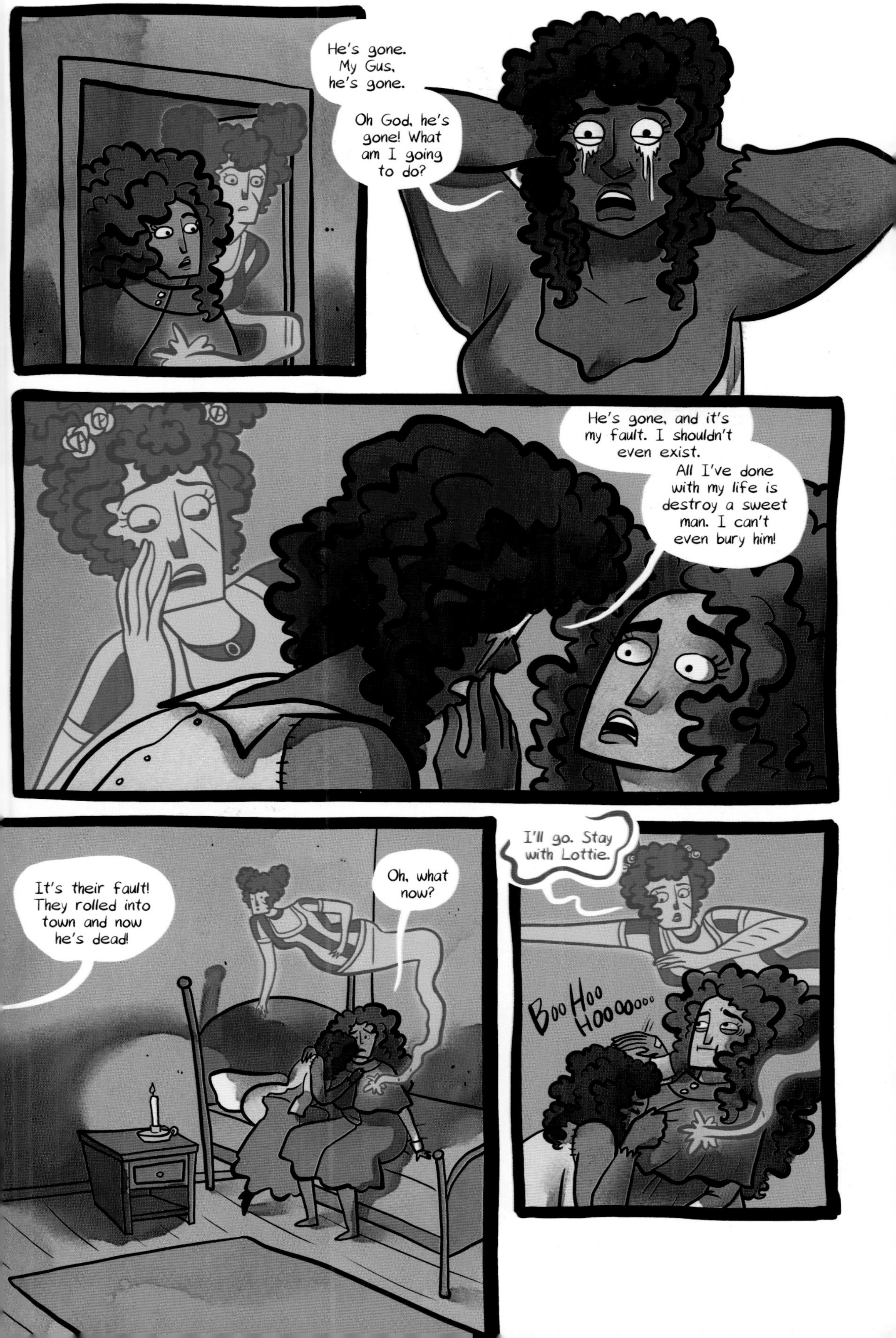
He's gone. My Gus, he's gone.
Oh God, he's gone! What am I going to do?
He's gone, and it's my fault. I shouldn't even exist.
All I've done with my life is destroy a sweet man. I can't even bury him!
It's their fault! They rolled into town and now he's dead!
Oh, what now?
I'll go. Stay with Lottie.
BooHoo HOOOOooo

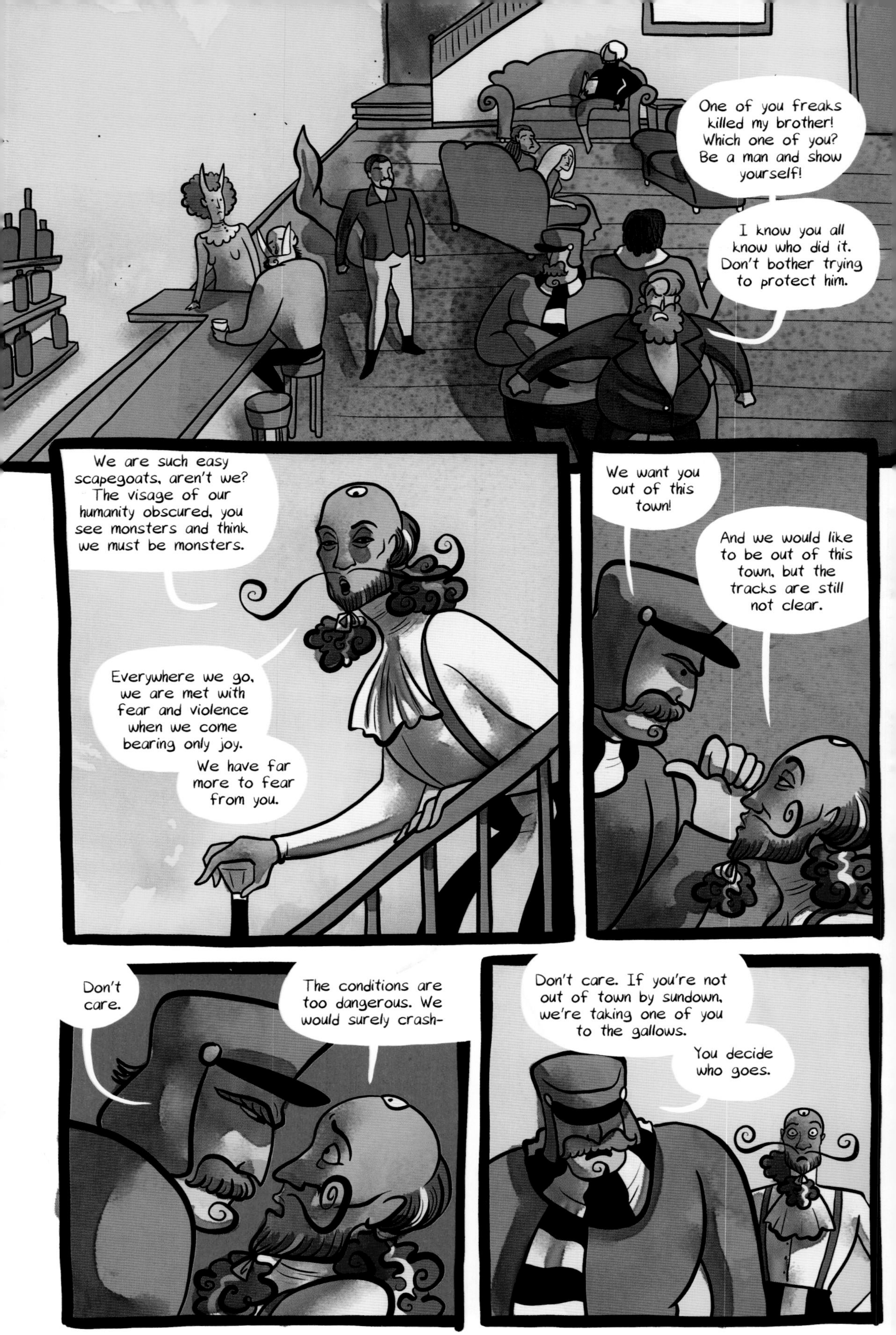

One of you freaks killed my brother! Which one of you? Be a man and show yourself!
I know you all know who did it. Don't bother trying to protect him.
We are such easy scapegoats, aren't we? The visage of our humanity obscured, you see monsters and think we must be monsters.
Everywhere we go, we are met with fear and violence when we come bearing only joy.
We have far more to fear from you.
We want you out of this town!
And we would like to be out of this town, but the tracks are still not clear.
Don't care.
The conditions are too dangerous. We would surely crash-
Don't care. If you're not out of town by sundown, we're taking one of you to the gallows.
You decide who goes.

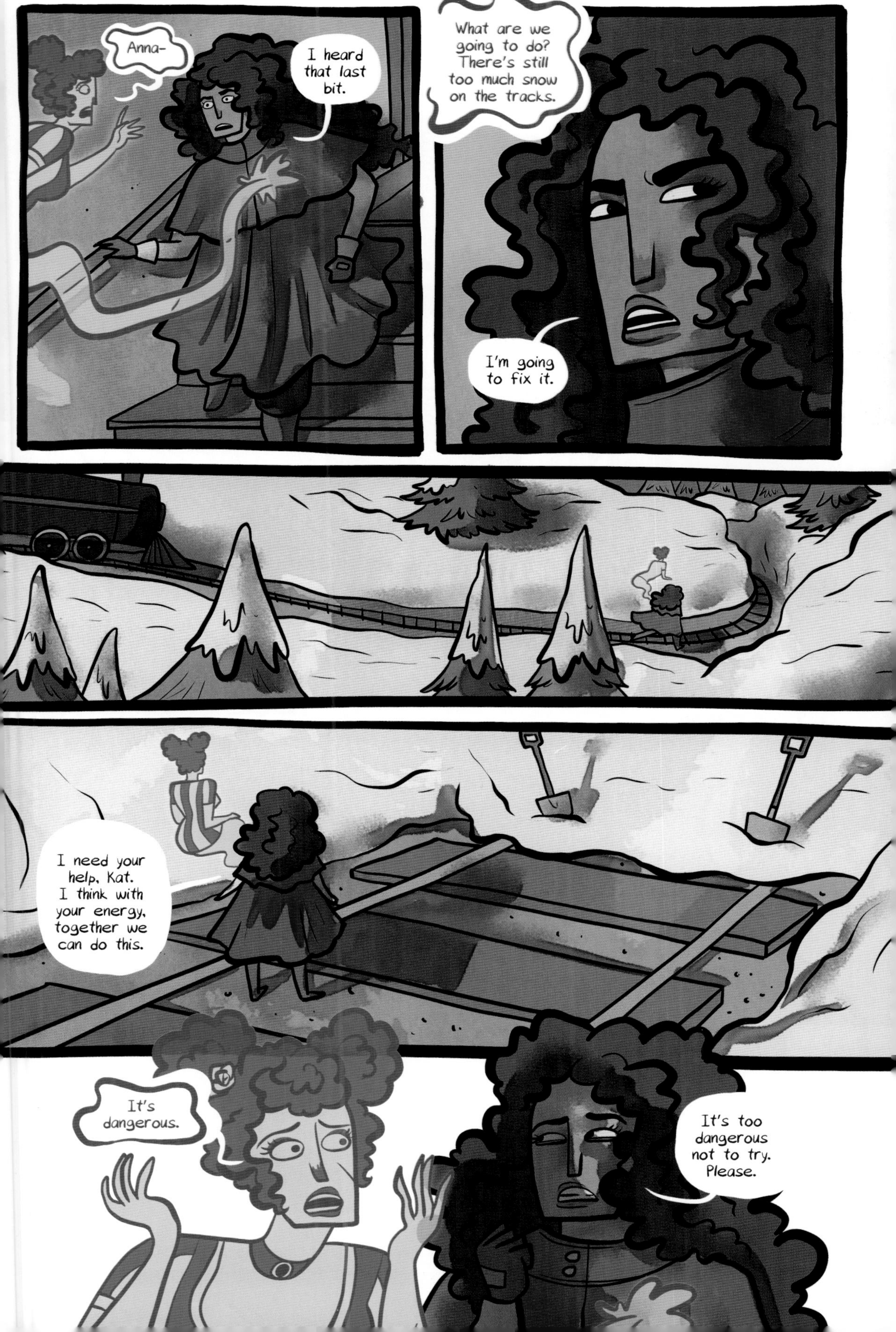
Anna-
I heard that last bit.
What are we going to do? There's still too much snow on the tracks.
I'm going to fix it.
I need your help, Kat. I think with your energy, together we can do this.
It's dangerous.
It's too dangerous not to try. Please.

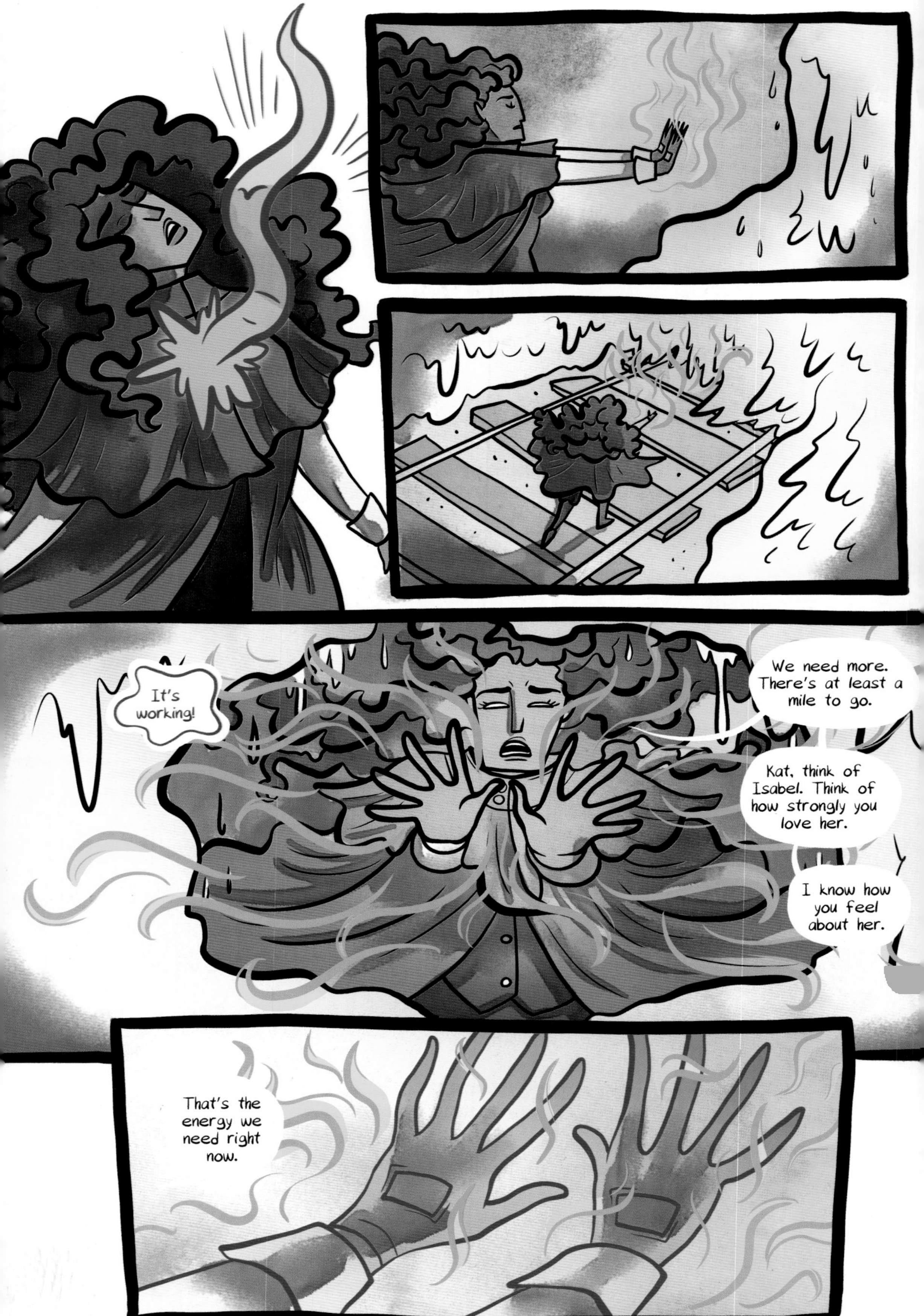
It's working!
We need more. There's at least a mile to go.
Kat, think of Isabel. Think of how strongly you love her.
I know how you feel about her.
That's the energy we need right now.

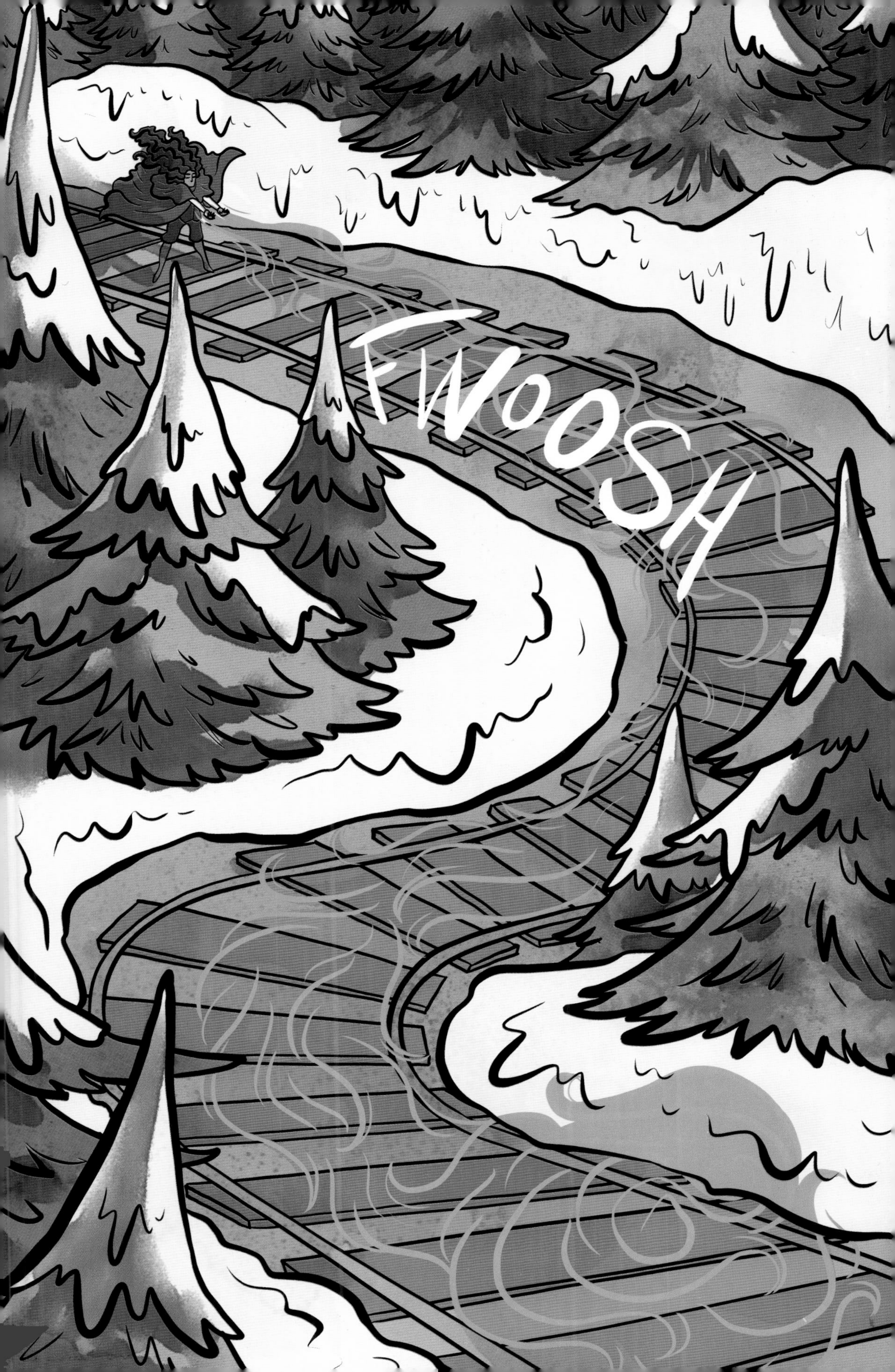
FWOOSH

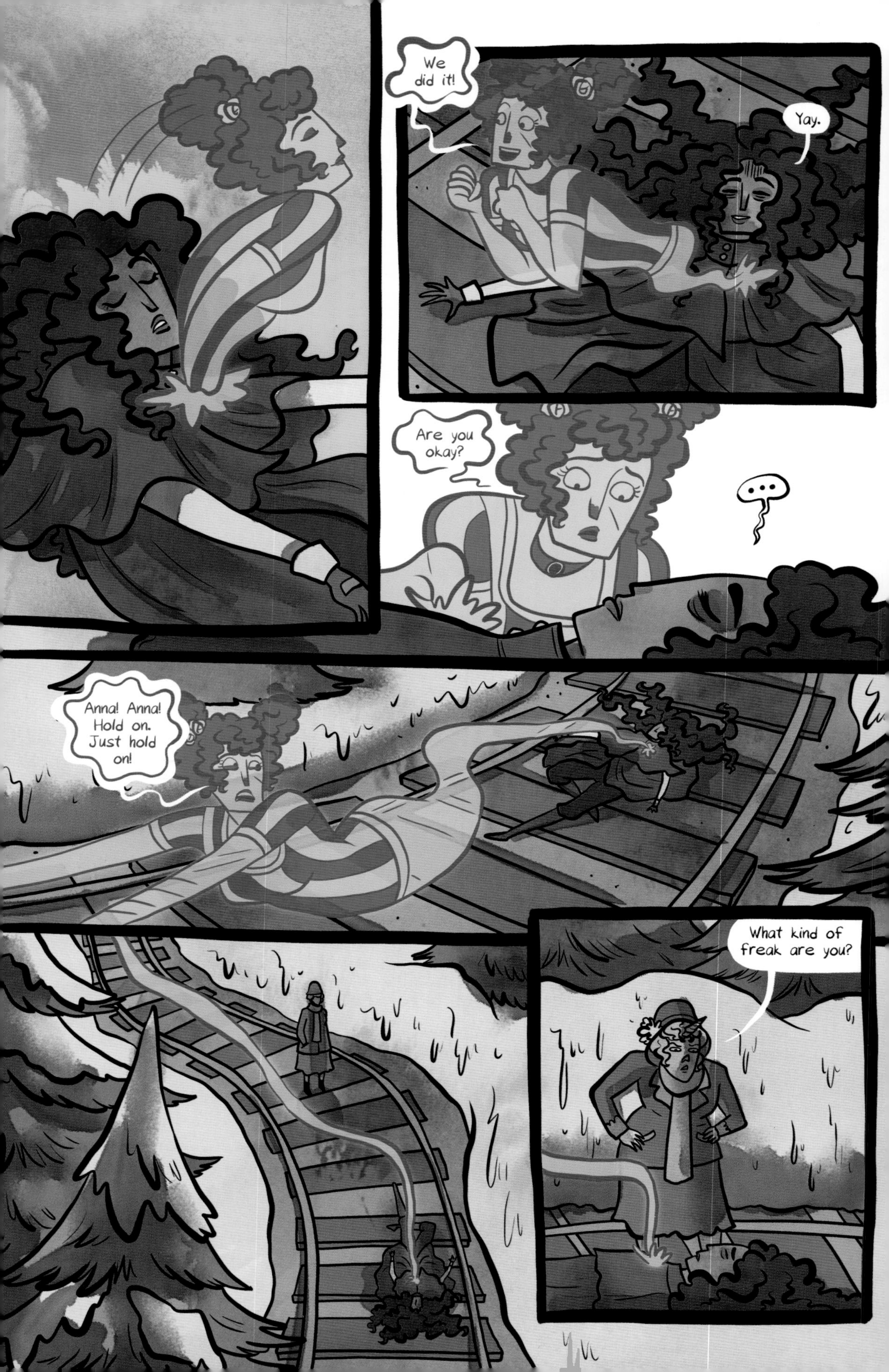

We did it!
Yay.
Are you okay?
...
Anna! Anna! Hold on. Just hold on!
What kind of freak are you?

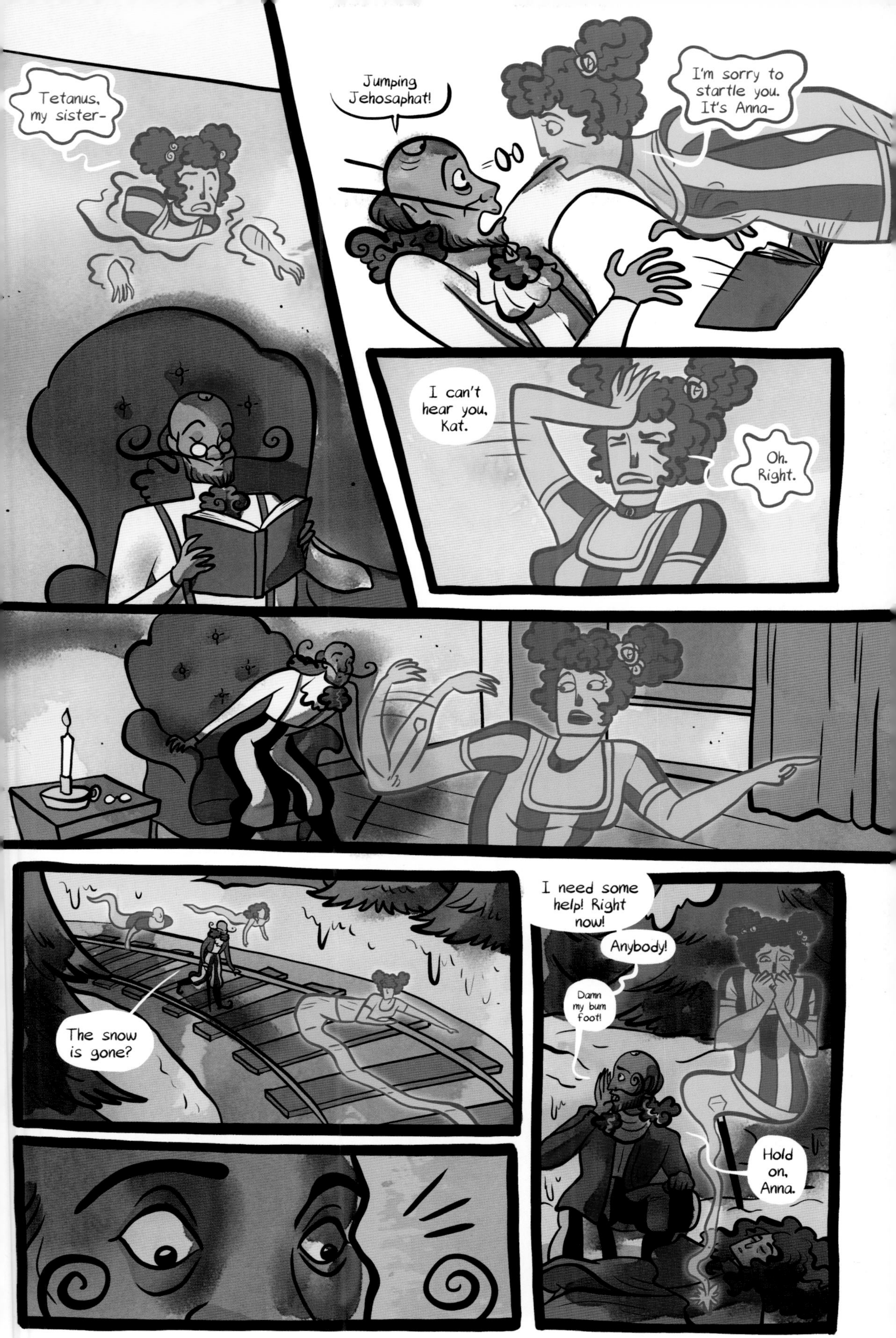
Tetanus, my sister-
Jumping Jehosaphat!
I'm sorry to startle you. It's Anna-
I can't hear you, Kat.
Oh. Right.
The snow is gone?
I need some help! Right now!
Anybody!
Damn my bum foot!
Hold on, Anna.

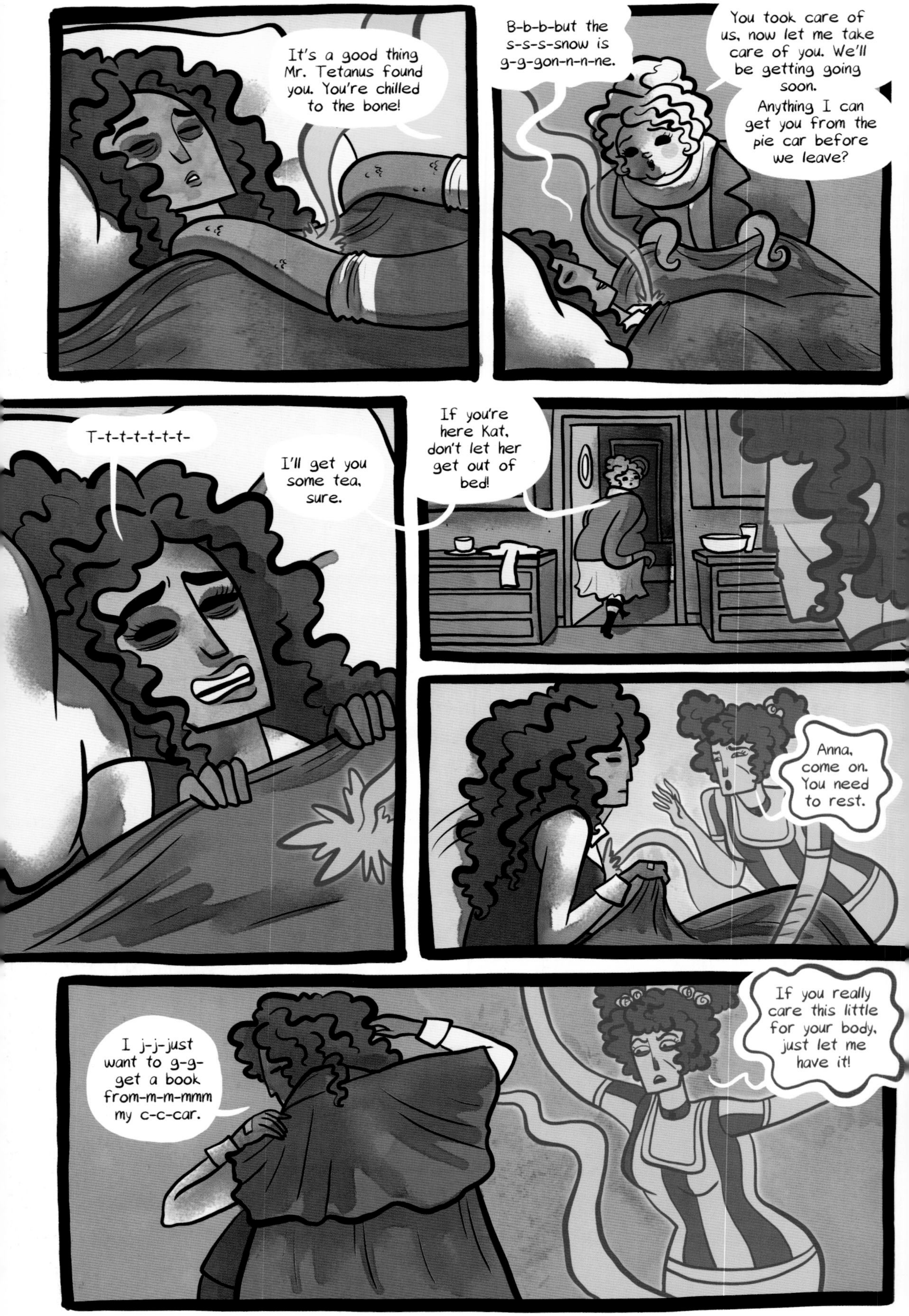
It's a good thing Mr. Tetanus found you. You're chilled to the bone!
B-b-b-but the s-s-s-snow is g-g-gon-n-n-ne.
You took care of us, now let me take care of you. We'll be getting going soon.
Anything I can get you from the pie car before we leave?
T-t-t-t-t-t-
I'll get you some tea, sure.
If you're here Kat, don't let her get out of bed!
Anna, come on. You need to rest.
I j-j-just want to g-g-get a book from-m-m-mmm my c-c-car.
If you really care this little for your body, just let me have it!

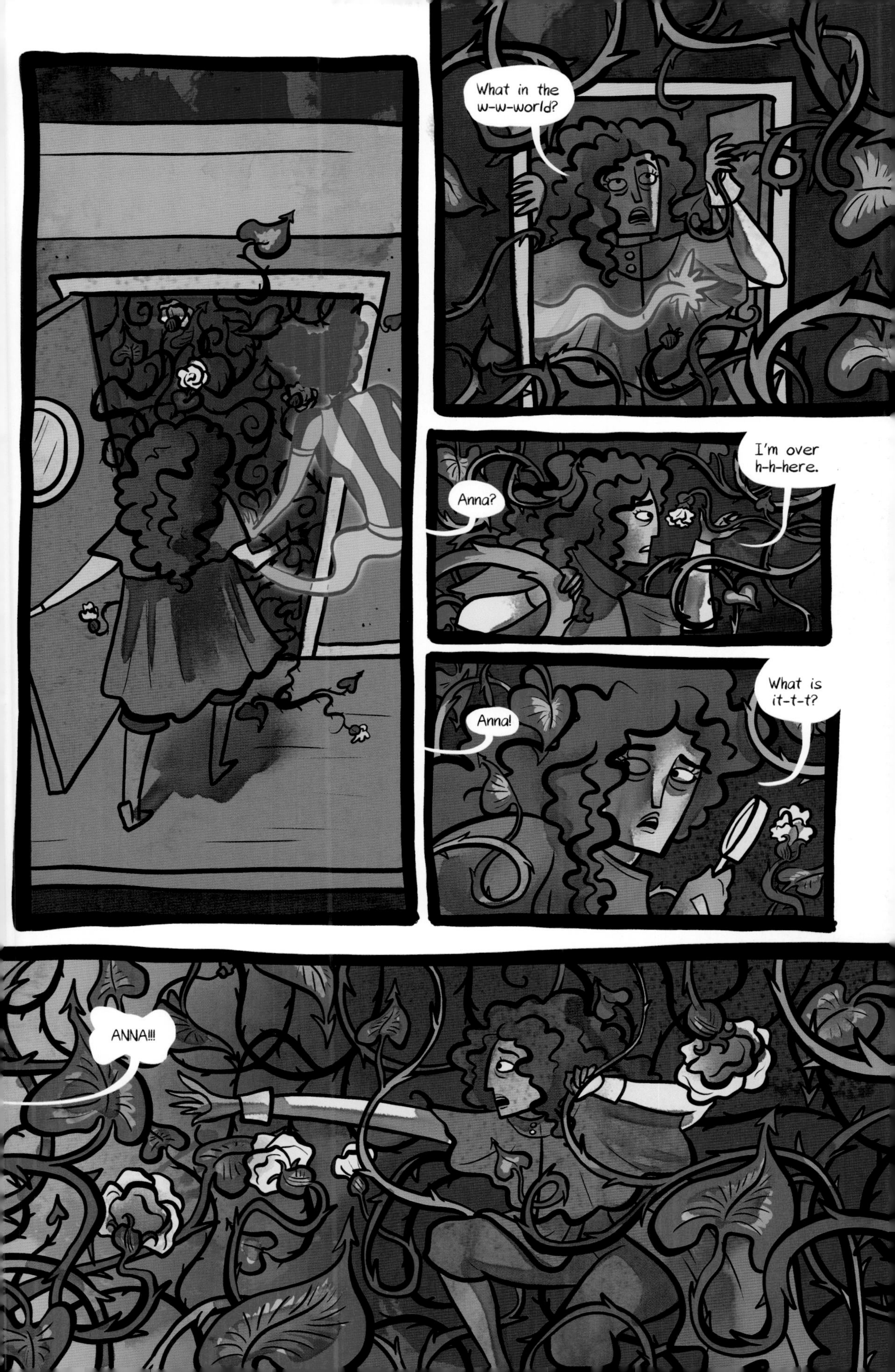
What in the w-w-world?
Anna?
I'm over h-h-here.
Anna!
What is it-t-t?
ANNA!!!

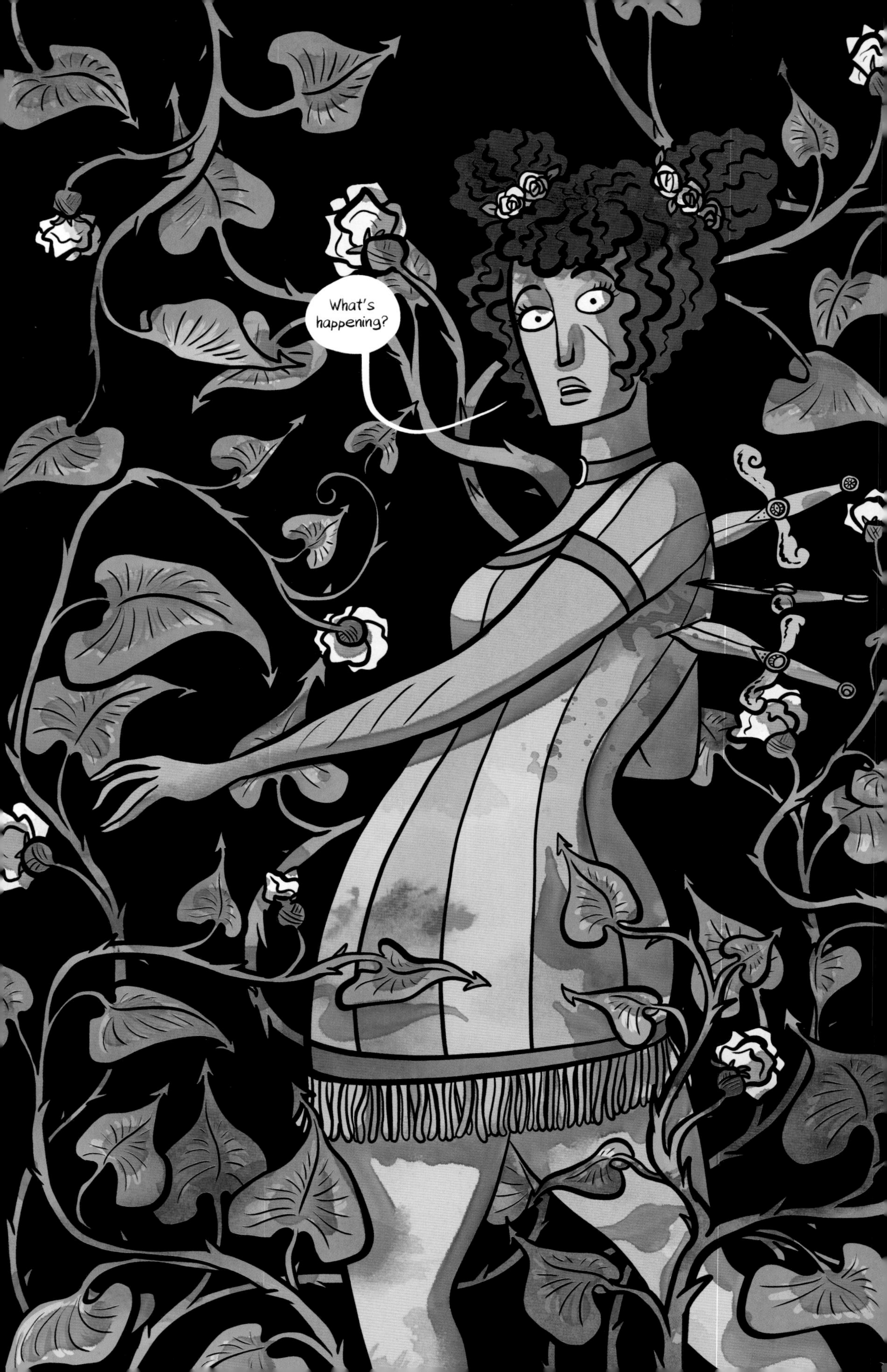
What's happening?

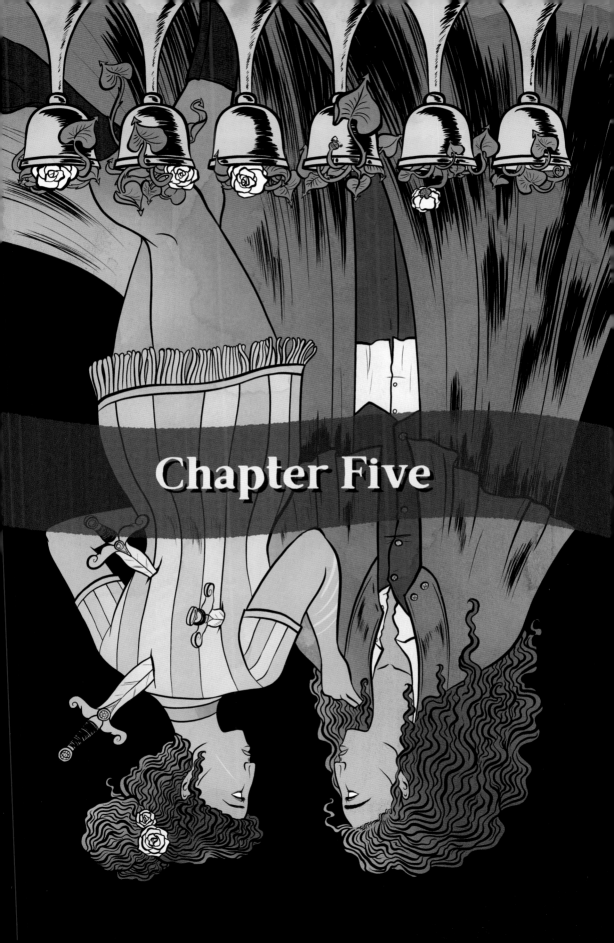

Chapter Five

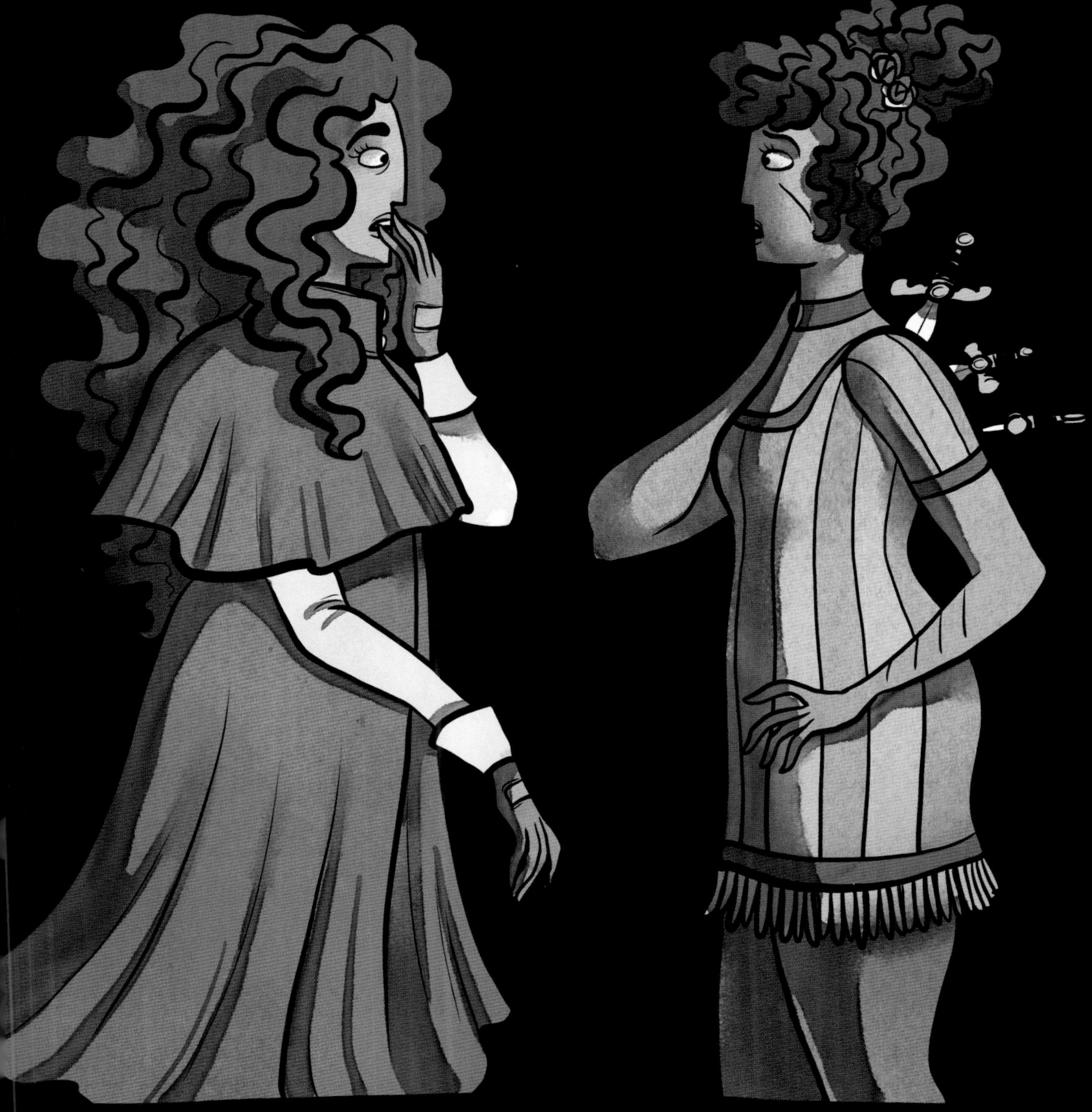
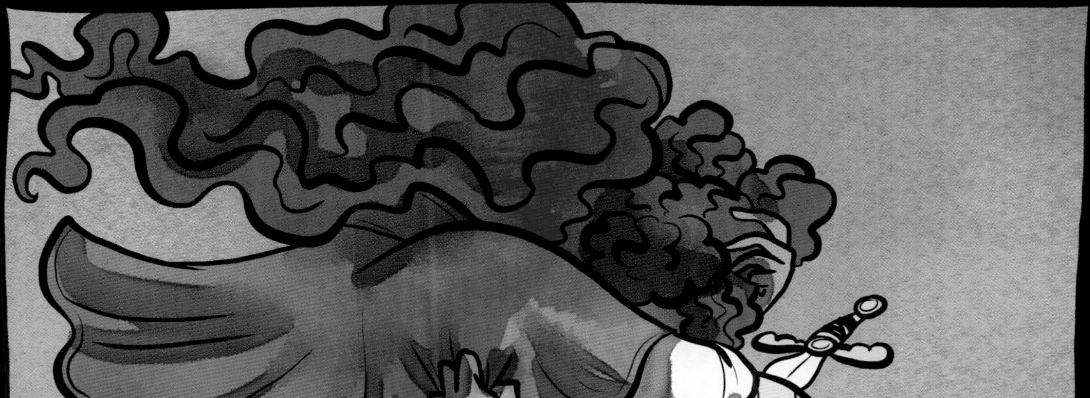

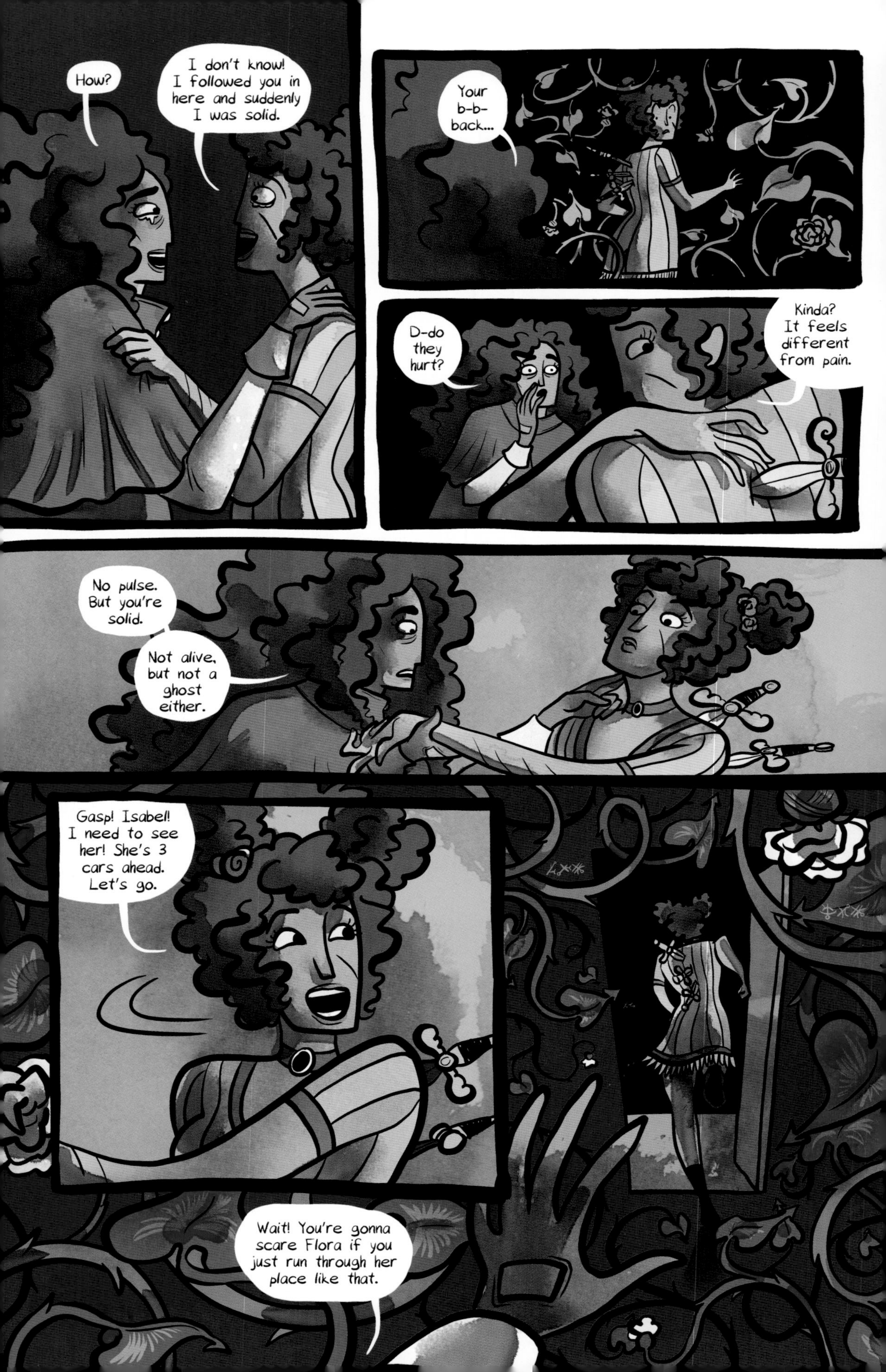
How?
I don't know! I followed you in here and suddenly I was solid.
Your b-b-back...
D-do they hurt?
Kinda? It feels different from pain.
No pulse. But you're solid.
Not alive, but not a ghost either.
Gasp! Isabel! I need to see her! She's 3 cars ahead. Let's go.
Wait! You're gonna scare Flora if you just run through her place like that.

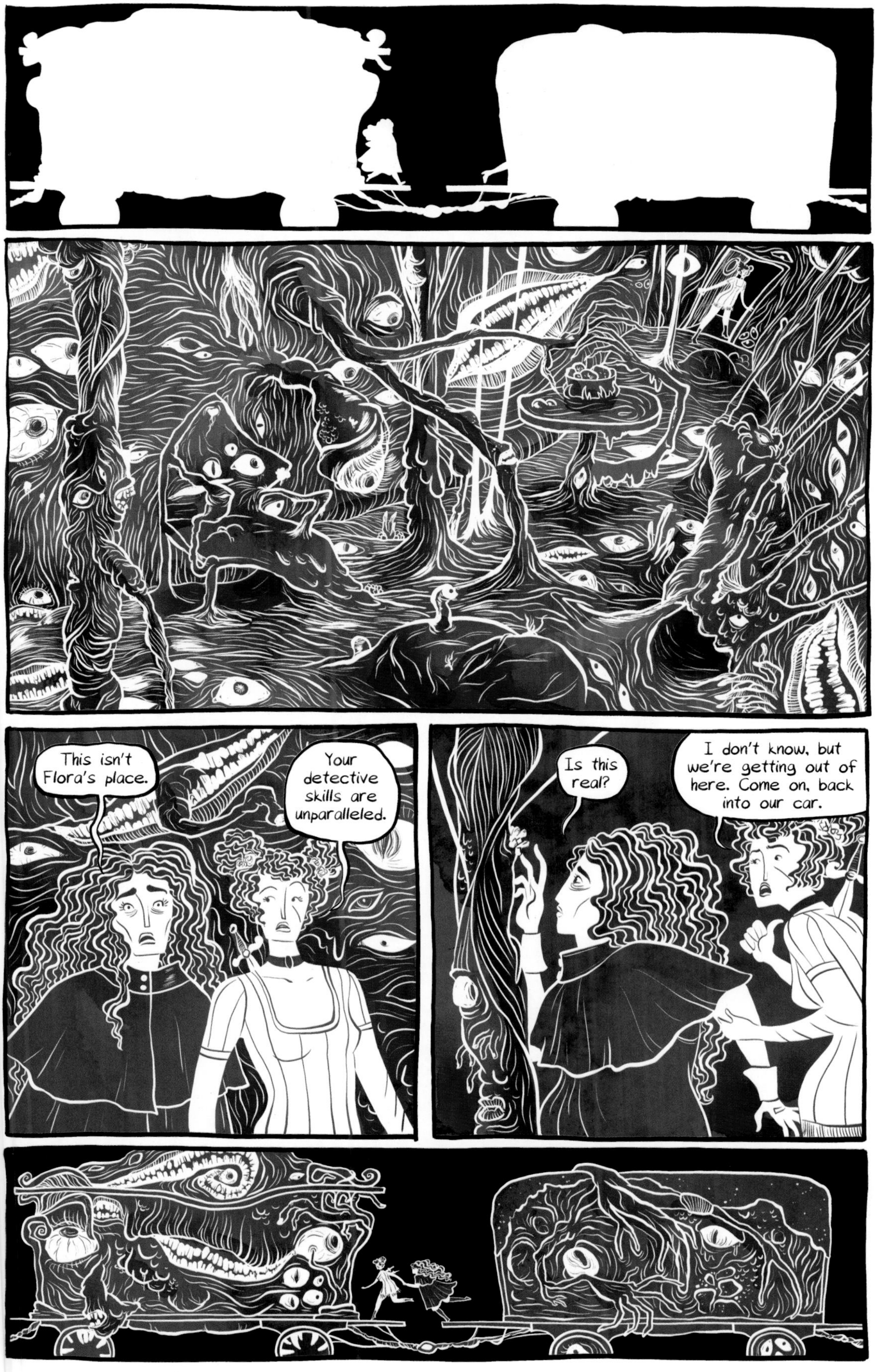
This isn't Flora's place.
Your detective skills are unparalleled.
Is this real?
I don't know, but we're getting out of here. Come on, back into our car.

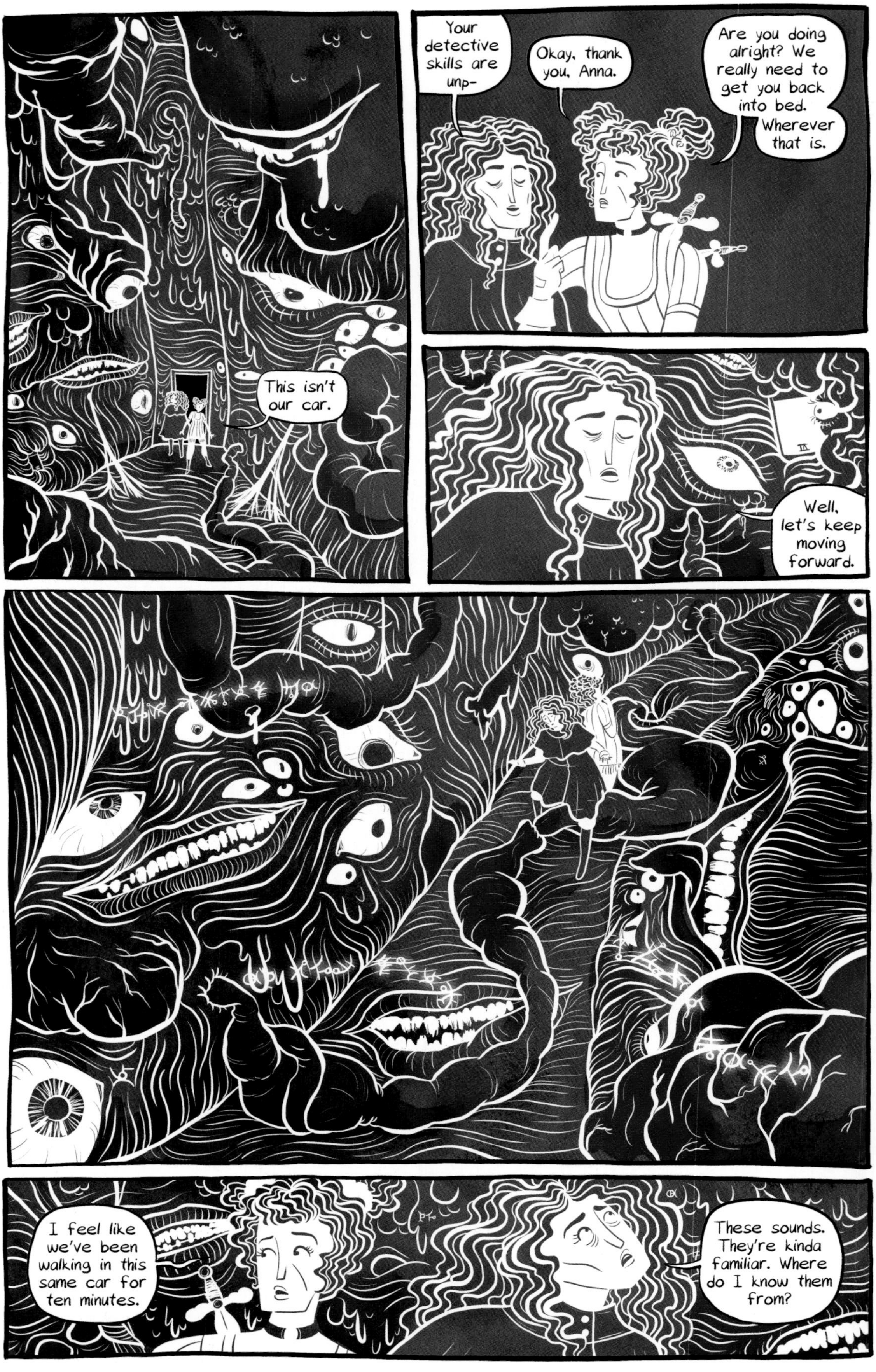
This isn't our car.
Your detective skills are unp-
Okay, thank you, Anna.
Are you doing alright? We really need to get you back into bed.
Wherever that is.
Well, let's keep moving forward.
I feel like we've been walking in this same car for ten minutes.
These sounds. They're kinda familiar. Where do I know them from?

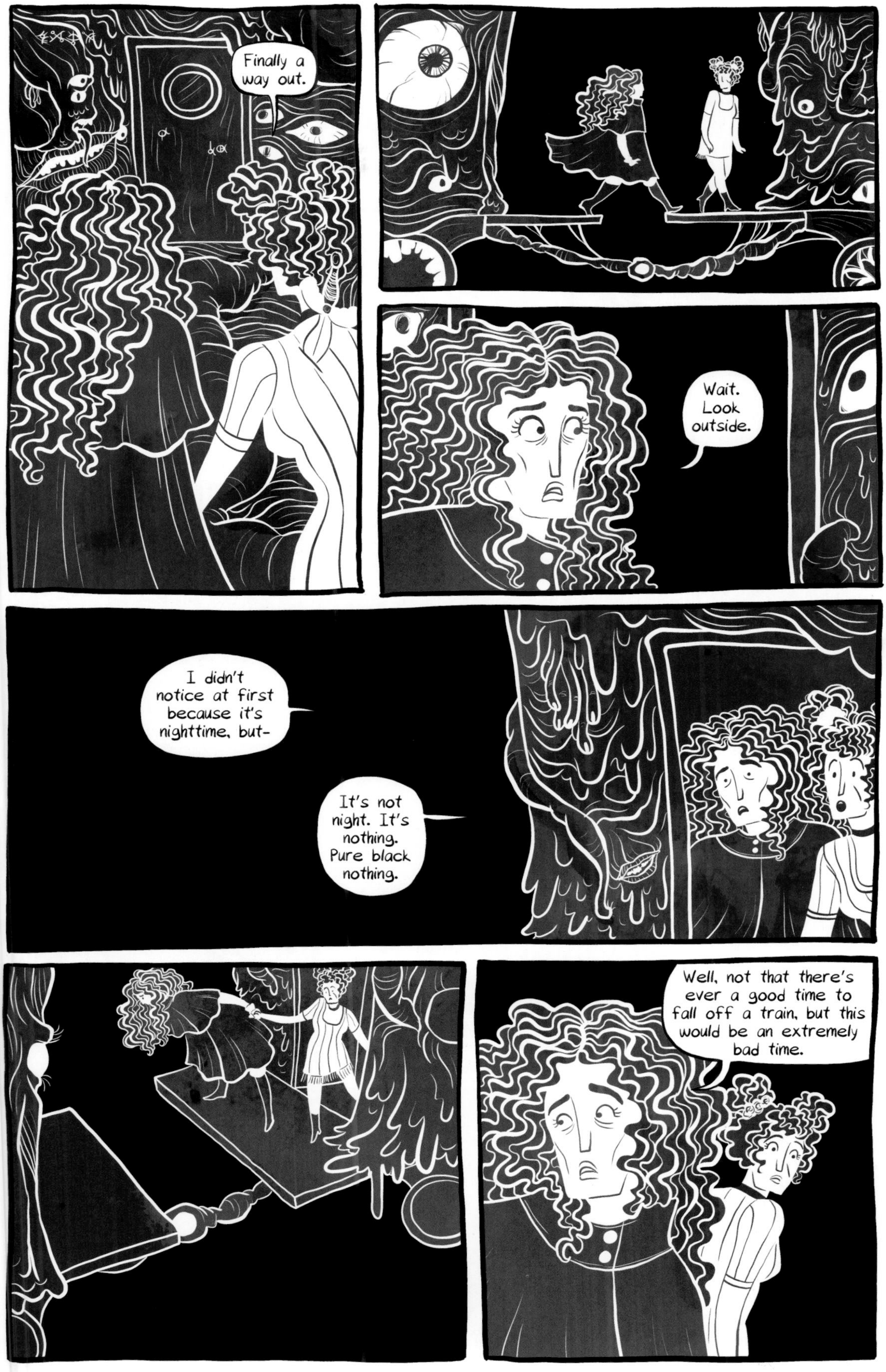
Finally a way out.
Wait. Look outside.
I didn't notice at first because it's nighttime, but-
It's not night. It's nothing. Pure black nothing.
Well, not that there's ever a good time to fall off a train, but this would be an extremely bad time.

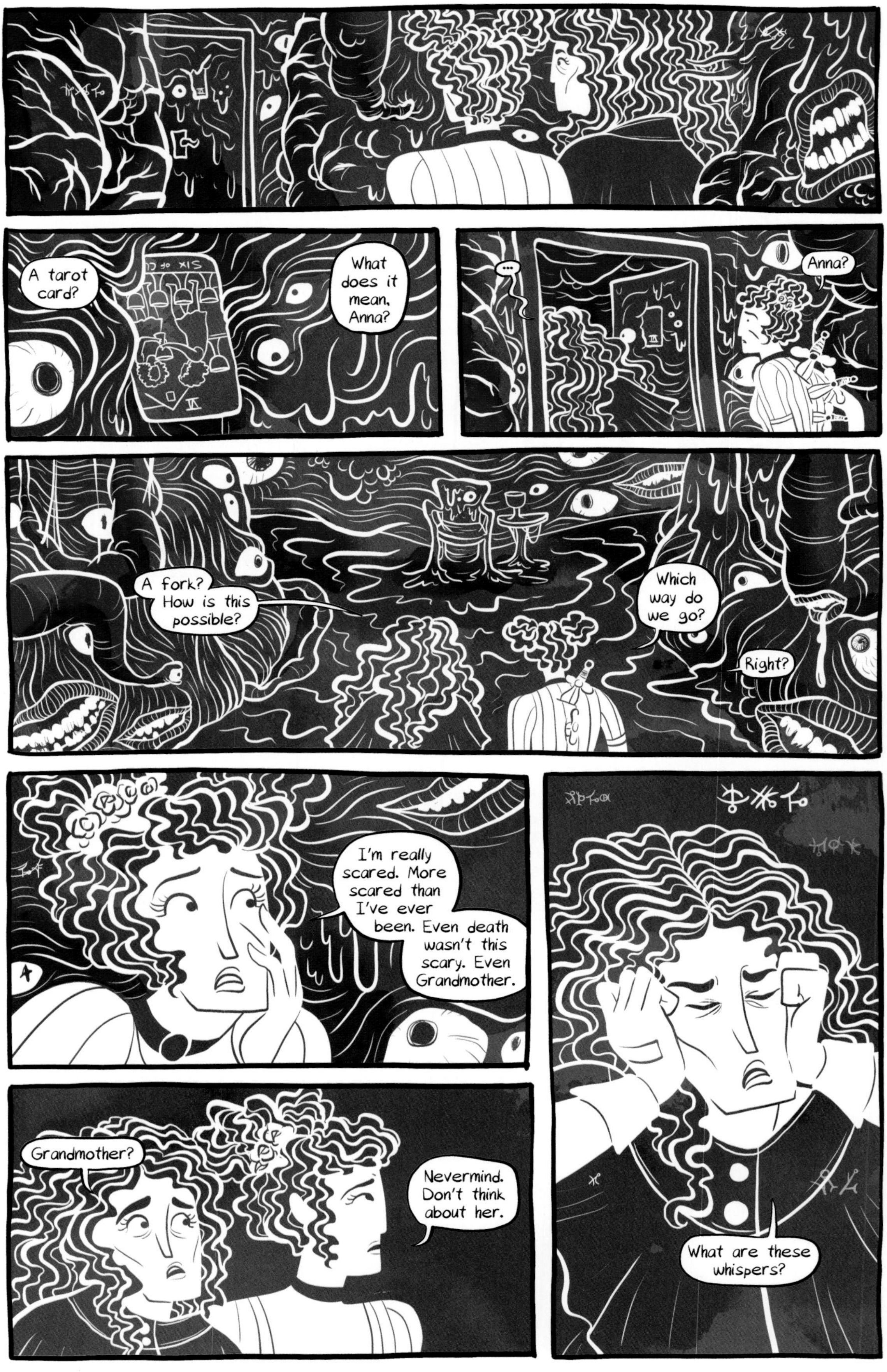
A tarot card?
What does it mean, Anna?
...
Anna?
A fork? How is this possible?
Which way do we go?
Right?
I'm really scared. More scared than I've ever been. Even death wasn't this scary. Even Grandmother.
What are these whispers?
Grandmother?
Nevermind. Don't think about her.

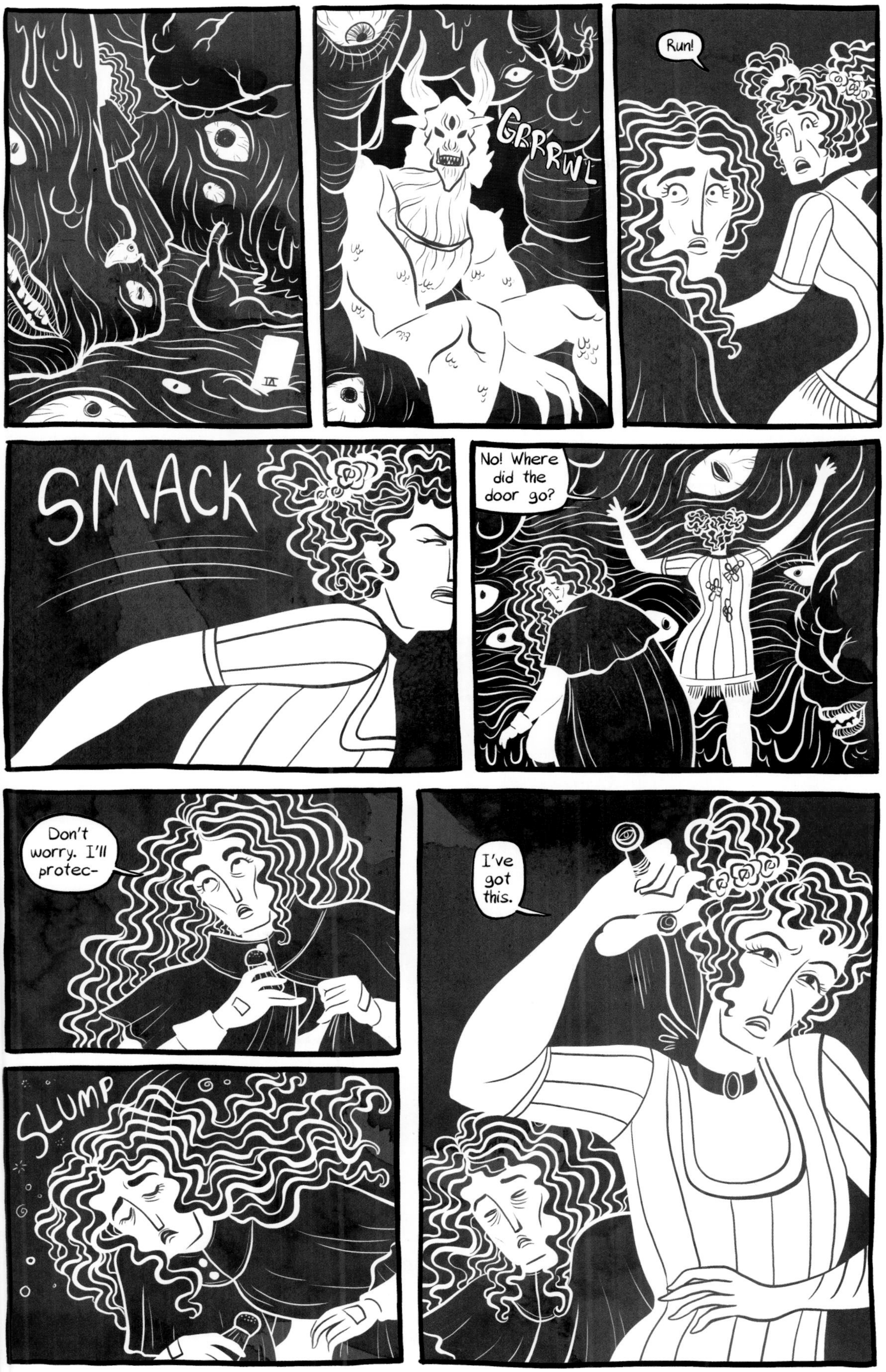
GRRRWL
Run!
SMACK
No! Where did the door go?
Don't worry. I'll protec-
SLUMP
I've got this.

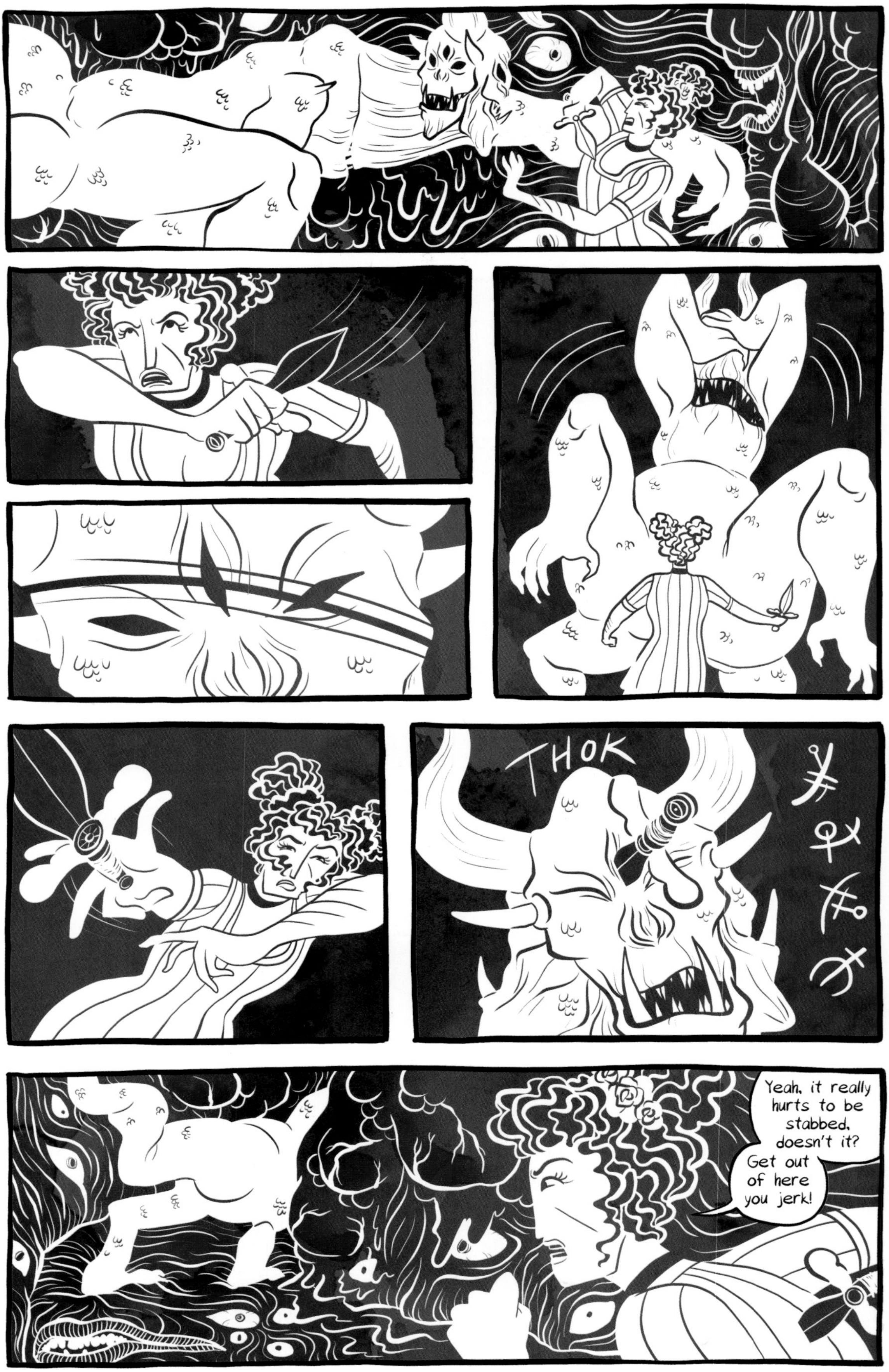
THOK
Yeah, it really hurts to be stabbed, doesn't it?
Get out of here you jerk!

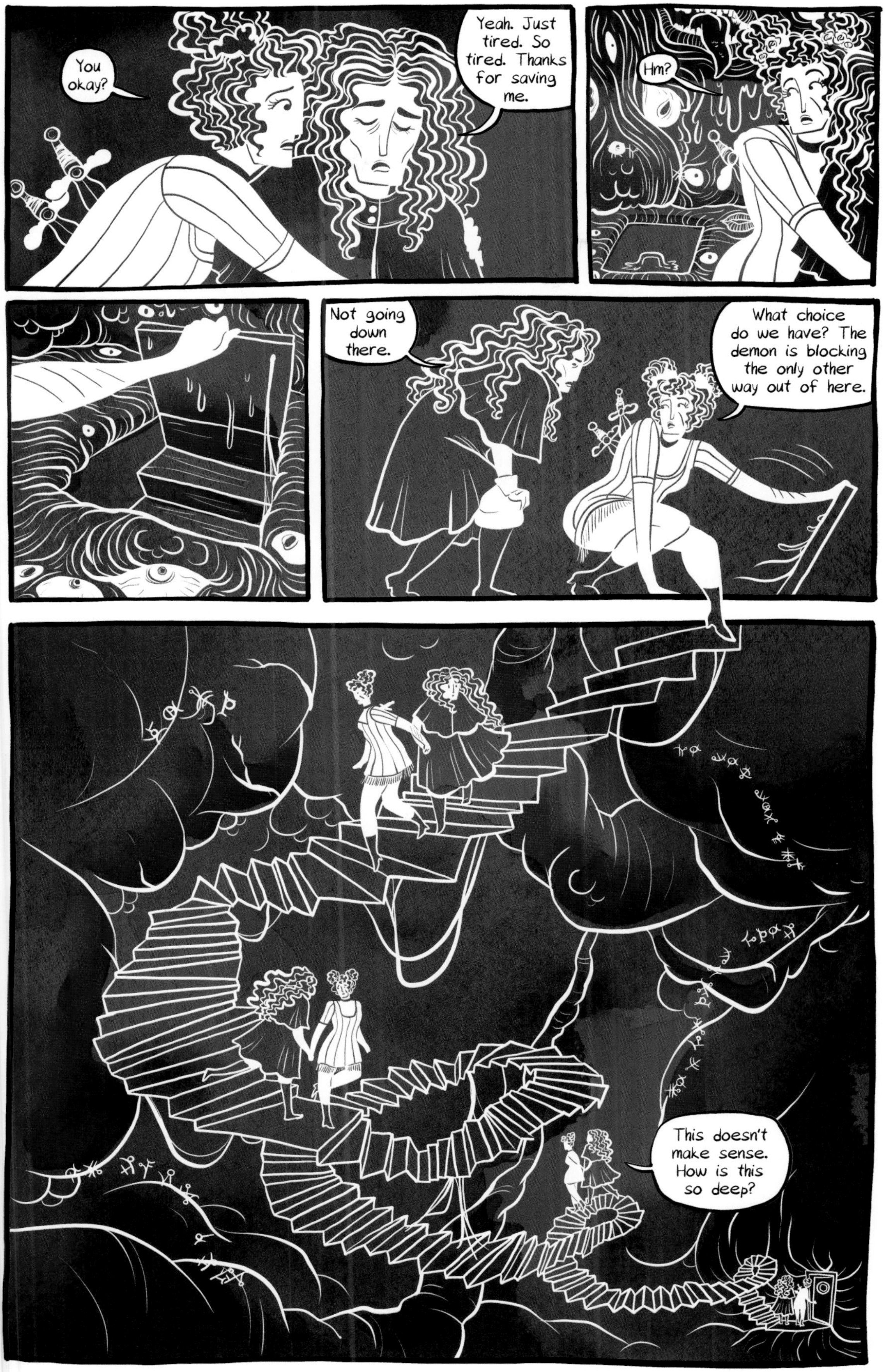
You okay?
Yeah. Just tired. So tired. Thanks for saving me.
Hm?
Not going down there.
What choice do we have? The demon is blocking the only other way out of here.
This doesn't make sense. How is this so deep?

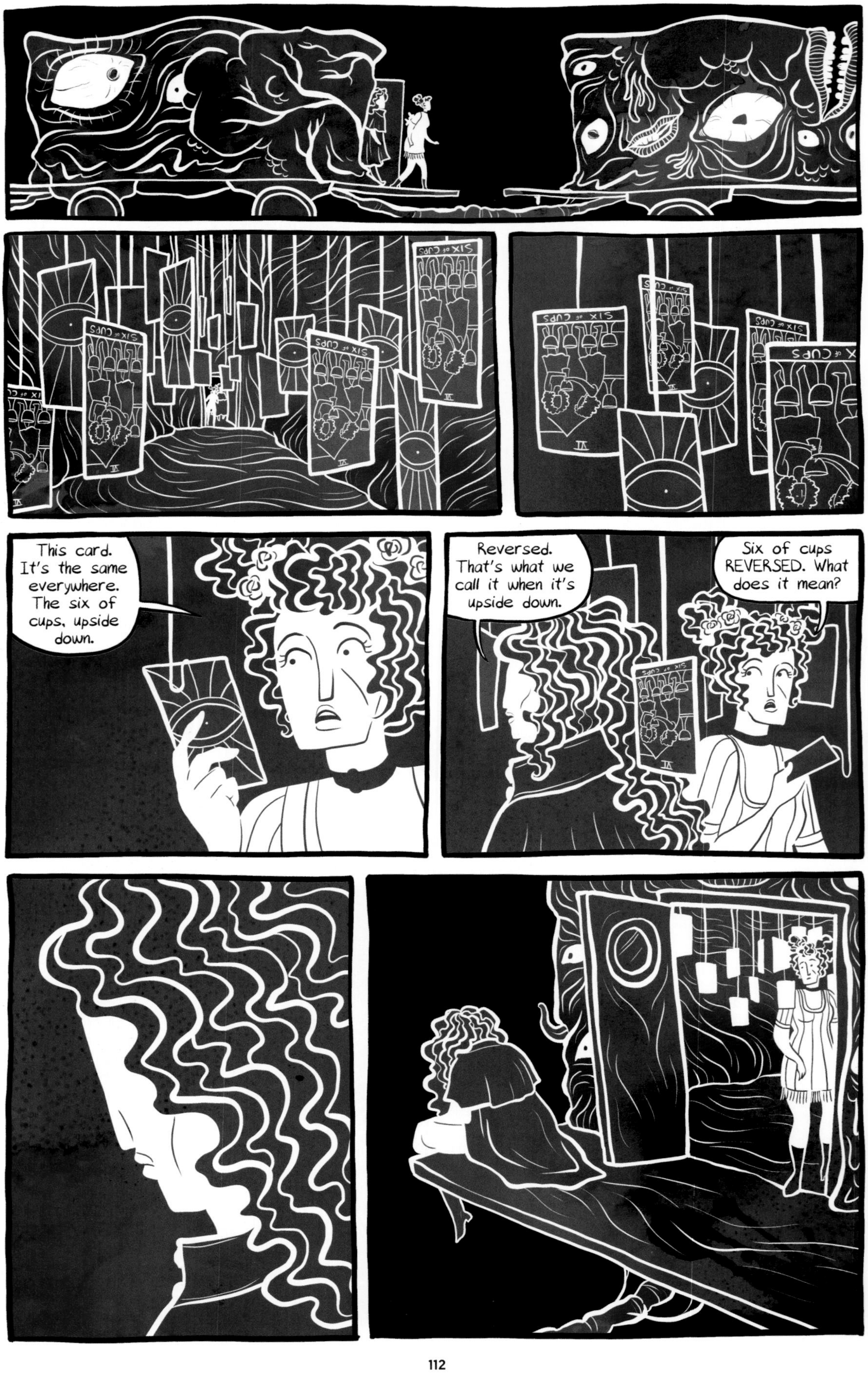

This card. It's the same everywhere. The six of cups, upside down.
Reversed. That's what we call it when it's upside down.
Six of cups REVERSED. What does it mean?

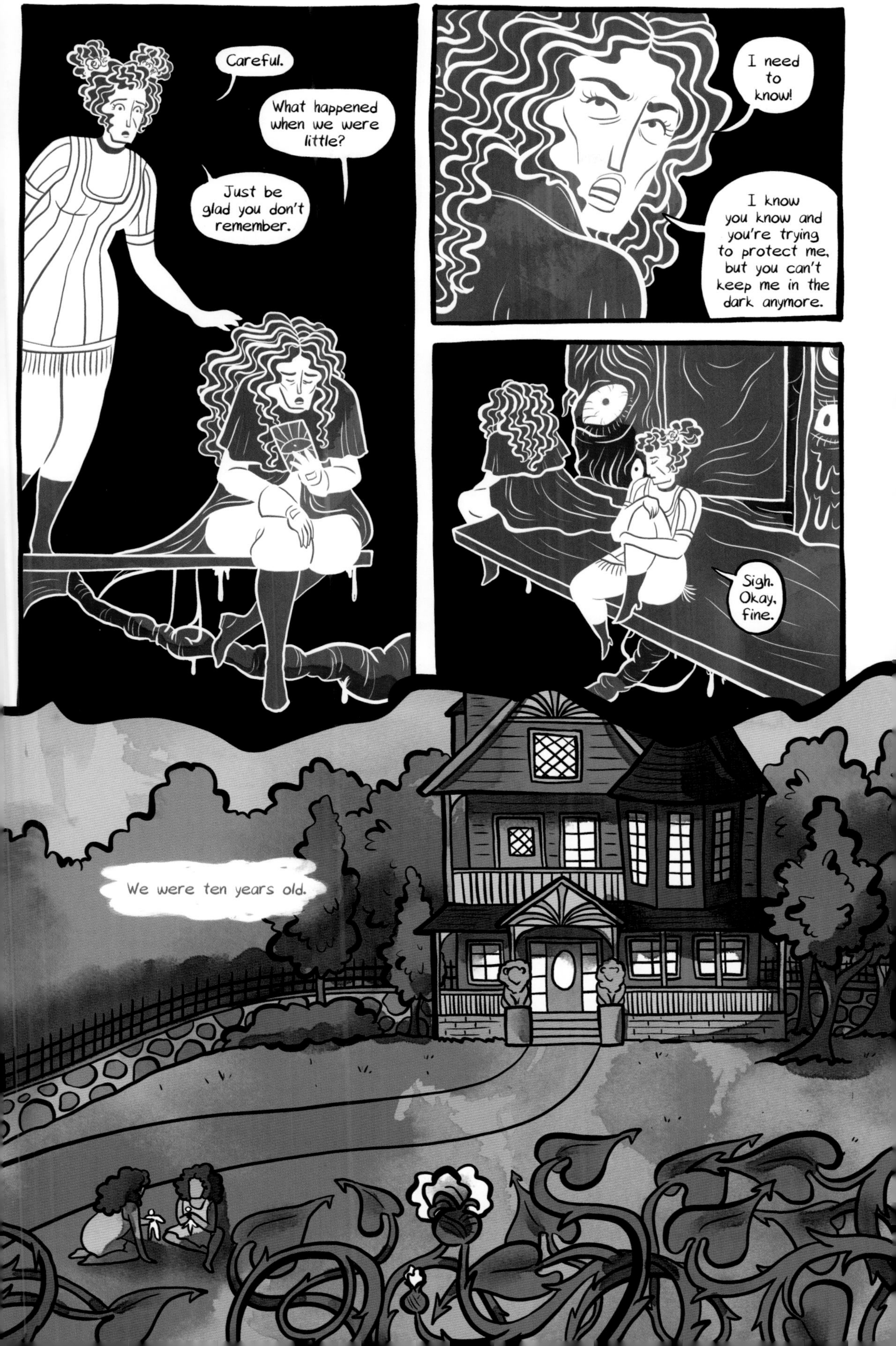
Careful.
What happened when we were little?
Just be glad you don't remember.
I need to know!
I know you know and you're trying to protect me, but you can't keep me in the dark anymore.
Sigh. Okay, fine.
We were ten years old.

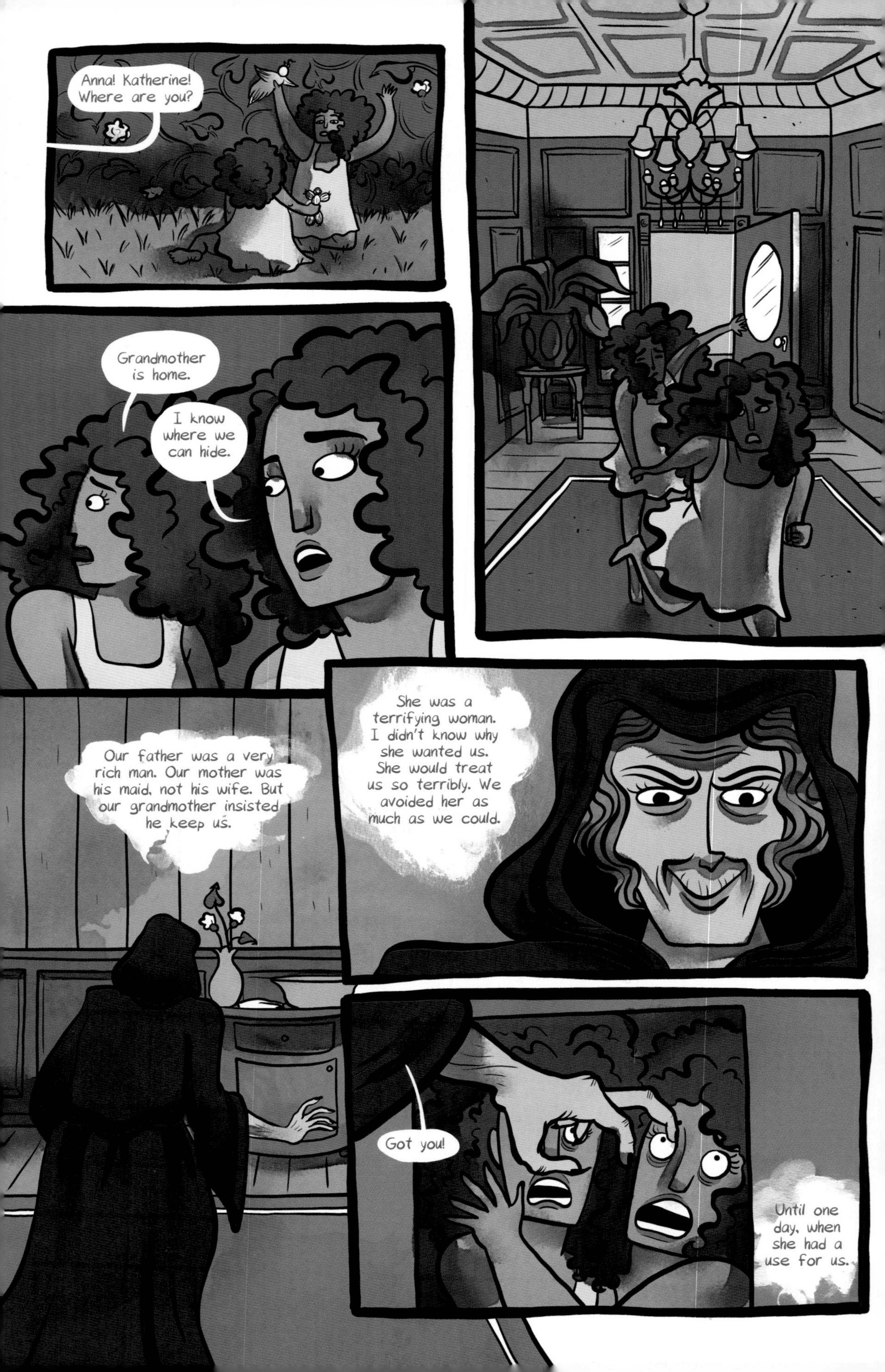
Anna! Katherine! Where are you?
Grandmother is home.
I know where we can hide.
Our father was a very rich man. Our mother was his maid, not his wife. But our grandmother insisted he keep us.
She was a terrifying woman. I didn't know why she wanted us. She would treat us so terribly. We avoided her as much as we could.
Got you!
Until one day, when she had a use for us.

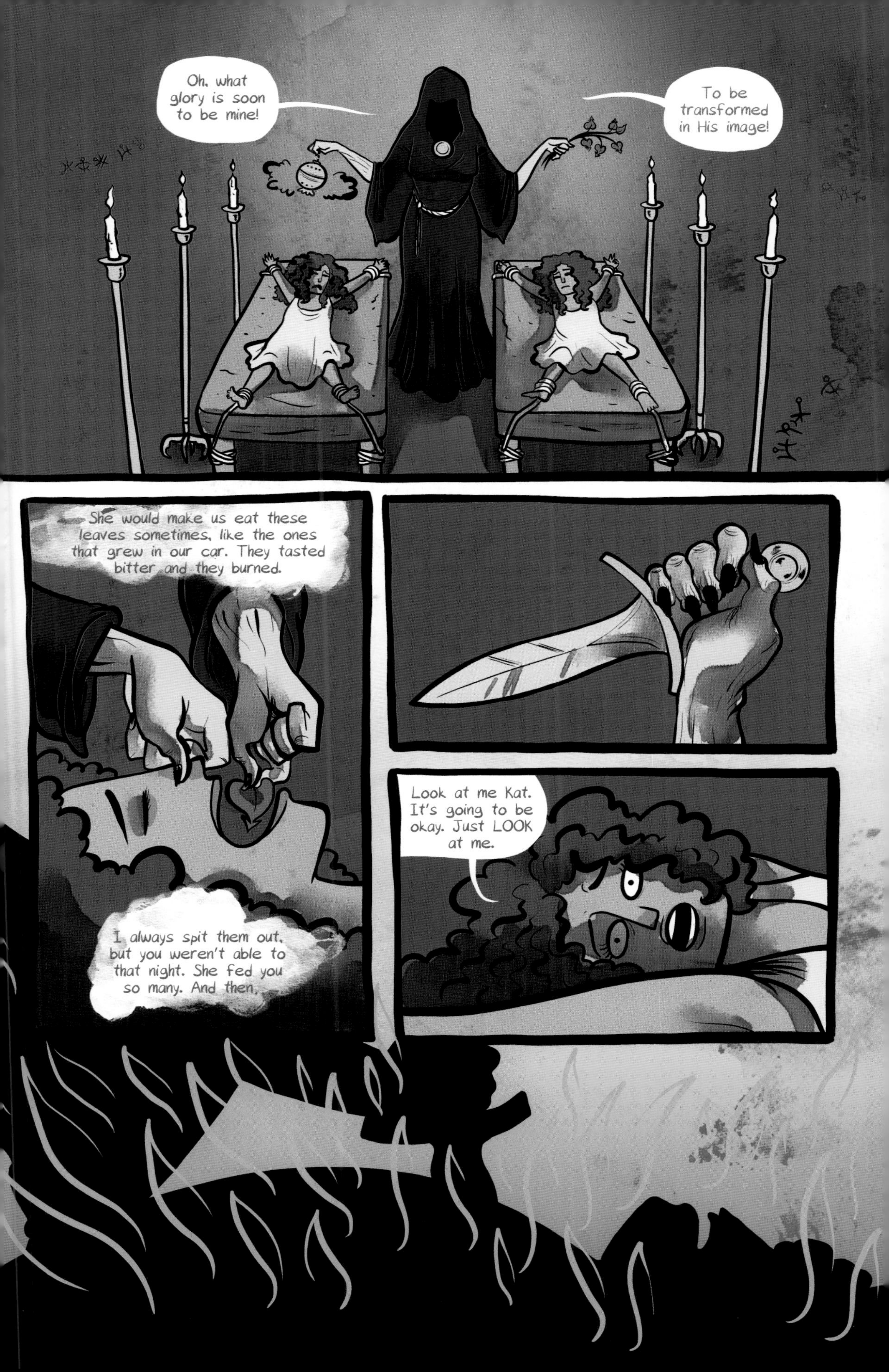
Oh, what glory is soon to be mine!
To be transformed in His image!
She would make us eat these leaves sometimes, like the ones that grew in our car. They tasted bitter and they burned.
I always spit them out, but you weren't able to that night. She fed you so many. And then.
Look at me Kat. It's going to be okay. Just LOOK at me.

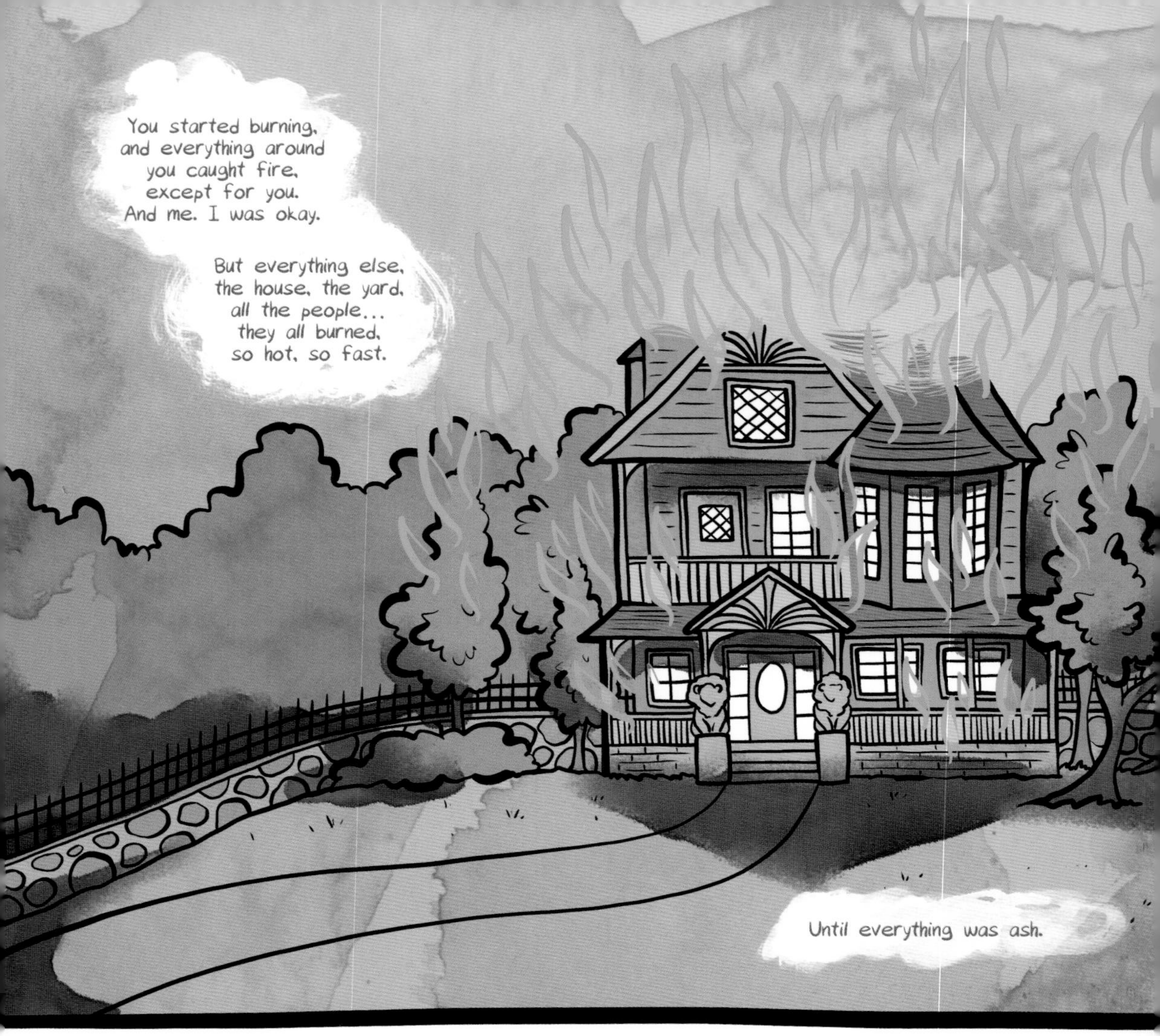
You started burning, and everything around you caught fire, except for you. And me. I was okay.
But everything else, the house, the yard, all the people... they all burned, so hot, so fast.
Until everything was ash.

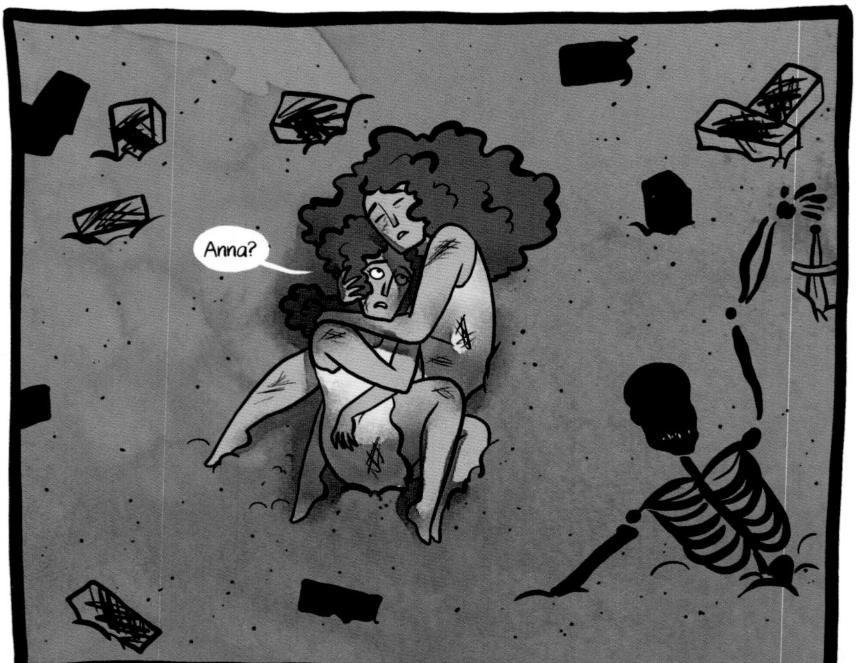
Anna?

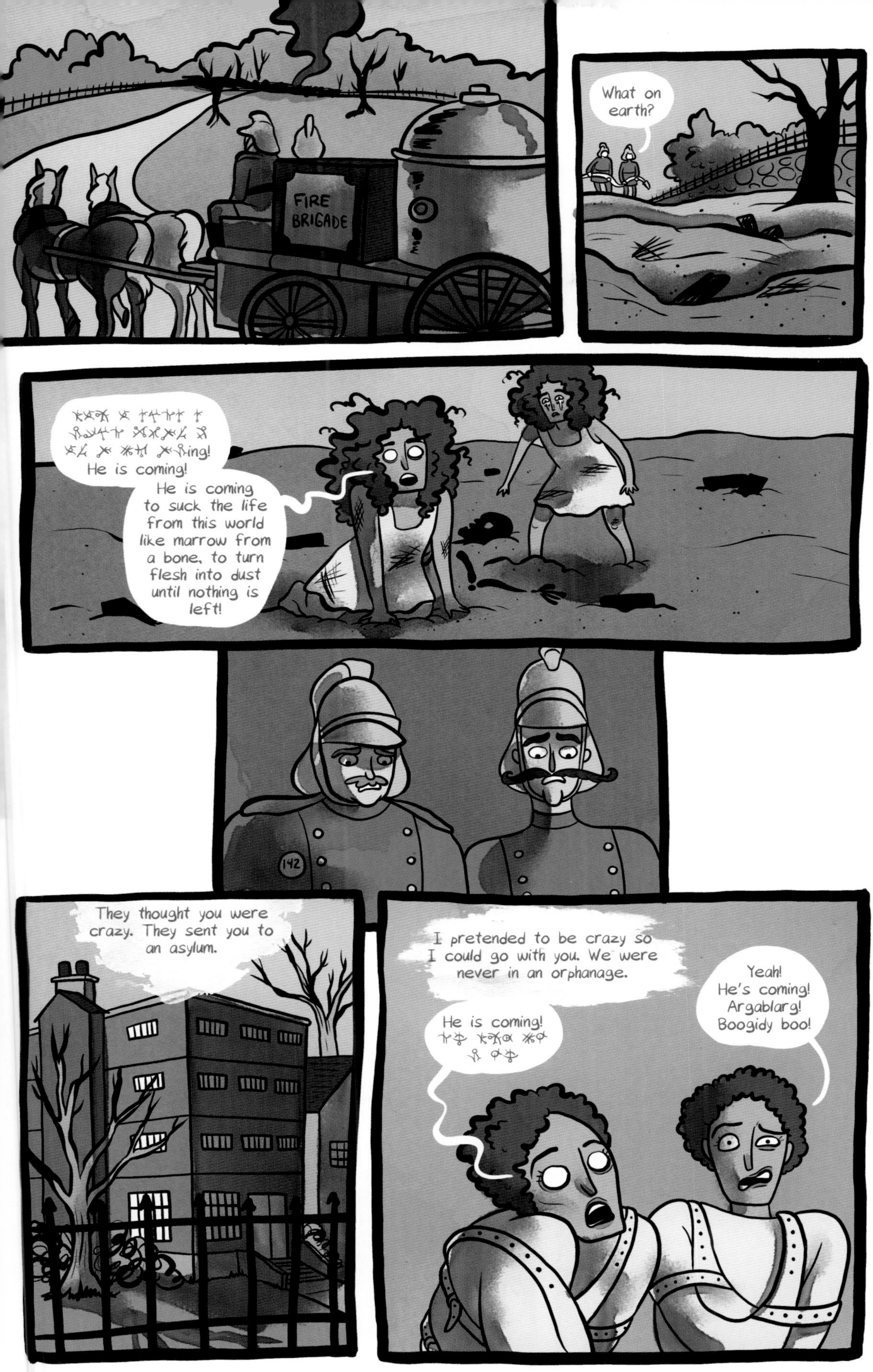
FIRE BRIGADE
What on earth?
He is coming!
He is coming to suck the life from this world like marrow from a bone, to turn flesh into dust until nothing is left!
142
They thought you were crazy. They sent you to an asylum.
I pretended to be crazy so I could go with you. We were never in an orphanage.
He is coming!
Yeah! He's coming! Argablarg! Boogidy boo!

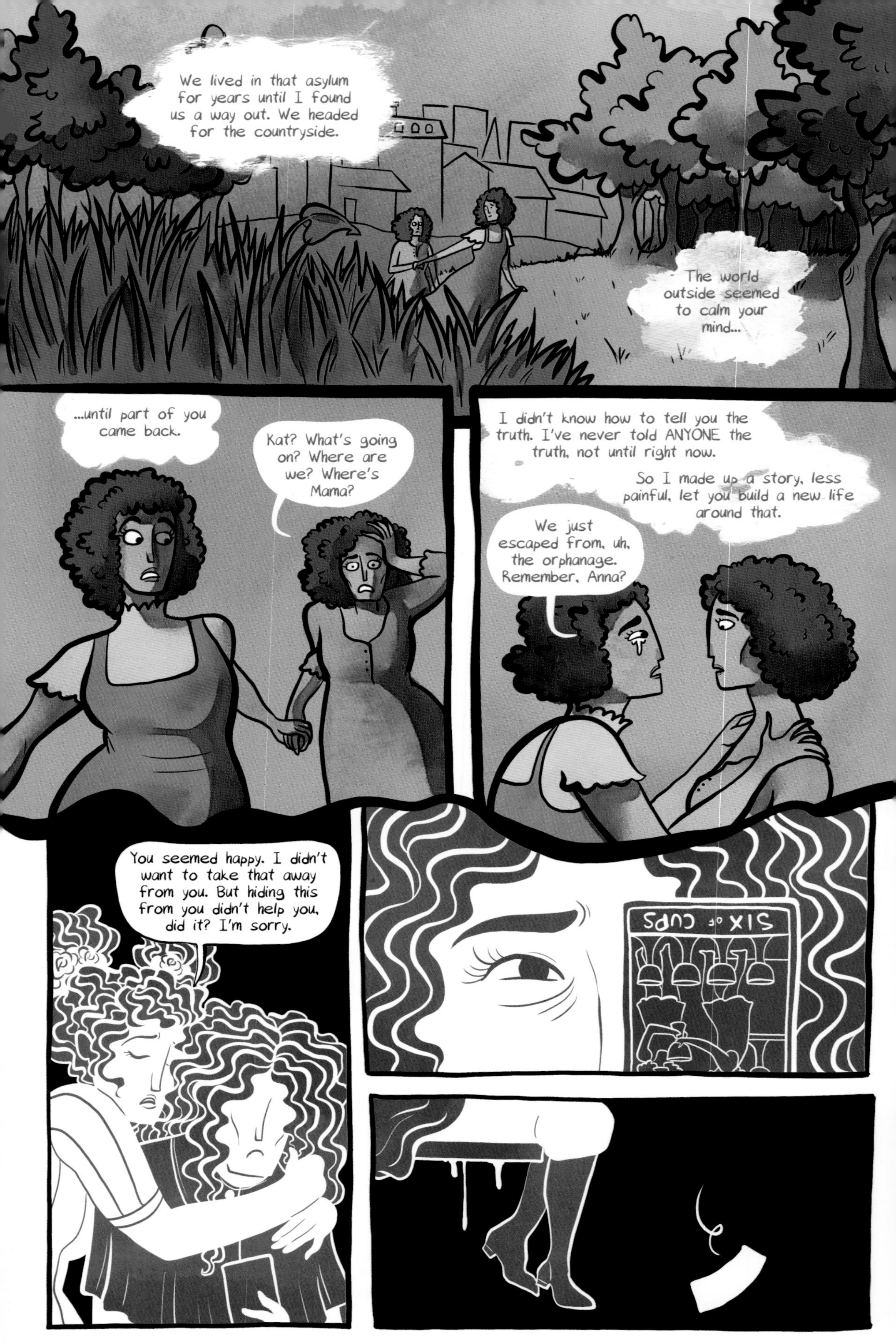
We lived in that asylum for years until I found us a way out. We headed for the countryside.
The world outside seemed to calm your mind...
...until part of you came back.
Kat? What's going on? Where are we? Where's Mama?
I didn't know how to tell you the truth. I've never told ANYONE the truth, not until right now.
So I made up a story, less painful, let you build a new life around that.
We just escaped from, uh, the orphanage. Remember, Anna?
You seemed happy. I didn't want to take that away from you. But hiding this from you didn't help you, did it? I'm sorry.
SIX of CUPS

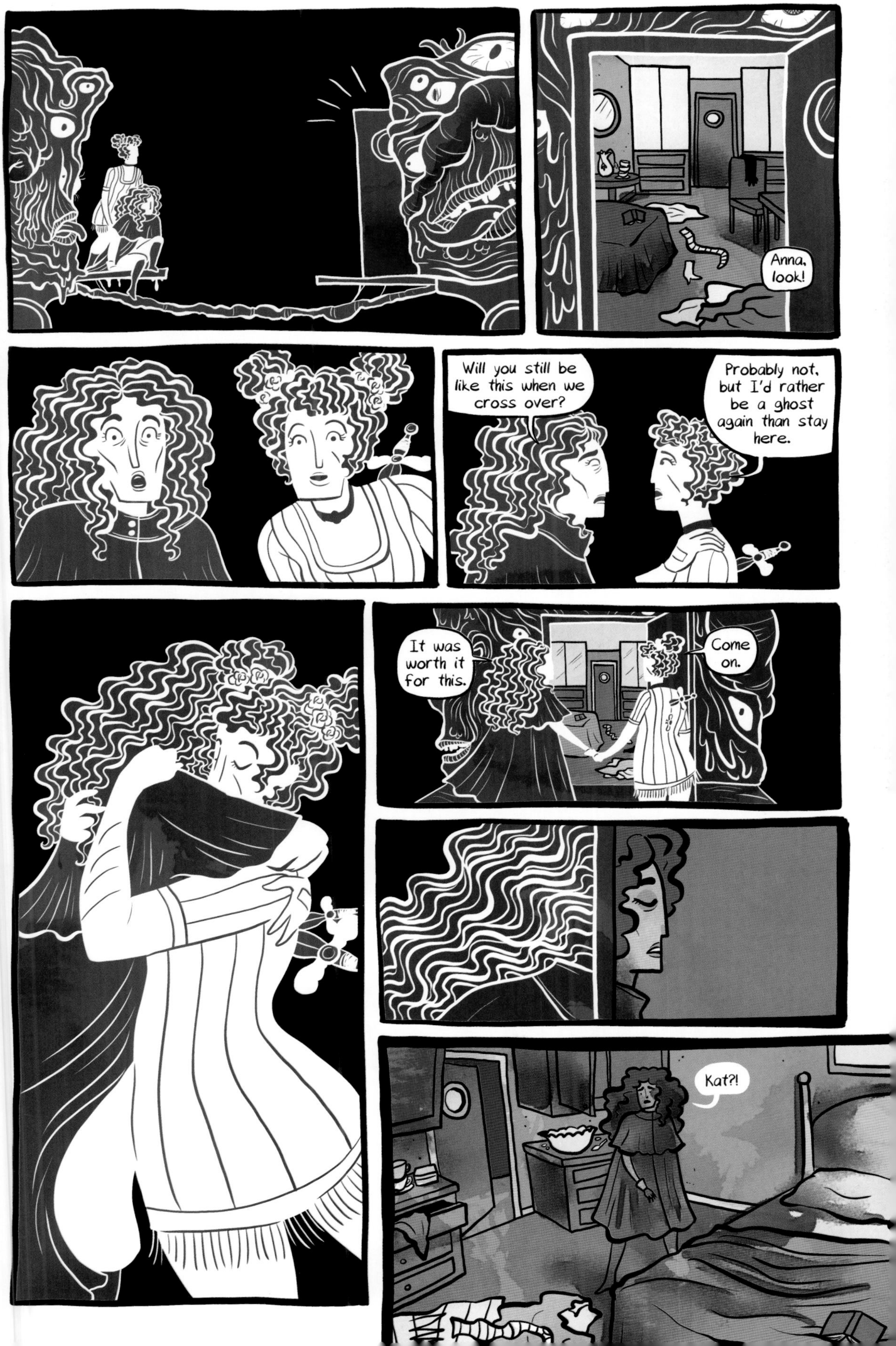
Anna, look!
Will you still be like this when we cross over?
Probably not, but I'd rather be a ghost again than stay here.
It was worth it for this.
Come on.
Kat?!

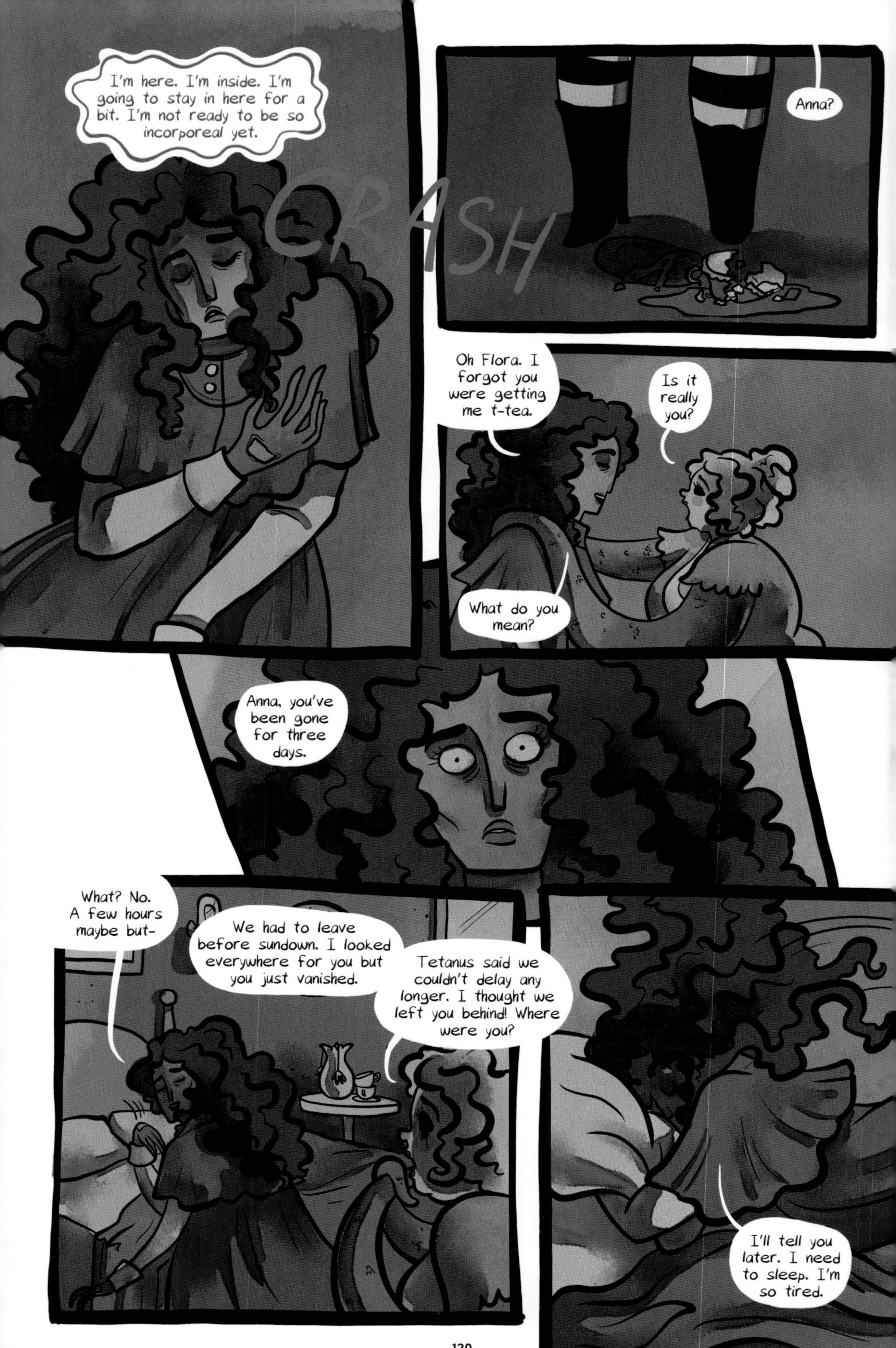
I'm here. I'm inside. I'm going to stay in here for a bit. I'm not ready to be so incorporeal yet.
CRASH
Anna?
Oh Flora. I forgot you were getting me t-tea.
Is it really you?
What do you mean?
Anna, you've been gone for three days.
What? No. A few hours maybe but-
We had to leave before sundown. I looked everywhere for you but you just vanished.
Tetanus said we couldn't delay any longer. I thought we left you behind! Where were you?
I'll tell you later. I need to sleep. I'm so tired.

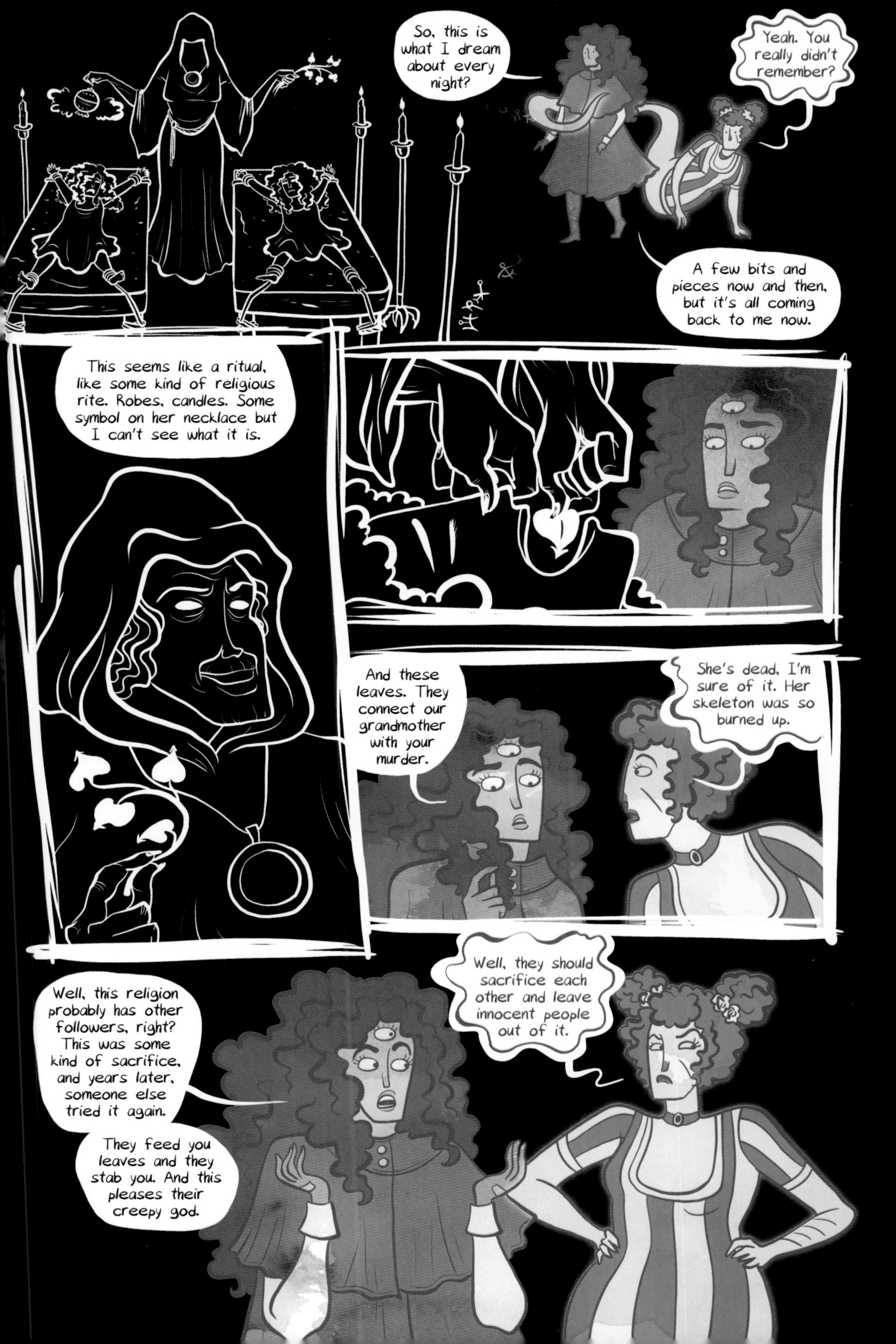
So, this is what I dream about every night?
Yeah. You really didn't remember?
A few bits and pieces now and then, but it's all coming back to me now.
This seems like a ritual, like some kind of religious rite. Robes, candles. Some symbol on her necklace but I can't see what it is.
And these leaves. They connect our grandmother with your murder.
She's dead, I'm sure of it. Her skeleton was so burned up.
Well, this religion probably has other followers, right? This was some kind of sacrifice, and years later, someone else tried it again.
They feed you leaves and they stab you. And this pleases their creepy god.
Well, they should sacrifice each other and leave innocent people out of it.

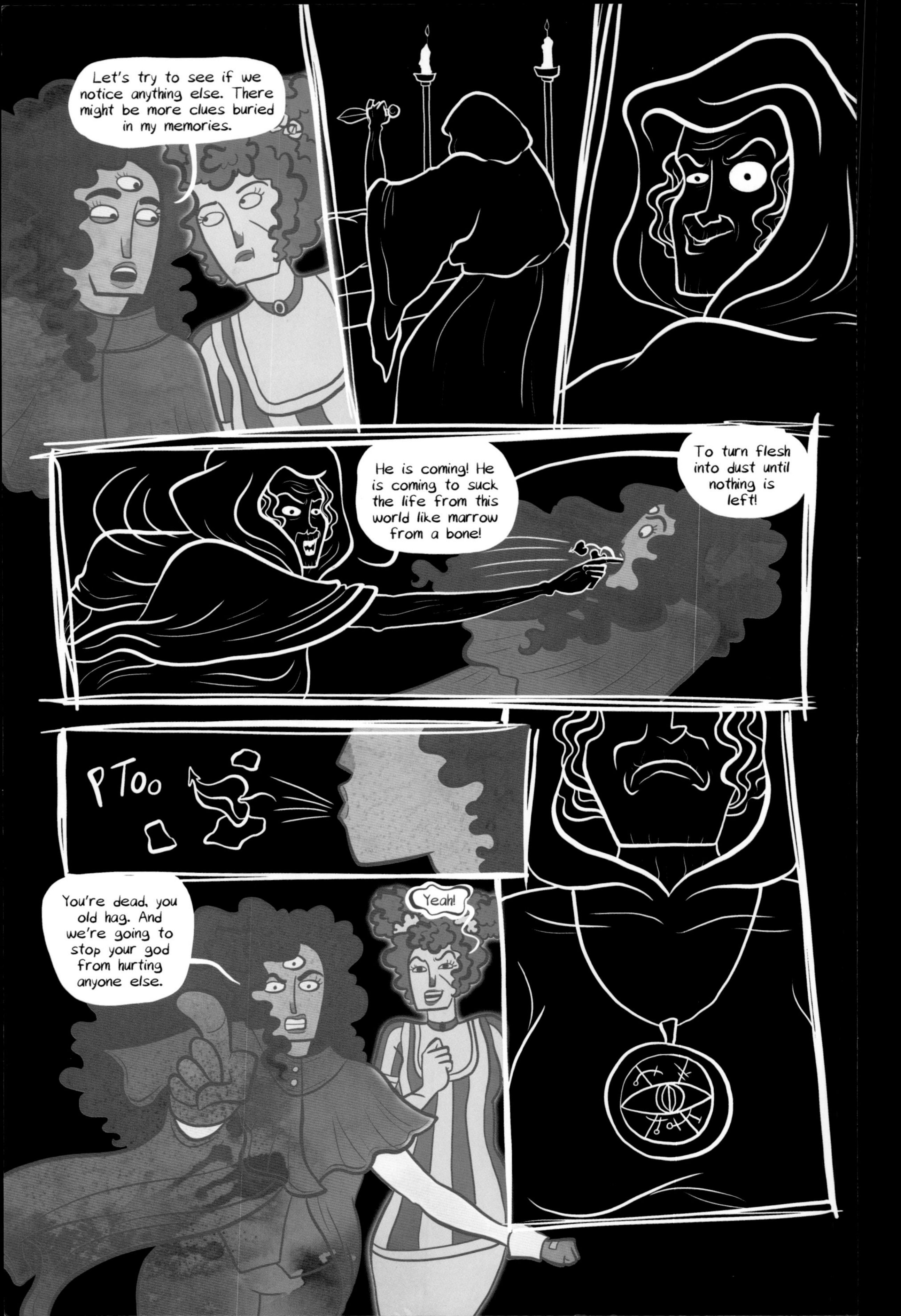
Let's try to see if we notice anything else. There might be more clues buried in my memories.
He is coming! He is coming to suck the life from this world like marrow from a bone!
To turn flesh into dust until nothing is left!
PToo
You're dead, you old hag. And we're going to stop your god from hurting anyone else.
Yeah!

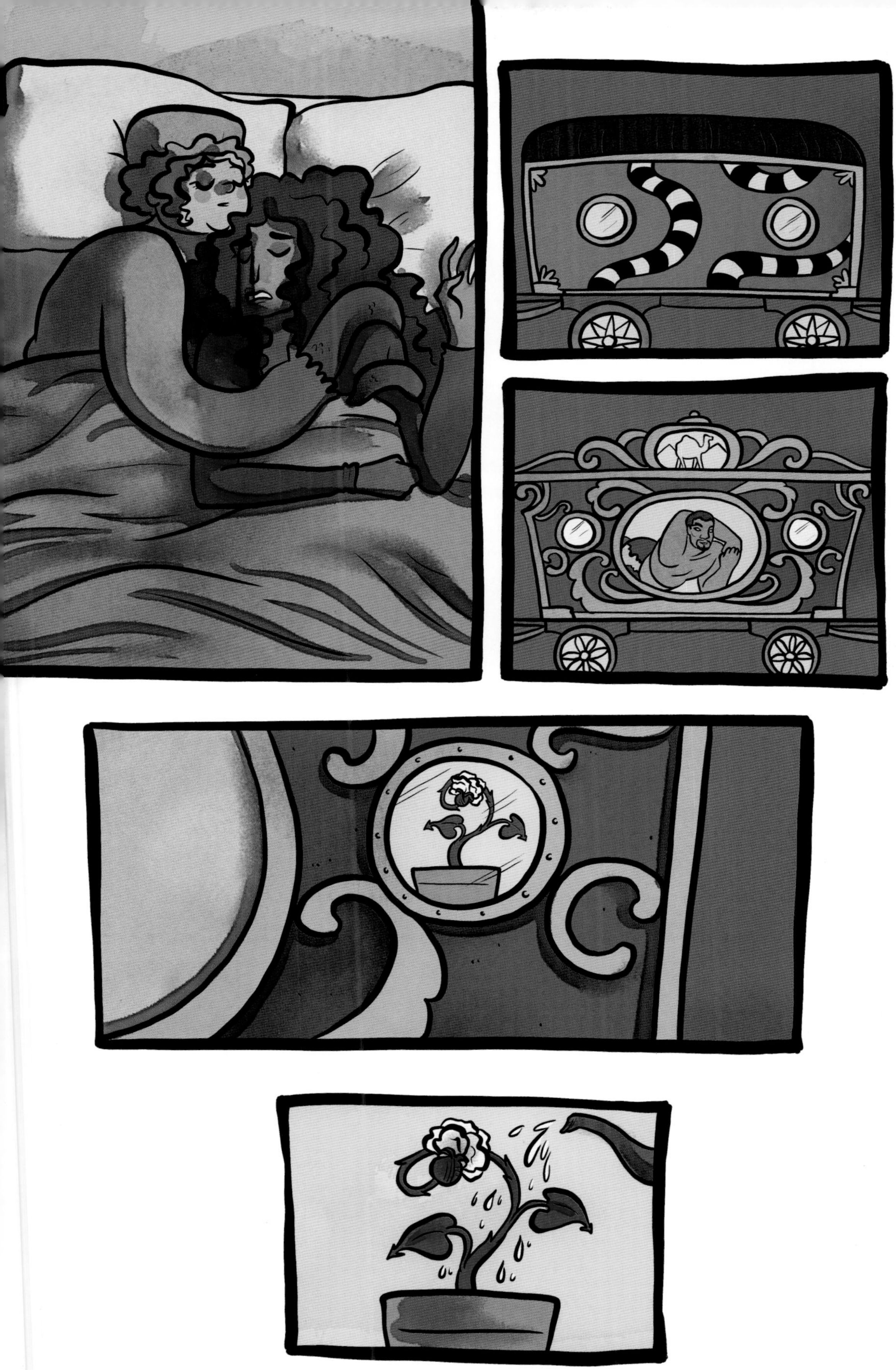

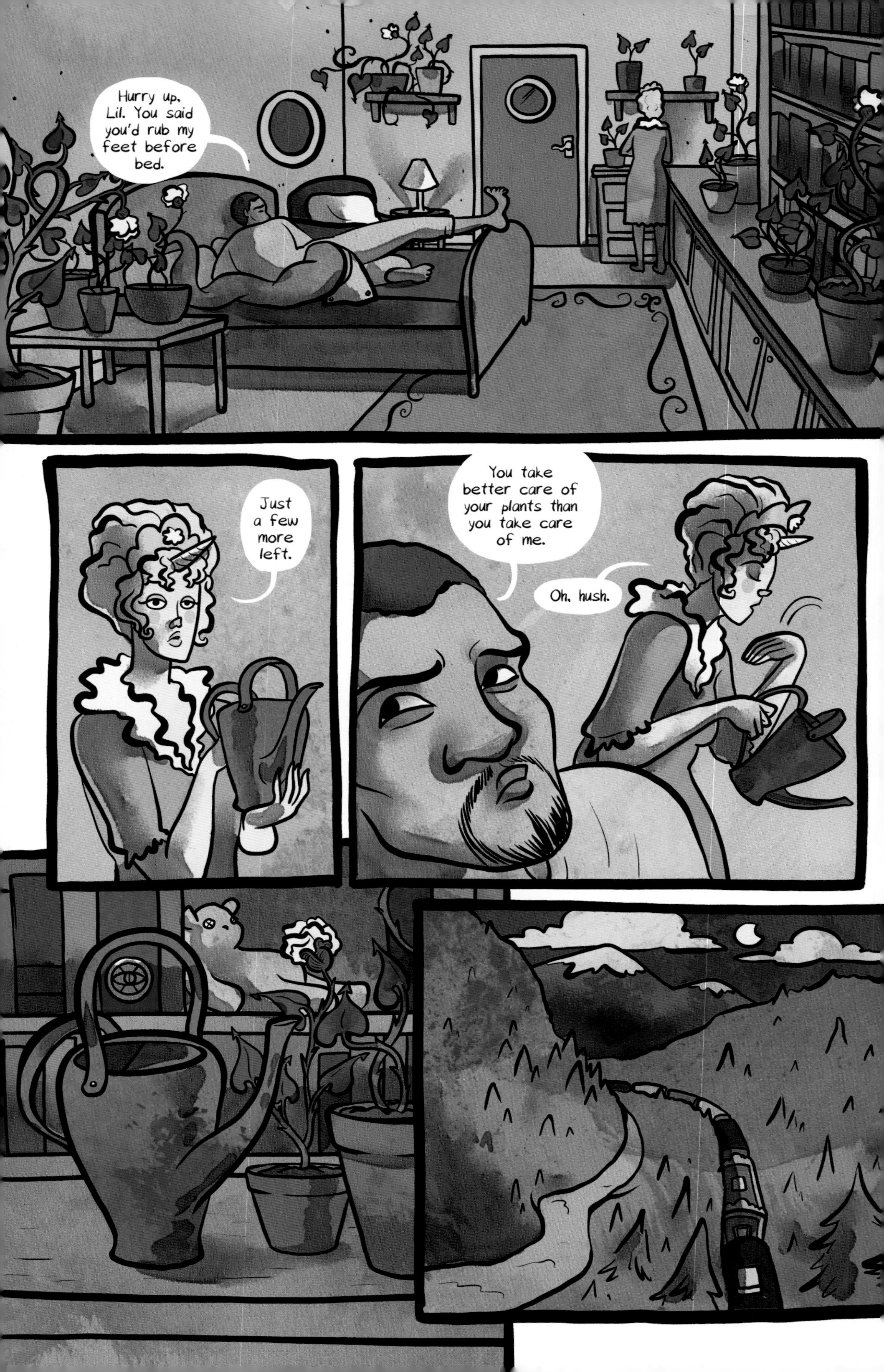
Hurry up, Lil. You said you'd rub my feet before bed.
Just a few more left.
You take better care of your plants than you take care of me.
Oh, hush.

End of Book Three

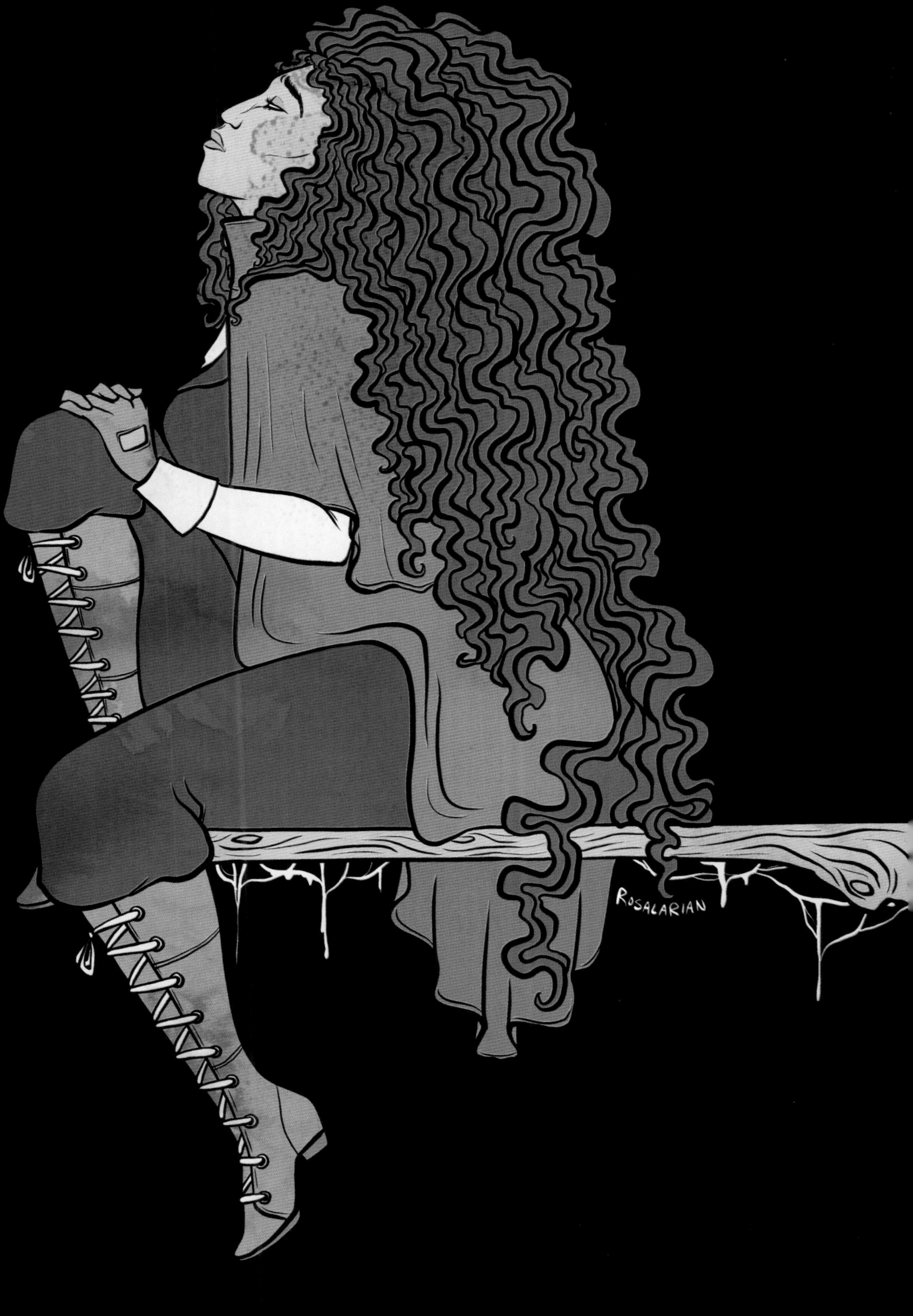
ROSALARIAN

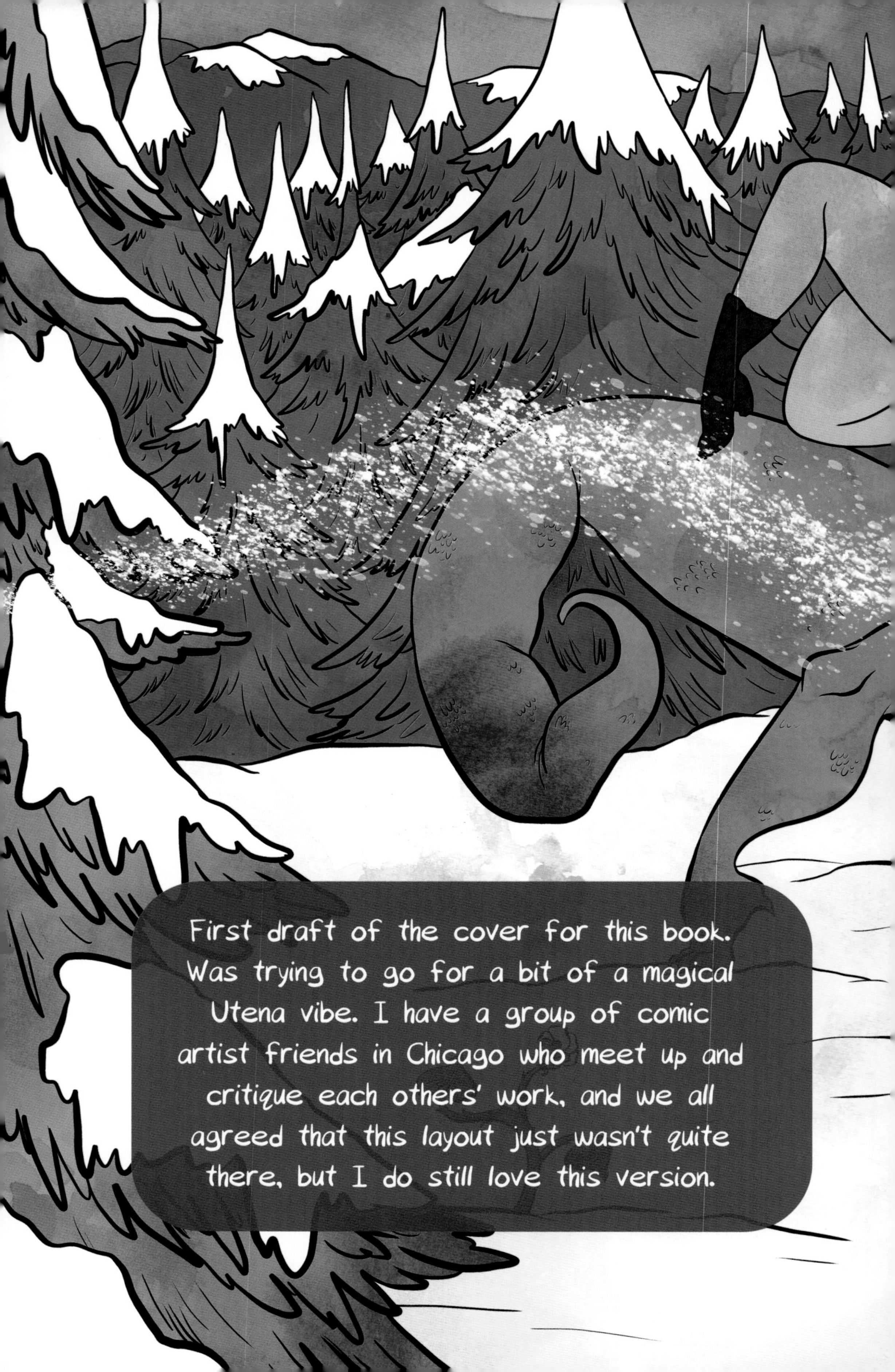

First draft of the cover for this book. Was trying to go for a bit of a magical Utena vibe. I have a group of comic artist friends in Chicago who meet up and critique each others' work, and we all agreed that this layout just wasn't quite there, but I do still love this version.

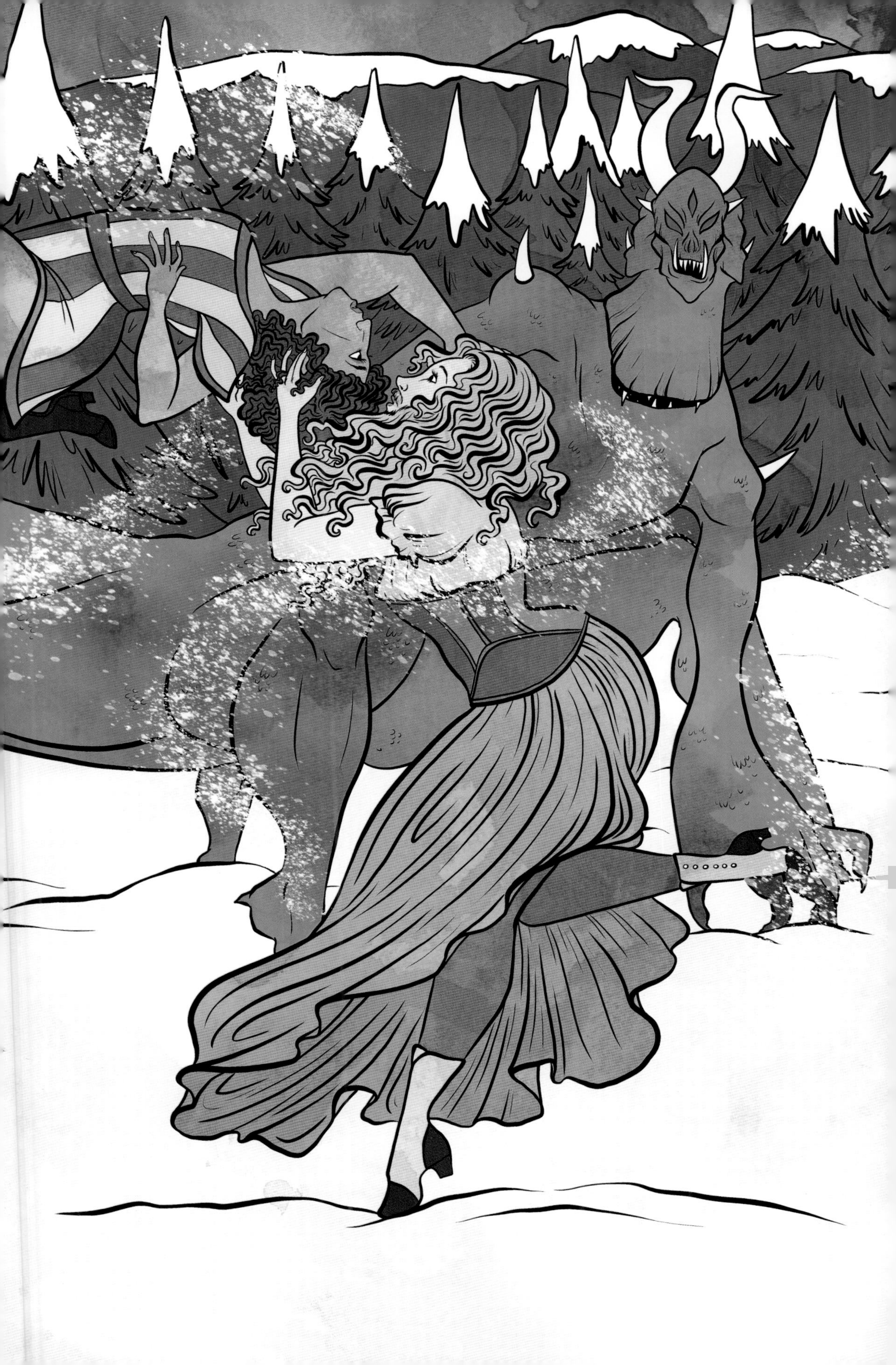

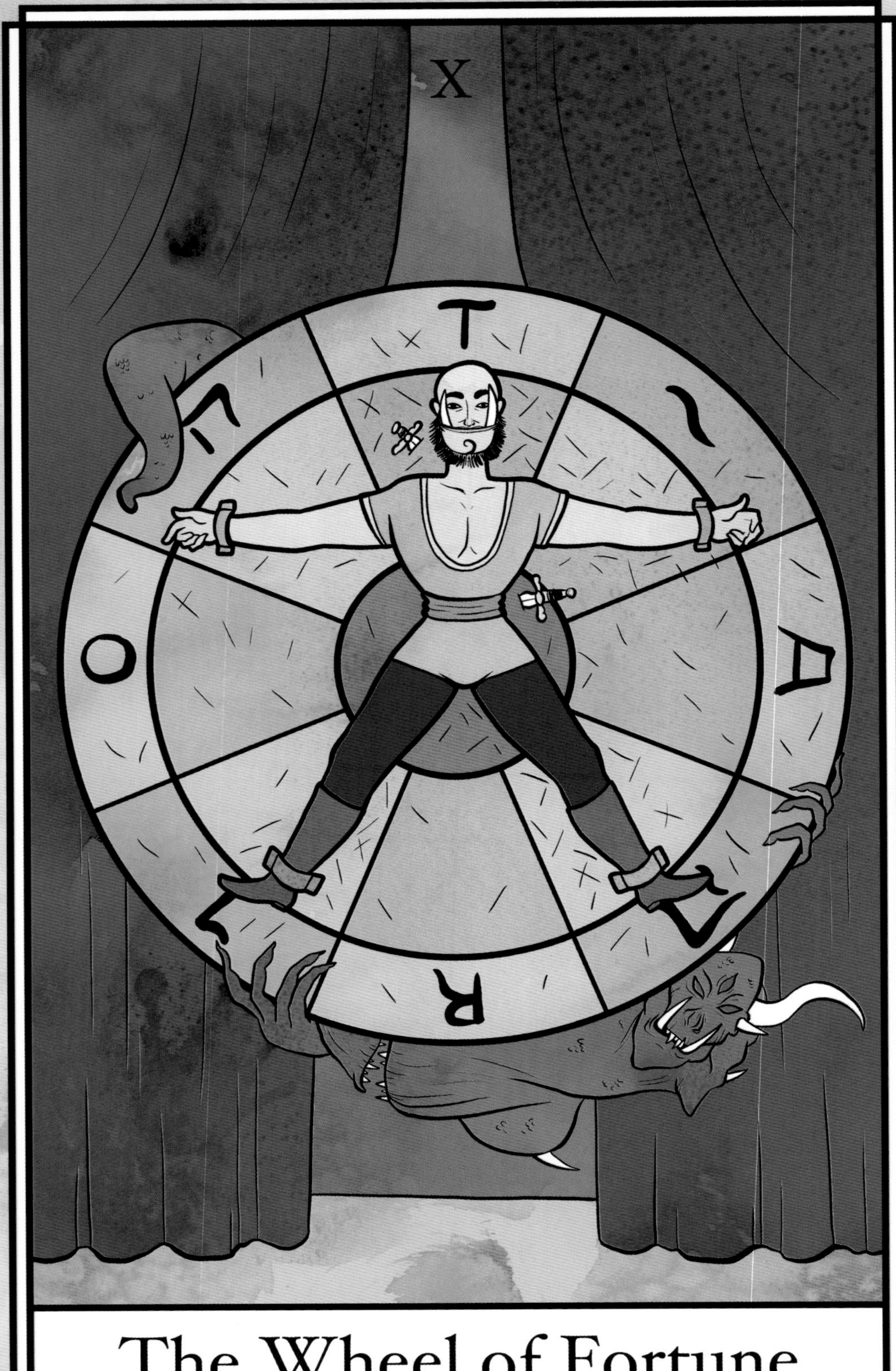
X
The Wheel of Fortune

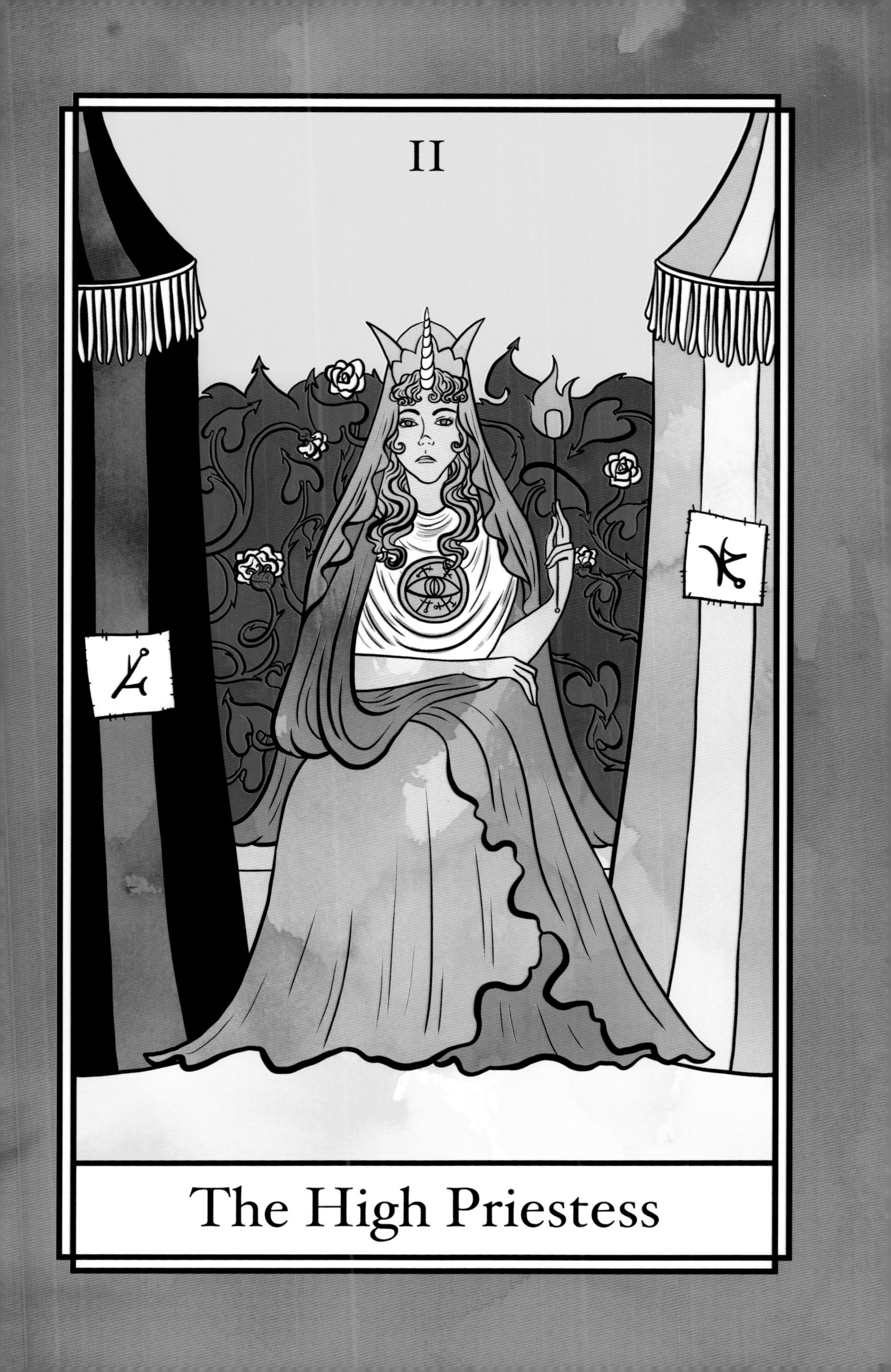
II
The High Priestess

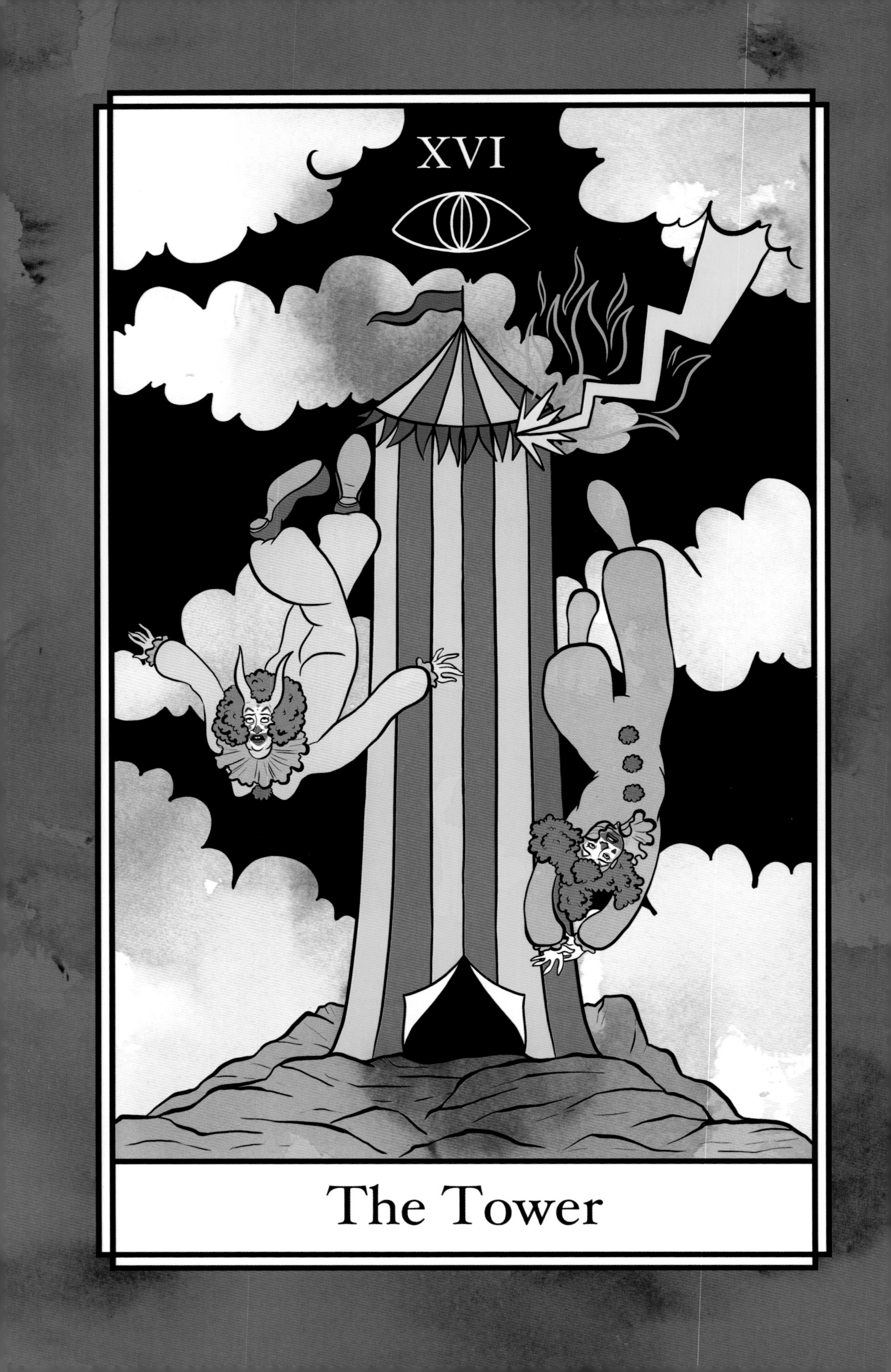
XVI

The Tower

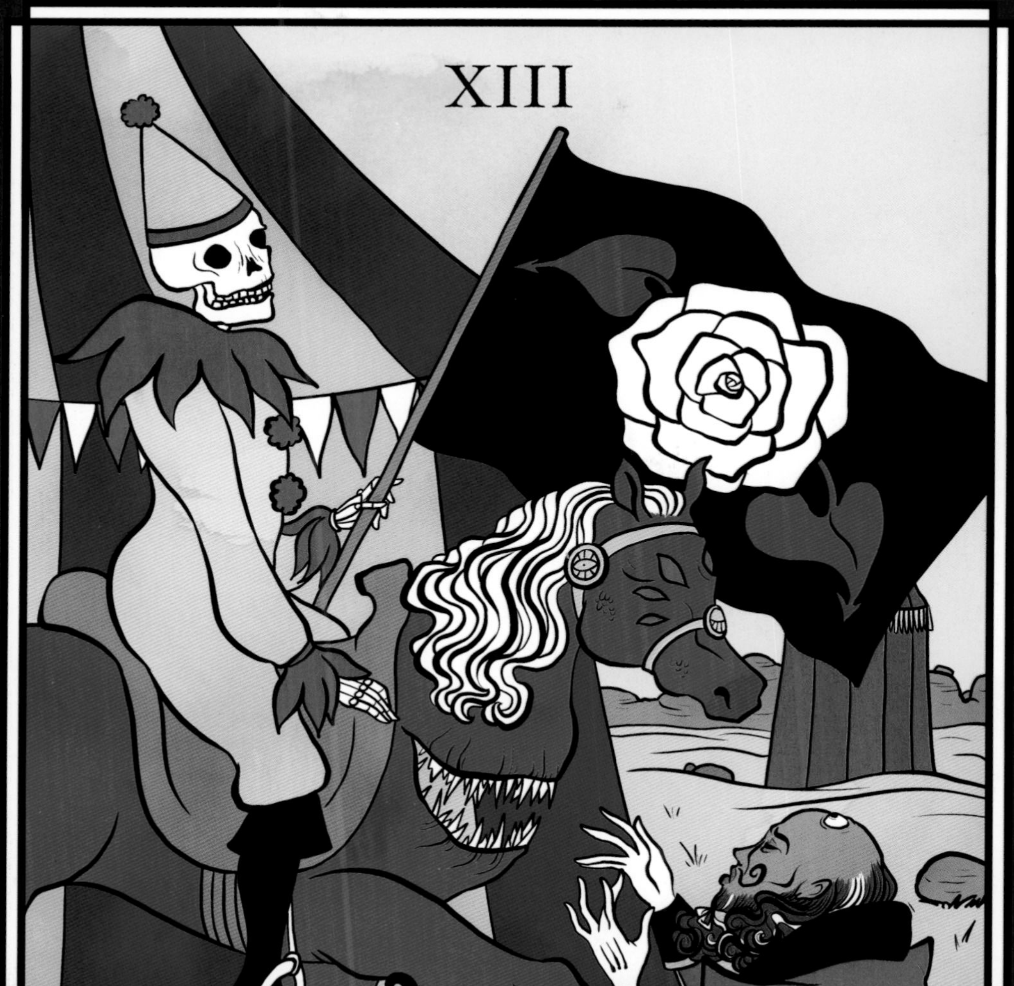
XIII
ROSALARIAN 2019
Death

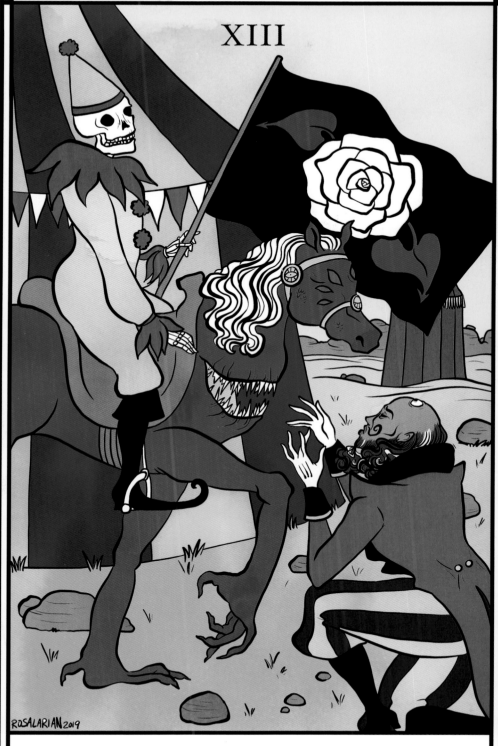

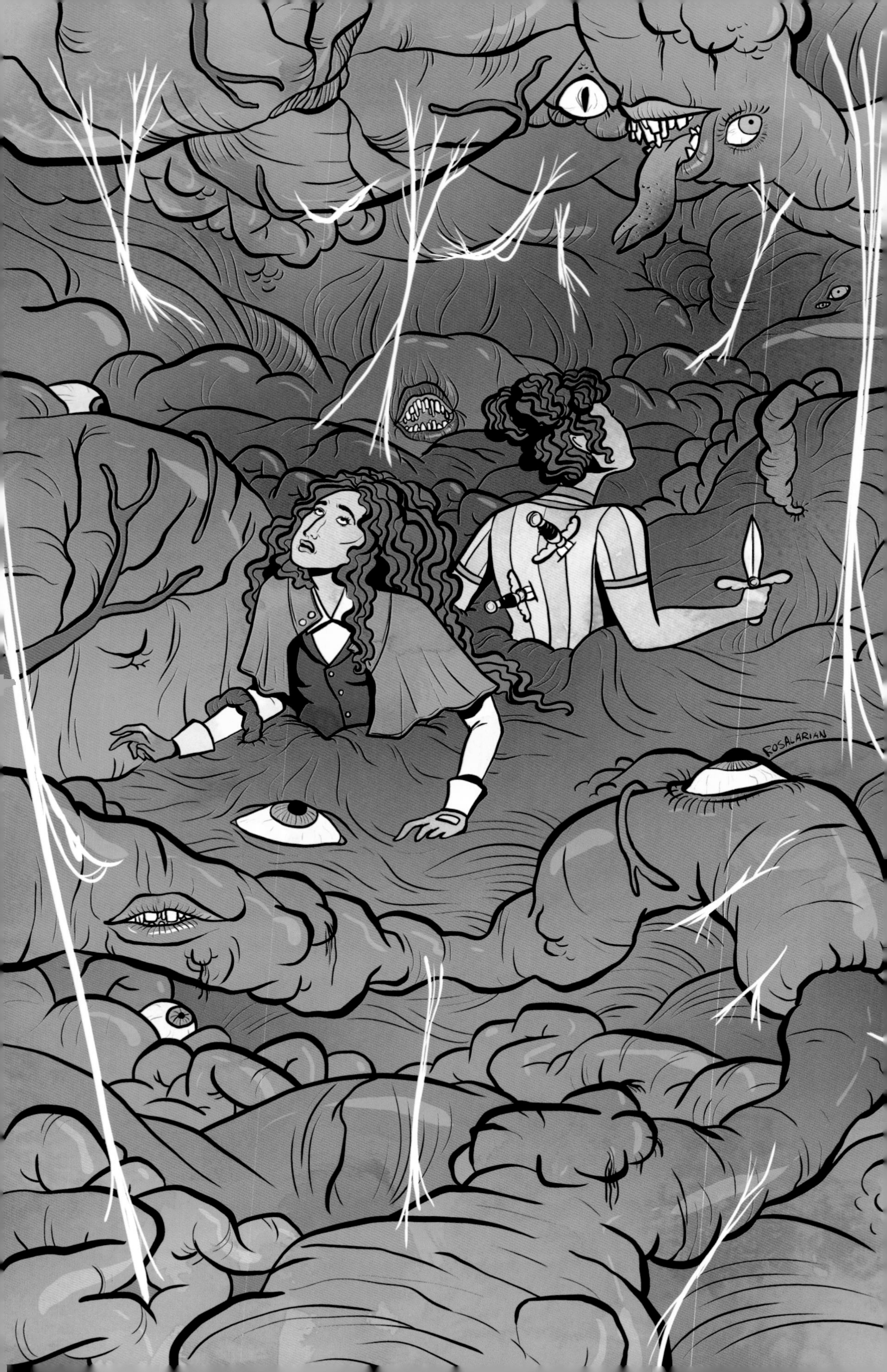
ROSALARIAN

Megan Rose Gedris has aspired to be a juggler, contortionist, gymnast, hula hooper, escape artist, magician, and fire spinner but instead she makes comics and does comedy and "performance art." She lives in Chicago.

See more of her work at rosalarian.com

Read more from Oni Press!

Spectacle
Megan Rose Gedris
Book One

SPECTACLE, BOOK ONE
By Megan Rose Gedris
The journey begins here!
ISBN 978-1-62010-492-7

Spectacle
Megan Rose Gedris
Book Two

SPECTACLE, BOOK TWO
By Megan Rose Gedris
The adventure continues!
ISBN 978-1-62010-599-3

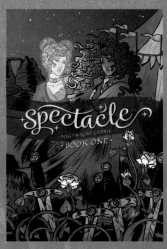

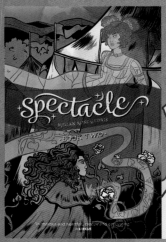

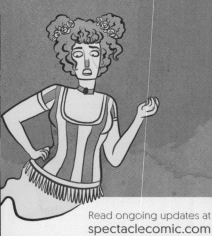

Read ongoing updates at
spectaclecomic.com

If you liked *Spectacle*, check out these other Oni Press books:

Kim Reaper
Grim Beginnings
By Sarah Graley

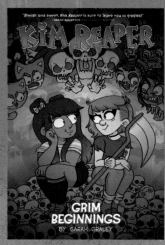

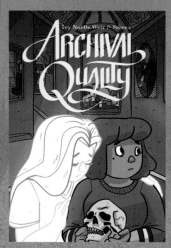

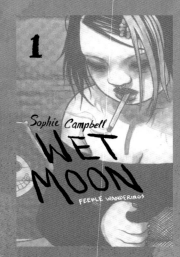

KIM REAPER, VOL. 1: GRIM BEGINNINGS
By Sarah Graley
An adorable and hilarious supernatural rom-com
ISBN 978-1-62010-455-2

Ivy Noelle Weir & Steenz
Archival Quality

ARCHIVAL QUALITY
By Ivy Noelle Weir & Steenz
An evocative ghost story exploring trauma and mental health
ISBN 978-1-62010-470-5

1
Sophie Campbell
Wet Moon
Feeble Wanderings

WET MOON, VOL. 1: FEEBLE WANDERINGS
By Sophie Campbell
A queer, swampy Southern gothic drama
ISBN 978-1-62010-304-3

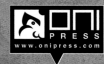

ONI PRESS
www.onipress.com

FOR MORE INFORMATION ON THESE AND OTHER FINE ONI PRESS COMIC BOOKS AND GRAPHIC NOVELS, VISIT WWW.ONIPRESS.COM. TO FIND A COMIC SPECIALTY STORE IN YOUR AREA, VISIT WWW.COMICSHOPS.US.